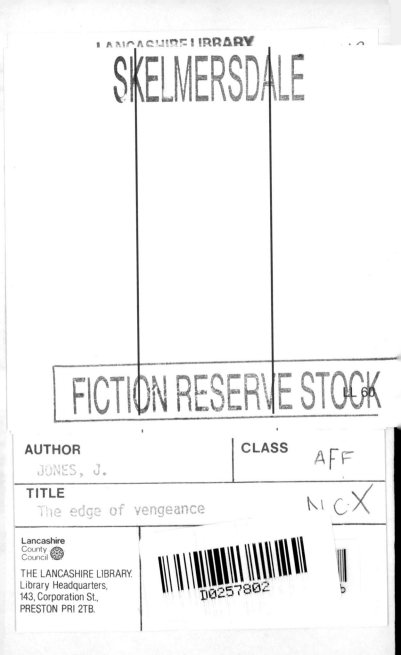

Jenny Jones was born in Essex and educated at
Loughton County High School and the University of
York. She now lives in Scotland and is married to a
musician. They have two children.

THE EDGE OF VENGEANCE is the second volume
in the *Flight Over Fire* sequence and follows FLY BY
NIGHT, her first novel.

Also by Jenny Jones

Flight Over Fire
Fly By Night

The Edge of Vengeance

Volume Two of
Flight Over Fire

Jenny Jones

Copyright © 1991 Jenny Jones

The right of Jenny Jones to be identified as the Author of the
Work has been asserted by her in accordance with the
Copyright, Designs and Patents Act 1988.

First published in 1991
by HEADLINE BOOK PUBLISHING PLC

First published in paperback in 1992
by HEADLINE BOOK PUBLISHING PLC

A HEADLINE FEATURE paperback

10 9 8 7 6 5 4 3 2 1

ISBN 0 7472 3714 X

Typeset by Medcalf Type Ltd, Bicester, Oxon

Printed and bound by
HarperCollins Manufacturing, Glasgow

HEADLINE BOOK PUBLISHING PLC
Headline House
79 Great Titchfield Street
London W1P 7FN

For Rosalind, with love

Contents

CONTENTS

PART TWO

Glossary and Main Characters

Eleanor Knight

Chorolon – a world governed by the flight of the Benu Bird.

The Benu Bird – the original phoenix. A blind hawk, whose cycle of birth, death and rebirth provides the framework for time to pass. It was captured by Lucian Lefevre (q.v.) for a period known as the Stasis.

The Stasis – an indeterminate length of time in Peraldon, the land ruled by Lycias (q.v.). During the Stasis no one aged, or died naturally. All creative life ceased. In Stromsall, the land ruled by Astret (q.v.), the Stasis was represented by an unending storm during the hours of daylight. People lived and died as usual.

The Boundary – a barrier of static time which divided Peraldon from Stromsall.

Lycias – The Sun God, whose great love for Mariana (q.v.) dictated the existence of the Stasis.

Astret – The Moon Goddess, to whom the unchanging sterility of the Stasis was anathema.

Peraldonia

Mariana – a mortal woman loved by Lycias. Mariana preferred her lover Idas to the Sun God, because Idas would grow old and share her own mortality. She died when the Benu was released at the end of the Stasis.

Lucian Lefevre – High Priest to the Sun God, Mage and brother to Mariana. He used magic to entrap the Benu Bird in the vanishing spiral of a sea-shell. In this way, Peraldonian humanity became immortal, and Lycias and

Mariana were given the freedom to love each other eternally.

The Emperor Xanthon – recently elected Sun Emperor of Peraldon.

Phinian Blythe – Peraldonian captain in the Warden's Watch, whose pregnant wife Karis was murdered in order to preserve the balance of immortality on Peraldon. He joined Eleanor Knight and Lukas Marling on the quest to find the Benu and so break the Stasis.

Elfitt de Mowbray – Peraldonian governor of Cliokest.

Imbert Cupere – Mage trained by Lefevre.

Edine Malreaux – Imbert's companion.

The Cavers – followers of Astret, marooned on the Peraldonian side of the Boundary during the Stasis and treated as despised outcasts by the Peraldonians.

Matthias Marling – a Caver Mage, responsible for bringing Eleanor Knight from her own world.

Lukas Marling – Matthias's brother. He befriended Eleanor after her arrival on Chorolon. They grew to love each other. His death was the price of the breaking of the Stasis.

Nerissa – Caver High Priestess to Astret, who threw herself out of a window on being granted the gift of seeing the future.

Stefan Pryse – Commander of the Caver Guard.

Thibaud Lye and Aylmer Alard – Caver Mages.

Haddon Derray – Caver warrior who travelled with Matthias through the Boundary to Stromsall. He fell in love with Coronis, a woman already pregnant by an unknown father. He decided to stay in the city of Bilith with Coronis and her father Ingram Lapith.

Coron – Coronis's baby son.

Jerenites – aligned to neither Lycias nor Astret. They loathed the Stasis because of the creative sterility, and were allied to the Cavers.

Thurstan Merauld – leader of the Jerenites.

Powel Hewlin – a Jerenite soldier.

Martitia Merauld – Thurstan's mother, killed by Fosca during the Stasis.

Jocasta Garraint – a Jerenite, loved by Lukas Marling until her death, shrivelled to ashes after a fight between the Jerenites and the Fosca.

Shelt

Torold Westray – Earl of Shelt.
Esmond Crinnion – Torold's lover.
Javon Westray – Duke of Eldin and Torold's brother.
Felicia – Javon's daughter.
Annis – Felicia's maid.
Kester Robard – Annis's lover and a captain in the Castle Guard of Shelt.
Feltham – Commander of Torold's personal Guard.
Gawne of Aquile – First Sea Lord (a Mage trained originally at the city of Peraldon).
Dederic – Sea Lord and Mage.
Fessil – Doctor.
Brice Lammon – apprentice Mage.
Olwyn Mittelson – a renegade Mage.
Ferant and Alex Aldrich – brothers, Mittelson's apprentices.
Jolin Rosco – rebel on behalf of the fisherpeople.
Philp Cammish – fisherman and rebel.
Jarry Lindel – rebel.
Vere Holtby – musician.
Ladon – a sea dragon.
Sharrak – one of the Parid.

The Eloish

Jerr Morrelow – traveller.
Irian Maryn – shaman.
Serethrun Maryn – Irian's brother.
Renferell Maryn – their father.
Brianne Querille and Enthor Farine – friends to Serethrun.
mereth – an eloish term to describe non-nomadic peoples, city-dwellers (derisive).

Smintha

Weard – The Fosca King's pupil.
Comyn Shreeve – a Caver.
Timon Lesterell – a Caver.
Hilde Nemen – a Jerenite.
Lily Herrys – actress.
Scurries – servants of Lefevre and his followers.
The Fosca – creatures engineered as fighting machines by Lefevre. They ride on dark angels, reptilian flying creatures.
The Fosca King – the flowery incarnation of Lucian Lefevre.

The Arrarat – sapient hawks.

Astrella – aligned to Lukas Marling.
Amery – aligned to Matthias Marling.
Ash – aligned to Eleanor Knight, killed at the end of the Stasis.
Adila

Prologue

Grass beneath her fingers, wet, short-cropped.

Not again, she thought. Not another bitter awakening.

As she pushed herself up to sitting, she saw, in the half-light before dawn, oak trees, chestnuts, the gentle rolling pasture of a familiar countryside.

She was home. Never had the word seemed so empty of comfort.

Not here, not now, please not now, she cried silently in the dark. She had prayed for this, a return to normality, and now it was empty, useless, a mockery.

She picked herself up. She was very stiff, deeply cold. She must have been lying there for some time.

She was wearing green silk again. It was wet and muddy. She stared at it blankly, her mind glancing over the implications.

Oh, why here? Why bring me back to *this*?

Her hands were shaking. She saw the hedge leading back to the garden, and started walking towards it. Only two steps, and she stopped, tears blinding, wretched sobs choking.

Lukas. Lukas, Lukas, Lukas.

A hopeless litany of grief, gripping her with an almost physical pain. She could not bear the weight of it. Her hands were clenched tight, so tight that she felt the nails dig into the skin.

He had lain twisted on the deck, blood soaking into the snow.

She had condemned him to it. She had been offered a choice, a free choice, and she had left him there, to die in the snow.

All joy was dead.

There was nothing to be done. She might as well go home.

Eleanor went back to the house in the end, as the sun began to rise. Past the shrubberies, down the path through the rose garden. To the terrace.

The ashes of the fire were still warm. She stared at it for a while, at the glowing embers, and the shards of coloured glass. Green, gold and brown, glinting sharply in the early light against dull stone.

Only then did she begin to realise how little time had passed. Only a few hours. The whole thing, all those extraordinary pressures and experiences were encompassed in the space of one brief June night.

Then she remembered. Time had not passed in Peraldon, not in any ordinary sense.

The house was in darkness now, but the back door was unlocked. She pushed it open, quietly moving through the sitting room, carefully stepping over the bodies sprawled on cushions, haphazard in sleep.

Her bag was under the hall table, where she had left it long ago. It felt unfamiliar, the neat velvet satchel embroidered with sequins.

Her car keys. Would she still know how to drive? How much had she changed?

Someone stirred in the dining-room. A door swung open and a man stood there, blinking in the sour dawn light.

It was Lewis. He looked at her and laughed, a little unkindly.

'Not quite the party you expected, Nell? Did you think I'd spend all evening looking for you? Who was it then? Poor old Rob, or have you got your claws into someone else?'

She couldn't speak. She pretended to search the bag for the keys and her hair fell forward, masking her face.

He'd opened the door for her. Quickly she ran past him, out onto the driveway.

She heard him laugh again as the door closed.

PART ONE

Chapter One
Lammon

The Boundary was broken. The Benu Bird was free once more.

In Stromsall, the northern continent of Chorolon, it became clear as soon as the storm died that the Stasis had ended. Thoughtfully, a Mage of great power called for his apprentice. It was a matter of some urgency to know what had happened.

They were in a high tower of a Castle by the sea. Through the narrow casement window they could see a bright, almost full moon gleaming over rippling water.

A small fire burning in the grate set in the wall gave some warmth. The other fire, which had been built in the centre of the circular stone floor, was still smouldering.

Shards of coloured glass lay at its perimeter.

Gawne was staring out at the sea while Lammon cleared away the glass, reverently folding the remaining spheres and crescents in their velvet bags. Gawne's tall, high-hunched figure was black against the moonlight. He was silent and unmoving.

More secrets, more events of unknown significance. The high shoulders expressed a weight of responsibility, a serious purpose that Gawne did not trouble to reveal to his apprentice.

Resentfully, Lammon knew that he would be kept in the dark. That, yet again, no one would tell him what was happening.

There was a sudden drop in the temperature as Gawne moved away from the window and the cold sea air washed through the room. Lammon could feel those passionless eyes resting on him.

Unable to deny their pressure he looked up at the First Sea Lord.

'Sharrak will come,' he said softly. His voice, with its slow, unfamiliar southern accent, was quite without expression, his lined face unreadable. He was very old, older than anyone Lammon had ever known. The dry, wizened voice, high and humourless, continued. 'The summons was answered. My sweet lady will come to join us here in Shelt.'

Lammon would have liked to ask, who is Sharrak? But already the First Sea Lord was crossing the room towards the door.

He cleared his throat.

Soundlessly the tall, hunched figure turned towards him. 'Lammon.' He spoke without inflection. 'Be patient. Men of action are always in the debt of men of power. A Mage will always prevail.' The door opened; soundlessly, in a drift of grey silk, Gawne left the tower.

Lammon's hands were trembling. Impatiently he turned back to the glass shapes on the floor. They lay in a spiral pattern of power, and the fire was still warm.

Did he dare? Could he risk it? Almost without thinking, quickly and impulsively, he leant over the fire, breathing life into the dying flames. He held a globe in one hand, a crescent in the other.

Obscure words muttered, a mind only half prepared, a rite crudely, recklessly executed . . .

He threw the glass shapes high through the air, diamond bright shapes spinning through dark, cold air; the arcs intersected.

Glass shattered and scattered and, in that moment of blazing chaos, Lammon saw a picture lancing through the dark air.

A flash of prevision, a scene imprinted on the memory like light. It happened so fast that he almost missed it, but the brief glimpse was enough.

A marriage. A central point, a conjunction between past and future. A meeting of male and female, the culmination of a great chain of events, inexorable and aweful. And in the future, leading away from the marriage, he saw a dynasty established, a line furthered to reflect down the long ages.

And Brice Lammon, the last member of the family

disinherited by strangers, turned away from the fire and glass in sickness and disgust.

The crown of Shelt to stay in the hands of the usurper's family! That was what he had seen. The line of Torold and Javon Westray established over his beloved city of Shelt.

A small man, Lammon was used to being disregarded. He had lowered his eyes, quietened his voice, when the conquerors came. He had watched the Sea Lords welcome the two brothers Torold and Javon as the secular power in Shelt. They had been impressed by the brothers' military prowess. Pathetically impressed. Nothing was too good for them.

Torold was installed as Earl of Shelt. Lammon's own family, who might reasonably have expected to have a role in the governance of Shelt, was ignored. The Sea Lords were seduced by the military power of Torold and Javon, and passed over Lammon's claim. They acted always on the advice of Gawne, with his high hunched shoulders and strange knowledge.

They hoped to use Torold's highly trained troops to secure their position.

Lammon knew them to be foolishly optimistic. Javon and Torold Westray were power-hungry thugs. Already Javon's empire covered most of southern Stromsall. Lammon hated the idea that Shelt should be merely a province in someone else's territory. He knew that the Sea Lords were putting themselves in the debt of a voracious barbarian.

He kept cool, although his calm, unflurried exterior hid a seething ferment of hatred and resentment. Most of the time, he concealed it well. He worked hard, and through sheer tenacity won for himself the place of apprentice to the First Sea Lord, Gawne.

Gawne was his only hope. A Mage trained in Peraldon had to be special, had to have knowledge wider and deeper than the Sea Lords. His passionless eyes saw more than mere appearance. Lammon knew that Gawne would keep Torold in his place.

But still the First Sea Lord shared nothing with Lammon. He was only an apprentice, and no one else told him anything.

He put resentment aside. Quickly and efficiently he executed the menial tasks the Sea Lords gave him, biding

his time, watching, learning their skills. He was waiting for
his chance, the chance to rid Shelt of the usurpers.

Brice Lammon was not a wise man, nor was he particularly
skilled in the execution of the Rite. He had been careless and
hasty, preoccupied with ambition and resentment, and so he
missed the last lingering series of images fast fading from the
air over the fire.

Sharrak pauses in its headlong flight to the north. A strange
collection of thought and will, of shifting matter and uneasy
stability, the Parid hovers on the outskirts of the ruined
citadel that is Cliokest, and watches the devastation remaining
after that final battle.

Sharrak pauses, its attention caught and held by something
familiar. A figure – abandoned, discarded, on the snowy
deck of a small fishing boat – is drifting slowly out to sea.
The outline of an Arrarat hawk stands there, on guard.

The Parid hesitates, scenting the chill in the wind, the icy
summoning from the north, and looks at the man lying
twisted on the deck.

He was of significance, once. And the hawk still waits there,
close by the man's body.

A light smile drifts across the face that flickers between
beauty and its parody. Sharrak likes to meddle, to influence
events. More than anything, it wants to be a true god, with
power over the lives of mortals. It knows that the
manipulation of form, of creating likeness, is an essential
adjunct to divine power. And in the north there is a powerful
Mage, the one who has sent the summoning.

So Sharrak moves through the cold wind, lifting the inert,
bloodstained body onto the back of the Arrarat hawk, twisting
the icy hands in and out of the leather strap that runs over
the bird's shoulders.

At once the hawk takes off, unerringly following the same
chill wind that beckons to Sharrak.

Sharrak laughs, a sick sound in the dark night over
Cliokest, and follows.

Chapter Two
The Emperor

Later, another kind of crossing was planned to the northern, windswept continent of Stromsall. The newly elected Emperor Xanthon of Peraldon was an intelligent, subtle man. He was well aware that the Channel between Stromsall and Peraldon was not wide. He wanted to know what had happened in the north, what the Stasis had meant to the neighbouring continent.

Councils, advisors, Mages, priests, he consulted them all in turn. Storm, they said. Storm and violence, for the length of the Stasis . . . The Lady Astret, Goddess of the Moon, had hidden the light of the Sun in the reckless power of Her storm.

Xanthon listened to them all with courtesy, and made his own decisions. Clairvoyance and mysticism were all very well, but he wanted factual information. He wanted to know what had happened to the people of Stromsall, how the Stasis had affected their daily lives, from the merest peasant to the great barons.

From the centre of his palace of Solkest, in the capital of his Empire, Peraldon, he made ready to send ships with ambassadors, discreetly backed up by soldiers, to Stromsall.

His first priority was to investigate the extent of the military power of Stromsall. Already there had been rumours on Peraldon about the massive forces of Eldin. The Duke of Eldin, Javon Westray, ruled vast areas of territory. Xanthon, wise and prudent, decided to investigate his intentions.

There was one other reason for this decision. He was wondering if the traditions could be re-established. If the old custom of Sun Emperor and Moon Empress might be revived.

Traditionally, the Moon Empress had come from windswept moors of the north.

It was not to be. Even before the ships set out from Peraldon, the temperature was rising. To the east, great acres of forest were devastated by a sudden forest fire. Abruptly, amazingly, the sun's heat intensified.

The ships were recalled, the ambassadors set to other, more urgent, tasks. Irrigation, rationing, fire-fighting, conservation.

Peraldon was caught under the glare of a scorching sun, and there was no further energy or initiative to spare for wondering what was happening north of the Malith Channel.

The Emperor made one last gesture towards Stromsall. He was prepared to act on intuition. He sent the Mage Matthias there, to assess the situation. His advisors, priests and Mages were outraged. A Caver? A Mage dedicated to Astret? The Mage who had brought about the end of the Stasis?

For those very reasons, replied Xanthon reasonably. No one else would be acceptable. He knew that Matthias would do his best to bring about peace between the two continents. He trusted Matthias to act constructively.

Then the Emperor turned his back on the northern territories. He watched instead the fires burning, the sun blasting his Empire.

The Emperor dreamed.

He dreamed of a great house, carpeted with forest and desert, furnished with cities and villages, illumined by starlight lamps. He moved through the house, along wide, empty corridors set with open doors. He saw the contours of a thousand worlds.

None of them was his own. Each world was inspired by golden fire, enlightened by silver clarity. The balance fluctuated, wavering and uncertain. There were dark corners everywhere, but the Emperor knew that what he saw was miraculous and wonderful. He breathed deeply, walking down the corridors, mounting the stairs, crossing the hallways. Through open doors he watched the fall of fountains, the slow movement of glaciers, the bright arcs of stars and planets.

He wandered here and there, through countless galleries, opening myriad doors. In some places there were only gases, swirling clouds of blue and violet, or dry gold-dust spinning through a void. But however the glimpse was structured, there was always a tension holding it together. A polarity between golden fire and silver water.

At length he scented something in the air, something sour and wrong. He saw, in a room far down one of the corridors, that a fire was raging, blazing through the hangings, flaring through the green carpets of forest and field. In the dream, his breath was caught between terror and dread. He knew that place, knew what it was.

The smoke billowed and stained his vision. He began to run, seeing that the fire would soon devastate the room, even the calm darkness of its far corners. He saw that it would all be destroyed in a white-hot furnace of fury, that the only shaping to that world's future would be etched in falls of ash, in charred remains. The fire was reaching out beyond the door, flaring into the corridor, searching for someone . . .

He halted at the threshold, hardly able to see through the smoke. His eyes were watering and sore, his flesh shrinking from the wild and savage heat. He was terrified that the fire was looking for *him*, that the flames wanted to take him in payment. He was the Emperor, and this was his Empire. Was the fire also his fault? The flames gusted and surged, and then subsided, flickering at his feet. He felt nothing. They moved through the air around him and beyond.

The flames were seeking their prey somewhere else. He turned round, straining to see into the dark corridor behind him. The flames reached out around him, framing the Emperor in firelight.

He saw, in the distance, the figure of a woman. She was waiting for the flames, although she did not know it. She was far away down the corridor, in some other room, a dark, cold, lonely place, bright hair echoing the firelight. She was oblivious of the flames' desire.

The Emperor turned back to his burning Empire and knew what the flames demanded. He would have to bring her to Chorolon, so that the fire might quieten and subside. And as this knowledge crystallised in his mind, the doors along the corridor swung shut, one by one, closing away the infinite universes. He was left in darkness.

When Xanthon awoke, he called for his most trusted Mage and closest advisor. Imbert Cupere, a man with pale flowing curls and a fine, sensitive face, listened carefully to the Emperor's dream and in due course gave his advice.

The Emperor did not see him smile.

Chapter Three
Bilith

On the instructions of the Emperor Xanthon, as a messenger of goodwill, Matthias Marling was sent to Stromsall. He rode Alta, an Arrarat hawk whose rider had died on Cliokest. In this way no extra manpower was needed, no ship diverted from service. Matthias travelled alone, as ever, a Mage of unique power.

He had been chosen for many reasons. He could ride an Arrarat hawk, and he had been to Stromsall more recently than anyone else in Peraldon. He had broken through the Boundary during the last days of the Stasis. His friend, Haddon Derray, still lived there. He was known to be a loyal follower of Astret and would therefore be acceptable to the people of the northern continent.

Most important, however, the Emperor Xanthon recognised in Matthias a genuine desire for peace. He felt that he could trust Matthias not to do anything to endanger the infinitely fragile bond that now existed between the followers of the Sun King and those of the Moon Queen.

So, some four months after the breaking of the Stasis, Matthias retraced his steps towards the southernmost city of Stromsall, a city of tumbled stone blocks. He took with him a wooden staff carved into a vanishing spiral, and a letter from the Emperor of Peraldon.

Bilith was in mourning. White scarves were bright in the sunlight. Matthias had last seen the dull buildings drenched in rain, storm clouds hanging heavy. A marriage had taken place there. At the time, he had felt an unreasoning dread, as if he had known that something terrible would happen. Now, one cold and clear morning, as he approached the squat

sprawl of massive architecture that formed Bilith, he knew
it for a place of grief.

White cloths fluttered along the line of the battlements.
The city was deserted. Doors and windows were closed, the
streets silent. Alta put him down in the central square of the
city, a place usually thronging with people and animals,
traders, children, beggars. Under normal conditions, the
sudden advent of an Arrarat hawk would have been certain
to cause a sensation, if not outright panic. But there was no
one there. The wide expanse of stone was empty. Even the
beggars had gone.

He wandered through the streets, looking for Ingram
Lapith's house. And when he found it, set in huge blocks
of stone, half built into the city wall itself, he did not dare
go in.

White drapes shrouded every door and window. The silence
of the city was centred here. As Matthias had feared, the price
of saving Coronis from the Lake of Lallon had been high
indeed.

He smelt, on the cold bright air, burning. Aromatic wood
and herbs, the smoke of a funeral pyre. It drew him on, past
Lapith's whitened house, to the north gate of the city.

There was a man on duty there, but he stared into space,
ignoring Matthias. On the plain beyond the city, Matthias
saw the pyre, raised high above the heads of the crowds. The
flames had almost reached the top of it, and smoke disguised
what lay there.

It seemed as if the entire population were there, watching.
The crowds filled the plain, but there was no sound. People
stood silent, in small, huddled groups. As he drew nearer,
he saw tears on some faces. Many were in the colours of
mourning, white and grey. Somewhere, not far away, a child
cried.

He spoke to a young man near the gate, but he turned away
without replying. Everyone seemed stunned, in deep shock.
No one would answer him directly.

He moved around the outer walls of the city, trying to get
a better view. He pushed through the stricken crowds,
ignoring the rustle of disapproval. This was the silence of
mourning, the halting of daily life to pay respects to the dead.
A stranger, barging through their midst, was not welcome.

The silence endured long after he had found a vantage point, a little beyond the mass of people. Smoke rose high over the plain, very thick now. The air was sickly sweet with the stench of burning flesh.

Alta, the Arrarat who had borne him on this journey, was circling the city high above. No one looked up. For a moment Matthias paused, standing near the massive stone blocks of the city walls. With some urgency, and much disquiet, he sent his thoughts in a message of doubtful enquiry to her.

A flare of terror. And then something else, a sudden, rigid clamping down on the communication, like an axe-blow to the head. A whitehot iron band cut through his brain. He staggered, raising his hands to ward it off. He was gasping with shock and pain. He felt as if half his mind had been annihilated.

He sagged against the stone block, his knees weak, his mouth filled with nausea. Something was forcing its way into his soul and bringing with it the image of flame and fire . . . There were flames everywhere.

With effort, he turned his back on the pyre, his face against the cold wall of stone, hiding his soundless screaming. His hands were pressed nerveless against his temples, trying to stop the fire from bursting through his skull. He had dropped his staff, and the world was leaping, taking on the vivid action of the flames.

With shut eyes, he saw images strong as the pounding of hammers, crashing their imprint on his memory. He saw what was happening within the pyre. He saw a bloody birth in the centre of the fire. Saw a child ripped, torn from the burning body of its mother, seized by powerful arms, snatched away through the flames and up to the Sun.

Lycias? He could not speak, and his mind was operating in some other dimension, closer to madness than anything else. Lycias, Lord of the Sun, what are You doing?

The baby was glistening with blood, its hands flailing against the brightness. Its small mouth was open, gasping in the smoke, and he thought it might die, lost in the flames. He could not bear it to die, that precious, new, innocent life.

He held out his arms, begging now, to take it at whatever cost, anything to save it from the fire, but the brightness overwhelmed everything, and he could no longer see the baby. The vast heat was driving him back, driving him away.

He started to cry, mourning the disappearance of the child, rocking in tragic, desperate grief . . .

In this extremity, he did not at first notice the strange thread of excitement running through the firelight. The breathless, exultant parabola of some other mind, skidding through the dimension where Matthias's own mind was floundering in flames.

Strange eyes flared at him, dark, almond shapes of mischievous ill-will.

They pricked him back to sanity. The smoke cleared from his sight, the flames from his mind. Where was the baby? His eyes fell into focus; abruptly he pushed himself away from the wall, reaching automatically for his staff.

There was someone watching him. Someone curiously indistinct, a rather vague looking young man, dressed in nondescript clothes, a wide-brimmed hat on his head. The brim cast his face into shadow; Matthias could not see him clearly.

'Are you all right?' His voice was light and pleasant, but there was an odd accent to it, lifting the cadence at the end of the sentence further than the inquiry justified. 'An extraordinary amount of smoke, don't you think . . . A stranger here, aren't you? Have you come far?'

'Yes . . .' He struggled to communicate. 'Can you tell me where to find the Archon, Ingram Lapith?'

A pause. 'He burns now, even as we speak. Along with his pregnant daughter, Coronis . . .'

The crowd was breaking up around them. At last Matthias had an uninterrupted view of the pyre. The flames were dying down. Glowing drifts of ash lay beneath the charcoal timbers.

Matthias tried to collect his thoughts. 'I didn't know. I've only just got here.'

There was another pause. The young man tilted his head to one side, examining Matthias in a fashion he found disconcerting. 'Well, well,' he said softly. 'A number of contradictions, here. You have only just reached Bilith and yet you know Lapith was Archon. You have a Mage's spiral staff, but you don't know whose pyre we have just seen burn.'

Matthias leant back against the plinth. He needed more information. 'How did they die? What happened to Coronis's husband, Haddon? The baby?' But even as he said the words, he knew part of the answer. The young man was studying him, his head still to one side.

Matthias found words. 'Is Haddon dead, too?'

The man nodded. 'And the baby, so it is said. How could it survive the death of the mother?'

Matthias did not believe it. The baby was not dead, he was sure. It had been lifted from the fire in strong hands . . .

He came to a decision. 'As I said, I am a stranger to Bilith – at least, I have been here once before, but only for a short time. Would you oblige me by telling me what has happened here? Perhaps we could find some refreshment somewhere . . .?

'I doubt you'll find anywhere open today.' He pulled open his coat and Matthias saw a bulge in the deep pocket in the lining. The top of a flask. 'However, I have my own supply. Come with me.' He turned away, pushing through the rapidly dispersing crowds. Matthias followed, his thoughts in disarray.

They sat beyond the city walls, on the cold slope overlooking the plain. The man's name was Jerr Morrelow. 'A stranger to Bilith too,' he said, smiling in deprecation. 'But I have been here almost a week, and do know a little of what has happened.' He handed the flask to Matthias, who took a small sip of the fiery liquid.

'It started, I suppose, just after I arrived here. The Archon's daughter, Coronis, died. You knew her?' That strange, uplifted cadence again.

'For a brief time. She was pregnant then . . .'

'It was very sudden. There was a storm. She was struck, it seems, by lightning . . . The baby had no chance.'

Matthias stared unseeing at the vanishing spiral of his staff. 'She was married –'

'Yes. Her husband went quite mad, I heard. When the news of her death was broken to him, he ran from the city. No one has seen him since, but the feeling is that he is dead. The priestesses have said so.' Morrelow frowned. 'It was an artificial storm. A deliberate creation that was nothing to do with ordinary climatic conditions.' There was a faint tinge of regret in Morrelow's voice.

Matthias looked at him sharply. 'What happened to the Archon, Lapith?'

'The story put about was that he left the city to look for Haddon Derray. He was haunted, they said. Flames filled his eyes. I saw him go, you see. I met him on the road from Bilith, and he had no more idea of looking for his son-in-law than I had. A personal vendetta, that was what it was. Ingram Lapith against the Gods, exacting vengeance for the death of his daughter.'

'He knew it was not an accident, then?'

'There has been no *accidental* lightning in Stromsall since the storms of the Stasis began –'

'But the Stasis has been over for some time . . .'

The man shrugged. 'Who knows? Lapith thought it deliberate. He wanted revenge.'

'Against whom?'

Morrelow made no answer, taking a long drink from the flask in his hands. Matthias tried again. 'What happened?'

'He died. No one knows how. His horse returned to the city carrying a dead man. His eyes – were burnt out. He had set off to the Lake of Lallon, you see.

'He thought he might find some answer there, but we don't know if he even got that far. Shall I tell you what I think, Mage? The unbiased opinion of an outsider . . . I think that Ingram Lapith held the Sun God responsible for the death of his daughter.'

He was leaning back against the cold stone wall, and for a moment Matthias could see his eyes beneath the wide-brimmed hat. They were dark, almond-shaped, set on a slant and wholly untrustworthy.

'Who are you?' he breathed. 'How do you know these things? What manner of man are you?' For the entering of another's thoughts, a sharing of dreams and visions, requires more than ordinary skills.

Morrelow tilted the hat forward again and laughed. He stood up, replacing the stopper to his flask, and made an ironic bow.

'No man at all,' he said. 'Merely *eloish*. I walk with the nomads of the forested plains. At your service.' As Matthias watched, he seemed to be losing definition, losing solidity. He raised his hand, calmly and gracefully, towards the plain, and Matthias saw a ripple in the grey-green grasses there. Morrelow bowed once more. He pulled his cloak tight and tilted back the brim of his hat. He took a step down the slope, but then he turned back.

'And yes,' he said, smiling at Matthias. 'You are quite right. I too think that the baby survived. But what has become of it, I do not know. Try a little clairvoyance, Mage: I think the child might be of significance.'

And with that he moved swiftly downhill to the plain and Matthias saw the grasses part, drift aside, until Morrelow was well away from the city. Then the grey-green sea drifted together again and the *eloish* stranger had gone.

Matthias returned to the Emperor with no comfortable assurances, no proposals for terms and treaties. He had visited Bilith, had delivered his letter to the new Archon.

He would say little about what happened there. His friends there were dead, that was all. The new Archon was ill disposed towards Peraldon. There was no good news from Bilith, no hope for peace or reconciliation.

In his eyes, Xanthon saw a memory of flames and blood.

In his arms, Matthias carried a baby.

Chapter Four
Eleanor

Mid-December. Cold, bright days, breath steaming in sharp, smoky air. The city, gaudy with decorations and late-opening shops. Perpetually crowded, jammed with cars and people.

Eleanor would be staying with friends this year; old friends who had known her since childhood. Her parents were going together to the West Indies. On business, her father maintained. The kind of business conducted on the golf course, in the club room. They had invited her to come too, warily.

They had been relieved when she refused. This was not merely a business trip. A second honeymoon, they called it, another attempt to make a go of a stormy and unpredictable marriage. She had always felt superfluous to their conflict, and didn't want to be involved in this.

'You're sure, sweetie? You've been looking so run down lately, wouldn't a holiday do you good?'

'I've had a holiday.' Ungraciously. 'One can only sit on so many beaches in a year. Anyway, the sun doesn't suit me.'

Her mother nodded, sympathetically. Red hair and fair skin were a fatal combination in the tropics. Complacently she patted her own darker blonde hair and smiled.

'I expect you're busy at work, too,' she said. 'There'll be parties and lunches, that kind of thing . . .'

'She goes to too many already.' Her father looked up from the newspaper. 'Look at her, she could do with a good night's sleep. What time was it last night? Two? Three?'

'Half past three.' Eleanor lifted her chin, daring him to comment. For a moment their eyes met in mutual antagonism and then her father shrugged, returning to the business pages.

She didn't live with them, she was of age, they had no right to question her. She had the firm intention of going to every party, every play, film, dinner, dance, concert she could find.

There were too many hours in the day to fill. She found sleep difficult, and waking worse. Dream-haunted nights, memory-haunted days.

I will have My revenge, Lycias had said. And through every day the bright gaze stalked her, pursuing every thought, every emotion, until there was no hiding place anywhere. Even the ordinary circumstances of her daily life reinforced the brilliance of the threat. The summer had expired in a heatwave of extraordinary and debilitating power. Crops failed, rivers dried up. Hosepipe bans, water rationing. Bath with a friend . . .

'After work, let's go swimming at Nick's.' Her friends tried to amuse her, mystified by so much depression.

'Must we? Will Rob be there?'

'I expect so. What have you got against him now? He's always very generous.'

'Yes, but . . .' The last thing she wanted was an encounter with an old lover.

'Well, what about going to that new restaurant at Epping Green?'

'Chinese, Japanese, Italian, Indian, Nouvelle, vegetarian, pie and chips?'

'Joe said it was good . . .'

'I'm not hungry.'

Her exhausted mind plunged yet deeper.

Revenge. Was this how it would be exacted, in the dreary pattern of uncontrollable thought, uncontrollable memory, comfortless sorrow? The sun burned through the long days of summer, the interminable golden autumn. She paced dusty streets, conducted strangers round stuffy houses, talked about mortgages, contracts, stamp duty, interest rates and damp-proofing.

And everywhere she looked, the sun flared in brilliance in cloudless skies. Her palms were sticky with apprehension, her clothes tight and uncomfortable. She was irritable and cross, and burst into inexplicable tears at the least argument, the slightest setback.

She was so lonely. Any other grief and there would have been friends and family to console and understand. They were instead puzzled, impatient. As the summer blazed towards its stifling conclusion, they were also bored.

Who could understand a dream?

By the time the heatwave ended, she had evolved strategies. She needed her friends. That autumn, she tried to pretend that nothing had happened. It had been a nightmare, a bad trip. But every morning her resolve was subverted when she looked in the treacherous mirror and saw the scar, moon-shaped, still on her temple. Every day she had to realise afresh that, for her alone in the world, it had been no dream.

And then the wasted acres of time before she could reasonably find someone to talk to.

Her 'phone bill was ludicrous.

'Debs, darling, sorry to ring so early, but what are you doing this evening?'

'For God's sake, Nell! It's before eight! You woke me up . . .'

'Oh, I am sorry! Just quickly then, is anything happening tonight?'

A sigh down the line. 'We thought we'd go to that new film, that one about the schizophrenic . . . Do you want to come too?'

'Good idea, yes please. Shall we meet for a drink first? At the Goat and Compasses? I'll go there straight from work . . .'

'Oh, all right.' Deb's voice was less than enthusiastic. She rang off soon after.

Eleanor would have to leave Debs and Joe alone for a bit. By mid-December she knew that she could not afford to exhaust her support systems.

Even less could she afford to be alone.

Fortunately, the Goat and Compasses was already crowded by the time Eleanor got there, even though she was early. She bought herself a drink and sat at one of the small tables in the corner, where she had a good view of the door and of everyone else in this fashionable, tasteful establishment.

They were fashionable, tasteful people. Good leather shoes and well-cut jackets, stylish haircuts – very short or very long, the occasional masculine pony-tail — subtle scents, mineral water in many glasses . . .

Eleanor was on gin. Anyway, it looked like mineral water. Perhaps they were all really on gin, after a hard day in the City, at the company, the bank, the salesroom . . .

There was a shout of laughter from two people by the door. An elegant, slim man with long, blond curls was holding something behind his back, twisting round so that his companion could not reach it. She was laughing, cheeks pink, chestnut hair swinging in a straight bob around a delicate, vivacious face. The man took a step back, right up against the wall, and she began to tickle him, long fingers inside his loose, pale jacket.

He exploded with laughter and abruptly brought one hand round to defend himself. With the other he threw something high into the air.

'Catch!' he shouted.

It landed in Eleanor's hands.

A small shell, curved, creamy gold.

She stared at it, lying in her palm, intricate and ordinary.

'No,' she said. 'No, no, no!' Surging up, she flung it to the ground, the polished wooden floor, and brought her heel down on it, grinding it round and round. It splintered, scratching the wood, fine dust spraying around.

'Whatever did you do that for?' The girl was suddenly beside her, watching. Eleanor had not seen her move. Intent, she was, neatly made up, thin and long-legged. Not in the least angry.

Eleanor stared at her blankly. 'What? I — I didn't mean . . .' She took a deep breath, beginning to recover. 'Why — throw a shell? Why did you do it?' She looked at the long-haired man coming to join them.

They were both regarding her with curiosity. She was embarrassed now, nervous and angry. Had she made some stupid mistake?

The door swung open. She saw Joe and Debs come in, and turned away from the two strangers, scooping up her bag and coat. She muttered, 'I'm sorry, I didn't mean to break it — '

'Oh yes you did.' The man was blocking her way, his eyes cold as stone. He lifted his hand, and for a moment she thought he was going to strike her.

She could not move, held still by hard eyes . . .

He pushed her fringe aside, exposing her temple.

She would scream, she thought. She would run wild, break things, smash windows, faint, fall over, be sick . . .

She knocked his hand away and pushed past them, running across the floor to the door.

'Look, let's go somewhere else!' she cried, catching hold of Debs' arm. 'I'll tell you outside, I don't want to stay here – '

Before they could stop her, she had crowded them back through the door, out into the cold, dark street.

'Nell! What's going on?' Joe was irritated. 'I like the Goat, and I want a drink.'

'There's a man there – '

'So? What did he do, make a pass or something? Come on, you can handle things like that, Eleanor.'

'He was horrible!' She was between them both, still shaking, holding Debs' arm, making them walk quickly back towards the City.

In panic, she looked round. There was no one following them. The street was quiet, patterned with the lights from the pub. She did not even notice the rippling shadows that skimmed the wall behind them, following her every movement. She understood only one thing.

This could not have been a coincidence. Not possibly.

It was not over.

Chapter Five
Abduction

She went out to dinner next night, the night before Christmas Eve. Lewis took her, a question in his eyes.

She ignored it, although it was beginning to get difficult. She was lonely and knew that she needed companionship. This was all part of her self-protecting strategy. And she had always liked Lewis. The problem was that he was beginning to want more than companionship; soon she would have to find someone else, someone who would not demand too much.

The hosts were friends of Lewis's, newly successful interior designers. Their house was painted a delicate eau-de-Nil, their carpets all the palest of golds, shimmering in soft lighting. White lilies were the only flowers, in plain glass vases on empty shelves.

They were pale, precise people, Lorraine Charles and Steven Finley. Friendly, in a cool way. Interested in dance, in film . . . What did they know, thought Eleanor savagely, what did they know about anything?

It was bound to be vegetarian.

Lewis winked at her across the table as the *gougère* was served.

'No concessions to the festive season, I see?'

'What, crackers, turkey . . . I am sorry! Are you disappointed?' Lorraine smiled gently. 'Aren't you going home for Christmas, Lewis? Doesn't Mummy provide all your favourite treats then?'

'Too true. And once a year is quite enough.' He tipped back in the spindly chair, raising his glass of dry-as-dust white wine. Thoughtfully he regarded the room through the golden filter. 'But aren't you in danger of throwing the baby out with the bathwater?'

'I've always considered that a singularly revolting expression.' Lorraine was still smiling.

'No, seriously.' Whenever Lewis says 'seriously', thought Eleanor, he starts stirring. She laid her fork down, sighing. She wished she could feel involved in all this. She was barely even interested.

'Don't you ever feel you're losing touch? That everything is getting refined out of sight? So tasteful that there's nothing to get your teeth into?'

'How very carnivorous of you!' Lorraine stared at him. 'What do you recommend? A return to the earth mother?'

'Twenty years out of date, surely.' Steven's voice was calm. He was tossing salad in a bowl.

'Shall we show them our secret?' Lorraine looked at him. 'The skeleton in the cupboard?'

'Not now, we're still eating.'

'Oh, go on!' Eleanor pushed her chair back. Lewis was going to get embarrassing soon, and this was all too tame. 'What skeleton? A stripped pine door? Don't tell me, your flying ducks have come home to roost.'

'No, nothing like that – '

'Worse?' she said hopefully.

'Come with me.'

The *gougère* was deflated, the salad limp. They stood up and followed the neat figure of their hostess out into the hallway and up the stairs of the late Victorian house.

Eleanor smelt it before she saw it.

A Christmas tree, real fir, standing in the bay window of the main bedroom. Covered with glitter, baubles, tinsel. Gaudy, tasteless and gorgeous, fairy lights ablaze.

It was beautiful. Eleanor went up to it, looking closely at the little angels, the snowman, the partridge in its pretty nest.

'Oh look, a jack-in-the-box!' She was enchanted.

'This is my favourite – ' Lorraine pointed out a small silver french horn, tarnished over the years.

'Lovely, and real candles too! Will you light them?'

There were tiny silver candle-holders dotted all over it, with the stubs of white wax ready for lighting.

'I'll get the bucket,' Steven sighed with resignation.

'Okay, I apologise,' Lewis had his arm round Eleanor's shoulders. His hand was heavy and alien, but she tried to relax. 'You're not totally tasteful, Lorraine, even quite human in patches. Do we sing carols now?'

'Oh yes, I think so, don't you? As a penance . . .' She grinned at him, suddenly pretty. She turned off the fairy lights and then struck a match to light the candles.

Steven, returning with a prudent bucket of water, switched off the room lights.

In the sudden dark the tree glowed and glimmered, the baubles turning in the warm air currents, the tinsel shimmering.

'Beautiful,' said Eleanor quietly. A moment of peace, of calm. Then she saw it. A glass ball, spinning over the candle flame, reflecting light.

Glass over fire.

Lorraine's voice, a small, clear soprano − '*Joseph liebe, Joseph meine . . .*'

She stood, paralysed. She knew what was going to happen.

Then she moved, tearing herself away from Lewis, blundering across the room, out into the bright hallway, down the stairs, out of the front door.

Cold air hit her like a wall of ice. She began to run, slipping on the frosty pavement. Dark, suburban houses, rainbow lights in many windows. There were footsteps behind her, in the silent, freezing street. Lewis, catching up with her, grabbing her arm.

'Let me go, let me go, don't touch me − ' She was frantic to escape.

'What is it? What's wrong? Nell, what is it?' He tried to take her in his arms, but she lashed out at him, catching the side of his face with her ringed fingers, opening a long gash in his cheek.

Sobbing, she struggled free, stumbling away from him along the pavement, trying to get further from the danger, whatever it was, wherever it was. He leapt after her, catching both her arms, whirling her round to face him.

He was white with shock, blood tracking a thin line down his cheek. He stared at her as if he had never seen her before.

'Go away, Lewis!' Her voice was unrecognisable. 'Get out of my life. I've nothing for you, it's not safe, leave me alone!'

He wanted to argue, to plead, to take her home, to a doctor, her mother, a therapist, friends, anything . . .

She could see Steven and Lorraine looking out of their front door, wondering whether to join them.

A car started up further down the road, coming towards them. A taxi, old-fashioned, heavy, black. She waved it down, closing her ears to Lewis's protests, and jumped into the back, slamming the door behind her.

At once the driver accelerated, skidding on the icy road, swerving wildly. The taxi caught Lewis a glancing blow.

She saw him crumple on the pavement and lie unmoving.

'Stop!'

The driver took no notice.

'Stop, you must stop, you hit him!'

The driver turned round to look at her. He had long wavy blond hair.

'Where to, lady?' A small laugh. 'Not that it matters. No choices this time, no difficult decisions of world-shattering significance. At least, not for you.' He spoke calmly, watching in his mirror as she struggled with the door and window.

The glass partition had slid into place between them. She couldn't open that, either.

'Who are you?' She was shouting over the engine noise.

He didn't answer, glancing at the heavy gold watch on his wrist. She saw him frown, and then fell back against the seat as he slammed his foot down on the accelerator and the taxi hurtled on, straight through red lights.

'Christ!' She looked back at the clash of traffic behind them, the swerving, squealing blaze of lights and metal.

Then it was gone as he swung the wheel round and they skidded round a corner, dodging into a wilderness of back streets, down narrow domestic avenues and terraces, pretty Christmas trees a blur of coloured light in window after window.

She was hammering against the glass, bruising her fists, still shouting, although she knew he couldn't care less.

Out onto a main road again, and suddenly into the centre of an unmoving traffic jam.

'Fuck.' She saw his mouth silently frame the word, and his white fingers began to tap on the wheel as they inched forward.

She twisted round in the seat, trying to catch the attention of the driver behind, a heavy, blowzy woman with an elaborate perm. She faced stonily ahead, ignoring the car in front.

A frantic sequence of mimed gestures: help, please, get me out!

Someone else on the left-hand side, an elderly man in a felt hat, a warm overcoat. He looked away, embarrassed, and started fiddling with his radio/cassette.

On the other side a group of young men whistled and gestured. One blew her a kiss.

In the mirror, the elegant man watched impassively.

'Keep still,' he said, and when she paid no attention, still mouthing help, help, get me out, he spoke one word.

'*Rilyni*'.'

The seat beside her shifted, changed shape, grew into creatures that fell onto her hands, clasping them in clammy folds of skin, crawling over her, anchoring her so that she had to face forwards, her head held rigid in an alien grip.

She shuddered at the touch, the memory, the implication.

Scurries.

God help her.

Chapter Six
The Crossing

They drove through the night, out of London, through Epping Forest, out into the depths of Essex, and onto the motorway.

Shuddering with revulsion she did not think of sleep, her flesh mimicked and confined by scurries, but at some stage, exhausted, she found oblivion.

And dreamed.

Two men, looking at her.

One, wreathed in shadow, held his left hand awkwardly. It was heavily bandaged.

The other, clearer, with kind, familiar eyes, was holding a staff carved into a spiral.

'I'm sorry, Eleanor,' he said, and his voice was filled with grief. 'So sorry . . .'

'He's bringing you back,' the shadowed man said, and as he stepped forward, she saw it was Phin, but obscured by the shifting shadows, still. They lifted his hair, hung around his shoulders, falling along the lines of his clothes.

She looked for friendliness from him, for welcome and strength, but he gave nothing.

It was something to do with the shadows. She found her eyes turning away from them as if they were some obscenity. They were drifting over him, concealing and suppressing, draining all energy. He could give nothing to her.

'Phin! What's wrong, what's happening to you?'

'They're nothing to do with you,' he said, his voice flat with exhaustion.

'But you're going to have to come back,' said Matthias. 'I can't help it. There's a storm coming. I'm sorry – '

'Did you send him?' She was frantic. 'The blond man, does he come from you?'

'I can't explain that now . . .'

'Be careful, Eleanor.' At last Phin was speaking strongly, directly to her. It seemed to take a great effort, a battle against the shadows. 'Be very careful. It's more dangerous than you know . . .'

And then she was awake again, and the car was still racing along a motorway, and her hands were still clasped in a chill, alien grip.

Phin, what has happened to you, what is happening to me? What storm?

The driver was still looking at his watch, his foot hard down on the accelerator, flashing lights at people to make them pull over, barely slowing for roundabouts and junctions, ignoring every speed limit.

M11, A1 . . . she knew the route, recognised the names of towns and places.

'What's the hurry?' she shouted at him.

For once, he was disposed to talk.

'We mustn't be late . . .'

'What for?'

'The crossing.'

'What crossing?'

'To Chorolon. Where did you think?'

Where indeed?

'Why? Who are you?'

No answer. 'Why do you want me? Why me, again?'

He ignored her.

She sat there, rigid with dread. As the miles were covered, as she was taken further from her home, further from her carefully reconstructed life, she tried to think.

How could they do it, travel between worlds? It had taken the Benu, last time, to wrench her from her ordinary life, leaving her in Chorolon to secure its release in that strange, violent world. It was the Benu Bird who had dropped her casually back into normality, where she had thought herself safe . . .

How could *men* do such a thing?

* * *

They turned off the A1 somewhere in the Midlands, weaving through ever smaller roads, the countryside increasingly hilly.

The roads were still icy, but the driver made no concessions, still pushing the car, heavy and resisting though it was. It squealed round corners, lurched over hills, as he took every chance.

She was blank with fear now. 'I shall have My revenge,' Lycias had said. 'You will never escape. There is no way out . . .'

Especially not on Chorolon. A world where He had shape and form, and power to stop death . . .

A world where she had lost Lukas.

She had tried to fill her life with events and people, and it had been possible, some of the time, to forget what had happened. To put aside his smile and vivid eyes, and the feel of his long fingers stroking her hair . . . and his blood, spilling onto snow.

But in Chorolon his absence would surround her, would ache in the air she breathed, would cripple every step she took, every thought she had.

She would begin grieving again.

A great ridge, caught in the headlights ahead, reared sharply above a forested valley. The road twisted through trees, making straight for the slope.

The car skidded to a halt at its foot. A light shone by the side of the road. The door beside her was wrenched open, a blast of cold air stunning her to awareness.

The woman with chestnut hair was standing there, holding a torch. She watched as the scurries flowed from the taxi, releasing Eleanor's limbs. The man got out of the car. She tried to follow him, anything to get out of that black prison, but the woman pushed her back in, getting in beside her, slamming the door again.

She held a knife, sharp-pointed, at Eleanor's ribs.

For a long time they sat there in silence. The woman refused to answer any of Eleanor's questions, refused even to look at her. In the car headlights, Eleanor could see the man with long hair doing something with the scurries, sending them off into the forest. She could dimly make out a huge pile of twigs and branches in the shadows at the side of the road.

'A bonfire?' Eleanor asked the woman, her voice high and thin. 'You're making a bonfire?'

The woman ignored her. The man had his back to them, facing the monstrous pile, but Eleanor could sense that he was saying something, chanting something.

As she watched, there was a sudden rushing sound. The dark branches and twigs burst into flame, and the scurries were running back to him, elongated shapes of bark and bracken. They were gathering more wood, building up a fire of raging power, flickering in the night.

The man ran back to the car, wrenching open the door, letting the scurries flood in beside her once more. There were vague whispers of sound as they settled round her wrists and ankles, echoes, perhaps, of the man's chant. He started the engine, accelerating hard so that the wheels spun uselessly in the mud.

Then the tyres gripped. The taxi surged on, in a low gear to begin with, ascending the hillside.

The road zigzagged back and forth, rising steeply. He was going fast again, too fast for safety, skidding and lurching round the corners.

The car would crash, she thought. It hardly mattered.

At the top a long stretch of road reached out, pale in the pre-dawn light. Most of the plain was in darkness below them. But the fire was exploding with energy now, flares of lightning darting out into the sky, illuminating the bare branches all around.

The man glanced once more at his watch.

'Ready,' he said, and it was not a question. He took a deep breath, and Eleanor could see sweat on his brow. Then he stood hard on the accelerator, and the car picked up speed.

The woman sitting beside her was smiling, a curious, unaware rictus drawn back in fear.

The road before them dropped away, swinging sharply round the corner at the end of the bank, and they were going too fast to stay on it, the wind rushing past them, drowning the noise of the engine.

There was the fire, far below them, electrical flashes darting very high into the dark. It reached up towards them.

And as the taxi left the road, darting out high into the emptiness over the fire, her last memory was of the sun, bright and blazing, rising strong and implacable in the east. Over fire, they were flying into the sun's centre.

Chapter Seven
Chorolon

God, it was hot. The air was dry and gritty in her throat, her velvet dress unbearably constricting. Eleanor stirred uneasily, not opening her eyes, unwilling to start playing a part here.

Lycias's world. It had to be; she could feel the sun through her closed eyelids, burning, heavy overhead.

There were people talking a little way from her. She couldn't hear the words, but one of the voices was familiar. Her eyes flew open and she sat up in one movement. Sand, as far as she could see in every direction, the folds of dunes and valleys orange and gold. An empty, hot, sun-filled sky above.

She was sitting in the shadow of the taxi, incongruous amongst the dunes. The voices came from the other side of it.

She stood up, and as she moved a scurry detached itself from the car door and whisked round to the other side of the taxi. She found her eyes following it, unwillingly fascinated, as usual. The scurry flickered next to metal, acquiring hard edges, shiny surfaces, and the grain of sand hung round its base.

'Good,' said the man with long hair. 'What took you so long?'

She could not have answered him, for she recognised the man he had been talking to, the man dressed in light jeans and a white shirt. He was carrying a wooden staff, and was steadfastly refusing to meet her eyes.

Matthias.

He was looking at the woman, talking to her in a furious, rapid undertone. As she watched, he frowned and kicked something on the sand.

A shard of coloured glass. There were the remains of a huge fire all around them, smouldering logs, drifting ash.

'You used the Rite?' Her voice was strained. 'Matthias. Did you bring me here?'

Then he looked at her. His skin was darker than she remembered, his eyes that deep blue that so reminded her . . . There were new lines of anxiety on his face, but his expression was rigidly masked, quite neutral, as if she were a complete stranger.

'Matthias! What is this?' She couldn't bear it, the look on his face. She began to move towards him, around the car, but he stepped back from her, self-contained and wary.

As she watched in disbelief, he gave the low warbling cry that she heard so often before.

Arrarat! Of course, he was calling Arrarat for them both!

The sound of wings filled the sky as the far speck above the horizon grew and grew, a familiar pattern of grace and strength, coming for them.

A dark grey hawk, one she had never seen before, settled on the sand beside Matthias, cocking its head towards him.

Quickly, smoothly, not waiting for her, he swung up onto its back.

'Matthias! Wait!' She began to run, not trusting the look in his eyes.

At last he spoke to her, distantly regretful.

'I'm sorry, Eleanor. So very sorry. But there's nothing else to be done. Take care of the baby . . .'

And then the hawk spread its wings and leapt up into the hot blue sky, leaving Eleanor alone on the sand with the two strangers and their vile scurries.

'Matthias!' She was screaming now, hurling the word up into the sky after him. 'Don't leave me! Matthias! Come back!'

A blow across her mouth sent her spinning onto the bonnet of the car.

'Be quiet.' The man's voice was unemotional. 'You'll wake the baby.'

Her lip was split, her mouth bruised. Matthias had gone! He had left her!

'Baby?' she said. 'What baby?'

'This one,' said the woman, reaching into the front seat

of the car and pulling out a large bundle wrapped in blankets.

She laid it carefully on the sand at Eleanor's feet and then, before Eleanor could react further, got into the car and started the engine.

Quickly the man got in beside her, and in a swirl of sand and dust the taxi moved swiftly away, disappearing in moments amongst the dunes, scurries trailing in a stream after it.

She was left on her knees, incredulous, in the sand, under the hot sun.

A thin wailing cry from the bundle of blankets.

The baby was crying.

She stared at it, not wanting to touch it. How could they do it, leave her here in the middle of a desert with no water, no food, nothing?

And a baby. Whose was it? Where did it come from? What was she to do with a baby? She knew nothing about them, why should he tell her to take care of it?

Why had Matthias left her? How could he do such a thing?

There was the faintest whisper of wind against her skin. She looked up, and along the far line of the horizon saw the blue of the sky darkening with cloud.

The sand was hot and bitter around her, the wailing baby nagging, grating on her nerves, the air heavy and ominous.

There was a storm coming.

Chapter Eight
Wreck

Some months after Matthias left Stromsall with the baby, another *eloish* plainsman speculated on the origin of a storm.

It was blowing full in his face as he rode a cliff path, just south of the city of Shelt. Wind, rain and thunder. The sound of the waves below the cliff path was almost lost in the racket. Serethrun Maryn guided his horse along the narrow track and considered the storm.

Three alternatives. It could be perfectly natural, a chance meeting of air pressure and temperature. He dismissed this. There was a malevolence in the air, something of ill-will. Something that was also incompetent.

It could be a throwback to the Stasis, when Astret's storms had blocked the sun from Stromsall. This was also unlikely, for much the same reason. The Lady, even when enraged, managed things with more elegance.

That left the Sea Lords. A Mage-powered tempest of uneven, crudely directed savagery. Under normal circumstances the Sea Lords' brief was to calm the storm, but Serethrun knew that controlling the weather worked both ways. Anyone who could quiet a storm could also initiate one.

If it went on like this, there might even be a shipwreck.

He almost laughed at the irony of it. There he was, employed by the Sea Lords, complete with gaudy uniform and a city-trained horse, watching the coast in case of shipwreck, while one of them was probably responsible for these conditions. He felt a familiar contempt for the men who paid him. Dressed in grey silk, with distracting spiral staffs, so portentous, so deeply serious . . . Did *they* want to wreck a ship?

Preoccupied by such thoughts, Serethrun Maryn, ex-*eloish* plainsman, did not bother to look up into the violent clouds overhead. He did not see the great hawk swinging away through the air, buffeted by wind and rain.

Although he was no longer one of the *eloish*, following the seasons and the winds, it was still a matter of pride to understand the provenance of this storm.

All afternoon it had been brewing. Black clouds had raced over the city, bringing both hail and rain, while the wind had whistled under doors, rattling the windows, whipping the rubbish up into a whirlwind. People had lit their lanterns soon after the midday meal, calling their children, bolting the doors.

In the barracks Serethrun had watched the others playing cards as the sky darkened. A sign outside was swaying monotonously, a sharp, scraping sound. Lambard had challenged the flautist, Vere Holtby, who sometimes amused them for the price of a drink.

'Match that,' he said, and Holtby had tried. A thin, reedy melody, shrill and out of key, deliberately unsettling. In the end, they told him to stop.

Serethrun was not surprised when the call came. They drew straws for the various routes, but that settled nothing. In the end it was decided that Serethrun should ride the central track, nearest to the city. Lambard was allocated the stretch beyond the south brigg, Alwick rode the cliff on the far side of the northern promontory. Serethrun had the worst of it, the exposed central three miles. The cliff was at its steepest there. The path wound along a fragmented course, fractured by rockfall and landslip.

In the pitch dark, with the rain and wind in his face, concentrating on the path itself, Serethrun could barely make out the edge of the cliff, let alone a ship out at sea.

His role was that of watchman. Watchman of the unsteady sea and the ship-murdering rocks. He rode the cliff path, all three muddy, exposed, windswept miles of it, over and over again for the length of his shift. He wasn't complaining: the wild ride reminded him of other times, other ways. He could almost imagine he was back with the *eloish* again, riding fast through a storm . . . But now he was on the look-out, a guard employed by the city in case a ship should be driven onto the brigg.

There were no safe harbours on this stretch of coast. No sheltered havens out of reach of the deep-troughed waves and irresistible currents. In fair weather, ships with merchandise from the south had to anchor far out from the briggs, and small craft, launched from Shelt's shallow bay, relieved them of their cargo.

The coastguard's job was to warn the ships away, to tend the lanterns that kept them from the brigg rocks at either end of the bay. And to send out lifeboats, if the warning failed. A ship would have more chance on the open sea than trying to negotiate the bay of Shelt.

The Sea Lords of Shelt were supposed to help. Shelt owed its existence to the sea, after all, from the time when all its inhabitants had been connected, one way or another, to the fishing trade. The Sea Lords had been hard pressed during the Stasis, when the daily storms had almost wrecked the fishing fleet. But sometimes, Serethrun had to admit, sometimes the Sea Lords had been successful at subduing the daily storms of the Stasis. They became almost good at it after the arrival of the southern Mage, Gawne of Aquile.

But things had changed. The Stasis was over. The fishing industry was over too, to all intents and purposes. The Sea Lords had other priorities now: healing the sick of Stromsall. They conducted obscure rites for those who could afford it and watched their coffers fill . . . Serethrun regarded the whole process with suspicion. Chained to the earth, they were, weighted by greed. It seemed unlikely that they would bother with mere weather-work these days. The storm that darkened the air over Shelt that night was probably nothing to do with them.

So, who *was* doing this?

There had been a time, long ago in his other life, when Serethrun might have enjoyed the power of such a storm. Tonight he was irritated and puzzled by it. There was something in the air, something abnormal . . .

His horse stumbled, unnerved by a stab of lightning. Serethrun murmured reassurance to the creature. His hands were light on the reins.

'Who's there?'

A familiar figure galloped briefly alongside him, blond hair hanging straight, darkened by rain, scarlet cloak billowing. Mud splattered between them.

The shouted words were difficult to catch over the wind.

'Ship! Half-way across the bay, on a dead course for the brigg. Get down there quickly, see if you can help. I'll sound the alarm – ' Lambard spurred his mount on, vanishing into the dark towards the city.

Serethrun hauled sharply on the reins, forcing his horse round in a skid of mud, back the way they had come. There was a path down to the shore half a mile away, south of the brigg.

His mount was reluctant, but Serethrun dug his heels in. He had seen wrecks before on those rocks, ships from the east and south, even a clipper from Eldin once, and knew how little chance there was. For although the coastguard strung lanterns from the Castle, although the cliff riders were a regular institution, there was a growing problem with wreckers in Shelt.

Serethrun knew why it happened, and why it would continue to happen. If the fishermen were no longer allowed to fish, how else did the Sea Lords expect them to live?

Maverick gangs of wreckers threw the whole fishing community into disrepute. The great ships from the south, bearing their ailing princes and elderly earls – Shelt's new-found wealth – were such easy prey. Wrecking paid well. It was worth risking the heavy penalties exacted by the Earl and the Sea Lords. Shelt was ruthlessly policed by the Castle Guard, its people under rigid control. Serethrun was part of a repressive machine. It did not always come easily to him, but he did indeed loathe the wreckers. The waste of life was anathema to him.

Serethrun saw the undercut turf where the track led down to the beach. It was unstable and steep. His horse would never manage it. He slid off and began to run, half slithering over the mud, grasping at the scrubby grass to slow the speed of descent. The roar of breaking waves filled his ears.

The tide was not yet in: there was a narrow curve of sand beneath the cliffs before the rocks of the brigg began. He

raced across the bay. Still he could hear nothing above the
sound of the crashing waves. No screams, no shouts. No
splintering of hull and oars.

No alarm.

Surely it should be sounding by now, the great bell of Shelt?
Surely it should be tolling out across the city, from Castle
to harbour, calling all men to the aid of the ship? Calling the
Sea Lords to their posts? Wouldn't Lambard have set the
bell ringing within minutes?

He saw the ship then, dipping dangerously. Out of control,
almost on the rocks. A big ship, a schooner from the acres
of billowing white, driven onto a lee shore.

There was nothing the sailors could do, so close to the
brigg. Except perhaps throw a line to Serethrun, if he could
get close enough.

The sand gave way to tumbled rocks and sudden pools.
The brigg was dangerous in the dark, slippery with seaweed,
uneven and unexpected underfoot. It slowed him a little, but
not much.

Where was everyone? The Sea Lords. The coastguard, the
lifeboats. The fishermen, the scavengers, the curious
onlookers? That ship needed *help*. Part of his mind was still
waiting for the tolling of the bell, steady over the water, steady
through the city. But there was no sound of voices shouting,
no flash of lanterns swinging.

He looked up then, to the Castle, looking for the safe,
familiar, golden glow.

The Castle was in blackness. There was no lantern lit that
night. What had gone wrong? Was this treachery, betrayal?
What *were* the Sea Lords up to?

Only then did he hear the terrible, splintering crash of wood
on rock and the shouting from the men aboard the ship. He
was almost at the end of the brigg. Furiously, he put the
darkened Castle out of his mind.

He saw the ship shiver with strain, impaled on Mark Spar.
A wave broke at his feet. He turned his eyes away from the
ship's death, and concentrated on getting there. He fell, his
knee striking rock. A half-voiced curse as he plunged onward,
slipping on seaweed, scrambling . . .

The ship was listing heavily over the jagged point of the
Spar beyond the end of the brigg. It was on the verge of

capsizing, and the coastguard was going to be too late . . .
He couldn't bear it.

He saw men tumbling into the black water, falling,
discarded like rags. Others were clinging to the rigging, trying
to inch their way high above the churning waves. He was
running again . . .

There at last, hard-braced against the wind, at the end of
the brigg. The ship was only thirty feet away, but the water
between the brigg and Spar was a cauldron, waves clashing
with utmost force in every direction, the spray leaping high
into the night.

He could see the ship clearly now, the masts jutting at crazy
angles, rigging hanging like web, straining down to the deck.
Dark shapes were clinging there, wailing with terror.

They were *mereth*, helpless as children. He was one of them
now, he knew what it was like. Bound to the earth, to the
city, to their possessions and responsibilities, at the mercy
of the storm and the sea. They were screaming into the wind,
calling for their God, their mother, their beloved to help.

There was no one to hear but Serethrun Maryn, stranger,
one of them and yet not one of them, alone at the end of the
brigg.

A wave broke, drenching him. He was up to his knees in
water. He cupped his hands over his mouth, shouting at the
ship. 'A line! Throw a line!'

They could not hear him, but he saw one man understand
his intention, and drop down from the rigging onto the
deck.

He staggered as the ship shifted on the rock, struggling
to unleash a heaving line.

Serethrun watched, shivering. There was little chance. A
wave broke, almost knocking him over. He looked down,
searching for a more secure place.

He sees something.

Disregarding the crashing waves, Serethrun kneels, leaning
forward. He looks again into the water. In that moment of
confusion he sees a glimpse of white, drifting in the grip of
the tide.

A face flickers there. Awash with water, lost in waves,
pulled back again into the blackness.

He reaches out, stumbles, almost falls . . .

The sailor is still labouring to unleash the coil. At last he has one end free. He looks at Screthrun, his face twisting.

'Hoy! You there! Stand ready!' he yells.

Serethrun is kneeling on the rock, leaning forward over the dark waves. He is trying to reach the figure drifting there, but the sailor's shout makes him look up. He has to drag his eyes from the flickering white of her face – her! A woman, washed by the tide . . .

The line falls, close by his hand. He clutches at it but it has already dropped away.

Her face gleams again.

He does not see the line reeled in once more. Does not see the uncomprehending fear and bewilderment in the sailor's face as he makes ready for another attempt.

The ship is now shivering, a constant tremor of stress.

In the water again, Serethrun pulls on cloth, feeling it give, tearing. He lunges forward, grabbing for a better purchase.

The sailor throws the line once more, just as Serethrun hauls the body out.

For a moment, strange, unaccustomed indecision. He looks at the face in his hands, and recognises something he has thought lost forever . . .

The weighted end of the line brushes his arm, and he misses it. As it falls back into the water, he looks at the man on the ship. The sailor's face is grimacing with terror.

The ship shudders, a wrenching groan from buckling timbers, and slowly, slowly, slides back off the Spar, back down into the black water, warping as the waves crash over it.

The coastguard's team of volunteers arrived soon after, but it was too late. There were only two survivors: the woman, and an ordinary seaman called Berwick. By some miracle chance he had jumped from the rigging just as the ship capsized, and a freak wave had caught him up, hurling him high onto the rocks of the Spar itself.

His leg was broken by the impact, his ribs crushed, his skin lacerated. He lay motionless and barely conscious until the storm abated in the early hours of the morning and a boat was launched.

He babbled in fever, a mixture of nonsense and fear, and

no one took much notice until one of the nurses remarked on one phrase.

'The guiding light — we followed it, the guiding light . . .'

Wreckers. The rumour flared round the city.

Within a few hours, soldiers were hammering at Serethrun Maryn's door.

Chapter Nine
The Inquiry

'Lambard told me. He said he'd raise the alarm, that there was a ship approaching the brigg.'

'Call Lambard Bowen!'

Voices faded along distant corridors. During the pause Serethrun felt his hands grow sweaty, although the room was cold.

His immediate superior, Captain Niall, was in the gallery, together with Kester Robard, one of his colleagues. Not once had either of them caught Serethrun's eye. They had both refused to give evidence as a character witness, and that in itself was damning. Still reluctant to believe it, Serethrun looked up at them once more, willing them to acknowledge him. There was no flicker of recognition.

The ornate courtroom, all carved oak panels and heavy brass candelabra, was crowded. But it seemed to Serethrun that his words echoed in the chilly silence.

No one believed him. Nothing he could say would make any difference. He was *eloish*. He knew how the catalogue would go. Ambivalent, eldritch stranger. Dark-haired foreigner, from the northern plains, racially different, small-boned, almond-eyed . . . Not to be trusted, plainspeople. That's what they always said, and there was an element of truth in it. Thieving savages, ruled by black witches with enough power to rival the Sea Lords. That was a lie, Irian was worth more than all the Sea Lords put together, but he'd never told anyone that. He'd played the innocent, had brawled in the stables, joked in the dormitories and bars. It had taken a long time to win a measure of acceptance, through a combination of swinging fists and hard work. He had become one of them, and not one of them.

Today no one would believe him. He knew it with sick certainty. There was a mob outside the door. He could hear them, jeering in impromptu chorus.

But Lambard would tell them. They'd trained together under Niall, had diced and drunk long into the night, had always covered for each other where necessary. He had never seemed to care that Serethrun was different.

He wouldn't let Serethrun down.

Lambard arrived at last, and stood unsmiling in the dock, a tall, fair man with steady grey eyes and straight hair. Like Niall and Robard, he did not look at Serethrun.

'Lambard Bowen, Lieutenant in Captain Niall's company, coastguard rider . . .

'Yes, I was on duty that night . . .

'I heard nothing until the alarm rang – '

'You gave the alarm yourself!' Serethrun was on his feet, his voice low and dangerous. 'You saw the ship first, Lambard. You told me – '

'Sit down, Maryn! At once!' The Archon's voice halted him. 'Continue, Mr Garwood.'

The prosecutor Garwood glanced briefly at Serethrun and continued his questions. A small man, his voice was dry and precise.

'In your own words, if you please, Lieutenant Bowen. Tell the court exactly what happened on the night in question.'

And Lambard told of the waiting in the barracks, the small flautist, the drawing of the straws . . .

'Alwick took the stretch north of the city, Serethrun Maryn the central. I had the south patrol. Nothing had seemed odd, nothing unusual. No, there had been nothing strange about the choice . . .' But here Bowen hesitated and Garwood pounced.

'You drew straws, you say? Was this usual?'

'It's the custom. The three patrols are very different in character. And it depends on the wind, too. The central is usually reckoned the worst . . .'

'And Maryn drew that patrol?'

'Well, no. I'd got the central run originally, but Serethrun – Lieutenant Maryn – asked if I'd swap . . .'

At last Lambard looked at him. 'He said he wanted to get back to the city quickly after the shift. There was someone waiting for him . . .'

'Accomplices, I suppose.' Niall's voice broke in here, rough with disgust.

Lambard was still looking at Serethrun, saying nothing, while the Archon dealt with the interruption.

No, he had no accomplices, no friends, no lovers in Shelt. Only his father waited for him every night, gasping with bronchitis. Another lonely, dark-haired stranger in the city, a cripple in more ways than one. No one would bring soup, or make up the fire if Serethrun didn't.

He hadn't told them about his father. Meanly, he had tried to hide him away, that bedridden, difficult figure. He tried to pretend, when he was with the Guard, that Renferell Maryn didn't exist . . .

Lambard hadn't minded swapping; Serethrun would have done the same for him, after all.

'So, Serethrun Maryn rode the central stretch. What then?'

'Then . . . nothing. Until I heard the alarm.' Lambard shrugged.

'You didn't see the ship?'

'No. It was too dark, and the rain was heavy.'

'You heard nothing. No shouts, no sound of the ship on the rocks?'

'In that wind?'

Of course not. Serethrun himself had heard nothing until he was far out on the brigg. No one could have heard anything from the cliff-top.

But Lambard had told him there was a ship approaching. He had ridden past, scarlet cloak flying in the wind, and had gone on to raise the alarm.

The alarm that had not sounded till much, much later.

Why should Lambard lie? What was going on? Who had engineered that storm?

Serethrun was no longer sweating. He was beginning to feel cold. Furious. What was he doing here with these people? What were they to him?

He told his story, over and over, his voice level and undisturbed. Why should he show them what he felt?

It was his word against Lambard's.

No one would believe him, dark-haired *eloish* in a *mereth* city.

The evidence piled up. The watchman on the bell-tower had been told to raise the alarm by a builder, who had gone to check his scaffolding in the storm. No, of course he hadn't mistaken Lieutenant Bowen for a labourer. In that uniform? All gaudy like a maiden's prayer . . .

A further witness, one of the coastguard's men, a thin, wiry man with quick, darting eyes.

'Aye, I was first along the brigg.

'Yes, I found Maryn there, trying to help the woman . . . yes, he'd clearly been there some time.

'The ship had gone down by the time we arrived. There were a few barrels, some timber . . . nothing much – '

'The wreck was a little too successful, eh, Maryn?' The Archon stared at Serethrun over the top of his glasses. 'Where were your friends, Maryn? You were surely not alone in this?'

'I am no wrecker.' Serethrun consciously relaxed his hands on the rail. His voice was still quiet and even. 'If I had been wrecking, I would not have been alone. There would have been others . . .'

'I put it to you that confederates were on their way when the alarm went. They had not reckoned on it being given so soon. The labourer's sighting was pure chance. It spoiled all their plans and left you there to take the blame. Who were they, Maryn? The *eloish*, your own kind from the plains? Or were you in league with fisherpeople? I suggest you give us their names. It will be the worse for you if you don't.'

'No. You've got it wrong. I'm not a wrecker. I have no "confederates", *eloish* or otherwise.' He paused, trying to think logically. 'Why should I have gone down first, anyway?'

For an answer the Archon reached down below his desk and brought out a battered lantern.

'Recognise this, Maryn?'

'Of course.' There were thousands of them in the city, a common design. 'Everyone has lamps like that.'

'This one was found half-way along the brigg. It was still warm.'

He said nothing, refusing to accept the implications.

'You really must think up a better story, Maryn. This won't

do.' The Archon's words were mild, but his voice was contemptuous.

'Wrecker! *Eloish*! String him up, wrecker!' The mob outside were getting louder, and he heard the doors rattle with the weight of bodies.

'I swear to you I am innocent of this.' He felt his eyes narrowing, felt the anger growing.

He did not want to lose his temper here. They were *mereth*, crude children, unskilled, earth-bound city-dwellers. They were eager for him to betray himself. He would not give them that satisfaction. 'I did my duty. You would be better advised to spend time investigating that storm, and why there was no light showing from the Castle – '

The Archon was not even listening. A messenger was standing at his side, whispering in his ear.

For a moment the Archon looked across at Serethrun, his face unreadable, and then he pursed his lips. His hands were playing with a paper knife on the desk in front of him, turning it over and over in gnarled fingers. A long pause, ambiguous and weighty.

He stood up. 'The case is not proven,' he said. 'All charges are dropped.'

An extraordinary silence. The noise of the mob outside was suddenly hollow and meaningless.

The court rose, a rustle of confusion and whispers. Once more the Archon looked long and coolly at Serethrun. Then he gathered his papers and swept out, followed by the court officials.

'You can go.' A sharp voice, to Serethrun. 'Go on, off with you!' One of the Guard, sneering.

Serethrun stood motionless. He was free. For a moment he remained in stillness, his hands resting on the wooden rail. Then he raised his head, as if emerging from a dream, and stepped down.

He walked away from the dock, across the courtroom, through the rapidly dispersing crowd to the double doors.

Lambard, talking to Niall and Robard at one side.

A stupid confusion, a muddle. Would he ever understand them? A joke. That was it. An elaborate, tasteless, practical joke. Surely.

Their faces were caricatures to him: gross, sweaty. Their ways were alien, he did not know or understand them. But still, he had worked with these men, would work with them again. He walked up to them.

'Lambard . . . Why did you do that? What were you playing at?'

He searched the broad face, the grey eyes and fair hair neat and ordered, searching for comprehension.

'I play at nothing.' Lambard looked at him for a long, unfriendly moment. Then he spat, accurately and deliberately at Serethrun's feet, before turning his back on him and walking away.

'Clear your things from the barracks, *eloish*. I want you out by four.' Niall was already turning away when Serethrun caught him by the arm.

'Didn't you hear? The charges were dropped. I'm innocent . . .'

'Case not proven, Maryn. The Archon said nothing about innocence. You're finished.'

The double doors swung open on the cold, damp morning.

The news had spread and the crowd was already breaking up. Only a few stragglers lingered, huddled under umbrellas, collars turned up.

His face was burning as he walked away through them, and although the refrain was no longer shouted, he heard the whisper, souring the air.

Wrecker. *Eloish*. Wrecker.

Eloish

Chapter Ten
The *Eloish*

The barracks were virtually deserted. Everyone was out on duty, patrols, exercises. In the guardroom, empty chairs and tables were lined up in strict, four-square order. A cleaner leant on his mop, silently watching Serethrun clear his locker. There wasn't much; a spare shirt, socks, an extra jersey. No books, no letters from the family, no cards or dice: he was still too much the *eloish* plainsman to want to clutter his life with possessions. And who was there to write to him?

The cleaner had moved on. There was no rush. Serethrun's father would not be expecting him yet. He sat at one of the tables, staring blankly at the rain running down the window.

He remembered. Or was it a dream? Something in his blood, rather than his thoughts. Long ago, during the Stasis. There had been blizzards and storms throughout Stromsall, but that night all was calm.

The circle was complete. Serethrun Maryn, attended by his friends Mir and Enthor, waited beneath the broken tree for the decision.

Their eyes met in darkness. Whatever the decision, they would roam the northern wastes, sweeping through the storms of the Stasis. They would risk everything, running before the wind, dodging the lightning, chancing the thunder, to take what they needed.

But now it was quiet, quiet and still. They formed a triangle of strength, Serethrun, Mir and Enthor, waiting, watching the circle. The light that flared along each glance showed a moonlit world of frosty brilliance. Trees, their branches weighted by sparkling snow. In the calm of midnight, Mir greeted the calling owl. Enthor laughed silently with the distant hyena. The scream of a dying rabbit sang sharply through the frost.

Serethrun waited. The other *eloish* were also watching, resting in the curve of a branch, or standing motionless amongst the young, slender trees, elder and birch. The moonlight passed over them as the circles of women shifted, now showing silver, now blue. The hunched figure on the ground inside the circle did not stir.

Blue, silver. Serethrun's eyes drifted away from his friends, waiting in the forest, and returned to the circle. Not much longer, surely? He felt a rustle in the air around him. The others were approaching, and the trees and branches swayed in the cold light as the *eloish* passed.

Mir's left hand rested lightly on Serethrun's shoulder; Enthor was holding his right wrist. A clasp of friendship.

Silver, blue. Stillness, all around him. The forest was quiet. They were all with him now, waiting.

Silver, blue, black.

The circle broke apart, and the women turned around. Black faces and black bodies, moving away now from the hunched shape on the ground. Irian, moving with slow and secret grace towards him. Unhurriedly, she pulled the silver and blue cloak close over the sacred paint.

He looked for reassurance and comfort from her.

She smiled. 'Serethrun. Be joyful. You are free, now.'

In shock, he felt his face change. 'Renferell is *dead*?'

The word itself was alien to him. He had not thought their father so severely injured. Irian, his shaman sister, still looked at him, the same faint smile curving narrow lips.

How could she smile, with their father lying there?

The grip on his wrist tightened briefly, and then fell away. Mir's hand lifted from his shoulder. He stood free of them, but the words refused to come.

Irian shook his head. 'Not dead, no. But deathwards. He will never walk again – '

'You're a healer, Irian, do something!' He looked past her to the unmoving figure of their father. He saw sweat shining on the broad forehead, saw the eyes turned away from him, distant with pain. 'You've mended broken bones before now!'

'Not broken spines. We have no horses to carry cripples.'

A pause. 'Serethrun. Think what I am saying. You are free now.'

He shook his head, as if to clear it. In reality, he could no longer bear the way his sister looked at him. There was triumph in it, a challenge he did not want to acknowledge. He felt a movement at his side, and turned away from Irian.

'Serethrun. Come with me.'

It was Brianne. Dream-bright, shining Brianne. She had braided her hair with silver. Holding out her hands to him, offering him the gift of herself.

He had longed for Brianne . . .

'Celebrate your freedom,' she said. 'Come with me.'

He struggled against it. 'My father . . .'

She shrugged. 'The horses are gone. There is nothing else to be done. You are free now.'

He followed her away from their camp. She led him through frosty paths to the deep wood. Silver seemed to trail behind her, drifting towards him, drawing him onwards. A web of entrancement, recreating the world around him. Brianne was like quicksilver, and as unexpected. He wanted to hold her, to push inside the silvery essence, to pin her quivering and enraptured beneath him.

He knew that the others would wait for them. They would light the fires and pitch the tents, whisper together in the wild night air. Irian and the daughters would wash away the sacred paint, putting on their ordinary clothes and then they would all eat, and share the burning brandy. There would be rejoicing, for Serethrun was now free.

It was a celebratory event, the passing of souls to full power. Such a passing depended on the death of the mother for a girl, of the father for a boy. Their mother had died long ago, shortly after giving birth to Irian. His sister had been too little then for the weight of her newly inherited powers, and it had fallen to Serethrun to guard and guide her.

He had watched her grow with delight and concern. He loved her small hands, her wide, serious stare. As time went on, it became impossible to ignore the extent of her powers. She would be a shaman of extraordinary skills, he knew, but he was more concerned that she should be warm and well-fed. He had discovered in himself a passionate impulse towards nurture.

It was an impulse that moved him now.

His father. Still lying beside the broken tree, his spine splintered by the frost-riven oak. The *eloish* camp would be pitched a little distance from him. They would take him no food, no brandy or blankets to ease his death. He was no longer one of the *eloish*. He was deathwards.

Serethrun's steps slowed. He remembered those eyes, turned away. The hand, deep clenched, against the frosty grass. He did not even know how long it would take. It might be days . . .

He stopped. He saw Brianne pause and turn to look at him. As he turned, beginning to walk back towards the broken tree, he heard his name spoken once, her voice calm and unstressed. He would make his decision freely.

He avoided the camp, skirting the bright warm fires and the murmur of his friends. At the end of the path, just where it opened out into the clearing of the broken tree, he saw Irian. She too had left the camp. She was waiting for him. She had known that he would return.

She did not need to touch him. She never had. She watched steadily as he crossed towards his father's slumped figure. She waited.

Serethrun lifted his hand to Renferell's face. At his touch, clear eyes opened and stared at him, alert and intelligent.

'Go . . .' His voice was very faint.

Serethrun laid his hand over his father's. 'I'll get you to Shelt,' he said. 'They have *real* healers there.'

He looked up at Irian. Steadily she met his gaze. There was no understanding in it, no compassion. She spoke one word, '*Mereth*,' her voice cold and clear. She turned back towards the camp.

He stood up, then, slowly. His mind was flinching from the word. 'Irian? Little sister, what have you said?'

Mereth. She did not turn back, did not reply. She had disowned him, she had denied every connection. He could not move. Was this really happening?

He was severed from Irian, his sister, and from the *eloish*. To the clan he would henceforth be an outsider, because Irian's word was law and they would all obey.

Glimpsed through the trees, the people sitting round the fires of the camp were strangers to him. Wild *eloish* plainspeople, untrustworthy robbers and thieves. They were friends and family no longer. The forest was bereft of comfort.

The cold of the night began to bite. He took his cloak off and wrapped it round his father. His hands were shaking but it didn't matter. He was not sure what mattered at all now. His mind was in a turmoil. But as he looked at the flickering firelight through the frosty trees, he knew one thing. He held fast to it, the original impulse that had informed his life. His father should not die like this, alone and without comfort. He would take him to Shelt, find him healing and strength. He would not give up like this.

Life was worth something. It should not be discarded so casually.

It was very cold now. He thought that perhaps he should make a fire, but he had no will for it. So he spent the night constructing a dragging stretcher, while the word *mereth* rang round his brain in patterns of distress.

In the morning, he manoeuvred his father onto the woven pallet of branches, ignoring the fury in the injured man's eyes, and began to pull.

He pushed the table away and left the guardroom.

The rain had stopped. He walked through the streets of Shelt, through the winding passages and cramped alleys he knew well. In the window of a baker's, he saw his face unkindly reflected.

Dark haired, slant-eyed. *Eloish*.

Outsider in every way.

Chapter Eleven
Eviction

'Where have you been?'

Slant eyes followed Serethrun round the room.

'Why are you home so early? What are you looking like that for?'

He didn't want to speak, didn't want to look at the crooked, ruined figure on the bed. He hung his cloak behind the door and unbelted his sword.

The room was unusually tidy, the bare boards swept, the thin curtains tied back. The cups had been washed and were hanging on hooks. But the flavour of the room was the same, the scent of smoke and stale sweat, sickness and bad cooking. Sour smells, not amenable to superficial tidying.

The fire needed stoking. Serethrun bent down, picking up the poker, turning it in aimless hands, staring blindly into the red coals.

'Well, my *mereth* son? Do I have to find out myself?' A crash as the old man on the bed pulled at the table at his side and sent it flying, cup, water, medicine, books.

The blankets were neat about him, the grey sheets folded back, tucked in tightly.

'Who told you?' Serethrun's voice was low and savage. 'Who's been here with the tittle-tattle? Mother Paskell and her god-awful crew?'

'Wrecking, eh? Wasn't your pay enough? Keeping your father must cramp your style, spoil the cut of your coat. Not enough money to treat the girls, impress the lads – '

'Is that what you think? That I would do such a thing?'

'Didn't you?' The old man was leaning back on his pillows, exhausted. Serethrun bit back the bitter retort. He could see the sheen of sweat on his father's brow, the thin hands clutching at the covers.

'Of course not,' he said more calmly. 'Lambard lied. Or someone was setting me up.'

'*Eloish*.' The old man nodded. 'Serethrun. Let's get out of here. Back to the plains, anywhere else but here. You should never have done it, it's never worked, nothing's been any use since the accident . . .'

'I was accepted in Shelt, the Guard took me on. This last year hasn't been bad.' This was true.

'But now what will you do? There's no work in Shelt except for soldiers and servants, as you well know. And you're different. *We're* different. They'll notice you in the street, black hair . . . A scapegoat, you'll be, they'll load all the misery onto *you*. We'll have to leave.'

Confined as he was to the room, largely neglected by neighbours, friendless and powerless, Renferell Maryn knew about the *mereth*, the city dwellers. It was all that remained of an understanding that had guided the clan over the wide plains, through the deep forests. He had led the *eloish* with ruthless intelligence and skill, dodging the storms or skimming within them, always living at the edge of experience. He applied this passionate will to the people around him in Shelt, and found them to be *mereth*: earthbound, inadequate, predictable and uninteresting.

Serethrun knew that Renferell furiously resented his helpless existence in Shelt. But would he have preferred death? Serethrun was not so sure. Renferell had energy and quick wits, and there had always been the hope that one day they would have enough money to finance the healing . . .

'We should get out of here.' His father's eyes were gleaming with eagerness. 'There's no point in staying now, we'll never be able to afford the attentions of a Sea Lord. Let's go. Back to the plains. Anything would be better than this.'

This was a new twist to a familiar refrain. As Serethrun picked up the table and mopped the floor, he wondered if his father was right.

Weeks it had taken them to reach Shelt, tramping the cold forests, sheltering where they could from the ceaseless storms.

There had been no other way, no other choice, if Renferell were to live, because the *eloish* never rested, never stayed still.

Serethrun did not rest on that long journey either. Their only hope on reaching Shelt — one that only just paid off — was that the Castle Guard would be in need of manpower. They were in luck, because the city was in a state of insurrection. Too much unemployment, poverty, bad housing: Shelt was a city on the verge of civil war.

They took Serethrun on. Ironically, it was only possible because of his alien, *eloish* background. Before their horses had been stolen (requisitioned, said Torold, Earl of Shelt), the *eloish* had learnt to ride in a fashion unknown to the city people, without saddles, whips or spurs. Serethrun relied only on the intuitive knowledge that always existed between the *eloish* and their horses. He was a wonderfully skilled horseman compared with the men of the city, controlling any horse to an extent judged uncanny by his fellow Guardsmen. And in Shelt the horses were needed not only to ride the cliffs, but also to patrol the streets, to move quickly from one part of the city to another: the Castle Guard was responsible for maintaining the peace, and it was an uphill struggle. They needed their horses.

That had all taken place a long time ago. It had taken two of those years to win a smile from the men who shared the barracks with him. But this last year had been good, and he had thought himself secure at last. A place in the fabric of city society; respect, if not friendliness from the men in the Guard. A regular income to support his father, and enough left over to save for the healing.

And now, one word had ruined it all. Wrecker. He could still not quite believe it. He had almost started to forget that he was different, *eloish*.

A thunder of knocks on the door.

Serethrun dusted the table, replacing the books and bottle of pills, taking his time before going to answer it. It could only be trouble.

A small man, greasy grey trousers and shirt, thinning mousy hair and narrow, foxy features. The landlord.

'What kept you?' he said belligerently. 'Hiding the evidence?'

'What are you talking about?'

'You know.' Sharp eyes flickered over the room. 'I need
this room. Your lease is up.'

'On the contrary, it's got six months to run.'

'I need it. Today.' He drew from his pocket a small pouch
of money. 'Here's a week's rent in lieu of notice.'

Serethrun didn't move. 'What about the contract?'

'What contract?' The man lifted his chin, meeting Serethrun's eyes. '*I've* no contract. And you'll not find a lawyer
in the city who'll back up any forgery *you* may produce.'

'The charges were dropped.' Serethrun's voice was patient,
deliberately neutral. 'I have done nothing.'

'You'll not find a lawyer to back that up either.' The man
spoke without heat. 'Get back to the plains, *eloish*. That's
where you belong.'

Two weeks later, Serethrun Maryn was sitting in a bar
watching everyone else get drunk. He had spent the last of his
money on a glass of brandy. It would have bought a loaf of
bread for his father. They would start to go hungry next day.

Serethrun was philosophical about it now. He could steal,
scavenge in dustbins – it was no worse than watching every
penny draining away, waiting for the supply to run out. He
hated scrimping and saving, it took too much mental energy.
And he wanted his mind clear. He wanted to find out what
had happened. It simply had not been a natural storm;
someone had framed him. There had to be an answer to it
somewhere.

The noise in the bar broke through his thoughts. The room
was crowded, the low ceiling lost in smoke. The trestle tables
were still scattered with the remains of the stew, but no one
was eating at this stage. Drinking was the serious business
of the evening.

The dark-curtained doorway to the right of the counter was
temporarily unattended. The girls were all busy for the
moment, and didn't need to tout for trade.

A row was in its infancy. Two men a little way along the
bar from him were starting to shout, their words rising above
the general chatter. Serethrun watched dispassionately as the
older of the two slammed his fist onto the counter, springing
to his feet.

'Shit, what do you mean, some other way? Are you

frightened or something?' He had short, greying hair, small, hot, black eyes, a bulbous, misshapen nose. He was built like a bull, head sunk deep into heavy shoulders, arms swinging wide to sweep a glass onto the floor.

The other man spoke too quietly for Serethrun to catch his words, but whatever he said inflamed the other to a flaring pitch of violence.

'Fool! It would never work, you know it wouldn't!'

'Perhaps you're the frightened one.' The second man was standing now, looking frail and insubstantial beside the brute strength of the other. He was dressed in patched, shabby clothes, jersey and jeans, like nearly everyone else there, but his eyes were watchful, contained.

Serethrun drank his last mouthful, looking away. Another brawl. It was nothing to do with him. In the Castle Guard he would have intervened, bringing order – if he had been there. But he wouldn't have been, of course. He had never frequented bars like this then, even on police duty.

The large man was still shouting. Predictably, he threw a punch at the other, who sidestepped it neatly and then responded in kind. He didn't miss, but it had little effect. The man with the grey hair came at him like a battering ram. They were locked together now, and people had cleared a space around them, watching with interest. Even Serethrun looked up, curious to see how long it would take for the heavier man to prevail.

It didn't happen like that. In a weird, sideways movement too quick to follow, the thin man had kicked his opponent's feet from under him. He overbalanced, crashing into a chair, and lay there for a moment, stunned. Blood trickled from the side of his mouth.

The thin man turned back to the bar, coolly ordering another drink. The landlord was nagging, demanding money, but without heat. It hadn't been a serious brawl. Only one chair damaged, a couple of glasses broken. The onlookers turned away.

But then Serethrun saw the big man stir, and caught a glint of light in his hand. A knife had appeared there, small in the bunched fist. Without pausing to think, Serethrun pushed the thin man to one side, and the knife thudded harmlessly into the counter between them.

For the briefest of seconds the thin man looked at it, quivering in the wood. Then he said a word, quietly, almost under his breath, and there was a small hissing sound. Under Serethrun's eyes the metal blade of the knife fizzed and smoked, and crumpled away to nothing. The hilt fell with a clatter to the floor.

No one else had seen. Only the man still crouched on the floor, and Serethrun.

Serethrun's eyes moved to the thin man's face. He stared back, impassively, and then slowly dropped the lid of one eye.

'Drink?' he said, not bothering to look as the large man clambered to his feet.

'You don't want nothing to do with this bastard,' he said to Serethrun. 'He's a con-man, a trickster . . .' The bluster faded away as he looked at Serethrun. Thoughtfully he wiped the blood from his chin. Something was flickering at the back of the black, beady eyes. 'Hey, I know your face, *eloish*, I seen it somewhere . . .'

He fished in a pocket and brought out a crumpled piece of paper. Pushing between Serethrun and the thin man, he straightened it on the bar, pressing the grubby folds flat. 'There,' he said. 'I reckon you deserve each other. Traitors both.' He spat on the badly produced picture, turned away, laughing to himself, and walked out of the bar.

Serethrun looked at the paper, a small handbill of the sort circulated by illegal political groups. His own face stared back at him from beneath the grime and spittle.

'WRECKERS IN CASTLE PAY', ran the headline. 'The Castle's Guard, that noble instrument of oppression, has lately found itself unwelcome publicity in the trial of Serethrun Maryn, one of its brightest young scions . . .'

It ran on, a heavily ironic account of the trial and subsequent acquittal, ending on a sour note. 'Thirty seamen died on the *Mirabelle*. Maryn, protected by the Castle Guard, goes free. Why should we endure this injustice? Maryn is an *eloish* plainsman . . . jobs, protection, freedom for the *eloish*, while the fishermen of Shelt are denied work, robbed of liberty and life, oppressed and ignored! Now is the time for change! We must unite!'

He reached out, weary and cynical, to screw it up, but the thin man's hand held his wrist fast. 'What's the rush?' he

said quietly. 'Don't you want to know who is circulating
this?'

'What's it to you?'

The man shrugged. 'Chad's knife might have found its
mark.'

Serethrun shook the hand off. He was cold with fury. It
made his voice acid sharp. 'Of course, a Mage who knows
words of power needs that kind of help . . .'

'Another drink, friend?' The man ignored the sarcasm in
Serethrun's voice. 'Come on.' Smoothly, he guided Serethrun
across the floor to one of the shady alcoves, somehow
acquiring a full bottle of brandy, sweeping up the handbill
on the way.

'I'm Olwyn, Olwyn Mittelson.' He leant across the narrow,
stained table, pouring a long drink for Serethrun. His eyes
were pale, colourless, and still distant, although his words
and actions were friendly.

Serethrun watched him curiously. He was more deeply
shocked by that handbill than he cared to admit. The only
thing that had made the last two weeks tolerable was his
anonymity. He had pulled down the hood of his cloak, hiding
his hair, and no one had stared at him in shops, at the market,
in bars. He had been refused work, but the employment
problem was desperate in Shelt anyway, and he had not taken
it personally.

But handbills like that had a habit of cropping up
everywhere, in every sector of society. People would be on
the look-out. He would be a marked man, visibly on the
outside of society. There would be no chance at all of finding
work, of any kind at all, whatever he did. It would be
desperate.

He would have to leave Shelt, return to the plains . . .

His father. It wouldn't work. Serethrun could do nothing,
go nowhere. He drained the glass, unaware of the pale eyes
studying him.

'Disguise.' Mittelson's low voice drifted across the table.
'Dye your hair, grow a beard, change your name. No one
will know.'

Serethrun looked at him, his mouth straight and unsmiling.
'No,' he said slowly. 'I'm innocent. I didn't do it. It's a lie.'
He uncurled his clenched fingers. 'I will not pretend, will

not lie to get work. I need to find out why first. There's some reason for this. Getting a job can wait.'

'You are either arrogant or foolish, Serethrun Maryn. You will starve before you find out anything in Shelt.'

Olwyn Mittelson leant back, his eyes still fastened on Serethrun with their curious, pale gaze.

'What do you want?' Serethrun poured more brandy, refusing to meet that unsettling stare. 'Why are you bothering?'

There was a small silence. The thin man's hair was lank and greasy, too long, unkempt. His nose was thin, unexpectedly aquiline, his chin pointed and narrow. His face seemed to slant towards the eyes, and the eyes gave nothing away.

'I'll be here next week,' he said at last. 'If you want me . . .' He stood up, pushing back the chair, and to Serethrun he suddenly appeared tall, tall as a tree, thin and unknown. He smiled to Serethrun briefly, turned and walked away through the crowded bar.

There was almost a full bottle left.

Serethrun began to empty it.

Chapter Twelve
Smintha

The baby had black eyes. It had stopped crying as soon as Eleanor picked it up, although she was clumsy and unwilling.

Matthias had left her, had abandoned her. Had performed the Seventh Rite – or whichever one it was – to bring her here, and had then just left.

She couldn't believe it. Why had he bothered? She would surely die here, in this heat with no water.

Unthinkingly, she held a finger out to the baby, who immediately clasped it. Babies always did that, she knew. As if it would help.

Its tiny hand was hot and clammy. It must be roasting, she thought, all those heavy blankets. She knelt on the sand again, the sweat running into her eyes as she leant over and unwrapped it.

Two layers of woollen blanket and then a thin cotton nightgown over heavy, damp, towelling nappies. The baby, a boy child, crowed with pleasure, kicking its legs as she freed them.

It had black hair, black eyes, a golden brown skin. It would stand the sun much better than she . . . She left the nightgown in place and borrowed one of its blankets to drape over her own head. It didn't seem to mind, laughing at the sky, wriggling and kicking.

She watched it for a while, thinking.

Matthias was Lukas's brother. He would not have brought her here to die. There had to be some reason, some solution.

Perhaps there was a town, just beyond the dunes. Civilization within easy reach. Perhaps she was panicking needlessly.

The clouds on the horizon were getting heavier, the faint whisper of wind against her skin more constant now. She picked up the baby, abandoning the soiled nappy, and slung the blanket over her shoulder so that the baby's face was shaded.

Then she began to walk over the sand, following the tracks left by the taxi, not looking back to where the ruins of the bonfire lay.

Of the four beings watching Eleanor Knight's movements during that walk, only one wished her well.

And as that one had no body to speak of, it was unable to act in any very positive way to help her. Instead it concentrated on finding a way through to Eleanor's thoughts, where it might offer a little hope, a little encouragement.

The child, of course, would need nothing. Calmly and quietly it lay there, watching the sweaty face above slowly growing pink with exertion and sunburn. It was happy, waiting.

Eleanor was a different matter. The being fluttering around the edge of her understanding quivered, almost failing in the knowledge of what Eleanor would need.

For it knew the future, as someone had once promised it, explicit in dreams, disguised on waking. As it lived only in dreams now, it never knew the consolation of waking.

The God Lycias watched with satisfaction. He also knew the future, better than the dream that was all that remained of Nerissa.

He smiled, the soft lips full and curved. Pleasure and cruelty combined in flickering firelight over the flawless face.

There was a chance, of course, that she might escape the fate He foresaw. There was always a chance, with the Benu free to wing its way across the world, beyond the power of the Gods.

But He doubted it. The odds were stacked high against her, and there was a storm coming. Either way, it would be of interest.

He might even play a part. This was an attractive thought; He would accompany her through the hot desert sands and deserted city. He had promised Himself a game of revenge, after all.

He was looking forward to it.

The Fosca King, on its leafy throne in the Palace of Blood, used clairvoyant powers and watched Eleanor struggling across the sand with the baby. It was avid and eager to interfere in this interesting situation. It hoped to find, through Eleanor's presence on Chorolon, some way to regain the favour of its former master, the Lord of the Sun.

It smiled to itself, a ripple running through the smooth, flower-petal face. Fortuitous events, happy conjunctions. And yet, how much of it was pure chance? The Emperor's dream, yes, that could be considered a gift, a sudden illumination of the will of God. But Imbert's presence at the Emperor's court was part of a careful strategy, a strategy planned long ago, well before the Fosca King had left Peraldon.

In his previous incarnation as Lucian Lefevre, the Fosca King had recognised certain qualities in the handsome young student of the Peraldonian College. Imbert Cupere had intelligence, passion, flexibility, subtlety – and, most unusually for an apprentice Mage, a lover, Edine. Intrigued, Lefevre had also detected an overwhelming ambition. Such a man might well be useful to the High Priest of the Sun, the Lord of Love . . .

He had instructed Imbert (and, indirectly, Edine) in the arts of disguise and concealment. He knew that Edine was clever for a woman, nearly as clever as the man. Indeed, in some ways she was more adept at artifice than her lover. He taught them how to blend with other societies, how to pick up the signals, use the systems. How to wait and watch, observing and mimicking the small signs which betrayed how others lived. Through the intermittent prescience that had informed his life as Lucian Lefevre, he knew it would one day be useful.

He had introduced Imbert to the newly elected Emperor Xanthon as a valued advisor. And then he had left the city of Peraldon in search of the Benu. He had hoped that the Emperor would learn to rely on Imbert, and so he did. The first person to be told of the Emperor's dream was Imbert.

It was Imbert's interpretation of it that guided the Emperor's actions . . .

The Emperor and Imbert had jointly decided to compel Matthias's help in returning Eleanor Knight to Chorolon.

None of them knew anything of the Fosca King's interest.

It had been an unlikely, uneasy alliance. Imbert, Edine and Matthias. Who would have thought that the Emperor could have held such a thing together?

But what should the Fosca King do now to turn this interesting situation to its own advantage? How to make the best of these disparate, unruly elements?

It decided to send a wraith, an imagined creature, to attend Eleanor. A counterfeit being who existed only through a bewilderment of the senses. It would appear human, would even sound and smell human. But it would be merely a projection of the Fosca King's mind, a conjuration by the Great Mage. It would give the Fosca King continuing influence, subtle and hidden.

The Fosca King wanted amusement.

It had no equals now, only servants. It needed company, someone to share its loneliness. It had been a very long time, after all, since it had enjoyed a civilised conversation with anyone . . .

Sourly it regarded the marble-lined hall, the incense burning in golden vessels of elaborate design, the shadowy shapes that stood attendant amongst the trees and blooming plants.

It wanted more, now. This was not enough. Ultimately it desired the God's love, of course. That was why it had delighted in Eleanor's return. Like the Emperor, the Fosca King wanted an offering . . . In the short term, however, the wraith would provide interest.

If only Matthias were here.

Then there would be something to discuss.

Far away, in the neglected corridors of Cliokest, Phinian Blythe paced up and down, waiting.

The Emperor Xanthon sat in state in the Great Hall, attended by his priests and Mages. In uneasy groups around the walls, the Cavers and their allies waited, amongst them Stefan Pryse, Thurstan Merauld, the two Mages, Aylmer and

Thibaud. Sigrid was there, too, the newly elected priestess of the Moon.

He would not join them, yet. Phinian Blythe was no longer fit for human company, and preferred solitude. But waiting was never pleasant, especially when expecting bad news.

He heard the bell from the look-out tower, the agreed signal. Matthias was back. He joined the others then, standing at the back of the Hall in the deep shadow, where no one would have to look at him.

He saw the wide double doors at the other end swing open, and the slight figure of Matthias standing there, tense and angry.

A silence. The Emperor was leaning forward, frowning with concentration. He raised one hand, and Matthias walked steadily towards the elaborate throne.

'Well, Matthias? Did it work? Did you find her?'

'I found her.' Matthias's voice was quiet, but bitter, everlastingly bitter. 'I brought her back. It's all set up, just as we agreed.'

'And Imbert? Where is he now?'

'He sends his deepest apologies to his Emperor. He and Edine wish to explore the ruins beneath Smintha.' A tight reined-in formality in Matthias's voice. 'He says there is much to investigate there – '

'And besides, he will want to observe what happens. He will let us know . . .' The Emperor leant back on his throne, sighing with relief.

Someone else stood forward, and laid a hand on Matthias's sleeve. 'The baby?' Sigrid, the recently inaugurate priestess of the Moon, was looking intently at him.

He barely glanced at her. 'She has the baby. As arranged.'

There was a muttering around the Hall, a murmur of distress and disagreement.

Suddenly Matthias swung round, his eyes blazing, his staff pointing to each of them in turn: priest, Caver, warrior, Mage.

'What's the matter now? You've got your scapegoat, what more do you want?'

They stared back, helplessly, and no one noticed one of the Cavers at the back slip out of the side door, calling for an Arrarat hawk. No one saw bird and rider leap together

into the hot blue sky or realised that Eleanor would soon have
a Caver companion, a friend who would act from the best
intentions.

Matthias was looking across the Hall to the man standing
in the dark. There were no possible words to span the gulf
that lay between them now.

Phinian Blythe, wreathed in shadow, turned away and left
the Hall.

Unfit for human company. Shrouded in memory.
Unassailably lonely.

The fourth being interested in Eleanor's progress across the
sand brought the storm with him.

It flowed from his heels and shoulders, lightning darting
from his hair, thunder rumbling in his breath.

He lived in the storm now, haggard-eyed and sleepless. He
had no rest and no peace, no light or relief. He had roamed
the wide plains, devastation in his wake, for months, not
knowing where to go.

But now he had a focus. He knew where the baby was,
carried in unwilling arms across the vast desert.

He was running wild across the sand, and the storm sprang
from his heels.

There was a city, just as Eleanor had hoped.

From the top of one of the higher dunes she could see it,
stretching away into the distance, a regular pattern of roads
and flat roofs radiating out from a central point. It glittered
in the sun. Abandoned. Silent.

The desert was eating away at it, the drifts building up
against the low-slung, pale brick houses. There was no one
there at all, no animal or bird. No trees or plants.

Water? Was the glittering light from pools or rivers?

The baby was beginning to whimper again in her aching
arms, and her own throat was harsh and dry. The sun was
beating down on her, an almost physical weight. The blanket
over her head and shoulders kept slipping. She could feel her
skin flinching, drying, burning. There must be water here,
somewhere. A well, a pool . . .

She was so hot. At least she could leave the baby in shade
while she searched. Eleanor stumbled down the side of the

dune, sand filling her shoes. She had tried to take them off
at one point, but the sand was too hot. She was glad now
that she had kept them on, for the sand soon gave way to
burning stone underfoot.

She wandered a little way into the town, unnerved by the
vast, empty silence of the wide roads and shady, flat-roofed
houses. She was strangely reluctant to enter any of them,
although the sun was high in the sky, the heat tangible all
around.

The baby was crying in earnest now. She would have to
do something about it, find it something to eat or drink. She
would have to explore one of the houses.

She chose one at random, a pale yellow brick building,
bordered by a neat white stone wall. It was just like a hundred
others, as far as she could see.

The door was unlocked. She pushed it with her foot and
it gave slightly, wedged by the sand that had drifted through
the cracks. She leant her shoulder against it and forced it
open.

'Hello?' she called, although she knew there would be no
one there. The house, and the city, were held in sun-blasted
silence. She found herself in a long, low, dark room, blessedly
cool and shady. A stone floor, whitewashed walls, Sparsely
furnished, but comfortable. There was a couch against one
of the walls, coloured blankets and cushions tumbling over it.

Sighing with relief, she put the baby down. She didn't
know if it was old enough yet to roll over but she wedged
it with cushions anyway. Immediately, it stopped crying. It
really was a remarkably good baby, she thought,
remembering harassed friends with fractious offspring. So
long as you do exactly what it wants, it never cries. Perhaps
all babies were like that, and most parents just bad at picking
up the signals. Perhaps Eleanor was particularly sensitive to
a baby's needs, particularly good with children . . .

Entranced by this new and unfamiliar vision of herself, she
wandered through the house, opening all the cupboards and
doors, looking for something to eat or drink.

One room was a kitchen, with a few dirty pots and pans
littering the tops. Dust and sand lay on every surface. A pile
of dusty plates stood in a basin beneath a pump. Sudden hope
gripped her. She rushed forward.

The pump spluttered, and ejected a cloud of dust.

She hadn't really expected anything else. What she really wanted was a bottle of water, fruit juice, anything.

There was no food or drink anywhere. She opened the doors to cupboards, and found nothing useful, although one of them contained steps downwards to some kind of cellar. It appeared to be quite empty.

People must have packed in a hurry, she thought, to have left things in such a mess. Perhaps there would be more in the next house.

She went through another door and discovered that the house was built around a courtyard. A bright pool of blue shone there. A *pond*? In *this* heat? Hardly believing it, she found her way into the courtyard and ran over to the glistening circle of light. Not water; glass. Shielding her eyes, she discovered that a sheet of heavy glass formed an artificial, ornamental pool. It was too bright, too uncomfortable to observe for long. Stones were set in a sun-ray pattern all around it, distorted somewhat by the layers of sand. She couldn't begin to imagine why it was there. An insoluble puzzle.

Shrugging, she climbed over the low stone wall into the next house. The doors weren't locked there either. It was much the same as the previous house, complete with mystifying artificial pool. There were no dirty dishes beneath the pump. That one didn't work, either. There were no supplies, anywhere.

She was about to move on to the next house when she remembered the baby. If she wasn't careful, she'd forget which house it was in.

She returned over the walls between the houses, back to the original house.

No sound; it must have fallen asleep.

The long, low room, the cushioned couch.

But no baby.

Only a small damp patch, to show where it had been, and a discarded blanket.

Father and son played together, in light and joy. The baby laughed and gurgled, reaching with warm hands towards the loving face smiling at it.

The Father sang for the baby, and flowers bloomed all around it, filling the air with sweet scent. There was music everywhere, music for dancing, and so the Father held the baby in His arms, waltzing and spinning through the rainbow air.

Their love was mutual and extraordinary.

A concentration of delight.

Chapter Thirteen
Hilde

There was someone there. The sudden, uneasy conviction that was she was being watched. Eleanor looked up from the damp blanket and saw a figure silhouetted in the doorway.

For a moment there was silence. The voice, when it came, was quite neutral. 'You look hot. Are you thirsty, too?'

'What do you think?'

The thirst was not the worst thing about all this, but it was the most urgent.

'I know where there's water. Come on.'

Eleanor followed the old woman out of the door, with hardly a second thought. She couldn't stay there, after all. And she didn't know where the baby had gone . . .

The woman was dressed in a dark linen robe, stained round the hem with dust. There was a belt around her slight waist and a silver-embroidered reticule hung from it. Her iron-grey hair was piled high on her head in an elaborate knot. Her hands, blue-veined and stained brown with age, were knobbly at the knuckles.

She moved rather slowly, leaning heavily on a silver-topped cane. She looked only once directly at Eleanor, but her gaze was steady and considering, if a little faded.

'There was a baby here − ' Eleanor found herself blurting out. 'I was given a baby to look after, and now it's gone.'

'Rather careless of you, don't you think?' Pale grey eyes regarded her impassively. 'Not your own baby, I assume, or you'd be more upset. Whose is it?'

.'I don't know. I was just given it. I shouldn't be here anyway, I belong somewhere else.'

'We all do.' The woman paused at the edge of the road, looking up and down its hot, empty expanse. 'No one belongs here any more, it's a ghost town.'

'Why are you here then?' They had turned onto the road, following it further into the town. The woman crept along, as if her feet were painful. The cane was clearly essential to her.

'This is a place of significance.'

'What *do* you mean?'

The woman paused, gazing vaguely out over the dunes. 'It's difficult to explain . . .'

'Well, what are you doing here? Who are you?'

'You're very inquisitive.' The woman's voice was briefly severe.

'I'm Eleanor Knight,' she offered.

The woman smiled. 'I know,' she said. 'My name is Hilde Nemen. I've come to find you.'

'Did Matthias send you?' Incredulous hope in her voice.

'Ah, Matthias . . . I know him well, but he did not send me. It's not his way. Look, we're nearly there.'

The road was narrowing, the buildings rising higher on each side. Glass glinted on many of the roofs, dazzling in the sunlight. The grid pattern of roads and houses was lost as the street began to twist.

They walked on for some time past empty shops, boarded-up cafés, disused temples and halls. The windows of houses gaped.

'There used to be a well . . . ah yes, there it is . . .' the woman's voice trailed through the dry air. 'It's a deep one, it ought to be all right still . . .'

The narrow passages had opened out into a large circular arena, surrounded by colonnaded buildings. Mosaic swirls of colour paved the immense expanse, just visible under the drifting sand. To one side, an imposing temple stood. Marble columns supported a soaring roof, set with glass tiles.

A statue of Lycias the Sun God stood there, looking out over a city glittering with glass.

Eleanor squinted against sunlight. She looked up at that well-remembered face, the curling lips and implacable eyes and, for a moment, she was aware of the uneven beat of her heart, the clamminess of her palms.

'What is this place?' she asked the woman. 'Where are we?'

'It's called Smintha. The desert city of Peraldon. It has a certain reputation . . .'

But Eleanor never asked about Smintha's reputation. Under the colonnade to one side of the arena she saw an ornamental well. Sand clung to the stone wall surrounding it, so that it appeared to grow from the ground. It was shaped like a water-lily, the delicate stone petals unfolding beneath an elegant, wrought-iron canopy. A bucket hung there. A carved wooden cover lay over the well, protecting it from dust.

Eleanor ran to it, almost falling in her hurry. She tore the cover off, letting it roll to the ground, grasping the bucket, throwing it down into the depths, the handle on the windlass spinning wildly.

Only then did she think to check that the rope was securely attached. It was whirling round, too fast for the eye to catch. Unthinking, she made a grab for it, and the rope tore through her hand, burning it.

She gasped, stumbling back, her hand clutched to her breast.

It was too much. The pain was vivid and her throat was burning, and Matthias had left her, and Lewis had been run over and the baby was gone.

And Lukas was dead.

She stood there by the well as the bucket splashed into water, and sobbed. Salt tears stung in her palms. She forgot Hilde, who was watching curiously.

'So careless . . .' In the end the woman had moved and was now standing beside her, the bucket of water in her hands. She held it out to the girl. 'It doesn't help, crying. Here, try this.'

Eleanor put her wounded hand into the water and then scooped some up to her mouth.

A quick movement at her side. The bucket was dashed from her hands, thrown violently down into the sand, all the water spilling.

Aghast, she looked up into the furious eyes of a man with unruly red hair and blazing green eyes, a wiry, power-filled figure.

'Why did you do that?' she yelled at him, tears and water mingled.

'Why do you think this place is deserted? Where do you think everyone is?' He was shouting too. 'The water's bad here, poisoned!'

'Nonsense.' The woman's voice was still calm. She picked up the bucket and lowered it into the well again. 'The fountains dried up when the heatwave started. But the deep wells are still safe . . .'

'Put your finger down your throat. Now. Make yourself sick. Or shall I do it for you?' He stepped towards her, and she glanced frantically from one to the other.

'One mouthful won't hurt. Leave her alone.' Another man, dark and unknown, was standing further along the colonnade, looking across the closed corridor to them.

He spoke mildly, but there was an edge to his voice, one that allowed no leeway.

'She'll be poisoned!' The red-haired man had taken her hand, pulling her towards him, reaching for her throat. She began to struggle, lashing out at him.

The other man stood still for an instant, sighed, and then came running, crashing into the red-haired man, knocking him over onto the ground.

The arena, so calm and empty, was now given over to noise and action. There was a brief, ugly scuffle, the two men rolling over in the sand, colliding against columns, cursing, kicking and grunting.

'Here.' Hilde was standing next to her, a full bucket in her hands.

Eleanor stared at her. Then she understood. She took the bucket, untying the rope. Two steps, and she emptied it over both men.

Brackish water mixed with sand and grit. She could hardly see what the second man looked like through all the mess. She thought he was older than the other, dark-haired, rather thin.

The pair of them sat in the dust and looked at her. Under other circumstances, Eleanor might have laughed. But she was beginning to feel rather odd. She moved backwards and sat down on the rim of the well. Her stomach was churning around, and saliva filled her mouth.

She was going to be sick.

The old woman was watching her. 'Don't let them upset you,' she said. 'They're only men.'

Her voice was cool, and sensible. Eleanor had drunk only one mouthful. She was strong and healthy, and never came down with odd maladies in foreign lands. She took a deep breath, and began to feel better. She leant back against the post, watching the two strangers.

The red-haired man was both furious and puzzled. He stood up, ignoring the other, his green eyes darting around. Often they rested on her own face. He was waiting for her to collapse, she thought resentfully.

Well, she wasn't going to. And to prove it, she picked up the bucket, tied it to the rope and began to lower it again.

The other man had climbed to his feet, brushing down his clothes. Pyjamas, thought Eleanor, diverted. He's wearing pyjamas. Pastel-coloured, loose cotton jacket and trousers. A dark man, standing tall against the Sun so that she could not quite see his face.

His teeth gleamed briefly.

'Hello, Eleanor,' he said. 'Welcome back.'

'Who are you?' It sounded rude, but this was getting ridiculous.

'My name is Comyn Shreeve. Matthias sent me.' A flood of relief. A friend, at last!

'He did not! I don't know you! He sent me!' The red-haired man was shouting again, but Comyn took no notice. He moved towards Eleanor and reached out. He took her hurt hand and held it gently for a moment.

Hilde was watching them all, standing just beyond the well, amongst the pillars. She was leaning heavily on the cane, her face unreadable. Her hands were trembling.

'Your hand . . .' The dark man was smiling at her, while the other almost danced with frustration. 'How is it now?'

His voice was low and gentle. She turned her palm over, staring down at the skin.

There was no mark there, no rope-burn, bruise or scar. Just the old familiar lines, curving round the thumb, straight across the palm, spanning its width.

She looked up at him, and he smiled again.

'This water is indisputably safe.' He had pulled a leather flask from a rucksack leaning against one of the pillars. He offered it to her.

She had seen this man with the cool smile before. She could not remember where or when. But he was no stranger to her.

It was then that the storm hit them.

Chapter Fourteen
Felicia

The girl sitting by the closed window still felt weak. It was taking so long, this recovery. To be sure, she had never had to recover from a shipwreck before, but Felicia was used to feeling ill. Clammy waves of weakness every month, nausea, cramping pains, migraines, fevers. She could count on the fingers of one hand the days on which she'd felt entirely well.

It was why her father Javon, Duke of Eldin, had sent her to Shelt.

'The Sea Lords of Shelt, they'll stop all this nonsense.' He had barely looked up from the map he was studying. He had never really believed that she felt ill so much of the time. Making a fuss, he'd called it. Spoilt. Looking for attention.

A mother might have sympathised more. But her mother had died when she was only six months old, and the succession of nurses and governesses who had brought her up were far too in awe of her father to give her the comfort she craved.

Javon had been looking at boundaries, as usual. 'The sensible thing,' he mused, 'would be to align with Hoel. Then we could pen the plainsmen in, and all those troublesome raids to the north could be stopped . . .'

He remembered she was in the room. He rarely gave up.

'Look,' he said, pointing to the chart on the desk. 'You see what I mean?' He jabbed a finger at the northern boundary. 'Hoel's got a son, he's only nine, so we'd have time to get you into shape . . . Don't look like that!'

She tried not to flinch when he was speaking, but failed. His face changed.

Instinctively she stepped back, rounding her shoulders,

raising her arms in front of her face, warding off the blow she knew was coming.

Her father's lips were compressed with irritation, his hands bunched into a fist. But today Javon held back.

'Why you?' he said intensely, not for the first time. 'Why not a son, a boy I could teach, ride with, laugh with? It's not your fault, you don't have to tell me. I get counselling all the time. But it's bloody hard, a sickly pale little thing like you . . . It's not just that you're a girl, there are girls who hunt and ride, who dance the night through, and have great, bouncing babes. But you – you'd crumple up if a man touched you.' He sighed. 'What am I to do with you? I need to marry you off, form an alliance, consolidate the borders, establish a lineage. Lady knows, it's precarious enough. But who would look at you? I can't blame them, a puff of wind would blow you over.'

He stared at her, the familiar shrinking form, pale hair drifting over her shoulders like water. Javon sighed. 'Go and lie down somewhere. Leave the window open, get some colour in your cheeks . . . Go on, get out of here.'

A reprieve. Felicia fled to the sanctuary of her own quarters, and tried to stop shaking.

Javon Westray, Duke of Eldin, was a slight man, narrow-shouldered, thin-fingered, who moved with whiplash energy. With his younger brother, Torold, he had fought against his own liege-lord to win the domain of Eldin, after the death of the previous Duke.

The fighting had endured for much of the Stasis, a long drawn-out war of considerable violence, set against the constant raging of the storm. Vast areas of the northern territories were laid waste, thousands had lost their lives. Javon had spent a long time hunting out and destroying any surviving opposition. He had not rested there.

He sent armies to help Torold carve out his own territories in the north, but they were not needed. Javon discovered, with amazement, the unique talents of the Sea Lords of Shelt.

Shelt. The city perched on the edge of an immense ocean. Its Castle stood on the headland of a jagged promontory, a tumble of varied and broken strata. The brigg extended out into the sea, almost submerged at high tide, treacherous and dangerous for any approaching ship. The rest of the city sprawled down over the cliff towards the River Shellet, a wide, lazy estuary prone to unexpected floods. It spewed out into the bay.

Beyond the river lay the rocks of the south brigg, the twin of the promontory beneath the Castle. Between rocks, river and sea, Shelt was at the mercy of both flood and tide. The storms of the Stasis had brought its inhabitants, largely dependent on the fishing industry, to the brink of poverty. They had given every power, every honour, to the Sea Lords, and waited for them to work deep, old magic.

The Sea Lords controlled the weather. They took the energies of the storm itself and bent it to their own designs. It did not always work, for the storm was wild and unpredictable, but there were notable successes. The Sea Lords' skills, impressive though they were, owed nothing at all to the shamans of the nomadic *eloish* tribes in the far north. The Sea Lords used their own magic, and distrusted the ancient rituals.

It was Gawne who set them onto other paths. It was Gawne, the foreigner Mage from the south, who insisted that they investigate the arts of healing. He knew so much. The Sea Lords were aware that there were whole areas of understanding still hidden from them. Gawne, with his Peraldonian training, knew about Synchronicity, about the creation of monsters, about scurries. Before the Stasis he had worked closely with the High Priest and Great Mage Lucian Lefevre.

There was something about the sea-water of Shelt, he had said. It would bring health and healing to those skilled enough to discover its secret.

Gawne was right. The Sea Lords found themselves able to restore life and health – for as long as the waters were undisturbed.

Javon heard of these unusual skills. He sent Torold to find out what was happening, and found a society torn apart. The Sea Lords, under Gawne, were under siege. The fisherpeople of Shelt were in revolt against their former protectors. They had been forbidden to fish the sea east of Shelt; and no one told them why.

Torold came prepared with a company of highly trained soldiers. He rescued the Sea Lords, and promised to stay, with his efficient complement of soldiers, on one condition. He was to become Earl of Shelt.

They agreed. There had been a brief struggle against the fisherpeople, but they were unable to match Torold's forces. Such was the Sea Lords' power over Shelt that there was virtually no other opposition. Torold became Earl of Shelt and the Sea Lords sighed with relief. They settled back and continued with their strange work.

Their miracles now were nothing to do with the weather. The Sea Lords, under Gawne, had a different priority. It was quite simple, easily comprehended, easily described. They were going to live forever.

And somehow they seemed close to the fulfilment of this desire, in part at least. The sea beyond Shelt became a place of healing, of regeneration. The news spread; the wealthy and aristocratic of Stromsall came flocking.

Javon, Duke of Eldin, thought about his sickly, ailing daughter, and came to a decision.

Javon was a hard, ambitious man, used to warfare, to treachery, to violence. He ruled Eldin with a grip of steel, and no one dared complain. To be fair, there was little need. Out of the wasteland of the civil war, a reasonably stable society had been dragged, protesting, into being. Javon had vision, an ideal that had underlined all his violence. No one would starve in Eldin, when Javon Westray became Duke. There would be schools and hospitals, festivals and tournaments.

He had realised all these ideals. He had even built for himself a light and airy palace of glass and pale woods, a palace which needed no defence beyond the power of his reputation. But his thin, ascetic face was furrowed by anger and disappointment, his mouth sneering. What use was it all, with no strong young son to inherit?

A weakling daughter was no good to him. He resented her green eyes, so like his own, her straight, baby-fine hair, her pale skin coloured only by the shadowing of blue veins.

He was glad to see her go to his brother's city of Shelt, where the Sea Lords under the Mage Gawne were skilled in the arts of healing. Glad to be spared her wispy presence shadowing the rooms of his palace, a constant reminder that his power would pass into unfamiliar hands.

*   *   *

Felicia sat in the chair by the window, far from home, waiting for the chilling waves of weakness to pass.

It was early in the morning, and the sun was only just higher than the line where sky met sea. But clouds were already racing across the pink-tinged blue, and the golden light was broken up, diffused. Although the window was closed, she could hear the wind whipping round the Castle walls, and the monotonous crash of the tide against rock and stone.

She avoided looking at the sea, raging far below her state apartment.

On her lap lay a sketch-pad. She had begun a likeness of the Second Sea Lord, Dederic. She had not deliberately tried to caricature the hook nose and sloping forehead, but somehow her pencil had taken over as usual, and Dederic, so solemn and magnificent, looked like an upset budgerigar.

She smiled. It was a small amusement, but one she found useful. In long ceremonies and meetings, as the prayers were chanted, the hymns sung, the treaties signed, the strategies discussed, she drew thumbnail sketches on the little pad that accompanied her everywhere, and the powerful men who ran her life were revealed as mammals, rodents, fish and fledgling, scrawny birds.

They lost some of their mystique that way. She didn't have to take them quite so seriously, certainly not as seriously as they took themselves.

She still did what they said, of course, but she knew really, deep down, that her drawings revealed part of the truth. They were like rapacious little animals, grubbing for food, grubbing for power. Playing games: they played with toys, and they thought she was one.

Perhaps they were right. She lacked the energy to show them otherwise.

There was a knock on the door and Annis came in, carrying a tray.

'Your medicine, my lady,' she said, swanning across the deep pile carpet, dark ringlets bouncing on her fine shoulders. She was not tall, but slender, softly rounded where the men liked it, red-lipped, rosy-cheeked.

In her more depressed moments, Felicia thought Annis had been chosen as her servant to emphasise the contrast. More often, she found Annis's vitality attractive, even cheering: the spring in her step, the laugh in her eyes.

Today it made Felicia feel tired, just watching her. She sat listlessly as Annis measured out the medicine, her eyes far away, watching the clouds racing.

A muffled snort from Annis. Felicia's eyes flew to the girl's face.

'Oh, I'm sorry, my lady – ' Annis was flushed with suppressed laughter.

Felicia looked down. The sketch-pad on her lap was still open, and Dederic the Budgerigar frowned at them both.

She closed it, considering a reprimand, but Annis spoke before she could gather the words.

'So *clever*! How ever did you get him so right? All that ruffled dignity . . .' She broke off, her hand over her mouth, suddenly realising what she'd said.

The reprimand died unuttered. Felicia couldn't be bothered. She would save it till she felt better . . . She leant forward and took the glass of medicine from the tray. She avoided Annis's eyes, drinking it down.

It was horrible, as usual.

'Will you come downstairs today, my lady?' Annis, all prim formality restored.

'Not today – perhaps tomorrow.'

'I'll open the window, shall I? Dr Fessil recommended fresh air – '

'No!' It came out louder than she intended. 'No, it's too cold. Leave it, please.'

'But Dr Fessil's orders – '

What could she say? That the sound of the sea made her sick, draining what little strength she possessed? That the damp seemed to gnaw at her bones, making them ache, and ache, until she could cry?

She turned her face against the high wooden back of the chair, so that the girl might not see how frightened she was.

Annis took no notice; her orders were clear. She knelt on the window seat, pushing up the iron catch, and swung the window wide.

Felicia closed her eyes as the noise flung itself through the room, the threatening crash of the heavy, beating waves, the violence of the wind, the clawing damp. Nausea welled in her stomach, trembled in her limbs.

Annis was watching her, a strange mixture of pity and contempt on her vivacious face. 'Is it the shipwreck, my lady? Does it still upset you?' Her voice was not ungentle.

'I – I don't think so. The sea – '

'Is our friend, our servant, the source of power . . .' The traditional formula.

What could Felicia say? The civilisation of Shelt was built on the power of the sea.

The trouble was, she was sea-sick – on land.

A slam, and the vile noise died away, the cold lost its bite. Annis had shut the window.

The physical relief was so great that Felicia unclenched her fists and almost smiled.

'Thank you,' she said with real gratitude.

'I won't tell anyone,' said Annis, bending to pick up the sketch-pad which had dropped to the floor in the wind.

'Nor about that . . .?' Felicia pointed to the caricature.

'It's no one I know,' she said, winking. 'Dr Fessil will be calling at eleven this morning. I'll open the window just before he comes . . .'

Felicia leant back in relief. An ally, in Shelt. Perhaps she might manage after all.

At ten to eleven, Annis returned to open the window. By the time Dr Fessil and Brice Lammon arrived, just after eleven, Felicia was crouched over a basin, helplessly vomiting up her breakfast.

They put her back to bed, Fessil and the apprentice Mage, took her temperature, her pulse, measured out medicine, and conferred, in whispers, at the other end of the room.

Felicia could not hear them there. The room was on a ludicrous scale, she considered. Heavy oak furniture, leaded windows reaching from floor to high ceiling. The carpet was a sickly shade of pink, the thick brocade curtains gold, green and rose. Felicia longed for her simple room back at home, the pale parquet floor and quiet colours, the tall, fragile windows and elegant arched ceilings. Here she was dwarfed by ponderous luxury.

'Fessil – ' her voice was no more than a whisper. Annis

heard her, though, and drew the doctor's attention.

He came back to her bedside, his face grave, the white bushy eyebrows drawn close together.

'My lady?'

'Shut the window; I feel better when it's shut – '

'She does, too.' Annis broke in.

The doctor turned and looked her up and down. Cold eyes grew icy with contempt.

'Forgive me,' he said, his voice low. 'I did not know that you were trained in the arts of healing. Tell me, Lady Annis, how you acquired such skills. In what colleges; at the knees of which great scientists and teachers? Or was it in the company of serving-women, prattling and gossiping?' His tone, so soft and courteous, was washed over by acid.

Annis flushed, but stood her ground. 'Lady Felicia is much better with the window shut. It's too cold for her. She wants it shut!'

'The Lady Felicia is in no condition to make an objective assessment of her situation.'

'And besides, nothing but good can come from sea air!' Fessil's companion, a slight young man, stepped forward, his eyes alight with zeal.

Annis barely glanced at him. The girl on the bed had moved her hand slightly on the sheet. Clearly she had had enough. She wanted them all to go away.

The doctor turned to her. 'Lady Felicia, with your permission, I will approach the First Sea Lord, the Mage Gawne. I feel the time has come for a consultation.'

There was no reply. For a moment the doctor waited, watching the small movement of her breath with a practised eye.

'The Lady is asleep. Perhaps it is as well. I will consult her uncle.' He turned, his floor-length gown dragging heavily across the rose carpet. 'Come, Lammon. We have difficult news to report.'

'Indeed.' The younger man sighed, but his bright eyes gleamed with enthusiasm.

As the two men crossed the floor to the door, Annis tried to keep close, to hear their conversation. They drew together, ignoring her, silently closing the door in her face.

*   *   *

The corridors were deserted. No need for guards to attend the Lady Felicia: so honoured was she that almost all her wishes were fulfilled. She had asked for quiet, for one trusted serving maid; and these two she had received. But her father Javon had commanded medical attention to heal his ailing, feeble daughter. His brother, the Earl of Shelt, called his greatest and wisest doctors, and they conferred, long into the night.

There was one such conference that night.

Three men round a table: Fessil, tall, white-haired, commanding, noble; Lammon, trainee Mage, young and eager with smooth, tidy fair hair and clear eyes.

And a third, always in shadow, grey hair bordering a greasy skull, sunken hollow eyes, bowed shoulders: the First Sea Lord, Gawne of Aquile.

The Earl of Shelt was there too, of course. Felicia's uncle was a large man, richly dressed, uninterested in such discussions, pacing the room restlessly.

'Do your best, naturally. I don't care what it takes. Just make her better.'

'It will not be easy.' Fessil regarded the heavy gold rings on his elegant hands. 'There is no strength there, no resistance to infection, no willingness to try –'

'She resists only the sea.' Gawne's voice was dry, expressionless.

'The shipwreck cannot have been a pleasant experience.' Fessil's hands were framing an arch on the table. 'She was near to death.'

'It was weeks ago! She should have recovered by now! What do I pay you for, Fessil? My brother, Duke of Eldin, entrusts his only child to us for healing because of our great and renowned skills – and what happens? First her ship is deliberately wrecked by our "loyal" subjects, and she only just survives. And then, instead of a steady return to health, she ails and sickens! This is embarrassment on a major scale! Hell! What if she dies?'

The Earl of Shelt flung his hands wide with theatrical horror. He knew his brother well.

'She will not die.' Gawne stared at the Earl of Shelt with distaste. He did not like melodrama.

'I wouldn't like to bet on it.'

'She was saved by the sea, from that wreck. Why should not the sea save her again?'

'A Marqun?' The young man, Lammon, was leaning forward, the bright eyes gleaming. 'Would you risk it?'

Gawne looked only at the Earl. 'If my Lord permits . . .' The sunken eyes betrayed nothing. The high hunched shoulders framed a neutral face, a mask of hidden potential.

Torold stared at him for a moment, halting the restless pacing. 'Is it a risk? Would it make her *worse*?'

'Probably . . . not.' Gawne stared at him, unblinking.

'She's not strong enough!' Fessil was frowning.

'She's making no progress using conventional methods,' Lammon said. 'We have nothing to lose – '

'I don't know . . .' The Earl of Shelt looked at the three men at the table with unaccustomed indecision. Gawne stood up and met his eyes.

Torold, Earl of Shelt, was a big man, but Gawne towered over him, hunched though he was. He was thin to the point of emaciation, dressed in grey silk shot through with green and blue, the traditional garb of a Sea Lord. The silk hung in drifting folds, blurring outlines, softening the effect of the skeletal frame.

'We will hold the Marqun tomorrow,' he said, unblinking. 'Full moon. The time is right.'

Without waiting for a reply, he turned and swiftly left the room. The three remaining men looked at each other. Torold sighed. He was Earl of Shelt, brother to Javon Westray of Eldin. He could order what he liked. The Sea Lords ruled Shelt courtesy of *his* soldiers. He did not have to do as the Sea Lord said.

'Tomorrow, then,' he said. 'We'll hold it tomorrow.'

Annis had stared at the door, shut in her face, and then had made a small gesture, sharp and obscene at the blank wood.

She returned to the bed.

Felicia's eyes were open. 'They will hold a Marqun,' she said. 'I think it will kill me.'

'My Lady! They only want the best for you.'

'It will kill me,' she said again, and tears began to roll, unheeded, down white cheeks.

Chapter Fifteen
Storm

The Storm-bearer hit the city at midday, when the sun was at its worst. The sand that billowed in vast clouds ahead of him had blanketed most of the buildings and he screamed with frustration at the lack of definition.

His scream drew the sand into a whirlwind dance, spinning high in the air beyond the city boundaries, enclosing it in an impenetrable orbit of grit, shutting out all light.

The streets and buildings lay naked before his feet.

He tore wildly down the long avenues, and lightning stabbed his steps into the stone. His hands reached for wall and roof, and they crumpled beneath his touch.

He smelt water, sour water in the wells, and threw thunderbolts into their depths.

The baby was hidden from him. Someone was hiding it, and the Storm-bearer would raze the city rather than lose the child again.

He cared nothing for the other creatures who crouched terrified in basements and cupboards, the desert rats and sand-snakes; lizards and scorpions; Eleanor and the others.

He blasted through the city centre, and the larger buildings there collapsed in clouds of dust. The narrow alleys around lay spread-eagled beneath his red-rimmed stare.

The baby was hidden. The Storm-bearer began to howl, ripping at the fabric of reality.

This was not tolerable.

The baby and its Father revealed themselves then, framed in a glittering, high-arched doorway.

The Storm-bearer flew over the shallow steps, his ruining hands stretched wide to seize the child.

The Father smiled, pleasantly.

'How does it feel, never to rest?' He enquired politely.

The stained hands were reaching out, about to grasp the black-eyed baby, falling forward at it.

The Father was still amused. Confident. Smiling.

But the baby was watching the Storm-bearer seriously, a slight frown on its golden-brown face. It opened its own fragile hands in a wide embrace, welcoming the storm, and its Father did nothing to stop it.

The Storm-bearer halted, tears running over the ravaged face, and took the child, falling to his knees.

The wind died, the lightning and thunder ceased.

For a while, the Father let the other hold the baby. He was not always cruel. Or was this just another refinement to cruelty?

The Storm-bearer looked up into the pitiless gaze.

'Begone,' said the Father. 'Leave this place. There is no peace for you here.' Or anywhere, He might have added.

Reaching down, He reclaimed His son. And the Storm-bearer grew in power, surging to his feet, the wind howling through his hair, the storm at his heels.

'Begone,' said the Father once more, softly.

The Storm-bearer began to run, hurling down the broken streets, screaming his agony out into the desert. The hot sand changed into monsters around him.

There were monsters clinging round Phinian Blythe, too. They were almost familiar companions by now.

In a crowded citadel of towers and arches, full of old friends and new enemies, he walked alone. Day after day, he paced the small circumference of his tower, and prayed for release.

He hardly noticed the sun burning the sea outside. He paid no attention to the difficult clashes between Cavers and Peraldonians. No one wanted his help, anyway. No one could bear his presence. What could he do, afflicted as he was?

Broken oaths exact their own retribution, Sharrak had said. Blythe had not understood what it meant at the time, but he had indeed failed to kill Marial for Sharrak, as promised. It had seemed trivial amongst the weight of so many other crimes. And later, when he was lying ill at Cliokest, after the Benu Bird had been released, he had thought that the paralysing injury to his left hand would be retribution enough. Marial had lost his left hand, after all.

But then Marial had died.

Would the shadows that surrounded Blythe hound him to death? Was that how it would go? They were too heavy for him, hanging round his shoulders, crowding out his thoughts.

Some called them Children of the Night, but he saw them only as shadows. Shadows which held him apart from the rest of the world.

Every sense was distorted by their presence, every thought interrupted by their chattering. Usually they draped his shoulders and head, washing over the skin of his face, darkening and clouding his eyes. Sometimes he felt that he would suffocate, that the stench from their breath would cause his lungs to fail, and he would struggle against their weight. But whenever he moved his hand, feebly trying to ward them off, they would flow along his arm, and deprive his fingers of volition.

He tried to kill himself, when he realised that they would not go away. He had arisen from weeks of illness, to find that the nightmare shapes of his fever still surrounded him. The shadows flickered over his face, clinging to his limbs, making any action or comfort impossible.

Weeks had passed, months of punishing, enfeebling heat, and every morning he had hoped that the glaring sunlight would burn through these shadows of the past, hanging so heavy about him, like iron weights. But nothing would move them, nothing release him. In the end, he sharpened a knife. He stood at the window, thinking of Karis.

Chattering, the shadows had clawed at his hand until his fingers opened and the knife clattered to the floor.

He did not hear the door open. Through a daze of weakness and despair, he did not see Matthias standing there.

No-one ever came to see him now. The others, even Thurstan, could not bear the presence of the twisting shadows, hanging round Blythe's shoulders, masking his eyes.

'Phin . . .' The quiet voice behind him made him spin round, and the shadows fell into place, like the swing of a cloak, rippling through the air.

He saw Matthias's eyes glance away for relief, to the floor, the ceiling, anywhere rather than at the Children of the Night. Dark eyes fell on the knife, gleaming dully on the stone floor.

Matthias bent to pick it up, turning it over in his hands.

Blythe wondered if he'd comment. And then, as Matthias looked directly at him, realised the Mage's thoughts were taking a quite different direction.

'Phin, they want me to bring Eleanor back.'

'Why?' His voice was cool, but his emotions were not.

'Why do you think?' Matthias walked past him to the window, turning his back on the shadows. Blythe admired his nerve. 'Look at the sun. Feel the heat. Smell the stench.'

They were standing in one of the high towers on Cliokest, and below them, where there had once been a pretty bay of blue and green waters, was now a dry wasteland. The sea had retreated to a thin line of silver in the distance. The rotting carcases of fish and other animals now scattered the cracked surfaces. A heat haze, yellow and grey, hung over it all, a pestilential pall.

Blythe had barely noticed it, obsessed as he was by the shadows. He had heard people crying, had intellectually known that there was much suffering. But he had no energy to spare to consider why.

'Revenge,' said Matthias. 'As Lycias promised. And as Eleanor is not here, He's taking it out on us.'

'You cannot possibly do it.' Blythe was frowning. 'She has already been through quite enough. She broke the Stasis!'

'No one has forgotten. They think it's her fault. That it is up to her to set things right, bring about a change.'

'Whose idea is this?'

'Our esteemed Emperor. He had a dream, a dream of significance. All his advisors and Mages and priests and courtiers are delighted. Especially Imbert Cupere, and that's something else again . . . They all agree. A scapegoat is required. They want me to organise a re-run of the Seventh Rite.'

'Why *you*?'

'They're short of Mages experienced in Synchronicity. No one knows what has happened to Lefevre, and although Imbert has many talents, skill in Synchronicity is not one of them.'

'Surely you will have nothing to do with this!'

There was a pause. When Matthias spoke again, his voice was very quiet. 'The price is territory for the Cavers. A Temple to Astret on Peraldon. Reinstatement of all the old rights and customs . . .'

'There must be other ways! The Emperor cannot *want* the situation between Peraldon and the Cavers to continue!'

'No, but he is a desperate man. There were forest fires in Albe last week. Vast areas laid waste, and it's not out yet. And plague is spreading from the south. Soon the city of Peraldon itself will be at risk.'

'It's nothing to do with Eleanor! She's paid a hell of a price already!'

Matthias said nothing. His eyes were running over the shadows, as if trying to get used to their changing, amorphous shapes.

'Revenge,' he said at last, 'or retribution? What are you living with here, in this tower, Phinian Blythe? You told me once that they were the shadows of a broken oath . . . But surely this is excessive. No promise could be worth so much. No. The Children of the Night are perhaps part of the same pattern, Lycias's vengeance. Eleanor might also free you . . .'

'I would not ask it of her!' And then the shadows crowded over his eyes and face, slimy on his skin, sickening the air with their breath. Impatiently he shook his head, but they shrilled and chattered in his ears, robbing his mind of thought.

Matthias was looking at him with such pity.

'She will have to return,' he said. 'This is no answer, after all.' He put the knife gently down on the table and moved towards the door.

'Matthias!' The effort was almost too great, the shadows so heavy over him. 'You must not bring her back. It would be evil, an act of selfish cruelty!'

'I know . . . I know.'

The door closed behind him.

The red-haired man had seen it first. He was standing in the dust outside the temple. He lifted his head, listening to the wind, and then shouted. He pointed, and everyone, strangely drawn, followed the direction of his gaze.

Above and beyond the high buildings around the arena,

the sun was being blotted out. Like a moving mountain, an immense cloud of sand was blowing towards the city.

Ignoring the others, he took Eleanor's arm, hustling her over to the Temple, weaving through the high columns, between shady walls.

She was not sorry to go with him, for the air was already choking with sand. He pushed open one of the heavy, ornately carved double doors, and guided her inside. It was light and airy there, a long room, curving at one end to echo the shape of the arena. It was filled with benches, all facing towards an altar at one end. There were heavy marble statues of Lycias standing in niches; murals and raised reliefs of scenes she did not recognise on the walls. Over the altar, the golden gleaming head of the Sun God looked down on the empty benches. There were doors to either side of the altar, emblazoned with more representations of the God.

The sand was scything through the crack beneath the door, splattering like hail against the windows. A crash as one of them broke, spraying glass over the room. The sand was everywhere now, a dense whirlwind driving through the building. She held her hands over mouth and nose, trying to filter out some of the sand, her eyes half-closed against the wind-driven grains. It was almost impossible to breathe. She leant against the wall.

The red-haired man was struggling with the door to the left of the altar. It was bolted. For a moment he wrestled with the catch, swearing under his breath, but then it gave, and he flung the door open.

The noise outside was growing into the terrible power, a roaring scream on the edge of desperation. It was as if the storm had a human voice, a human dimension, fragmented and agonised, expressed in the whirling sand all around them.

'You'll be safe here,' he said, gently pushing her towards the door.

She did not doubt him for a minute. It was simply not bearable, the sand filling one's lungs, and the voice screaming through her mind. Eleanor was almost glad to run into the black depths, stumbling down curving stairs.

'Stay here. I'll come for you when it's over.'

The door slammed behind her, all light immediately extinguished.

She was alone.

Why hadn't he joined her? Why had he stayed out there, exposed to the storm? Who was he, anyway? For a moment, she was overwhelmed by it all. She leant back against the door, thinking. At least the sand was no longer blowing . . .

But there was a smell, a dreadful stench in the cellar. Rotting meat, rotting cabbage, she couldn't tell which. And it was stifling hot, and far too dark. She could see nothing at all. Her heart was thudding painfully. She felt a huge mistrust of this place.

Rather than risk what she might find at the bottom of the steps, she had stayed at the top, close to the door.

The voice was still screaming out there, an inhuman weight of anguish, caught up somehow in the sandstorm. She felt herself begin to sob again in sympathy for such misery. But she didn't want to see who or what it was. She had more than enough to cope with on her own account.

There was a bolt on her side of the door too. Driven by the terrible sound, she leant hard against it and it rasped into place.

Putting her hands over her ears she went a little way down the stairs, just far enough to be out of reach of the sound. She could not tell how far down the stairs went. And then discovered that she needed to hear what was going on: she could not bear to be both blind and deaf. She lowered her hands, feeling cautiously behind her, and explored the dry stone steps. Just dust and sand, nothing else. She sat down and waited, shuddering.

It took a long time, but at last the screaming outside died away and the storm seemed quieter. Perhaps they would come to get her soon . . .

And then what? What was she doing here, who were these people? What was she going to do next? Her hands twisted together. She was filled with misery and doubt.

Were they going to put her through it *again*? She wanted her home again, the lonely, desperate flat, the meaningless job. At least she knew what she was doing, she had some control. Here, yet again, she was at the mercy of forces she did not understand.

Sitting on the steps in the dark, she made a decision. This time she would not be a victim. Not in any way. She would be aware of the issues, she would work out what was happening. She had been here before. She knew this world, knew how it worked.

And an idea formed. Although Matthias had abandoned her, she was not friendless on Chorolon. She would go and find Phin. She would make these people take her to him.

She took a deep breath. It felt much better to have some definite plan.

It was then, in the calm of the storm, that she heard the movement beneath her, on the steps below. Not the scamper of rats or mice, but a slow, sliding movement, as if some wounded creature was dragging itself over stone.

She was on her feet, at the top of the stairs in an instant, wrestling with the bolt. It was jammed. She started hammering on the door. No response. Again, 'Help! Someone! Let me out, quick, let me out!'

Her voice was high and unsteady while her fingers tugged at the rusty knob of the bolt. It refused to move. She forced herself to silence, straining every nerve to listen.

'Please . . .' A thread of a voice, uneven and faint. 'I won't hurt you . . .' It took a long time to say that.

'Who are you?' Her own voice was not much steadier.

'Please, help me . . .'

She could not tell if it were a man or woman. It didn't matter, perhaps, for whoever it was was clearly in extremis, in need of help.

Slowly, anxiously, she crept down the steps, testing each tread with her foot. 'What do you want? Are you hurt?'

There was a pause, and then the voice spoke again. 'I'm trapped here, I'm ill, I can't get out . . . They left me – '

'Locked you in?' She was horrified.

'They thought I might try to get away . . .'

'What's wrong with you?' Eleanor had stopped on the steps, her mind leaping to possibilities. Plague. Leprosy. Madness. Why else leave someone sick behind?

'I was left as a sacrifice, an offering.'

'What!' She couldn't believe it.

'To the Lord Lycias. So that He might relent.' There was another convulsive movement, much closer to her this time, on the steps just below.

'Please help me.'

Eleanor bent down, gently reaching out her hands towards the person on the steps.

Her fingers touched cloth, and then whoever it was moved again, and a thin hand reached for hers.

The skin was hot and dry, burning with feverish heat. The hand lay passive in her own, and she heard the faint sound of crying. She lifted her own hand, and stroked long curling hair back from the burning brow. There were tears on the cheeks.

'Hush, don't cry, I'll help you.'

There was something in the voice she found inexpressibly moving. Something that communicated itself directly to her. She knew this woman, understood everything about her.

'What is your name?' she asked.

And then there was the sound of pushing at the door, and it flew open, light flooding down the steps to where Eleanor knelt by the woman. Figures at the top of the stairs. She had no time to wonder how the bolt was released.

She looked only at the woman lying at her knees.

Red-gold hair, grey eyes. A moon-scar on the left temple. The face she saw in the mirror every morning: herself.

The woman's legs were all twined around with green leaves and creepers, binding her into immobility. And, as Eleanor watched, frozen with shock, the grey eyes closed, and the already thin flesh began to melt away, to burn and char, blacken and dry out, dissolving in dust, falling from the bone.

The hand she still held became dry, ashy and insubstantial, until there were only bones, and then those too crumbled, desiccated dust, falling to the floor.

The twining greenery sank onto the step, empty.

There was nothing left of the woman who had been herself.

Her head turned away, helplessly, and she found herself staring up the stairs to the open door.

Two men stood there, one dark, the other red-haired.

They had seen it all. And neither of them looked in the least surprised.

Chapter Sixteen
The Three

She stood up slowly, letting the leaves fall into the dust.

A long moment, caught out of time, as she looked at the two men. Light was glinting on the red hair of the younger man, skimming darkly over the other.

They were connected, she thought. An undeniable and extraordinary intuition. They knew each other well, were together in some subtle way she did not understand.

No one moved.

Then she spoke, quietly, her voice very steady.

'Who are you?'

Like a song their voices chimed together.

'Friends. To help you.'

She pointed to the red-haired man.

'Why did you put me *here*? With *that*?' She would not look back at the drifting dust, falling back into the chasm beneath them.

He came down the steps then, and took her hands. He was pale, his green eyes scanning her face. 'I did not know – did not realise what would happen, what you are.'

'What do you mean?' She ripped her hands away from him. She could not bear his touch.

'A scapegoat,' said the other cool voice from the top of the stairs. 'That's what you are, Eleanor Knight. Do you know what this place is?'

They were standing on a spiral staircase, curving in a wide, shallow arc down the side of a deep pit. It lead down into indeterminate depths. A bizarre setting, but it didn't matter. What did matter was that this was the Temple of Lycias. She didn't need to say it.

She wanted him to move out of the doorway, so that she could get past. She started to climb the curving stairs, pushing past the red-haired man. She hardly registered the other staircase winding clockwise from the other doorway.

The man at the top stood aside. He was called Comyn, she remembered.

'*Do* you know? What you've just seen?' He was looking after her as she walked away through the Temple.

She would not look back at him, not reply to this.

She knew what she had seen. She knew the message of that burning, dying figure.

It was a promise for the future. What would happen. A scapegoat, Comyn had said.

For Lycias had promised revenge, hadn't He? And it was perhaps sweet for the God to show His victim what her fate would be.

She went out into the sun.

Comyn found food for them; some kind of lizard creature which he roasted over a small fire.

He told her about himself. He was a Caver, a friend to Matthias and Lukas. He had seen Eleanor during that brief stay at the Cliff, but had not spoken to her. He was a healer, brought in to attend the injured Fabian. He had seen her in Margat's cave, lonely and frightened. Didn't she remember? He had heard Matthias's announcement that she had been brought back to divert the revenge of Lycias. He had decided to come and help her. He knew none of the others.

The red-haired man was called Timon Lesterell. His story was virtually identical to Comyn's. He was a Caver, come to befriend her. She had helped him from his Arrarat hawk on return from the raid on the Ferry. He had been barely conscious, but Eleanor had been kind . . . He said he had never seen Comyn before, and knew he was lying. His green eyes were bright with anger and suspicion, glaring at the dark man, who took no notice.

Hilde, the elderly woman, said that she came from Jeren. She was a close friend to Martitia; indeed, they were cousins. Like the others, she claimed to have come solely to help Eleanor. She did not recognise either of the men.

At least two of them had to be lying. Their stories were

mutually contradictory.

The Cavers had been a close-knit community, existing in hardship and pain together for the timeless length of the Stasis. They knew each other well, depended on each other. It was not conceivable that they should fail to recognise each other here.

It was almost as unlikely that they should not know Hilde. It was true that Cavers and Jerenites rarely met; but there had been a regular traffic of information between them.

Lukas, at one stage, had loved a Jerenite.

Jocasta, blasted by the Moon.

They had lit a fire in one of the smaller squares, some distance from the great arena outside the Temple to Lycias. They told their stories as the meat roasted, justifying and arguing.

She left them, in the end, after the meal she could not eat. Timon had wanted to come with her.

'The city is dangerous,' he said. 'And although the storm has passed, I do not like to leave you alone . . .'

'But I don't know who you are,' she said. 'Why should I trust you?'

He shrugged helplessly. She walked away.

The silent city waited for her. She avoided the central avenues, where the buildings had collapsed into piles of rubble, and instead paced other wide streets and deserted parks. There was ornate and beautiful stone-work everywhere: statues, fountains, benches. She saw faces cast in bronze, figures of animals and fish adorning the lifeless cascades. As the shadows lengthened towards evening the shifting light gave the carvings an odd illusion of animation. Drifts of sand softened every outline, running through mosaicked pavements where people had once walked.

The backstreets were dark and narrow, although even here the buildings were rarely more than two storeys high. In the late afternoon light the painted shutters and doors were tinged with quiet colour. Terracotta, ochre, olive and gold. She ran her fingers over the blistering woodwork and peeling doors and wondered where everyone had gone.

She was roaming the streets aimlessly, trying to order her thoughts, trying to separate panic from her distrust of her three companions. She needed to be cool and logical. There

had to be some answer. Matthias would not have brought
her back without some reason. She was clinging to this
thought.

At the back of her mind there was another, nagging worry.
What had happened to the baby, where had it gone? Whose
was it? She could not bear it to be abandoned, lost in this
burning desert.

The rapidly falling dusk blotted out the memory of the sun.
As the moon rose she came to the circular arena once more.

At first she nearly turned and retraced her steps. But the
empty expanse seemed innocent of threat. And it was clear
of the shadows which haunted the city, a wide theatre for
light and space.

She hardly glanced at the statue of Lycias on the roof of
the Temple. It was only stone, she thought. It would not hurt
her.

She moved down the colonnades and out onto the mosaic
patterns. The moon was almost full, a generous silvery light,
the night all around embroidered by stars.

Why did You kill Jocasta? she thought. It could not have
been only to humiliate me. There were other ways of doing
that; You didn't need to kill Jocasta, who adored You.

No, came the answer, spinning on a moonbeam. But Lukas
had to be free.

Free to be loved by you.

Or your choice would not have been significant.

The moonbeam dissolved into the greater light, and Eleanor
sat on one of the steps and thought.

She had always blamed Lycias for everything. She had
thought that all the misery of the Stasis was the result of His
own wilful obsession. But now she wondered if Astret, the
Lady of the Moon, might not be equally ruthless, equally
dangerous.

Setting her up, from start to finish. Using her. As Matthias
seemed to be, and everyone else.

Except Lukas. And Phin.

She would not be a victim again. Would not be their
scapegoat, play their games.

She turned her back on the Moon, and Lycias's temple,
and walked purposefully back through the streets to her three
treacherous, lying companions.

* * *

All night she kept it up, sitting under the strange stars, the strange moon, in a deserted city.

What was the name of Letia's Arrarat? What lies in the seams of a Caver cloak? Who was Richenda? How did Albin wear his hair?

She searched her mind, trying to remember tiny details. But she had only been at the Caves for a few hours. And the Jerenites had kept to themselves, preoccupied by the exigencies of their situation.

More painfully, she willed herself to remember the stories Lukas had told her during the time they had loved each other on the island south of Cliokest.

The first raid on Peraldon. The Cavers' strategy at the battle of Philus, during the Banishment War. Fishing with Matthias.

'Stop it, Eleanor.' Timon reached out and put his arm round her shoulder. 'You don't have to go on with this. You won't find out anything this way.'

She wiped away the stupid tears. They had all been word perfect. They knew everything she did, and very much more. She couldn't trip them up that way.

'All right,' she said. 'You all say you're here to help me. Prove it. What I want is to find Phinian Blythe. Take me to him.'

The three of them looked at each other.

'Eleanor – ' Comyn came forward. 'He's – not free.'

'What do you mean? In prison?'

'Worse than that . . . Haunted, you might say.'

'The Children of the Night have him.' Hilde spoke with regret.

'Children of the Night?'

So they told her. And she forgot about their treachery and lies, and cried herself to sleep, inside a deserted house, on a stranger's bed.

Chapter Seventeen
The Well

'How deep is it?'

'No one knows. No one wants to find out. There's a vast superstition against exploring underground. Even Sharrak refused to go to the bottom.'

'Couldn't you make it explore?'

'I? Make Sharrak do anything?' De Mowbray gave a short bitter laugh. 'My control of Sharrak is strictly limited. And you, Merauld, have never even met it. You have no idea what the Parid are like.'

'Aylmer could help. Or Thibaud.' Thurstan Merauld was rather close to the edge of the well, looking down over the low parapet into its web-festooned depths.

Both men were standing at the top of the tower jutting from the forest east of Cliokest, the entrance to Sharrak's well. They had crossed the long walkway from the citadel early that morning, before the sun's heat became too intense.

Steps led down the outside of the tower, deep into the ground. In his frequent visits to the southern province of Mavrud, Lucian Lefevre, the High Priest to the Sun, had insisted that living quarters be maintained near to the Parid's home. He had spent some time there, at one stage, experimenting with his creatures. He had spent yet more time far away in the desert city of Smintha, conducting the Rites of the Lord Lycias at the sweltering, sun-drenched Temple there.

De Mowbray had heard rumours of underground chambers beneath the Temple as well – some even said that an entire city lay underground there – but he had never been to Smintha. He had always had enough on his hands at Cliokest.

There was some significance in what happened underground, something De Mowbray did not understand. But he wondered, like Thurstan, as they watched the landscape fry beneath the heat of the sun, if some answer did not lie in the cool depths, sheltered from the incinerating heat.

De Mowbray had always tried to avoid Sharrak's well. He mistrusted his own abilities to control the Parid and rarely visited it. He had not been here since the Stasis had ended: there had been no need, for Sharrak had gone.

But not for long. It would be back, he thought. And then he would indeed be glad of a friendly Mage. It was one reason why he had been prepared to collaborate with the Cavers and their allies. It went some way towards explaining why he was here now, talking civilly to someone he had not long ago dismissed as an insignificant barbarian.

The two men were lightly dressed in cool, loose clothes, both immaculate in crisply pressed linen. De Mowbray was looking at Thurstan with some amusement, although the situation did not really merit levity.

The sun was beginning to beat down on them. He wished he'd remembered his hat. There was no shade where they stood, although the surrounding trees were not yet dead. Those with deeper roots had found moisture underground. Leaves rustled softly around and below them.

The forest had given Thurstan an idea. During the dreary sessions, thrashing out terms and treaties, de Mowbray had noticed him staring out of the windows towards the trees shimmering in the distance. They were green and cool, welcoming, while the grass on the mainland shrivelled and the crops died.

'Matthias is the only Mage who might be effective against the Parid. And he is being — difficult, right now.' De Mowbray drummed his fingers impatiently against the stone. It was all very well, planning to use the Parid's home as an actual well, but Sharrak would hardly take kindly to the idea.

Thurstan sighed. He bent down and picked a pebble from the ground and leant over the parapet, holding the stone over the drop. Then he released it, waiting for some distant sound to tell him that it had reached the bottom.

He had tried it before, like everyone else. But there was never anything.

De Mowbray's voice was dry. 'It's your own fault, you Jerenites and Cavers. So eager to break the Stasis, and then so surprised when Lycias takes His revenge. What did you expect?'

'We're one stage further on.' Thurstan had turned round, leaning against the parapet. Hard blue eyes gleamed in sun-burnt skin. De Mowbray wondered fleetingly if he ever smiled. 'We solved one problem, the hardest of all. No one ever pretended that that would be the end of it.'

'So you just keep going, digging for water, arranging territories, rebuilding temples, and put your faith in some vague hope that it will all be all right in the end?'

'What else can one do? What would you do?'

'I don't think I would put my trust in the scapegoat theory. It's too simple.'

Thurstan turned round again, looking down into the well. He didn't trust it either. And that was why he was pushing hard for everyone to learn to cope with drought.

He was full of ideas. Plans for irrigation channels, dams and reservoirs. Precipitation projects. De-salination plants.

It would be something to unite them all. At last, Thurstan had found a mission that was something more than trying to preserve the Jerenites from extinction.

He found he could work with de Mowbray, that eminently practical man. Never one to repine in a crisis, when the Stasis broke and Matthias was revealed as a Mage of incomparable power, de Mowbray had cut his losses. Under the instructions of the Emperor Xanthon, he had drawn up a provisional treaty. He was instrumental in persuading the Peraldonian territories to confer with the Cavers and Jerenites.

They were still a very long way from reconciliation. Not only had the Peraldonians had to come to terms with their own mortality, they now had to contend with drought and plague. The Cavers were held responsible, as indeed they were. Only the commands of the Emperor had prevented outright persecution.

But as the sun assaulted the land and dried up the lakes, it had become essential to discuss together what to do. De Mowbray had found the Jerenites more approachable than

the Cavers, who were still so obsessively loyal to Astret.
Thurstan and the other Jerenites had declined to take an
interest in religion, which made them possible colleagues.

'Well, Sharrak's not here now. Let's take a chance and get
on with it.' Thurstan pushed himself away from the parapet
and looked down at the winding staircase. 'How far do the
steps go down?'

'Quite a way. About five hundred feet. But it will do no
good. Sharrak will return. And Matthias is no help at all at
the moment.'

Watching Phinian Blythe from a distance, Matthias found
himself almost envying him.

The shadows that surrounded him were exacting their
price. Blythe was paying, working through the debt, in
sleepless, haunted agony.

But Matthias was free. No one hung on his shoulder
whispering poison into his ears, stealing the sweetness from
the air he breathed. No one said to him, you are at fault.

Instead he heard, again and again, Eleanor's desperate cry:
Matthias, don't leave me! He saw her face, thinner than he'd
remembered it, drawn with bewilderment and fear.

With every instinct he wanted to go to her, to help her.
His brother Lukas had loved her, and that meant much to
him. He missed Lukas more than he had anticipated. It was
a betrayal to Lukas's memory, leading Eleanor into such
danger. He should go to her, give her every help . . .

But that would ruin it all, would devalue her role. She had
to be left alone to face Lycias. He had promised Xanthon.
He had acquiesced to a dreadful bargain, to an appalling
misuse of power. It was done now. She was here, and Lycias
would be watching . . .

That evening, unable to bear it any longer, he locked the
door to his private quarters, in the same wing as Blythe's.
In an austere room, uncarpeted, uncurtained, he looked for
a long moment at the sliver of moon just above the horizon.

Then he built a fire, and concentrated.

It was easy for him now. The flight of the Benu had released
in him extraordinary power, revealing the paths to vast
perspectives, faceted dimensions. He had been frightened at
first, disturbed by the potential of it all. He had not wanted

to tap such dangerous visions, had not wanted to use it at all. But every event compelled him to explore.

His power was the deciding factor in the fragile peace that existed between the followers of Astret and Lycias. The Emperor's Mage, Imbert Cupere, had been fascinated by it. Even Xanthon had recognised it as invaluable. They would not leave him alone. There was no way out. Now Matthias was going to use his power for a different purpose.

He had no need of glass toys for this. Just clear concentration, and a leap of the imagination, magnified in firelight. He knew how to focus it, knew where he wanted it to be.

It came: the moment of vision, the impossible knowledge.

He saw Eleanor and her three companions. He recognised them all.

A friend, someone he trusted, whose heart would surely be broken, already in deadly peril. Already – ? *Corrupted*? Was that what he saw, a distortion – possession? A creeping horror, this . . .

A wraith, sent by the Fosca Lord, oblivious of Matthias's vision.

And Lycias, disguised, looking back at him. Smiling.

He threw sand on the fire, and walked to the window. The room, already stiflingly hot, was now impossible. He flung open the window and looked out at the darkening sky, the slight moon just rising.

'Astret.' He spoke softly. 'Where are You now, now that she needs You?'

But there was no answer in the silver glow. No consolation, no hope. He turned back to the fire and his breath caught.

The face of the Sun God still watched him, caught in a shimmer of light over the smoking fire. The eyes were alight with cruelty, the fine lips curving dangerously. There was something predatory in the glance: the powerful, malicious control of the hunter.

Waiting for Matthias.

As he watched, caught helpless between one thought and the next, the vision disappeared. Shuddering, he drank the wine put ready on the silver tray without taking the elementary step of scanning it for poison.

Preoccupied with dread and guilt, he wanted oblivion, deep rest, so that he might think clearly next day.

But there was no peace that night in the citadel of Cliokest.

At midnight the assassins struck.

There was more than one traitor within Cliokest. The gate to the causeway was left unattended. Thirty men, Peraldonian trained, with sharp swords and daggers. Through the stable blocks, the warehouses and barracks, gathering others on the way.

'We will die, because of them.'

'Our hair will go white, our hands ache with arthritis. We had eternal youth, and now we are doomed to death.'

'It is the fault of the Mage Matthias and his friends.'

'They must pay!'

A hand over the mouth, a blade across the throat.

'Taste the death you wished for so much!'

A pillow held down, rigid and unforgiving.

They were quiet at first, and some ten Caver men and women were killed silently as night.

Then one rolled from his bed, alerted by the scent of blood. Or was it the scrape of a blade dragged from its scabbard?

He ran to the door, shouting, running onto the smooth steel of the others waiting there.

But Thibaud Lye had heard, and the blood-reek was now everywhere. A message, instantaneously, to Aylmer and Matthias: '*Assassins! Quick! Alert the guard*!' And Aylmer at once ran to Stefan and Thurstan, and bells began to ring, voices to shout.

But Matthias slept on, drugged and unknowing.

And Phinian Blythe opened the door to the bitter enemies who had once been his friends.

He hoped they were still his friends. That they would draw the quiet blade keen across his throat and release him.

They could not believe their luck. The great Mage, the man who had compelled the release of the Benu, given extraordinary power in that one act, dazed and enfeebled with drugged wine.

Three men broke into Matthias's room. One was tall, wearing an unusual, patterned leather jerkin, his hands wide

and ham-like, reaching immediately for the spiral staff by
the bed.

The other two were younger, eager and passionate. They
would have plunged sharp knives straight into the unstirring
figure on the narrow mattress, but the other halted them with
a few words.

'Don't hurt him. He's coming with us. Tie his hands,
carefully now! A blindfold over his eyes . . . that's it.'

A great Mage has power concentrated in his eyes. Always
cover his eyes, and never let him near his staff . . .

He had learnt his lessons well. He had had a good teacher,
a being which had mastered powers greater even than
Matthias.

He was the Fosca King's pupil.

His name was Weard.

Elfitt de Mowbray tried to stop them, yelling from the top
of the stairs above the Great Hall.

'This is madness! What can you hope to achieve?'

Twenty-five men were running down the causeway, back
into the forest, pursued by Stefan Pryse and others.

Weard stood apart from his two companions who were
bundling the prone figure in blankets. His hands ran over
the light wood of the staff, tracing the pattern of the spiral.
His mouth was slightly open, tongue moistening lips.

Experimentally, he jarred the staff against stone,
murmuring words de Mowbray could not hear. Lightning
flared from the tip of the spiral, singeing the embroidered
tapestries on the walls. There was smoke, and the smell of
burning.

'The Stasis, Elfitt. The Stasis again, of course.'

And then, laughing gently to himself, he turned and
followed his men out onto the causeway where the Fosca were
waiting, while de Mowbray and his men found their limbs
encased in iron.

The shadows lifted from Blythe's shoulders, a weight of
anguish suddenly gone, and flew across the floor to the two
Peraldonian assassins standing there. They had no time to
react, no idea what was happening.

The Children of the Night worked silently, dragging their

nails through flesh, wiping soft mouths over eyes, nose and mouth, clogging them with foetid slime.

Blinded, suffocating, the men stumbled to their knees, flailing wildly with maddened arms. The Children laughed.

Blythe watched, unable to move, even though they no longer disturbed the lie of his hair, the line of his vision, the clarity of his thought.

The Children of the Night began to flense flesh from bone, tearing through muscle and nerve, pulling apart sinew and tendon. It was a very long time before the ruined bodies stopped twitching and writhing.

Blythe had not moved, watching blankly.

When they had done, the Children waited for a moment, looking across the room to him, blood tainting the shadows red.

Then, in a rush, they sprang across the room to settle in their usual place.

Hanging on his shoulders.

Breathing in his face.

Trailing blood and agony.

Exacting their price.

Chapter Eighteen
The Marqun

The Marqun was held by the light of the full moon.

A secret gathering. Only the Sea Lords and their acolytes were permitted to attend.

Torold, Earl of Shelt, was left to pace the battlements of his Castle in the company of his elegant lover, Esmond Crinnion. And although his eyes constantly searched the far horizon, he did not look back over the city, sprawling like an architect's nightmare towards the river. The great houses there soon gave way to cramped tenements, which in their turn degenerated into the chaotic, ramshackle dwellings round the Grey Bridge. The bright moonlight cast into sharp relief the edge of a wall, the line of a roof-top, the domes of the Temple . . . It gave to Shelt a filigree gloss of glamour. An unreal, theatrical sparkle.

From the battlements of the Castle, Torold might have watched the life of his city, might have observed the disarray of Shelt's night-life, the aimless gangs of youths, the noisy bars with their brawling customers, the lonely patrols of streetwalkers, the shuttered shops and heavily barred doors.

But that night, together, Torold and Esmond looked only northwards, towards the Bay of Marqun. They could not see anything in the pale moonlight, but nonetheless their eyes constantly scanned the bleak rocks which fragmented the coast in that direction.

Within the Castle, far removed from the restless city, Annis was flirting with Kester Robard, the ambitious, good-looking young captain in the Guard. But although his arms were strong and his body warm with desire, her heart wasn't in it. She kept seeing Felicia's face, white and haunted, steadfastly resisting the Sea Lord's proposed treatment.

There had been a scene, that morning. Gawne, the First Sea Lord, with Fessil and Lammon. Felicia, supported only by Annis. There was not even the pretence of honouring her wishes.

Felicia had spoken out strongly, more passionately than Annis had ever heard, trying to change their minds.

'I *know* it will not help! I *know* it is wrong!' She was shaking with foolish weakness, frustrated and furious.

'With all respect, my Lady, you must allow us to know our business.' Gawne's voice had been arid as usual. There was no leeway in it, no possibility of debate.

Nonetheless, Felicia had tried. She had used every argument.

'My father . . . would not want you take risks!'

'There is no risk. The sea will not harm you, Lady, not while the Lords are there to direct the Marqun.' Fessil, coolly confident.

'You cannot be sure!'

'You must not question the Lords' power, Lady.' His white brows almost met over his nose. Annis wondered irreverently which animal Felicia would turn him into.

Lammon was muttering to Gawne, 'One might almost suspect the taint of heresy . . .'

Felicia caught the soft murmur. 'Heresy? What heresy? Is anything that goes contrary to the Sea Lords' will always defined as heresy?'

'The Sea Lords work with the power of the Lady Herself,' said Gawne. 'It does not do to question . . .'

'But it won't work, I know it will only make things worse! I only need to be left alone!' Felicia was increasingly agitated. It came to Annis that she was fighting for her life.

'You are wrong.'

'I know what I need! It's my body!'

'And our skill.' Gawne was severe. 'You know nothing of the rhythms of the tide, the source of our power. We know secrets as old as the sea itself.' He paused then, a weighty pause, designed to impress. He continued, his voice stained with acid, 'And it is a surprise to me, to all of us, that the daughter of Duke Javon of Eldin should be so faint of heart.

Your father would not be pleased to learn of your obstinacy, your cowardice.'

He had no need to go on. She had turned her face away, that pale, hidden face.

Leaving the room, he caught sight of her drawing pad, open on the table. Amongst many others his own face, horned like a goat, leapt out at him.

The cold eyes flickered with anger then, and Annis, watching him, had felt suddenly terrified for her mistress.

But she could do nothing.

The Marqun would take place.

A tide-pool, a circular expanse of water worn into rock at the side of the cliff, filled to the brim with glassy, cold sea-water. It was impossible to tell how deep it was.

The twelve Sea Lords stood at its edge, on the slippery, green-stained rock. Each held a staff, wrought at the end into a vanishing spiral.

The tide was almost at its height, turbulent, hurling at the rocks. As yet the waves did not reach into the pool; they crashed forcefully against the tumbled strata just below the rim, and the calm pool was undisturbed – for the moment.

Felicia stood between Gawne and Dederic. No longer could she think of the goat, the budgerigar. Her eyes were drawn irresistibly to the cool depths at her feet, the gentle shadows of weed and rock.

She knew what would happen. They would warp it. Conjure the calm water to febrile life, creating a whirling pool of energy and power. And she would be thrown in, into the vortex of their creation, of the men's making. It would fasten onto the patterns of her being, drawing out her individual, unique quality. The vortex would spin it all around, dissolving it into power. Into force.

She would become their creature, their creation. Something of force and energy, directed by them. She would act in their world, become a part of them. Fit for their society, a part of the world as created by man.

And what would there be left, after that?

A toy. Someone to be married off, to secure important boundaries. A breeding machine. Producing children to serve political ends.

She clung to her weakness, to her ill-health. She need take no responsibility then, for furthering the whole sorry system.

The tide was almost overlapping the brim. She caught her breath. If she screamed or shouted, no one would pay any attention. She could not run away, there was nowhere to go, only slippery steep cliffs rising sheer around them. The boat that had brought them all there had vanished round the headland long ago. She would have to go through with it, and she would die. She did not believe that the force contained in the crashing waves could have anything to do with healing. It was entirely destructive, entirely dangerous.

The twelve men around her raised their staffs, and she felt the monstrous power shudder in the air.

She would die. She could not resist this, could not maintain an identity against this force.

The tide rose, and the first wave spilt over the rim of rock into the pool.

It did not just sweep in, and retreat. They, the men, made it swirl round, around the circumference of the rock, vanishing inwards. And the next wave, and the next.

She was half-fainting at the edge of the pool, trying feebly to push back through the wall of men. Her mouth was full of the taste of salt, blood anticipating water: water in her mouth, her throat, her lungs. Her eyes were losing focus, irresistibly drawn by the pattern of foam and wave. Her head felt as if it were spinning around and around, tracking the movement of the everlasting spiral.

'Oh, no, please, no, not this . . .' She was staggering at the edge, her limbs like water, drawn into the whorl of energy.

She saw Gawne look at her, eyes blank with power. No help there.

And the moon above, cold, distant.

Another wave. Again and again, the spiral whirled at her feet, gaining strength and power. And just when she felt that her feet were disappearing into the maelstrom, she felt a hand, light on her shoulder.

'May the sea take you,' said the dry voice in her ear, and she lost her footing, sliding across uneven, slippery rock into the vortex, down, down, to whatever waited at the bottom of the whirlpool.

* * *

They thought she was dead, at first. But Gawne knew better.

'She won't die, not this one. The sea did not take her before. It would not take her now. But it might . . . change her . . .' He looked down at the frail figure under warm blankets on the bed.

The fire was roaring, the curtains drawn. Annis watched the unmoving body on the bed, eager for some sign of life, while the Sea Lords conferred with Torold.

He had been shocked when they arrived back at Shelt, carrying his niece wrapped in Lammon's cloak.

'This is a *cure*?' he had shouted, surprised by the strength of his feeling for the girl. 'You've killed her!'

He could see no breath, no colour anywhere.

But Gawne had been firm. 'Warmth, rest, peace . . . she'll recover. And she will be different. You'll see.'

'A sea-change,' Fessil had nodded in confirmation. 'It has never failed.'

But Annis, watching the white face and colourless hair, thought that they might be wrong, this time. Felicia had not changed, not at all. All they had achieved was to weaken her further, taking every last degree of strength from her.

And what would be left when she awoke?

Chapter Nineteen
The Fire

There was a fire at Serethrun's lodgings.

Lodgings was perhaps too fine a word for the place, a run-down shack set on the river-bank beneath the arches of the Grey Bridge.

Other vagrants lived there, in tumbled dwellings of rotting wood and scrap metal. They were alcoholics, drug addicts, the lame, blind and leprous. The wily, small-time criminals and the mildly insane.

No one else would give him a roof. That spiteful, bitter little handbill seemed to have found its way into the hands of every potential landlady, every employer. Serethrun walked in shadows, avoiding the abuse and violence, the taunts of children, the sneers of women.

And his father watched with a curious satisfaction, almost glad that his fine son was now reduced, as he was, to dependency.

Serethrun had been out that day, slipping through the back alleys, searching rubbish tips, stealing where he could the small amount of food necessary to keep his father alive.

He didn't care if he ate or not. He was distracted by a determination to discover what had happened. Ideas of revenge filtered through his mind but he dismissed them. He saw instead, in his dreams and his memory, that pale face, washed with water, surrounded by sea.

Who was she, what was she? Just as the storm was not natural, so he knew that she was not pure *mereth*. There was something else there, something that matched with the water, breathed with the tide. He wanted to find out more about her and what had happened to her.

No one would tell him. Her name was never mentioned in the reports of the wreck and trial. Either she was totally unimportant, a serving maid perhaps, or of greatly exalted rank. Anyone else would have been used by the Sea Lords to justify the continuing oppression of the fishermen.

There was no way of telling. He tramped the streets of Shelt and the reflections in the dark glass of shop windows showed him pale hair streaming, frail limbs drifting.

He could not admit his unreasoning obsession to his father. There were other motives that Renferell would understand, however.

'I'll find out, you'll see.' He tried to sound positive and encouraging. 'The ship was deliberately wrecked, of course. There was some reason for it, someone hoped to gain something by discrediting me . . .' He poked the small fire in the grate.

The figure slumped on the pallet in the corner laughed, a dry, humourless bark.

'How will you do it, looking like that?'

Serethrun's clothes were stained, his boots needed repairing. His hair was unkempt, unwashed, too long, his fingernails broken and dirty.

How could he say it? There was nothing to be done while his father still lived. He wanted to take a risk, break into the Castle, find a Sea Lord . . .

They would know, they *must* know, what had happened that night. A Sea Lord had set that storm going, no one else would know how to do it. And a Sea Lord would know who had ridden the cliff path, scarlet cloak flying, to give the alarm. Would even know why he, Serethrun, had been set up. Framed.

Even more puzzling, why he had been acquitted. They would not let him in at the monthly courts. An *eloish* plainsman, dishonourable and subversive. He would have to break into the Castle somehow.

He had to find out who she was.

His chances of success were negligible. And then, who would find food for his father? The old man was coughing again. This riverside shack was probably the worst possible place for him to be, damp, dirty and draughty.

What could he do? With furious, frustrated energy, he

built up the fire and then slammed out of the door.

He tramped the streets that rainy night, walking quickly to keep warm, with no aim or object in mind. He preferred to be out, even in the city, where the wind and rain ran free. If he had found the discipline of the Guard difficult, the exigencies of poverty were worse. He hated the way he had to think, all the time, of how to get food, how to keep his father warm.

It was a relief to follow the wind down the long alleys, to drift with no purpose, like a leaf through a forest.

He passed the taverns and hotels, the shut-up shops, the tenement blocks and shanty town that had sprung up round the harbour.

Lost in reverie, he did not notice the two men watching him, first from the bridge over his shack, and then again at various points through the city. They were not following him; but here and there their paths crossed, and Serethrun would turn aside, his eyes dark and withdrawn, pressing on regardless.

One of the men was Olwyn Mittelson, tall and frail. The other, equally tall, but moving with careless grace, used an alias.

He too was a stranger in the city. Separated from home, family and lover for reasons he did not understand. He frowned as he watched Serethrun fling himself down the lonely alleys, kicking at cans. He was not without compassion.

He too had lost much.

The fire started when Serethrun was far away, over by the harbour. He was walking near the quayside, where rows of deserted fishing boats were beached high out of reach of the tide.

The rain was a steady drizzle now, plastering down his hair, running into his eyes. Light from a few windows glimmered briefly on the damp pavements. He walked through rubbish, through puddles and gutters, unnoticing.

He was too far away to hear the shouts and screams, the calls for help.

At last he returned, in the early hours of the morning, and smelt the smoke hanging heavy over the riverside area, acrid and harsh. Through the dark, damp air he saw unfamiliar outlines, the unusual line of the bridge's arches clear and uncluttered. There was nothing left of those few, disreputable shacks but a pile of rubble.

He ran. There was a group of men rooting around in the smoking remains, and he recognised one of them, an undersized pick-pocket with only one eye.

'Jacko, what happened?' Cold gripped him now.

The little man looked at him, his head on one side, his mouth working as he chewed at a straw.

'Your father's dead,' he said at last, the words almost incomprehensible. 'The roof fell in before anyone could get him out.'

'Dead?' Serethrun repeated the word mechanically. For a moment the pattern of his thoughts halted.

'They took the body to the paupers' cemetery. No one knew where you were. Rattner named it.'

Jacko regarded Serethrun with curiosity. Sympathy did not often form part of his emotional vocabulary, but he had liked Serethrun Maryn, respected the way he had put up with the constant nagging of the old man.

Sympathy was not relevant here. Jacko turned away, slightly shocked by what he now saw in the dark-fringed eyes.

Serethrun had started thinking again. He could find out what had happened, who she was. He could clear his name, could even leave Shelt. Return to the plains. Become one with the *eloish* again.

His father was dead, and now everything would be all right.

The two tall men caught up with him just before dawn.

He was wandering again, the ceaseless tramping of dull streets, but now his step was full of energy, of purpose. He was almost happy.

'Serethrun Maryn.' Olwyn Mittelson stepped out of the shadow, blocking his path. The other man was lounging against the wall of the alley, hands deep in pockets.

Serethrun halted, his eyes suddenly wary. 'You! What do you want?'

'Do you want to get into the Castle?' The words were softly spoken, but Serethrun felt them reverberating everywhere.

'I . . . don't know . . .'

'Clear your name? Reinstate yourself?'

'I'd rather – go home . . .'

'Home? Where is your home?' The other man pushed himself away from the wall, coming forward so that the light from the window above just caught on his straight, fair hair.

'What's it to you?' Serethrun didn't know what to make of these two, the thin man who could dissolve metal with a word, the other whose blue eyes seemed unnervingly to plumb every depth.

They were trouble, these two. He didn't need them. He would pack his things and return to the plains. It was where he belonged.

'You are needed here.' Olwyn Mittelson still spoke softly, but there was sympathy in his eyes.

'What? What are you talking about?'

'There has been a miscarriage of justice. There is much wrong in Shelt. There is something for you to do here.'

'Who are you?' He stepped away from them, wary and watchful.

'You know my name.'

'Come on, Olwyn, be fair. That's not what he means.' The fair-haired man was almost bored by the conversation. 'We have a proposition for you, Maryn. You would do well to listen.'

'No. I'm leaving. I'm going home.'

Mittelson was about to speak, but the other man forestalled him, holding up an eloquent hand. 'Leave it, Olwyn,' he said. 'Wait – '

'There's not much time!'

'There's enough. Let him go.'

For a moment the two men looked at each other, and then Mittelson stood aside, nodding.

'If you change your mind – we mean you no harm. And can be found, most evenings, at the Fish and Net . . .'

Serethrun stared at them for a moment, and then turned on his heel, pushing through the narrow alleyways towards the west gate.

The gate to the plains. Where the *eloish* ran through the wind.

The way home.

* * *

Serethrun left the city and stood on the hillside beyond the city walls, on a slope of green and grey, while the sun rose behind him.

The wind was blowing through his hair, flapping his untidy clothes. His people were probably camped in the east, in the shelter of Selby Forest. It was spring, after all. Soon they would be able to move further north, up towards the wind-strewn tundra north of the Pallon Crag. He would rejoin them, forget the *mereth* city, laugh with the running deer and calling owl.

He experienced an almost physical pain, the bitter ache of longing. He wanted it so much, to be *eloish* again. The wind was calling him, almost as strongly as it used to . . .

He saw the wind ripple through the long grasses of the plain, and it looked like water. The surface of grass moved in washes of grey-green colour. He remembered the sea, darker than this, washing over rock at the end of the brigg.

And the woman, her face white and fragile beneath the waves.

He had been dishonoured, framed, discredited. But she had been almost murdered. The men on the ship had been murdered.

The storm had been an artificial creation. He was sure of it, he knew all about storms. One or more of the Sea Lords . . . Mittelson was right, there was great evil in Shelt.

He found his mind returning again and again to that pale face. She had been beautiful, drifting so lightly through the waves, and the sea was part of her, extending out from her flowing hair . . .

This was getting fanciful. She was probably some spoilt, rich, city-bred brat, anathema to everything he valued.

He thought again of those two men. They had not been unfriendly, only unknown. There had been something about the man with fair hair that he had liked.

Perhaps he would try the Fish and Net. See what they wanted. He would rejoin the *eloish* later. There was still time.

That evening, the man living under an alias also stood outside the city, looking out into the wilderness around. He stood on the cliff-top, looking east towards the darkening sea.

An observer on the rocks below would have seen a gaunt

figure, dark shadowed against the setting sun, a cloak fluttering in the onshore wind. Waves were crashing below in a foam of white but he did not look down. He was still and unmoving, a black silhouette in the vivid light.

For a long time he stood there, framed in the hectic light of the setting sun, staring out into the cooling air. Then, as the last of the sun's rays sank below the horizon, he turned, with a kind of impatience, and walked away down the cliff, back to the city.

'Disguise,' said Olwyn Mittelson. 'I can change you so that you'll not be recognised . . .'

'What, a false beard? Dye my hair?'

'Don't knock it.' The fair-haired man, who had introduced himself as Jolin Rosco, was half laughing at Serethrun's outrage. 'It can be very effective.'

They were sitting in one of the alcoves at the Fish, a bottle of brandy half finished between them.

'Why are you doing this? What do you want?'

They had given him a warm cloak to replace the one he'd lost in the fire, bought him food and drink, leaving him with money in his purse.

'What are you buying?' Lulled by the food and warmth, it sounded churlish.

'You want to talk to a Sea Lord, find out why you were framed, don't you?' Mittelson spoke quietly. 'Do you think they're just going to sit down across a table from you and tell you why? You'd never get near them.'

'But what do you want?' Why was he so evasive?

'The Sea Lords . . . are taking a dangerous course. Dangerous to the lives of the ordinary people of Shelt, dangerous to the plainspeople, the *eloish*, to everyone who comes into contact with them . . .'

'The shipwreck . . .' Unwillingly he saw that image again, of the woman in the waves. 'That storm was artificially constructed. The *Mirabelle* was deliberately wrecked.'

Mittelson's pale eyes did not blink. 'Yes. And you are *eloish*, after all . . .' His voice was very quiet. He glanced suddenly at the fair-haired man at his side. He seemed to come to a decision. 'We need the *eloish*, Serethrun. In order to overturn the Sea Lords, we need the plainspeople.'

'Who, exactly, is "we"?'

'The fishing community of Shelt. The people who have been dispossessed by the Sea Lords.'

'Give me one good reason why the *eloish* should help the citizens of Shelt.' Serethrun was watching Mittelson carefully, warily.

'They need horses, don't they? To follow the ancient paths?'

Yes, they needed horses. They had not needed to be so – cruel, when they still had their horses . . .

'Serethrun. This is the bargain. We will undertake to return to the *eloish* their horses, if they will fight with the fisherpeople to depose the Sea Lords.'

Serethrun let out his breath, leaning back.

'Madness,' was all he said. Suddenly, he saw it all. They were rebels, working for some underground revolutionary organisation. The whole thing would be violent and risky, doomed to almost certain failure.

They wouldn't help him; they would only use him.

'Think about it.'

Rosco was looking at him, and Serethrun found himself unable to meet those compelling blue eyes.

'What's it to you? Who are you?'

Mittelson answered. 'Don't you want to know what's going on here? There's so much wrong. That shipwreck . . . Where did that storm come from, where did it go? The *eloish* might know. Their shaman women could counter powers like that. Don't you want to go home? Don't you want the *eloish* to ride once more? Don't you want to ride with them?'

The questions piled up, and Serethrun had no answer.

Rosco was sitting back, taking no part in the discussion, still watching him in that unnerving way. Serethrun dragged his eyes away and found himself looking at Mittelson's hands lying calmly on the table.

The index finger casually traced the figure of a spiral on the uneven surface. It took on a life of its own. Fascinated, he could not look away. He watched the pattern, swirling round and round and, like a whirlpool, it drew him in.

'You're an unprincipled bastard.' Rosco's eyes were cold.

'You're complaining?'

'No. Come on, let's get him home.'

The two tall men, one on either side, slung the slumped body of the younger man between them, and crossed the floor to the door.

No one saw them go. No one noticed their faces.

Protected by the spiral, they went out into the night, and moonlight shone all around them.

Chapter Twenty
Kidnap

Alone, she lived in sea-water. It ran through her veins, flowed under her skin. As the tide moved, so did her breath.

There was a fire in the room, but she could only recognise cold. No part of her was now capable of sensing heat. There were warm blankets and sheets around her, but she only knew the wash of waves over her skin. Soft dry hair clouded her unmoving head, drifting as seaweed over the pillows.

She had no strength to move her hand, to lift her eyelids. The only movement was of sea-water, welling from beneath her eyes, flowing ceaselessly over her face. Two days she had lain there, silent as driftwood, and now they were beginning to leave her alone. Through the sound of water washing within and without her, she heard their anxiety.

They had slapped and shaken her, massaging and pummelling, trying to force warmth into chilled limbs. They had given her medicines, stroking her throat to make her swallow. And bread, soaked in honeyed milk.

She hardly noticed what they were doing, aware only of the tide in her veins, the eternal murmur of waves turning and returning within her.

But the movement of sea-driven breath was becoming fainter.

The tide was going out.

'It took place three nights ago. She's still unconscious.'

Vere Holtby, the flautist who sometimes entertained the Castle Guard for the price of a drink, leant back in his chair, watching the effect of his words.

There was a brief silence. Mittelson sighed. 'It's too soon. We're not ready. It's asking for trouble – '

'There will be reprisals.' Holtby nodded in agreement. 'But on the other hand, will she survive this kind of treatment?' He asked the question of the smoky, noisy air. The three men were sitting round a table at the Fish, the drinks on the table before them untasted.

'Oh, I think so.' Mittelson's pale eyes were unblinking. 'But it is a risk. Perhaps we should act now. Get her out.'

'Who are you talking about?' Serethrun Maryn looked up from deeply abstracted thoughts.

He had decided to stay in Shelt. He had recovered his senses after that meeting in the Fish to find himself thinking more favourably of Mittelson and Rosco. There was injustice here in Shelt, and treachery. He had always known that. All that had altered was that he now felt that he should do something about it.

He remembered nothing of moving spirals, of pale eyes blinking. Although he had no reason to trust men, Serethrun Maryn found himself listening to Olwyn Mittelson.

'The Lady Felicia Westray. Duke Javon's daughter.'

'Where have you been, Maryn?' Vere Holtby was laughing at him. 'Chasing the wind or star-signing?'

Serethrun stared at Holtby, unsmiling, unspeaking. Holtby shrugged and took a long drink.

'You've met her before, Serethrun,' Mittelson went on, smoothing it over. 'She is the woman you saved from the wreck.'

It was a shock, harsh as lightning. Serethrun sat bolt upright and paid attention.

'They're killing her.'

They dyed Serethrun's hair brown and gave him a knife. He knew his way round the Castle, had been on duty there often before. That was why they had chosen him. He had not been reluctant. Serethrun Maryn wanted to be the one to rescue Felicia.

He wanted to see if the bones of her face were as fine as he remembered. If her hair was as silky and straight as he thought. He wanted to know the colour of her eyes.

She would be in the east wing, where the honoured guests

were always housed, close to the sea. They decided to waste
no more time, and borrowed one of the illegal boats hidden
in the warehouses by the harbour.

They stood on the rocks below the sheer walls, and Serethrun
looked up at the window, high above. The clouds were racing
across the grey sky, the wind chill and bitter around them.
The stone wall was running with damp, slippery with lichen.

He wondered how they expected him to climb it. There
were no handholds. But even as he thought, there was a sound
above and a rope snaked down. It was an inch thick, knotted
at intervals. He pulled hard on it, and it hung steady.

'Where does that come from?'

Mittelson gave a small smile. Wind was lifting through his
grey hair, and his pale gold eyes gleamed at Serethrun. 'We
have friends, you know. We're not alone in this.'

Rosco was not there. He had a meeting to attend. He had
wished Serethrun luck, and used an archaic phrase: 'May the
Lady go with you . . .'

'Lady go with you . . .' echoed Mittelson, and Serethrun
began to climb.

He was still fit, although the last two weeks had taken the
edge off his strength. He moved quickly and neatly, unwilling
to remain exposed on that storm-battered sea-wall for long.

Mittelson would wait, for an hour or so. It wouldn't take
long, the Mage had assured him. She would not be guarded.
A serving-maid, perhaps. The doctor would have called
earlier in the day.

A hundred feet, the rope cold and harsh beneath his fingers,
damp with moisture.

He tried to remember what had happened, how he came
to be climbing a knotted rope, rescuing – or kidnapping –
Duke Javon's daughter.

But he found it hard to appreciate that she was a figure
of political importance. Mittelson had explained, carefully,
a thousand reasons why they should abduct the Duke's
daughter. A lever, a bargaining counter. The traditional
hostage role.

All Serethrun could remember, to the point of obsession,
was her face, drifting in water.

'There is a connection.' He had tried to articulate it to

Mittelson that afternoon. 'It would be appropriate . . .'

He had stopped. Mittelson wasn't listening anyway. He was climbing the rope because of this unreasonable, absurd, intuition. He was not sure how significant it was.

The tall casement window was open. He clambered onto the narrow ledge outside the room, and wondered who had hooked the loop of the rope round a stone bollard on the battlements. There was a hawk, winging in the wind-driven clouds far above him, but he didn't look up.

He pushed the window wide and went in.

The room was hot, stifling hot, even though the window had been open. A fire blazed in the grate, and heavy velvet curtains hung over the door, shutting out any through-draught.

The girl lay motionless on a four-postered bed, rose pink brocade all around. She was grey against the pillows, shadowed with blue-green, ashy hair spread wide on white linen.

For a moment he stared at her, surprised. She was just as he remembered but he didn't want to touch her. She was too fragile. She would melt beneath his fingers, drain away like water over stone. He could not possibly just put her over his shoulder and climb a knotted rope out of the castle.

There were footsteps outside.

Quickly he stepped behind the hangings at the back of the bed, so that he was standing just behind her head.

The door opened. A young woman, richly dressed, a lady-in-waiting. Dark, curling ringlets, a neat curvy figure and bright eyes. She was flushed with some emotion — anger, he decided, observing her through the narrow opening at the side of the bed.

She was followed by a tall, gaunt man dressed in silvery silk, and another, broad-shouldered and energetic. Torold.

Serethrun knew him from parades and formal ceremonies. Usually he was seen at a distance, usually stern and dignified. He was almost beside himself with fury.

'What news then, Gawne? Any change? What's going to happen next?' His deep voice was uneven with the power of it.

'She will recover.' Dry as dust, Gawne was quietly confident.

'She's dying, man, fading away! Use your eyes!'

'She merely rests. Our purpose is accomplished.'

The words were ambivalent. He did not trouble to disguise it.

The girl was standing by the bed, close to Serethrun. He could smell her warmth, sense her indignation. She said nothing, but her hands, clasped one over the other, were white at the knuckles.

The old man in grey bent over the bed, lifting one slack eyelid. He straightened again, rather quickly. 'Another Marqun might make the difference – '

'Never!' Torold was pacing the centre of the floor, avoiding the bed. 'I'll write to Javon. He'd better know what you've done. That his daughter is dying.'

'She is not dying!' The grey man's voice was sharp and acidic. 'She is fated to much more than a meaningless death in Shelt! We have seen –'

'What have you seen?'

He had stopped pacing, was glaring across the room, looking straight at Gawne.

'She will not die. Not yet.' The first Sea Lord lifted his chin, daring Torold to question further.

Sighing with frustration, Torold resumed his pacing.

The girl was bending over the bed, tucking in the sheets with curious tenderness. Serethrun looked away from her, almost resenting her movements, the golden skin and rosy cheeks. She was so different from that other fragile figure lying there.

'If she dies,' Torold's voice was shaking, 'I'll see you beg, Gawne, don't mistake it.'

The other man did not even bother to reply. He picked up the white hand on the sheet and concentrated on the pulse.

'She will not die,' he repeated. 'You need not imperil your soul with heresy.'

'Heresy!'

'Calling into question the decision of the Sea Lords. You would do well to moderate your responses.'

'Shit!' A crash as Torold violently and deliberately swept a flower vase from the mantelpiece. Daffodils and broken china littered the carpet, dank water staining the pink wool. 'You take too much on yourself, Gawne! You owe Javon for your position here, and don't you forget it. You are his to command!'

'But time has passed, my Lord Torold. We have moved on. I do not think I need to point out what *your* position here owes to *me* . . .'

The girl at the bed moved nearer its head, so close that Serethrun could have touched her shoulder just by leaning forward a little.

The grey man barely blinked. His voice continued, steady and characterless. 'Unity, Torold. That's what it's all about. Remember the forces that could be ranged against you – and us. The Lady is a jealous mistress. We need each other. You know it.'

'Think what Javon will do if she dies!' Torold's dark eyes were intense.

'But she won't.' Gawne spoke as if to a child. He turned to the girl standing by the bed. 'And if Mistress Annis here repeats one word of what she has just heard, she will live to envy the dead.' A thin smile flickered on his death's head face. He reached out one bony hand, caressing the girl's flushed cheek.

Serethrun could feel her revulsion, her hatred and fear.

'Leave the window open, my dear,' he instructed. 'Fresh air – now, that's the thing.'

'She'd better have shown some signs of life by tomorrow, Gawne. I'm warning you. Or I'll send you back to Javon, and you can explain to his face that his daughter is dying!'

The Sea Lord just looked at him until, discomfited, Torold turned away and left the room, slamming the door behind him.

'Remember, Annis. These are not games for pretty maidens to witness . . .' Gawne smiled at her, a thin distortion of warmth, and left the room, closing the door quietly.

'Damn, damn, damn!' The girl was shaking with impotent fury. She rushed across the room to the broken vase, and knelt down, beginning to clear it up.

Serethrun could hear that she was close to tears. Trusting to intuition, he stepped out from behind the bed.

'Don't cry – '

She straightened up, spinning round in one smooth

movement, and he could see that she was going to scream.

Instantly he was across the room, his hand over her mouth.

'Quiet,' he whispered. 'I won't harm you, or your mistress.'

He saw from her eyes that she understood him. Cautiously he moved his hand. She stepped back from him, moving towards the door. Her voice was light and petulant.

'That's what they all say.'

'Who?'

'Men. All of them. They won't harm us, it's for our own good, we don't know any better . . .'

Suddenly she dashed for the door, flinging it wide.

He caught up with her in a moment, pulling her back into the room. Fortunately, the corridor outside was deserted.

'Don't be a fool!' He was holding her tightly now, his hands imprisoning her wrists.

She aimed a kick at him, and there was a brief struggle. They finished up against the far wall, near the open window. He had her arms twisted behind, her wrists in one hand.

The sound of the sea outside swept into the room, angry and violent. The girl stopped struggling, suddenly unresisting.

'Shut the window!' she said urgently, and Serethrun dropped his hands, looking at her uncomprehending.

'It's the Lady Felicia! The sea is killing her, listen to it – '

The tide below them roared and crashed. Serethrun could almost feel the whole Castle shudder at the power of it. He didn't know what she meant, but every instinct agreed. He had to use all his strength to pull the window shut, bolting it against the wind.

Annis was back by the bed, looking at the figure lying there.

'I've come to get her out,' said Serethrun. To his surprise, she sighed.

'Let's hope you're not too late.'

'You're not going to try to stop me?'

'You heard them. Torold and the Sea Lord. They'll kill her between them, all for pride.'

Serethrun was untying the rope round his waist, brought for the purpose. Something in the girl's voice made him look at her.

'You'll have to come too, won't you? They'll blame you otherwise.'

She stared at him. A short, bitter laugh escaped her.

'As soon as I saw you, I knew. I knew this would be the end of everything.'

'Or the start . . .'

Serethrun wondered why he had said that, as she helped him lay Felicia's unconscious body across his shoulders, tying her in place with rope.

Once more they opened the window and the noise outside hit them as violently as a blow.

And yet, as soon as they were outside the Castle, on the narrow battlements, the wind died. And as Serethrun swung himself onto the rope and began the slow climb down, his shoulders aching under Felicia's slight weight, the tide below calmed to a quiet, gentle rhythm.

Mittelson helped them untie the girl, and laid her in the bottom of the boat. Watching him, Serethrun noticed more than tenderness and care in his actions.

There was awe.

Reverence.

Chapter Twenty-one
The Arrarat

'Where are we?'

Comyn squinted up at the early morning sun, shading his eyes, before answering her.

'You still want to go to find Blythe?'

'Is it far?' Eleanor was sitting in the shadow of a doorway watching Comyn prepare breakfast. He was heating up water for coffee over a small fire. There were biscuits, olives, pale, creamy cheese and oranges. He had come well prepared.

There was dust mixed with sand on every surface, on stone and pavement, wall and window-sill. They were in a small square some distance from the Temple of Lycias. There was a well there, but he had used water from a flask.

Timon and Hilde had gone for a walk. To look for the baby, Timon said.

She had watched them incuriously. She felt no desire to go with them, although she also was worried about the baby. Her mind returned to it constantly. Whose was it? Were its parents searching, grieving, frantic? Matthias would know, he had given it to her in the first place. But Matthias was no friend, no help. He had abandoned her, and the baby.

None of her three new acquaintances had any answers either.

She had decided to try to tackle Comyn alone. She knew that she would become confused if she tried to talk to more than one of them at a time.

She didn't understand who these people were, or what they wanted. Their stories, so alike in the details, were inherently contradictory. Only one of them could possibly be a friend

– and she had no means of knowing who he or she was. They could all be lying.

She wondered briefly if it would be better to strike off on her own across the desert, but it was not an idea to entertain seriously. She had no illusions about her ability to survive in a world of arid, empty heat. Whoever these people were, they were at least company against the desert.

Although it was early, the sun was already ferociously hot. Her velvet dress was crumpled, dusty, and stained with sweat. For a moment she remembered the baby, kicking its brown legs in the warm air, free.

Why not?

She stood up and went over to Comyn. 'Have you got a shirt or anything I could borrow?'

He smiled sympathetically. 'It *is* hot, isn't it? Here, try this.'

He fished in the wide canvas bag at his side, bringing out an unbleached cotton shirt. She reached out for it and then halted.

'It's all right, it won't bite you.' The words were light, but his voice was serious. 'You'll have to make up your mind, Eleanor. Either you trust me – us. Or you don't. If you don't, you shouldn't share our food, wear our clothes, fall asleep near us or relax in any way. You'll crack up in two days that way. Or you can take the chance that one of us at least is looking out for you, trying to help . . .'

'You?'

'What do you think?'

He was taller than the others, moving with a contained energy. Short dark hair, intelligent hazel eyes. He always spoke quietly.

There was something hidden about him. A reserve, something she didn't understand. She almost liked him, but there was no real way through to him.

She took the shirt, not answering. In the shade of the doorway she stripped off the velvet, discarding it without a second thought.

It was a relief, precise and sensuous, to feel warm air move freely over her skin. The shirt was loose, wide and long, reaching almost to her knees. She rescued the belt from the green dress, tying it around her waist.

When she returned, Comyn had drawn a map, scratched with a stick in the sand.

'This is where we are now, in the ruins of Smintha. One of the far outposts of the Peraldonian Empire. Here − ' he pointed to a little heap of stones some distance away, 'this is Peraldon, and here, across the sea, is Jeren. The Cavers' island, where you first arrived, was just north of Jeren . . .' A little cross. 'And much further south, on the same latitude as Smintha, is Cliokest. That is where Phinian Blythe now lives, and those of the Cavers and Jerenites who elected to stay.'

'What happened to the others?'

'Some returned to Jeren, others ventured further afield. As you can imagine, there is much resentment against the Cavers for ending the Stasis. There are other lands dedicated to Astret, in Stromsall, the northern continent. There are a few large cities in the southern reaches and on the coast but most of the rest of it is given over to nomadic plainspeople. I believe there's some fishing on the eastern coast, but the seas are unreliable.

'It was always a turbulent place, full of aggressive, land-hungry barons, and I doubt that the Stasis has improved matters. Little is known about what goes on there now. Traffic has only just started moving between north and south. Since the Boundary broke, of course.'

'How far to Cliokest?'

He looked at her, sighing. 'A long way. Two hundred miles, at least.'

Not far, if you had cars, aeroplanes or trains. Daunting, for Eleanor, on foot.

'How did *you* get here?'

He raised an eyebrow at her. 'Arrarat, of course.'

Arrarat! *That* would be the way to tell which of them was trustworthy.

And then she heard it again, the sound for which she had been unconsciously waiting.

The baby was crying again.

Timon was carrying it this time, stumping furiously towards them down the street from the Temple. Hilde was trailing far behind him, struggling to keep up.

Timon was hot and perspiring, scowling at them both. Unceremoniously, he dumped the baby in Eleanor's lap.

'There,' he said. 'Now, look after it this time!'

Her mouth dropped at the effrontery of it.

She stood up, leaving it carefully on the step. 'Why on earth should I?' She couldn't believe it. 'It's not my baby, I know nothing about babies. If you're so worried about it, you look after it!'

'Really, what a fuss.' Hilde had caught up with them, slightly breathless, but still calm. 'Comyn, what else have you got in that capacious bag of yours? Milk, water, cereal?'

'Milk? In this heat?'

Of course not. What else could they give it? But as they turned to look at the baby, it stopped crying, waving podgy fists in the air. It was frowning, making shapes with its hands, watching them with concentration.

'Well,' said Eleanor, 'it's happy enough for the moment.'

'Why don't we explore some of these houses? We might find something it could eat.' Hilde had lowered herself tiredly onto the steps by the well. She was white with exhaustion and heat. Her skin had a faint sheen, like wax. She waved away the cup of coffee Comyn was holding out to her, and took a small pleated fan from her reticule, slowly waving it back and forth in the oppressive air.

'Okay, but in a minute.' Eleanor looked at them all. There was something about the mere idea of the Arrarat that gave her courage. Or was it the way the baby waved its hands, that look of intense concentration?

'How did you both get here? Comyn came by Arrarat, he says. What about you?'

'Not another bloody inquisition!' Timon scowled at her.

'It's not unreasonable,' said Hilde. 'I also was brought here by Arrarat . . .'

'But the Jerenites don't ride Arrarat!' Triumphantly, she thought she had caught one of them out at last.

'No, of course not. But I was lent one by Caspar – you remember Caspar, don't you? Margat's son. Lukas's nephew. He sent his love . . . Adila is her name, a fine, chestnut hawk –'

'*Mine* is chestnut!' Timon's chin was jutting aggressively.

'Show me, then.' She felt sure that she would know if they

were true Arrarat. No one could copy that bright strength.

'Oh, all right.' In one smooth movement. Timon had scooped the baby up again. 'Come on.'

They walked through the city in silence. Comyn had wanted to call his Arrarat there and then, but the others had all felt that open spaces would be more suitable.

The baby was enjoying the outing, laughing and cooing in Timon's arms.

Eleanor walked alone, behind the others. She watched the three figures ahead almost dispassionately. Heat shimmered around them, blurring the outlines. They appeared almost dreamlike against the baking stone of the city. More vivid to her, more real, were her memories.

She thought of Phin, in the grip of extraordinary torment. He had been such a friend to her, chosen by Astret to break the Stasis, just as she had been. She remembered that journey south from Jeren, his arms round her waist, his voice in her ear. She could not bear him to be hurt. Still suffering, after he had been through so much.

In this world, everyone she met and loved suffered. It was almost as if she were cursed. Know Eleanor Knight, and pay for it. Die.

Oh Christ, Lukas! I need you so. Was it worth it, breaking the Stasis, losing you? We're going to meet Arrarat hawks today. You were with me when I found Ash, my midnight hawk.

Ash died too.

Eleanor barely noticed that they had passed through the wide gate in the city walls. Dusty pavements beneath their feet gave way to drifting sand. They walked out into the desert, the wide, burning spaces hard and bright about them.

Then she heard Comyn call the familiar Arrarat summoning. Timon joined him, and then Hilde, wavering, unsure in the brilliant stillness.

She had shut her eyes, dreary, weary tears on her cheeks. She heard the beat of wings, knew that if she looked up there would be familiar shapes on the horizon.

But not Ash. Not Astrella with Lukas. No one she loved, no one to love her.

A sudden scream, high and extreme. The cry of an angry,

surprised Arrarat. She looked up, her eyes narrowed against the violent sun.

Three vast winged creatures, wheeling in wide arcs far above them. They were too high to distinguish markings or colour; three dark hawks swung on the back of powerful thermals, warily circling each other.

As she watched, her breath caught, she saw two of them dart in as one on the third. She saw it lift suddenly, strongly, even higher away from them.

The other two surged after it, screaming in the thin air. It swerved desperately and then drew its wings in, plummeting in a sheer fall, down, down towards the people standing below.

She could hear the rush of air, the scream as it dropped to the earth, and the other two followed close on its tracks.

And then she saw. The two pursuers were not Arrarat. One was a reptile: leathery wings, scaled body, red eyes, avid mouth. The other was a raven, black and glossy.

She could hardly bear to watch. The Arrarat was deep chestnut with golden eyes. Falling, it seared through the air like a fire-brand, bright and glowing.

At the last moment, only yards above their heads, it lifted once more, and she felt the wind in her hair. It was off again, skimming low over the dunes and city, swerving and dodging, while the others followed close behind.

Oh, let it escape! Let it be free, winging on the light air. Let it go, let it go . . .

It vanished into the heat-haze over the desert, low over the horizon, winding between dunes, and the other two shrieked in pursuit.

Her three companions seemed immobile with shock. They remained in stillness, watching the line of the dunes, waiting for the reappearance of the Arrarat.

It would not come back. She knew it. The Fosca angel and the strange raven would not allow it to return. Probably, they would not allow it to live.

'Adila!' Hilde's voice, desperate and frail.

Timon ignored her, holding the baby as if for comfort. His bright eyes searched the horizon, still scanning the sky for the Arrarat's return.

Comyn turned to look at her. His mouth was straight and unsmiling. He said nothing, waiting for her reaction.

She looked up at them, at their pale, shocked faces.

'I hate you,' she said. 'I hate you all. I wish you'd all go away and leave me alone. I don't need you, I don't want you.'

I want only Lukas, and Ash, and Phin.

I want only Lukas.

Chapter Twenty-two
The Caravan

She turned back towards the city. Where else was there to go? It shone white and golden in the sunlight, the glass-tiled roofs gaudy in the brilliant sky. But as she watched it, something changed. It lost the straight geometric lines she was used to. Instead a heat-haze drifted over the low-slung buildings. Only the gleaming towers arose above the shimmering mists. It was beautiful, in a way.

There was a disturbance in the haze at the desert gate. At first the clouds of dust and sand disguised what was happening, but then she saw, and heard, something all too familiar.

A black London taxi, chugging across the sand. At the head of an unruly procession leaving the city. Huge creatures moved slowly with uneven, ponderous gait, vast heads dipping with each step, armoured tails trailing a wide swathe through the sand. She saw light glance from shiny, scaled skin, viridescent and subtle. From a distance they looked like great lizards, reptiles of the sun, anachronisms from another age.

They were surrounded by tawdry clutter. Haphazard constructions were roped to their backs: crates, tents and pagodas. Torn rags of cloth fluttered, bells jangled. Fraying banners waved from the top of tall poles. And all around a milling crowd of people and animals, laden by bundles and bags, pots and pans, led other animals: goats, sheep, horses.

The caravan was sullenly tramping through the desert, a noisy, stinking, drab procession, creeping out into the heat. She could smell the stench of it, even though there was no wind. Hot animal smells, dung, sweat, sour cooking. Blood.

'Who are they? Where have they come from?' She was amazed.

'Underground . . .' She hardly caught Hilde's soft voice. 'That's where they all went, when water became scarce. The people of Smintha went underground, but I don't know why they're leaving now.'

Timon touched her hand. 'Eleanor,' he said, quietly. 'Please . . .' He was looking at her seriously, a question in the green eyes. She nodded, and so he gave her the baby again. It was asleep.

He drew from his belt a serrated knife, standing slightly in front of her. Comyn was to her right, Hilde behind. Comyn too held a serrated knife.

The taxi's horn was blaring, harsh and strident, its engine a low rumble. The sound was nearly lost amidst the other noises: the jangle of pans and bells, the heavy tread of the great beasts, the ceaseless murmur of all the people, cries and shouts and moans and arguments. Drums were beating, carried by armed men on horseback, riding up and down the caravan, keeping it all moving, all in place.

'Where are they going?' She whispered over the baby's head to Timon.

'I don't know.' He was squinting against the sun, his left hand shading his eyes, his legs wide-braced, tension in every muscle.

She didn't like taxis, or the people who rode in them. At the sides of the procession, streaming back towards the city, she saw serpentine ripples in the sand, fanning out. As if a thousand snakes were escorting the procession, accompanying it from the city.

Or as if it were all growing from the sand, created out of the burning haze . . .

The taxi suddenly accelerated, swerving away from the head of the procession, coming straight for them in a cloud of dust.

Behind it, like the wash from a boat, trailed a pattern of rippled sand. The taxi squealed to a halt only feet from them, but the wave of sand swept on past and around them, circling them completely.

Timon reached out for her, pulling her close to him. She

could feel Comyn's breath just beside her, sense that Hilde was trembling.

As they watched, the wave-shape changed, rearing up over them, drawing in power from the surrounding desert, growing and swelling, a wall of sand. At its crest, it took on a different character.

Scales, golden and russet, sweeping smoothly over a muscular body. A head, forming in lines of savage artistry. A mouth, wide, with forked tongue and back-turned fangs.

Eleanor shrank away from it, crouching low over the baby, trying to protect him. She felt, rather than heard, a movement beside her. Timon was leaping, hurling defiance at it. She could not bear to watch.

She saw a figure through the windscreen of the taxi, making shapes with his hands, spinning them around a wooden spiral. Creating the sand-snake, imagining, inventing, and controlling its action.

She heard a sudden dry hiss, virulently powerful, ripping through the air, and a scream from Timon.

She had to look; over her shoulder she saw him thrown back to the sand, discarded, his upper arm torn open in a long, spurting gash.

The taxi door opened. A man stood on the sand beneath the snake, holding a spiral carved staff. He had long curly brown hair hanging in greasy curls, a patterned leather jerkin, bare, sunburnt arms. Large, heavy hands.

'Well, well, well,' he said, smiling. 'What a find. Eleanor Knight *and* the baby!'

She looked around frantically for the others. The sand snake had closed in, separating her from them. She could no longer see Comyn or Hilde behind that glistening wall of neat, overlapping scales.

And Timon, beside her, was on his knees, his right hand clasped to his arm, trying to staunch the flow. It spurted between his fingers, blood soaking into sand. As Lukas's blood had soaked into snow . . .

Her heart was beating wildly. She looked down at the baby, still sleeping in her arms. As she watched its small face crumpled up, screwing into a pattern of lines and furrows. It began to scream.

Slowly, she stood up. The sun was beating down, a

relentless pressure over them all. She lifted her eyes to meet the man with the staff, and came to a decision.

'Here you are,' she said, walking forward. 'You take it.' And while he watched her, his thick lips curling in amused contempt, she thrust the yelling, damp bundle into his arms.

Its flailing hands struck against the spiral staff.

The sound of distant bells and an explosion of light. A sweeping cool wind around them all, a sudden clarity, wiping away the dust and heat and stink.

The staff shattered into a thousand splinters, spinning over the sand, settling in jagged shards around them. The sand-snake collapsed, vanishing back into the desert at the instant of the staff's destruction.

She was dimly aware that Comyn and Hilde were there, but receding from her, and that even Timon had become insubstantial, fading into the desert. All conflict, all vivid life was held between the man, the baby and herself. She could not drag her eyes away from him, away from the terrifying expression on his face.

The man stared at the splinters, then at the baby and lastly at Eleanor. He let the baby fall on the soft sand, and took a step towards her. She could smell his sweat, sour and pungent.

She had never seen such fury in anyone's face.

She put up her hands, but he was already hitting her, lashing out in an uncontrollable frenzy, battering her face, her body, kicking and punching and beating.

Her last thought, as she sank to the ground, was to wonder why no one was helping her.

The sense of painful, jogging motion lived in her nightmares before she awoke. Drifting through layers of unconsciousness, all she knew for a long time was that she was moving, thrown from side to side, and that every jolt hurt. She was made of pain.

It was hot and airless where she existed, the taste of blood in her mouth, her body throbbing, aching, bruised, wrenched.

It was dark. At least, when some form of consciousness prevailed, she could see nothing. Or were her eyes injured? She tried to move her hands, but they were held immobile behind her back, drawn together by chains. There were manacles round her wrists, anchoring them together. She was lying on a hard, rigid surface. It was moving around, constantly tipping and jerking, and with every movement she rolled and slid, landing with a thump against the unyielding walls of her prison.

She scrabbled with her fingers, trying to find something to hold on to, to stop this terrible rocketing around; but there was nothing to grasp. Nothing beneath her fingers but splintering wood.

She tried shouting, screaming with all her strength, but her voice was rusty and hoarse and no one answered. She heard drums outside, a monotonous, insistent rhythm, and shouts and cries. The sound of harness and hooves on hard-packed sand. The jangle of pots and pans, the murmur of voices. The caravan.

She was hurting all over, sick with pain in her head and stomach, raw, open wounds battered by the ceaseless falling and tumbling.

Her prison was too large for her to wedge herself against the sides, to stop the dreadful plunging. She had no strength for bracing herself anyway. She could not even protect her head, with her hands pulled tightly behind her. She tried to hunch her shoulders but she could not hold the position for long.

After an intolerable age of chaos, the inevitable happened. Her lolling head struck against the side of the prison, and there was another flare of pain, this time heralding oblivion.

When she awoke for the second time, it was still dark, and the floor was still tilting around. But instead of being flung all over it, she was held steady in someone's arms.

'Eleanor – ' A familiar voice, urgent and anxious. 'Eleanor, are you all right?'

It was Timon Lesterell.

She tried to say that it was a silly question but all that came out was a faint moan. A hand, warm and gentle, brushed the hair back from her face. Her own hands were still fastened behind her.

Why were his free?

He must have sensed the sudden tension in her, for his arms

tightened round her. 'Don't panic, Eleanor, it's all right, I won't hurt you. It's me, Timon.'

'Where are we?' Her voice was cracked and unfamiliar. She couldn't move her mouth properly, her lips swollen and bleeding.

'We're on top of one of those creatures, I don't know what they are. In the caravan, going east.'

'Where are Comyn and Hilde?' Her voice was only the faintest whisper. It was all she could manage.

'I don't know. I haven't seen them since the staff shattered. When that man . . .' He stopped for a while. 'Eleanor. I tried to stop him, but he has power.'

The man in leather, she thought, the man in the taxi. She felt Timon shift behind her, and remembered that he had been hurt too.

'The baby?'

Another pause before he answered. 'I don't know. I didn't see. Perhaps someone on the caravan has it.'

She could hardly concentrate on what he was saying. Everything was hurting too much. She lay back against him, knowing it was foolish. Why should she trust him?

The dark closed in once more.

As she drifted in and out of consciousness, the train of thoughts continued. Timon had tried to help her, had jumped at that sand monster. *He* had not vanished when the staff shattered. Perhaps he really was one of the Cavers, an ally and friend.

For all her weakness, she was aware that it would be easy to trust him. She wanted to so much. She could not endure all this on her own. She needed a friend. She had no strength to fight alone any more. She was too sick, too hurt. Her head drooped against his shoulder.

At some stage they stopped. Their prison held steady for a while. She heard shouting outside, and then there was the sound of wood scraping on wood, the rasp of a bolt being drawn back. One side of the crate suddenly fell open.

It was night. She saw flickering torchlight illumine unfamiliar, unfriendly faces, bending to lift her with rough hands. She was unceremoniously carried away from the crate, down a slope, dumped on the cooling sand.

Timon was moving stiffly, coming over to her.

She could not move, imprisoned in chains and weakness. Again, his arms around her, his voice in her ear. 'Don't worry Eleanor, I'll look after you . . .'

How could he, she thought? He's only one. And there were crowds of people around them, moving tiredly. They were building fires, preparing food, erecting tents. She heard the sullen murmur of their voices and the squall of babies crying.

There were men lounging close by, armed with knives, watching them. Their eyes glittered in the firelight. Beyond them, unlikely and bizarre, she saw the lizard. She watched dispassionately as it shifted its huge triangular, flat-topped head, stretching out towards the freshly killed goat carcase that had been placed before it. It had tusks, like an elephant, but there the resemblance ended.

Short, thick legs ended in horny digging claws. Its long flat tail was still curling viciously from side to side, sweeping sand from its path in its eagerness to get at the meat. Its hide reflected light in crazy patterns from the strange scales. They were raised like pyramids, sharp and pointed.

In the distance, further along the caravan, she could see another of them. People were swarming all over it, untying the ropes and chains which fastened another crate to the creature's back.

One side of it tumbled open, and she wondered who was in that one, but it was too far away to see clearly. One of the men stepped forward, leaning over her. Without speaking, he unlocked the chains on her wrists, but her arms were too cramped and numb to be moved. She began to cry with frustration and discomfort, tears falling into the sand, and Timon knelt at her side.

Very gently, very softly, he began to rub her shoulders, massaging them, gradually drawing her arms round. One of the men put a small dish of water beside them. Timon tore a strip from his own shirt, dipping it in, wiping her face, clearing away the blood.

She could see better then, for her left eye had been gummed up with blood. Timon was not in a much better state than she, bruised and battered, the wound in his arm stained and dirty. But he bathed her tenderly and helped her drink, spoon-fed her from the disgusting bowl of porridge that one of the men brought, coaxing her to accept more than the two mouthfuls which were all she could bear. He nursed her with the utmost patience and gentleness, ignoring his own condition.

She had no energy for speech, no energy for wondering where they were or where they were going or why.

The night was brief, harshly cold and clear. She lay shivering by the fire with Timon's arms around her, watched unblinkingly by one of the armed men.

She couldn't sleep, not properly. Every now and then she would lose herself in a kind of faint, but the pain in her ribs and stomach kept dragging her back to consciousness. At one stage Timon asked a man for bandages, medicine.

He laughed. But when the black sky began to lighten in the east, and the camp was dismantled, he agreed not to replace the chains before starting off again.

Held at knife-point, Timon carried her back to their prison, walking with some difficulty over the sharp pointed scales from the tip of the creature's tail, up to the wooden crate lashed over its hind-quarters.

Another day's journey. Another nightmare.

Timon fought for food and water whenever they stopped, arguing and cajoling. Once he was successful, and she gulped down almost a full tumbler of water before realising that it was between them both.

He brushed away her apologies as the lid was clamped down again.

'It doesn't matter about *me*,' he said. 'I'll be all right.'

'But what about your arm, that must hurt . . .'

'But Eleanor, I am here to help you. To protect. To be your friend. I've failed so badly that this is the least I can do. Let me make some gesture, at least. As proof.'

Proof? What proof did one need of friendship? Sharing water, arms around each other. Together in danger and fear. Other distinctions were artificial. This was her life, this jolting, hot hell of aches and pains, and Timon was her only friend, her only relief.

Chapter Twenty-three
Rebels

When at last the wash of tide had become no more than a gentle murmur on the edge of awareness, Felicia opened her eyes.

Light. Airy, warm light flooding in through wide-flung windows.

The walls were whitewashed, plain. Pale, scrubbed boards on the floor. No curtains, at the window or around the bed.

There was a man standing by the window watching her. For a long moment he looked across at her.

'Hello,' he said at last. 'How do you feel?'

His eyes were the most intense blue she had ever seen. Long straight blond hair fell forward across his forehead.

She didn't want to speak. She had no words, anyway. How to express rebirth? Resurrection? There had been a kind of death, and now she was alive again. For a while.

The sea still washed in her blood, still moved in her breath. Tears, in her eyes, were forever salt.

She turned her head slightly on the pillow, looking away from the man to the warm spring sunlight. The sky was clear and pale, neutral and undemanding.

When she looked back, he had gone. She had not heard him move.

In his place, Annis, bustling round, a warm hand on her forehead, an arm behind her shoulders.

'Can you drink this? Lady Felicia, please try . . .'

Warm milk, with a tang of something else. A drug? What would they do to her now?

'Don't cry, oh, don't cry. You're safe now.' The hands laying her back on the pillows were gentle and kind, but she

could not help it now, the foolish weak tears rolling down
her cheeks.

Safe now. What did Annis mean by it?

For how long?

There had been searches of course. Alarms rang, the city was
ransacked. And that not casually.

Felicia knew nothing about it, lost in the moving waves. A
tide of scarlet-clad soldiers swept through the city. Each tenement block was evacuated while the soldiers tore apart every
room. Groups of muttering people waited in the rain while their
homes were invaded. They glared at the soldiers, clutching thin
cloaks. But the real trouble was down by the river.

The Castle Guards focused their attention on the shanty
town round the harbour. There were no orderly evacuations
here: doors were kicked down, windows smashed. Sometimes
people resisted and there were fights and arrests. Nowhere
was sacrosanct. Even the deserted warehouse where the
fisherpeople worshipped Astret was ransacked, the hangings
torn down, the altar overturned.

Watching the groups of men breaking into houses,
throwing furniture out onto the street, Annis turned to
Mittelson. 'We should get out of here! Leave the city, they'll
find us!'

'The gates are watched. But there's no need to worry,
Annis, they search with blind eyes . . . No one will find the
Lady Felicia, or recognise you.'

She mistrusted the way he looked at her, but what choice
was there? Together they bundled Felicia into a small
chamber built into one of the walls of the cottage, a
smugglers' store. Olwyn Mittelson spoke, and the opening
disappeared into whitewashed solidity.

Annis watched with amazement.

'A trickster,' said Serethrun Maryn severely. 'But
useful . . .'

The men who thrust themselves in through the front and
back doors simultaneously barely looked at the old woman
bending over the pots.

Mittelson had given Annis drab rags to wear. 'Ash in your
hair, so . . . Look down, never in their faces, hold your shawl
like this, hunched over one shoulder – and there.'

Again Mittelson muttered a word and Annis felt her bones ache, her voice crack. She leant her uncomfortable body forward, reaching for a stick, watching the skin wrinkle on her hands, the knuckles thicken. She looked at him in panic. He dropped one eyelid in a slow wink. 'Don't worry, pretty Annis, it's only for an hour or so . . .'

She became old for the length of the soldiers' visit, and for the first time knew what it felt like to move slowly, with nagging, depressing clumsiness. To find her thoughts distracted by the flaws of her body. She was passed over, ignored as part of the furniture. Are the old always disregarded, she thought, in a sudden fury?

One of the soldiers looked at her.

She knew him, a friend of her lover. Some trick in her voice or the way she moved had caught his attention. She pulled the shawl closer and grumbled as she bent to pick up the chairs they had let fall.

'Wait a minute – ' He reached out, a large, confident man, and grasped her arm. She felt old bones ache and protest under careless fingers.

'What do you want?' she spat at him. 'I've nothing for you.'

He stared at her for a moment. Then his face relaxed and he laughed, coarsely. 'That's true enough!' He let her go, and she stumbled back against the dresser.

And after the men had gone, leaving the chairs tumbled, drawers emptied on the floor, rugs pushed aside, and Olwyn Mittelson restored Annis's youth, she retained an unusually mature understanding.

And something else.

She wanted to see her lover again.

'Men have fished these seas for a thousand years. Before the Stasis, fishing supported the entire community. The city of Shelt was essentially a village around a harbour, and all the men followed the tides, while their women gathered bait, repaired the nets, prayed when the storms began.

'It was not an easy life, the sea always exacted a price. Boats were lost, men sometimes drowned – but there was a purpose, a reason, and it seemed that the Lady of the Moon cared for them all. Families thrived down the ages, reaping the harvest of the sea and sharing it with family, friends and community.

'Twelve great families evolved. Through a combination of luck, skill, hard work, the right number of children at the right time, twelve families emerged as dominant.'

Mittelson shrugged, his eyes squinting in the sunlight. Felicia, watching and listening, wondered why he was telling her this.

'Some became more powerful than others. It is always so. Originally fishermen or boat builders, these men were ambitious for wealth and prestige. They retired from the sea, turning their attention to safer matters. But they continued to finance the fishermen, investing in new boats, insuring them against storm and accident. They explored trading routes with the rest of Stromsall. A feudal relationship, one might say. The Earl was traditionally elected from the twelve families, *by* the twelve families, together with the rest of the fishing community. There was at least a pretence of democracy.

'To protect their sea-borne investments, the twelve families began to investigate the paths of magic. Originally, it was the comparatively simple matter of influencing the weather. Warding off storms, turning the wind direction, dispelling fogs. They became known as the Sea Lords.

'But during the Stasis, the storms were no longer amenable to gentle suggestion. With ever greater vigour, the Sea Lords studied the transforming arts, and pursued the way of wind and tide. They began, under the influence of Gawne, recently arrived from the south, to investigate the arts of healing. Then, as now, the Sea Lords were entirely dominated by Gawne . . .'

'Where did you learn your magic, Olwyn?' she said suddenly.

He looked at her, briefly silent. His mouth smiled gently, but his eyes were cynical. 'Dear Lady Felicia, I thought you knew. I was a Sea Lord once. The giddy pinnacles of power, the grey silk robes, the pretty spiral staff, all were mine. Once.' His eyes blinked then, and he lifted empty hands to show her.

'They threw me out,' he said, and shrugged again. 'It was hardly surprising. I'll tell you why another time.' He sighed and continued his story.

'The Sea Lords turned aside from the will of the Lady, pursuing the paths of magic. They became divided from their own people, the fishermen and women. They forbad the fishing. It was a ruinous, crazed policy. It was at this stage that we – parted company.

'Dissension and division, you see. The pattern of the Stasis throughout our northern world. Men and women driven apart, driven into dispute and aggression. There was massive unrest in Shelt. And when your father Javon, with his brother, Torold, approached Shelt from the west, the Sea Lords welcomed Torold as the new Earl. He brought a force of highly trained men with him, you see.

'The only reason they countenanced Torold as Earl was because of his military strength.

'Do you know your uncle well?' He looked at her keenly.

Felicia shook her head. 'No. He was always off campaigning somewhere when I was a child. We didn't really go in for family reunions . . .'

She was sitting in a chair by the open window. A small fire burnt in the grate to her right, an absurd extravagance. Why have a fire burning while the windows are open?

For warmth, and comfort, and delight.

Annis had just come in, accompanied by Serethrun Maryn. As always he glanced at Felicia, his brown eyes quickly scanning her face. She smiled at him, and for a moment their eyes met. He said nothing, his strange, almond eyes deeply serious. She wondered what he was thinking, but it was always impossible to tell.

Mittelson's voice ran on undisturbed. 'Gawne is the enemy here. To you and to the fishing people of Shelt. The decision to halt the fishing originated with him. He wants power to remain in the hands of the Sea Lords, for various, complicated reasons. I shall not burden you with them as yet.

'One thing is worth pointing out. The Sea Lords are regarded now as heretics by the Lady's priestesses in Shelt. They trespass, so it is said, on essentially feminine concerns. They have taken for themselves the Rites of the Lady, and have ignored the claim of the priestesses. In fact, any suspicion that their power does *not* come from the Lady is now treated as heresy, and of course they have the Castle Guard, augmented by Torold's troops, to back it up. An ultimate irony, that . . . But the Rule of Astret was much diminished during the storms of the Stasis, almost as if the Lady Herself was turning Her attention to other matters. That is how a man like Gawne can come to power . . .

'If Gawne and the Sea Lords are dangerous to the ordinary people of Shelt, you must also remember that he has a personal vendetta against you.' He looked at her intently. 'His use of a Marqun in your case was unprecedented. Far too risky for someone in your state of health.' He still studied her, as if he might understand her soul. 'Can you really remember nothing of what happened?'

He had asked her this so many times. She felt herself begin to shake once more, the ridiculous betrayal of her own body. 'No. It's just a blank.' I don't even want to remember, she thought. It lies in a past I want to forget.

'Your family will not harm you, not deliberately. Torold wants you well for his brother's sake. And your father needs an heir, you must not think he hates you – '

'He wants a son.'

'His only failure is one of imagination. Of understanding. It is up to you to show him alternatives.'

'He would pay no attention to me.' She looked again at Olwyn Mittelson, so insignificant against the broad wash of sunlight from the window.

A Sea Lord. She was not sure whether she trusted him. He had been a constant companion to her as her strength returned. Mild and unassuming at first, he had gently drawn from her revelations she would have preferred to conceal. A clever man, she thought. Devious, cunning. But he was courteous to Annis, and showed more than that to Felicia.

Rosco, the man with blue eyes, was another matter. On his rare visits he paced the cottage with restless energy. She asked Mittelson where he went the rest of the time.

Meetings, said Mittelson. Rallies, committees – he was busy.

'But why?' she had asked. 'What is he planning?' But Mittelson always changed the subject, or went away.

Mittelson was a heron, she decided early on, tracing the outline of the sheet. Elegant lines, spindly legs, pale golden eyes.

She lived peacefully in the quiet airy room, while warm

spring light shone through open windows. The sea was not far away, she could hear the wash of high tide, but it was gentle here at the other end of the city. No high sea-wall held it back.

This was almost a shanty town, built around the neglected harbour. A haphazard collection of small cottages and back-to-back houses, narrow alleys and run-down shops. Here lived the men who used to fish before the Sea Lords forbad it.

Here there was unemployment and poverty. A dreary wasteland of empty days and grinding hardship. Some looked for diversion, turning to drink, the only cheaply available pleasure. There were fights, violent brawls. Felicia heard them shouting beneath her window sometimes, late at night, when the bar over the road made its first attempt to close.

An extraordinary world in which to find herself. No servants to run around after her, only Annis, her fine clothes scuffed by dusty floors, her face losing the elegant pallor of court life. No delicate foods to tempt the invalid. No pressures to get well, find a mate, marry, produce heirs, consolidate boundaries.

A mixed bag of people, Annis the only woman, kind and good-natured. For the first time in her life she relaxed, refusing to think about Torold, or her father.

She wondered about the dark plainsman who always watched her so steadily. She knew that Serethrun Maryn was one of the *eloish*. His slanted, saturnine eyes gave it away. She had heard so many rumours of the *eloish* that at first she was wary, dismayed by the quality of stillness in him. What savagery ran through his past? He never spoke of it, avoiding every conversation that touched the plainspeople.

He had been the one to pull her from the sea after the wreck.

'Twice you rescued me,' she said shyly. 'I hope they didn't give you too hard a time – '

'When?' He frowned at her, dark brows almost meeting over darker eyes.

'There was an inquiry, I heard. Something about wrecking. I asked that you should be released – '

'So it was you . . . ' A faint smile as he looked at her.

'Did it go wrong? Was it hard for you?' she said anxiously.

'It – would have been worse if you had not spoken,' he

said, and she wondered at the evenness of his voice. 'But I'm glad you're all right now.'

'It would have been rather a waste of effort otherwise, wouldn't it?'

He watched her calmly, as if waiting for her to say something else. Or perhaps he didn't understand: people so rarely understood her. But she saw Rosco, who had just come in, look across at her, his eyes crinkling up in appreciation.

'And wouldn't that have been a shame, now?' he said softly.

Chapter Twenty-four
Raid

Felicia was recovering. There was colour in her cheeks and she was no longer sick. For over three weeks she had been in the company of rebels, and she had never felt better.

Mittelson had been confident that she would flourish. He had brushed aside Annis's suggestion that a doctor should be called, supported by Rosco.

'Annis, don't you remember? The Sea Lords have the monopoly of healing, they and their acolytes; there *are* no other doctors, none with formal qualifications.'

'And anyway, the fewer people know she's here the better,' Rosco had added. 'Isn't it obvious?'

'Why did you kidnap her? For what purpose?' Annis didn't like him, this tall, graceful man whose eyes coldly mocked everything she said.

Serethrun Maryn had joined them then. 'Yes, why? I thought you were going to use her as a hostage, hold her for ransom, something like that . . .'

'Something like that . . . ' Rosco's long mouth twisted into a bitter smile. 'That might have won us a temporary victory, perhaps a brief cessation of hostilities. And then there would come the backlash, the restrictions and purges, the clamp-down on what little freedom we do have . . .'

'Won't it happen anyway?' Serethrun was frowning.

'They're waiting. Wondering what move we'll make.' Rosco looked from one to the other of them. 'And we need time, too. To make sure Felicia is well, and to prepare our own defences.'

'What has Felicia Westray to do with the fishermen?'

'Everything – and nothing. You will see.' And then Rosco had left the cottage, and did not return for some time.

Annis complained over supper later that week.

'It's so cramped here! Can't I just go for a walk? I could wear a hooded cloak – '

'They don't like strangers here.' Mittelson's voice was flat with refusal.

'They wouldn't even notice me!'

'It's a foolish risk . . . '

'I didn't ask to come here! What about my friends and family?' She pushed her chair back, scraping it on the bare boards. Felicia was asleep upstairs, Serethrun out with Rosco somewhere.

'Forget them. For the time being. One day, if it all works out, you can go back.'

'When? I was not made for this!' She waved her hand at the poor cottage, the cracked glass in the windows, the smoking fire.

Mittelson had stood up. 'Listen, Annis. Do you know what would have happened if we'd left you there?'

She remembered Gawne's fingers against her cheek and shuddered. 'But my family . . . '

'Will be reassured that you are with the Lady Felicia.' Pale eyes gazed at her unblinkingly. 'The only reason that there has not been outright persecution, a decimation of the fishing families, is that Felicia is assumed to be alive, with you in attendance. Torold will make no violent move while she is safe. And your absence is an additional guarantee of Felicia's safety.'

She knew he was right. But still she wondered if Kester, her lover, had found someone else.

A light tap on the door.

Mittelson opened it a crack, peering out into the drizzle. Then a slight, black-hooded figure stepped forward into the kitchen.

'Annis, this is Ismay, a friend of mine.' The woman stood still in the flickering firelight, pushing back the hood of her cloak. Annis saw wide grey eyes, heart-shaped face, a serious mouth.

'I have to go out tonight. Ismay will keep you company.'

Already Mittelson was moving towards the door, flinging a shabby cloak over his gaunt frame.

'Company — or is she a gaoler?'

He paused, his hand on the latch. 'Whichever you'll accept. Annis, you will come to no harm with us, I promise you. Trust us, and you and the Lady Felicia will be restored to your rightful positions. It may seem obscure now, but it will become clear. Soon, I hope.'

'I hope so too.' The woman Ismay spoke with a low intensity that caught Annis's attention. She hardly noticed that Mittelson had left.

'What are you doing with Olwyn Mittelson?' Annis stood in the doorway through to the other downstairs room in the cottage, blocking the way to the stairs.

She did not answer directly. 'You can trust Olwyn, you know. He means nothing but good towards the Lady Felicia.'

'So he keeps saying.' Sulkily, Annis stood aside and followed the other woman upstairs.

Felicia was awake, gazing dreamily at the fire. She looked up in surprise as Ismay entered. Visitors were unusual. Ismay had brought some knitting with her, a plain jersey made from dark blue wool. She sat in the window seat, placidly casting on a sleeve and chatted amicably. It made, thought Annis with irritation, a comfortable and domestic scene.

Felicia asked Ismay about her family.

Fishing folk, they were. Ismay was the eldest of six. Two little sisters had died in infancy; her three brothers had owned a fishing boat together with her uncle and father.

'What do they do now?' asked Felicia. 'Now that there is no fishing?'

Ismay shrugged. 'This and that. Davon sometimes helps at the bakery, Cal with the horses. My father — writes.'

'Writes? What does he write? Poems, plays?' Felicia was interested.

'Oh, articles. Pamphlets. That kind of thing.' Ismay put down her knitting and took from the pocket of her thin grey dress a small sheaf of papers.

She laid them on the bed and Felicia turned them over. Lurid headlines, emotive language.

'OUR LADY MOCKED!

'Distort the tide and the power of the Moon in our lives

is lost! Is it not plain, is it not clear that all our good fortune, our honest livelihood has been destroyed? And why? So that the Sea Lords may exert their evil power over the sea itself! What arrogance, what short-sighted foolery! Our Lady will not be mocked, our time will come!'

So they ran on. Felicia turned them over slowly, frowning slightly.

'Who are they for?' she asked. 'How do you distribute them?'

'It's not difficult. Rosco holds meetings, organises leafleting. There is much hardship. People always want someone to blame.'

'And the Sea Lords are indeed guilty, of course . . . '

'Foul heretics. Destroyers and fools.' Ismay looked directly into Felicia's eyes, a vivid passion gleaming in her own.

The pale, thin figure on the pillows leaned forward. 'Even Mittelson?' she said softly. 'Was he not a Sea Lord too, once?'

'Ages ago. He refused to go along with the ban on the fishing, you see. That's why they threw him out – '

Neither of them noticed that Annis had already slipped out of the door, taking her cloak.

Neither of them realised how little Annis trusted Olwyn Mittelson, nor how much she missed her lover.

It was cold outside, freezing fog replacing the drizzle. Some spring, Annis thought, pulling her cloak closer, hurrying through the narrow alleys away from the harbour.

She had only a vague idea of the direction, only an approximate idea of what she was going to do. She had no intention of deserting Felicia, nor of giving her up to the Sea Lords. But she did want reassurance, some proof that her old life would welcome her back when all this was over.

The streets were virtually deserted. It wasn't that late. Where was everyone? At home, crouched round fires, she thought. In bars, drinking. Not half running through obscure, unknown streets, going to find someone who had probably forgotten all about her . . .

A clatter to her left; a cat bolted across her path leaving a pile of rubbish upset, stinking refuse across the cobbles. Distastefully, she lifted her skirts and tiptoed her way through the mess.

The fog was too dense to see the shape of the Castle looming over the city, with its cluster of barracks and stables. She was trusting instinct to take her there, but it was not good enough.

After an hour of alternate running and walking she had to admit she was lost. The occasional people she passed stared at her curiously. Once she asked where she was.

'Jubgate Lane, lady. You shouldn't be here.'

'The Castle?' She stared uneasily at the man, whose broken teeth and thick lips distorted his words.

He nodded over his left shoulder. 'That way – but I wouldn't advise it tonight . . . '

She would have asked why, but he turned away, swiftly vanishing into the mist.

She was cold now, too tired to walk quickly, and the breath was sharp and harsh in her throat. Perhaps she should go back, return to Felicia. She stopped and looked around her. She would get lost trying to do that, too.

Then the explosion.

All sounds had been muffled by fog, but this burst through the night in a flare of flame and fire. She saw it, leaping into the sky above the fog, momentarily illuminating the black outlines of the Castle.

Debris was clattering down all around her: wood, metal, glass, stone. She shrank back into a doorway, her cloak pulled over her head, her hands shaking. What was happening, was it war?

And then people began to run past her, coming from the harbour area, running not away from the explosion, but towards it. She heard shouting and screams. The panicky stamping of horses in a nearby stable.

The debris was no longer falling. Trembling, still hidden in the doorway, she pushed her hood back and looked around.

There were people everywhere, roughly dressed working people. Fisherpeople. Plunging through the smoke and the fog, they were carrying weapons – swords, knives and bows; and then there were flashes of scarlet as the Castle Guard came running, cloaks swirling, blades bright and alert.

The doors to one of the warehouses lay in smoking ruins amidst the rubble of the walls. She knew it. It had been the armoury. The fisherpeople were stealing weapons and ammunition.

Suddenly she was pushed back roughly against the wall as three men pulled a cart through the narrow alley. It was heavily piled high with barrels and sacks, and the men grunted and strained at the ropes.

Why didn't they use horses? she wondered irrelevantly, pushing past them through the crowds towards the sound of the fighting.

It was foolish, of course. But she was simply curious, the ancient human instinct to watch the action, find out what was going on.

The alley abruptly opened out into a large square she knew well, the ordered gardens leading to the Castle. No longer elegant, they were full of fighting, shouting, the clash of swords, the sweep of red cloaks down the sloping ramp from the Castle, overwhelming the dark, struggling shapes of the fisherpeople.

Most of the action was focused by the entrance to the stables.

As she watched, horrified and fascinated, she saw a tall man moving very fast through the crowds towards the fighting at the stable door.

It was Rosco, followed by another familiar figure.

Serethrun, smaller, dark and intense, slicing through the mêlée.

The stable gates were bolted. At the same moment as she recognised the two men, she heard the crack of fracturing metal and looked to the side of the door. Mittelson was standing there, shrouded in black, pointing to the bolt.

It was crumbling beneath his fingers, dissolving, disappearing.

Rosco wrenched the doors open, and Serethrun ran through, followed by three others.

She pressed back against the alley wall, the back of her hand hard against her teeth. It was so dangerous, so foolhardy. What could they possibly hope to achieve?

And then there was a thunder of hooves, the pattern of red cloaks running and dispersing under the force of it. A flood of horses, black and brown, thundering across the square, led by one immense, chestnut stallion.

Serethrun, moulded behind the shoulders of the creature,

moving at one with it, guiding all the Guard's horses out across the square towards the west gate.

She had never seen the *eloish* ride before, without reins or saddle, so united with the animal that man and horse formed a complete entity.

Soldiers tried to stop them, leaping for their manes, running for halters – but the rush was too fast, too headstrong. They streamed through the city, down streets and alleys, well beyond Annis's view.

She saw the soldiers running from the Castle surround the stable area, a ring of men five deep. She wondered if Rosco were still in there, and Mittelson.

Without realising what she was doing, she began to move across the chaotic square, towards the ring of scarlet-cloaked guards.

And then she saw him, his back to her, the familiar broad shoulders of Kester, her laughing lover.

'Kes!' She couldn't resist it.

He swung round, his arms held wide.

'Annis! Oh, my love, where have you been?' He was lifting her from the ground, whirling her round, his arms so welcome around her.

'Annis!' Another voice behind her. Mittelson, standing there, an extreme edge of danger in his voice.

How had he got there?

Kes had put her down, was staring at Mittelson, frowning, reaching for his sword

Another hand suddenly grasped her arm, pulling her back into the shadows, wrenching her almost off her feet.

She struggled, screaming, and a firm hand fell across her mouth.

She bit it, hard, until the blood came, but whoever it was didn't flinch. Roughly she was pulled away from the square, back into an alley between two large houses.

'For Lady's sake, Annis, shut up!' An exasperated hiss in her ear.

She stamped hard on his instep, and the man cursed, swinging her round to face him. It was Rosco.

'Let me go! I want Kester!'

'You've probably killed your precious Kester,' he snapped, his face white and livid in the dark.

'What do you mean?' She was gasping with fright and fear. Where was Kes? What had happened to him?

Rosco had stepped away from her, back into the shadow, and she saw the glint of blood on his hand, where she had bitten him.

'Later.' He was looking beyond her to someone. She was not surprised to hear Mittelson's voice. He was breathless.

'Time to go home, Annis. It's late for little girls to be playing out . . . '

He too was angry, but not, she thought, with her. The furious retort on her lips died.

'Come on,' said Rosco. 'We'd better get back to Felicia.' He moved rapidly away from the wall.

'What's all the rush? You were happy to leave her alone tonight.' Annis was still refusing to move.

'Are you much better?' His voice was so cold. He turned and looked at her, and she saw that his shirt was ripped and torn, scorch marks on his jersey. Still holding her attention, he went on. 'This is not a game, Annis. We do not hide you and Felicia for our own amusement. It's crucial you understand this, for there will be reprisals now. The truce is over.'

'What do you mean?' An abyss of fear before her.

'Open warfare, now. The game, for real.'

Tramping through the narrow, deadly streets, she heard the murmur of anxiety behind closed doors, hidden sobs and anger on all sides.

The city was hostile. There was no peace anywhere, no place for laughter or love. She shivered with foreboding and quickened her pace to keep up with the two men.

She should never have left Felicia. No one was safe in Shelt any more.

Chapter Twenty-five
Journey

'You're not serious.'

This was a statement, not a question or a joke. Thurstan's words were cold and unfriendly, the essence of disbelief.

'Why should I stay? What is the possible point of staying here?'

Phinian Blythe turned impatiently back to the window, the shadows settling around him in an unlovely swirl. The distant forest with its yellowing, dying trees was alive with movement and activity. Great scars of red clay cut swathes through the trees. Thurstan's earth-works were making their mark on the countryside.

Thurstan was angry. He had been coldly, bitterly angry since the night of the assassins. It was more than a simple outrage and grief at the deaths of his people.

The abduction of Matthias was a blow of incalculable significance. Not only had he inspired an almost fanatical devotion in the Cavers — he had brought about the ending of the Stasis, after all — but he was also involved in close discussion with the Emperor.

Secret discussion. He had not told Thurstan the nature of the bargain with Xanthon. Thurstan knew the result; everyone knew the result: that Eleanor Knight was to be brought back to divert the wrath of Lycias.

But there was more to it than that. It was something to do with the baby. There was a mystery around that child, brought so strangely from Stromsall some months after the end of the Stasis. He suspected that Sigrid, the High Priestess to Astret, knew something of the answer, but she wasn't going to reveal anything to a Jerenite.

He was angry with himself for not realising how difficult
it was all going to be. He had thought, with the end of the
Stasis, the breaking of the Boundary, to make a decent life
for the Jerenites. Like de Mowbray, he had worked hard,
accepting difficult compromises in the cause of peace, to
construct a relationship. If the Emperor and Matthias had
taken it upon themselves to take decisions of mystic import,
Thurstan and de Mowbray battled with the day-to-day
problems.

Where people should live. What work they should do, how
lives should be ordered. How they were to survive under the
burning sun of Lycias. How they were to get water . . .

He was taken by surprise when the assassins attacked. He
blamed himself for not realising that it had been bound to
happen.

No one had ever thought that it was going to be easy,
exchanging immortality for death and old age. Few people
recognised the distortion that had been the Stasis. Only
childless women, the artists and musicians, and followers of
Astret had been sure.

Thurstan himself had come late to the realisation of its evil,
watching his people falling apart under the strain of
immortality. Life needed the rhythms of change, the
flowering and fruiting to be given shape by death.

But the assassins had been motivated by more than the fear
of mortality. It was more than a simple act of revenge.
(Though was revenge ever simple? he thought, watching the
shadows unsettling the air around Blythe.)

It had been an act of evil intent. Brutal and well-planned.
There had been a mind at work, planning murder, planning
abduction. It was abhorrent. Something he had not expected,
something evil. Something he could not control.

And now Blythe was leaving on a fool's errand.

'No animal will bear you.' All animals ran screaming from
the Children of the Night. Even the Arrarat would not carry
Blythe, burdened as he was by shadows.

'I shall walk.' He sounded so calm, so certain.

'But where? Where will you go?' Where could he go, so
afflicted?

'To the east,' he said simply. 'After Weard and the
assassins. To find Matthias, and perhaps Eleanor.'

'What could you do?'

He was a wreck now. Red-rimmed eyes, hollow with nightmares. Too thin, pale, almost grey-skinned. He was sweating, and Thurstan wondered if it was with the effort of not screaming, not howling. And his left hand, just a rigid, crippled claw, terribly scarred, unmoving.

'You're in no shape to go anywhere, far less tackle Weard.' Thurstan spoke gently.

'I cannot stay here!' The slow, quiet voice was edged with desperation. 'Think, Thurstan. Any action, any at all, must be better than *this*!'

The lonely tower high on Cliokest. The well-worn boards he had paced for months. The rumpled bed where he failed each night to sleep. The untasted food, left on trays outside day after day. The view from the window, over an arid, scorched countryside.

And the Children, whispering evil in his ears, clouding his eyes with horrors, befouling his air, his food, his water. Sliding across his skin, staying his hand from the knife, the rope, the window catch.

'I'll follow Weard. I may even find him, and Matthias. And Eleanor. She should never have been brought back, abandoned to the sun like that. The desert contains many secrets now.' He paused. 'And if I don't make it, well, it will be a relief, of course.'

It was said quite without drama. Thurstan left the room soon after that.

Poor bastard, he thought.

Three days later Blythe set off, walking to the Eastern Desert. Behind him trailed two horses, laden with water, food, tents, weapons, and Thurstan. They had argued over it, Blythe coldly listing all Thurstan's responsibilities, the numbers of people who relied on him, the treaties needing his ratification. Leaving was running out, he said. People needed him here, at Cliokest, at the junction of two worlds.

The world of the Cavers, darkly rhythmic, relying on the phases of the moon, the passing sequences of life. The world of Peraldon, shot through with clear sunlight and sharp intellect. It was difficult making a synthesis. And Thurstan was uniquely placed to bring it about.

But still, he left them to travel with Phinian Blythe. Stefan Pryse stayed behind, the Mages Aylmer Alard and Thibaud Lye. Sigrid Messure, who knew more than she would reveal. Powel Hewlin, to give the view of the Jerenites.

They crossed the causeway from Cliokest to the mainland, Thurstan some ten yards behind Blythe. Any closer and the horses would have bolted. It was a distance they were to maintain for a long time.

The Children allowed Blythe to use a staff. It was as tall as he was, but plain and straight, with no distracting spiral. He leant on it, and slowly, slowly, covered the ground.

Thurstan, leading the two horses, could have ridden. They were not heavily laden. But somehow it felt too selfish, too easy, to ride where Blythe must walk. When they stopped at nightfall, Thurstan nerved himself to approach the lonely figure.

He had tied the horses to a dead tree-trunk. He dare not leave them loose to graze, not with the Children so close. He carried bread and meat and water. Fruit, wrapped in cool leaves. He put them on the ground and stepped back.

'Go away, Thurstan. You don't have to see this . . . '

But he stayed, watching, as Blythe approached the food, reaching out his good hand, and the shadows swarmed down the length of his arm, extending out over the food, leaving a wash of slime all over it.

Only then was he allowed to touch it, soiled and ruined as it was. Thurstan saw him force himself to eat, forcing the stinking stuff down. Blythe looked up and saw his face.

'Go *away*, Thurstan. I don't need you here. You cannot help by watching.' His eyes were darker than the shadows around him.

Thurstan turned away, back to the horses, back to the sweet, clean air of the cool night. Was it a mistake coming? Could he be of any help at all?

Did it matter anyway? Perhaps it was enough just to know that he had not let Blythe travel alone with the Children. Perhaps it was all for his own peace of mind, so that he should not feel guilty.

As he pulled his cloak around, ready for the cold night, he took one last look at Phinian Blythe, sitting against a tree, his knees drawn up.

Only then did Thurstan see faces of the Children, distinct in the twilight. For the first time he saw clearly who they were.

A woman, black-haired and violet-eyed, heartbreakingly beautiful.

A thin man, eyes so old and sad that they made him want to weep.

And another man, someone he recognised, younger, strong and powerful, whose eyes were completely empty, void of all humanity. Idas.

Three faces. Their message plain: Love. Guilt. And Fear. Accompanying Blythe everywhere.

Next day, slowly moving out of the forest towards the desert, he asked Blythe who the first two were.

He said, as the shapes shifted around him, 'The woman – is my wife, Karis. She died long ago . . . ' His eyes glanced away. 'The old man was called Marial. His death was the price of my freedom from Cliokest. And the other you know, Idas . . .' He looked suddenly, severely at Thurstan. 'They are not *real*, you must understand. The real Karis would not – do this. She is not part of this, wherever she is.' His eyes had returned to the flickering shadows, obsessively tracing the outline of lip and cheek, cyebrow and ear. 'The Children only adopt meaningful shapes, you see. There would be no point in formless horrors . . . '

The sun was hard and bright overhead, the brown grass becoming sparse and scrubby beneath their feet. They were following the dried-up bed of a river, a narrow, cracked gully fringed by the skeletal remains of trees.

The river had been known as the Whiterod, rising in the foothills of the mountains. They were travelling due east from Cliokest, towards its source, along the deep valley between the mountains where the Stasis had been broken during that long night, months ago.

The mountain range extended for a hundred miles into the desert. After that, they would have no landmarks until they reached the ruined city of Smintha. A far outpost of the Peraldonian Empire, it had been cut off by the great heat. Poised on the edge of the desert, survival there had always been a precarious business. And when the rains had stopped

and its own river had dried, no one from Cliokest had
attempted the journey there. No one knew what had
happened to the people of Smintha.

There were underground chambers there, and even water
in the deep wells. It was likely that some had survived.

Between the mountains and Smintha was a hundred miles
of desert. A burnt-out no man's land which had once held
comfortable farms and vineyards. The drought had been
punctuated by a series of fires, sweeping across the mainland,
devastating the region. Those who had survived had also left.
Thurstan did not expect to meet anyone there. It would be
a difficult and depressing journey, he thought, and the worst
of it would be east of Smintha.

They travelled slowly, no more than fifteen miles a day,
most of it in the early morning and evening. In the heat of
midday Thurstan slept, a wide-brimmed straw hat slanted
over his eyes, leaning against a rock, a tree, a dry-stone wall.
Sometimes, infrequently, they came to a deserted farmhouse
and sat at a table, on chairs, avoiding the worst of the midday
sun.

There was a kind of peace in travelling. Partly because the
Children, although ever-present, were not actively hindering
this journey. They seemed almost to approve of the action,
chattering and laughing in Blythe's ears. And it was much,
much better to have to think of walking, step after step,
noting the position of the sun, the length of the shadows,
than to pace an empty tower.

The devastation of the countryside was a fitting setting for
him. He passed black charred fields, and the sun-baked
corpses of cattle, the encroaching sand, with equanimity. In
a green and fertile land, the Children would be an aberration.
Here, in a blasted and ruined country, they were at home.

What he could not bear was the way that his every thought
was interrupted by their faces. Watching Thurstan sleeping
one day, soon after they had started out, he found himself
remembering the island of Jeren with its extraordinary trees.
It was not a particularly pleasant memory, a time of illness
and confrontation, Thurstan cynical and angry; but, even as
he thought of it, the shadows crowded in on him.

Marial would be staring at him, pleading for mercy.

Karis, crying his name.

Idas, hungry for his soul.

And he would forget how he met Eleanor and Lukas, how he had been drawn in.

The shadows destroyed his context. The ordinary circumstances of his life, and the extraordinary, were discarded, rubbed out, crushed by the assault of shadows. He was left naked before the Children, his life stripped to its essential acts.

Sometimes, looking at Thurstan, he almost forgot who he was. Where they were going. Why they moved at all.

In this he was different from the Storm-bearer, who was also suffering under the weight of the Sun God's vengeance. The Storm-bearer had one, very clear, focus.

Find the baby.

There was a meeting one night.

Sometimes the Children allowed Blythe to doze, at least for an hour or two, but not that night. They were particularly active, had been all day, and Thurstan had given up.

'Forgive me, Phin,' he'd said, closing the door of the empty farmhouse. He had shown more courage than most in the face of the Children, had neither flinched nor looked away when Blythe spoke to him. He had not turned back to Cliokest. But it was not easy to be in the company of shadows, and that night his nerve had failed. He had shut the door between Blythe and himself, and had drawn a bolt across.

In moonlight Blythe had started to walk around the farm, over fields and ditches, along walls and through dead woods. He was tired, tired to death, his limbs heavy and sluggish, but the Children were fizzy with febrile excitement around him.

There was electricity in the air that night. He could feel it, sparkling along the stone walls, sizzling over the discarded farm machinery. He knew that if he touched the blade of the plough, or the handle of a well, he would receive a shock.

The moonlight was still hard and bright, sharply defining the shapes of leafless trees, of slanting roof. He tried to look up at the moon, remembering it for a friend, but the Children would not allow it.

Not with the Storm so close.

They dragged his head around until he was staring at the

small orchard of dying olive trees. Thunder was now rumbling in the air, wind beginning to rush through the trees, their dry branches rattling, cracking and snapping.

And then, as lightning blazed through the night, there was a sudden ripping aside of the dark, and he saw someone deep in the olive grove. A tall figure, his arms spread wide, the electricity sparking dangerously from outstretched fingers.

Blythe tried to step back, away from all that uncontrolled power, but the Children instead pushed him forward. He could hardly breath; the air was viscous about him, charged and potent.

The figure moved slowly through the olive grove towards him. As lightning blazed and seared, Blythe caught irregular glimpses of a face stretched wide in a rictus of fear and pain.

Wind was streaming from his wild hair, thunder underlined his breath. He was the Storm-bearer, but the storm was not all he brought to Blythe that night.

'There is peace' – the words howled through the darkly shattered air, and the Children mimicked them, repeating them like a song – 'in the child . . . '

At great cost, the Storm-bearer was sending the words through the storm, branding them onto Blythe's soul. The effort was etched in torment on the wreck of a generous and warm face.

'Trust the child – ' Still the words were wrenched out. 'And there will be peace.'

Lightning sprang at his heels and the Storm-bearer began to run, rushing down the olive grove towards Blythe, darting too fast to follow over hedge and fence.

He was running fast, and the storm was hurling behind him. As he reached the farmhouse, there was once more the sound of howling and the storm lifted him. Lifted him up high into the air, running high above the farm, the dead trees, the wasted fields.

He was still running, running over the stars and the face of the moon, never resting, never ceasing, touching the heavens with blazing light and ruinous thunder.

And Blythe, watching far below, found tears on his own face.

They were in sympathy for the Storm-bearer, enduring an eternal race.

And they were in relief, for the Storm-bearer had brought more than thunder and lightning.

He had brought hope.

When Blythe turned back to the farmhouse, he saw Thurstan standing in the doorway.

'Well, now.' His voice was softly considering. 'So that's what happened.'

'What do you mean, Thurstan? What do you know?'

'As much as you and perhaps a little more . . . '

'Did you hear all that?'

'It has not been a good night for sleeping.' Dryly.

'No . . . ' Blythe sat down on the bench on the verandah. For once the Children were quiet, as if sated by the evening's events.

'Do you know who that was?' Thurstan was watching him, his expression cool. Blythe shook his head.

'His name is – was – Haddon Derray. A Caver, a close friend to Lukas and Matthias Marling. Did Matthias ever tell you about Coronis?'

He may have done, thought Blythe, but the Children have stolen my memory and my thoughts. 'I don't know,' he said.

'When you were off jaunting around with Lukas and Eleanor, Matthias and Haddon broke through the Boundary to the Carald Mountains in Stromsall. To the Lake of Lallon, a place sacred to the Lady, Matthias wanted the Lady's promise of three days' dark – remember?'

Yes, that came back. A small crowded fishing boat off Cliokest, and his own act, pulling back a curtain and finding rain and dark where there should have been a dawn.

'He was successful, as you know.' Thurstan was sitting at the end of the bench from him, looking out over the desolate farm. 'But at the Lake he found a young woman. Coronis. She was pregnant, but Haddon fell in love with her. He decided to marry her and stay there in the city of Bilith. Matthias always spoke of it as if it was some dark tragedy. Haddon had usurped someone's place, you see.'

'The father of the child?' He spoke with difficulty, for the Children were beginning to stir again, to flicker and waft over his face.

'Yes. Whoever that may be . . . ' He stopped, frowning

with frustration. Sigrid knew. Sigrid and Matthias both knew who the baby was and why it was important. They hadn't told Thurstan. He continued. 'And now Haddon roams Peraldon, trailing thunder and lightning, looking for Coronis's baby.'

'What happened to Coronis?'

'She died.' Thurstan had moved away to the end of the verandah. 'And the baby – Eleanor has the baby.'

'*What*!' He was on his feet, the shadows spinning round him in a kaleidoscope of horrors, making him stumble, his hands to his face, trying uselessly to ward them off.

Thurstan was steadfastly looking the other way. There was nothing he could do, after all.

'The Council debated it. The Mages Aylmer and Thibaud. Stefan Pryse, Elfitt de Mowbray, Oliphant d'Albe . . . But the decision had already been taken by the Emperor and Matthias Marling. They *said* that if Eleanor were to be the scapegoat, then she ought to be involved in every way. That it would only work if she were involved, committed. If it mattered. Like it mattered with Lukas. They thought that the baby would draw her in, make her take part.'

Thurstan paused. 'I think that's just bluff. There's some other reason why Matthias brought the baby here from Stromsall, and it's not just to involve Eleanor Knight. I'm not too sure, myself, if that would work anyway. She doesn't strike me as the kind of woman to lose her heart to a baby just because it was there . . . '

She wasn't, of course. Eleanor Knight's first act with the baby had been to lose it, but they weren't to know that.

It was nearing dawn. Thurstan loaded up the horses once more and they set off, slowly winding eastwards towards Smintha, while the sun beat down and the shadows offered no relief.

Chapter Twenty-six
Moonlight

They moved rapidly through Shelt, but they were too late.

The streets near the shanty town were quiet, shut up and deserted. The fisherpeople of Shelt had closed ranks.

'All good citizens quiet in their beds,' said Olwyn Mittelson. 'I wonder how long they'll be left there.'

The door to the cottage was swinging wide, banging on its hinges in the onshore breeze. Firelight still flickered inside, and the men raced through the door, running up the stairs. Annis followed more slowly. She knew they were too late.

There was no sign of a struggle – but what struggle could the two women have put up anyway? A sudden silence from the room ahead, low murmurs. Annis went to join them.

Rosco, by the door, held out a hand to stop her. Mittelson was kneeling on the floor beside Ismay's body, immobile, his head bent. She had been strangled, her eyes staring, her face contorted and suffused with blood.

'Where are they?' Rosco, furious and bitter to Olwyn.

In shock, Annis did not at first notice what the Mage was doing. He was standing now, moving to the window, which he opened. For a moment there was silence as he stared out to sea.

He was so still that it was almost as if he were no longer a living creature. She saw his curious pale eyes sharply focused, locked on the turning tide, the monotonous crash of foam on the sands.

His hands, moving as if they no longer belonged to him, described shapes in the air, shapes she recognised with sick familiarity.

The fall of the waves, the curving fall of water. Curving inwards, ever inwards . . . spirals, interlocking, interweaving circles, leading beyond the scope of mind's concentration. Light seemed to radiate from his hands.

'Along the shore – towards the Castle . . . '

The words drifted from Mittelson, neutral as air. Almost simultaneously Rosco was pushing past Annis, down the stairs, out of the door, vanishing from sight.

Mittelson was after him in an instant.

They had both forgotten about Annis. She picked up her skirts and ran after them.

Olwyn Mittelson was using Sea Lord lore. He was still one of them. He would manipulate Felicia, just like the others.

Annis wasn't going to let it happen. When they'd got Felicia back, Annis would tell her all about it . . . If they got Felicia back . . .

Felicia's abductors had not gone far. Annis could see two people moving swiftly along the water's edge towards the Castle. One, wide-built with short-cropped grey hair, was carrying a lantern. She saw the soft fall of Felicia's hair over the shoulders of the other, an immensely tall figure with hunched, high shoulders.

Gawne, she thought, chilled. Gawne has her.

And then Rosco hurled out of the dark at the group and there was a shout, the scream of swords, and a sudden collapse into disorder.

There were only two of them, she thought. But Rosco is already tired. And Olwyn . . .

Whose side was he on, anyway?

Gawne had let the girl fall to the sand, had just heedlessly allowed her to drop. She lay unmoving, and Annis started to run again, her breath rasping in her throat.

The man with the lantern was on the ground, just beginning to pick himself up. The First Sea Lord was staring at Rosco, his strange spiral staff held out towards him.

Watching, Annis couldn't understand why Rosco was waiting, circling Gawne and Felicia. But then, as she got nearer, she saw that they were both surrounded by a spiral of sick green light, weaving around them, holding them separate and inviolate.

Gawne's other companion, the heavily built grey-haired man, was on his feet again, his sword drawn, about to launch himself at Rosco.

'Rosco! Behind you!' she shouted, and although her voice was breathless with running, he heard and spun round, lashing out with his foot, knocking the sword out of the other's hand.

They fell on each other, rolling over and over in the sand, struggling and kicking.

She wanted to get to Felicia, still unmoving, discarded on the ground, but the green spiral fizzed like fire when she approached.

And then its character changed. It became invaded with another weaving of light, another spiral coming from the shapes drawn in the air by Olwyn's expressive hands.

'Olwyn . . . ' Gawne's voice, long and slow, drawn out on a sigh. 'So, you're back. Misguided as ever. Loser Olwyn, fighting a losing battle . . . '

'Not this time.' Olwyn Mittelson was still crossing the sand towards him, and as he drew closer the light spinning from his hands became brighter, more dazzling.

Annis half closed her eyes against the shining whiteness of it.

A silence. A moment of complete and deep calm.

Annis opened her eyes and saw, far beyond the glittering figures on the beach, far away on the horizon, a change in the character of the night.

Stillness reached out and held the air quiet and unmoving. A breathless silence. Even the waves no longer tumbled.

A shaft of light shot out across the sea, out of the mist, clear, bright and merciless.

All other light was dull. This was an essence of clarity, a centre of power moving over water. There was no comprehending it, no way of containing this within the confines of thought. Annis felt her mind turn aside, retreat into whimpering passivity. She tried to cover her eyes but it made no difference. This was happening throughout her consciousness.

Eyes were shining, blacker than jet, blacker than night.

Wide hands were held open, stilling the tide. Something approached over the sea. A figure composed of light.

No one moved. Every possible course of action was denied.

Annis saw Gawne struggle to raise his spiral staff, to ward off his enemy. His sunken eyes were distorted and staring.

Rosco was standing, the body of the other man at his feet. His head was unbowed, his hands clenched fast at his side.

Mittelson, on his knees, like she was herself.

And Felicia, conjured to life . . .

A pale, insubstantial figure, she moved over water towards the Lady. Her hair was white, streaming in an unknown wind.

The Woman took Felicia's hand. There were no words, but the knowledge was clear. Trust them . . .

She stepped down from a wave, down to the earth, down to walk amongst mortals. She brought Felicia to Rosco, drifting over sand.

He was staring at Her, transfixed . . .

Astret, Lady of the Moon, caused Felicia's hand to move until it lay, passive and unresisting, within Rosco's clasp.

A web of light contained them, separated from everyone else. A tableau they made, a rich carving, ornate and unmoving against the night like a cameo.

Light glanced over the austere plains of Her face. The black eyes reflected only triumph.

Then She turned to Gawne. His staff dropped from nerveless fingers. He was gaping helplessly.

Begone . . . The merest flicker of attention, and an undeniable knowledge: failure is its own reward.

Turning, dignity and power dropping from him like a rag, he picked up his useless staff and began to run, loping away across the sand, long ungainly strides, back to the Castle.

A curious smile on Her face. Mockery? Satisfaction?

She leant forward. Her fingertips touched Felicia's. She was delicate as a surgeon.

The girl's eyes closed, her hands dropping to her sides, drifting gently down to the sand again, as if her limbs were water . . .

And then She was gone, all the cold light and clarity and triumph all vanishing.

Complete, unmoving silence for what seemed like a very long time. Then they breathed again, and Rosco bent down. He lifted Felicia in his arms.

Watching, Annis expected to see reverence, wonder – pity.

But the expression on Jolin Rosco's face was unmistakable.

Anger, raging fury. And dreadful, heartbroken grief.

Chapter Twenty-seven
The Palace of Blood

Caravan conversations over the days that followed:

'Where are we going?'

'East – to the Kingdom of Blood.'

'That doesn't sound very nice.'

'It isn't. It's the home of the Fosca.'

'Who is that man in the taxi? The one with the staff?'

'He's called Weard. He used to live in Smintha.'

'How do you know?'

'The guard told me last night when you were asleep.'

Eleanor slept most of the time, both in the crate during the day and at night under the cold moon. In this way her exhausted body sought relief and her mind found oblivion. She lost all track of time. There was only the heavy uneven rocking of the great creature's pace, and Timon's arms, never failing, around her, a place of sanctuary against the dark.

Thin porridge to eat every now and then. Sips of brackish water, never enough. She thought perhaps that a week had passed because her swollen face had subsided and she no longer tasted blood every time she spoke or ate.

'What's happened to Comyn, to Hilde?'

'I saw Hilde in the distance two nights ago. She was preparing food with some other women, further down the caravan.'

'Not kept prisoner? Free?'

'It was difficult to tell. They all moved like slaves, as if frightened.' His voice was severe.

'Poor Hilde . . . ' Tears again, weakness she could no longer control. 'And Comyn?'

'I don't know. There are other prisoners held on the beast

behind us, but I couldn't see clearly who they were. Two men, I think.'

'Why haven't they killed us?'

'Kill you? Eleanor Knight, who broke the Stasis? No, they wouldn't dare.'

'Why not? Who are they working for?'

'I think — but it's only a guess — the Fosca King.'

'Who is that?'

'It used to be a man called Lucian Lefevre. He was the architect of the Stasis, but he changed when the Stasis broke, and went to live with the Fosca.'

'How do you know all this?'

'Matthias told me. He understood most of what happened when the Stasis ended.'

'What will happen to me? Why do they still want me?'

His arms tightened around her, but he gave no answer. There was no answer that would not send her screaming into panic. 'I won't leave you,' he said at last. 'We'll manage it somehow. We'll get out . . . '

But the creatures kept tramping on, and the sun burnt through joints in the wooden crate, and there were armed men pointing knives and swords at them whenever they stopped. And where could they go? Every day took them deeper into a burning wasteland. No water, no food, no friends, no means of escape or shelter from the scorching sun.

'Did you know Lukas?'

'Everyone knew Lukas.'

'What did you know about him?' It was half suspicion, half longing which made her ask.

So he began. Some stories she knew, others were new to her. But he stopped when she started crying again and refused to go on.

'What's the point, Eleanor? What good can it do?'

She didn't know, but it felt like a sheet anchor, thinking about Lukas. As if he were the only solid thing on which she could rely.

'He's dead, Eleanor. You saw him die. There's no point in torturing yourself with memories.'

There was nothing to rely on now. Even the baby had disappeared. And Matthias had betrayed her, had ridden away on a beautiful Arrarat, leaving her in the desert.

She turned her face against Timon's shoulder, closing her eyes, waiting again for sleep.

Perhaps it was weeks, perhaps only days later, that the caravan reached the Kingdom of Blood. When the crate doors were flung open for the last time, Eleanor understood one of the reasons for its name.

The Kingdom of Blood was the colour of blood. Dry, rusty, red-brown blood, blowing as sand all around them. It clung like dust to great stratified piles of rock, which reared from the desert in grotesque columns.

They were in the centre of a vast plain. Barren and empty, it stretched for miles in every direction, fractured only by the irregular tumbles of rock and stone. Silence hung heavily over it. She could not imagine that any creature could live there, that any green thing might survive.

There was noise and activity all around them, but it seemed insignificant against the greater silences of the desert. People were running up onto the backs of the great creatures, untying the crates and bags and pagodas, throwing them rapidly down to the ground before leaping down themselves. She did not understand what the hurry was, staring at the creatures.

She had not seen them clearly before; the last time she had seen them in daylight had been at a distance, just outside the city of Smintha. Now, under the eye of an armed guard, she stood close to Timon and watched.

They were more like crocodiles than anything else, she decided, but the sharp scales raised like pyramids were unlike those of any reptile she had ever seen. The eyes were orange, fire-filled and glowing, masked by three lids, shading out the sun. The scales round the eyes were raised high in protection, like lunatic eyelashes, forming solid, spiky ridges. The teeth were long and pointed, irregularly spaced.

The ground was shaking under her feet. Turning, she saw more of them coming forwards to stand together. The guard motioned for them to move to one side, and she was glad to do so, for the huge, heavy tails were swinging wildly from side to side, sweeping great curves in the sand.

Then, astounded, she saw them start to run over the plain, thundering over the sand, stirring up great clouds of dust, towards a great mound of rocks. A dark cavern yawned

massively there, an entrance to somewhere else . . . The
creatures reached it in a cloud of dust, disappearing rapidly
into the vast hole. Within minutes they had all vanished.
Somehow, Eleanor knew that they had gone underground,
out of the sun.

She turned round to Timon, wanting to ask, what are they,
what is that place? But when she looked for him he had gone.
Standing there instead, holding out her arms, was Hilde.

'Oh, my poor girl! Your face!'

'What's wrong with it?' But she knew the answer as she
spoke. Her legs and arms were covered with a motley of
yellow and black bruising. Her face would be the same. By
this stage it looked far worse than it felt.

'Where's Timon?' she said, looking round.

'He's been taken to Weard. I've been sent to look after
you.'

'So they trust you?' It was not a point in Hilde's favour.

The old woman said nothing, but her mouth trembled and
her hands shook. Critically, Eleanor saw that her clothes were
torn and stained by red dust, that she had lost her gold-topped
cane and elegant reticule. The lines of her face were clogged
with dust, a blood-red tracery across the skin.

Hilde looked much older than she had at Smintha. Her grey
hair was escaping from its clasp, hanging in sparse strands
to her shoulder. She looked frail, tired and desperate.

Disappointed. It was a strange thing to read on this old
woman's face. Unthinking, Eleanor reached out to put an
arm round her shoulder, but Hilde stepped away.

'If you don't trust me, there's nothing I can do. And you
won't survive very long here, not trusting anyone.'

'That's what Comyn said.' But it had been Timon who had
held her steady, had shared water and food with her. Perhaps
Comyn would have done the same if he'd been there . . .
There was no answer to it.

Hilde shrugged. 'Anyway, you're to come with me. To
the Palace.' She stepped aside, and Eleanor at last looked
directly at the object of their journey, the vast edifice she
had first taken to be another cliff or a mountain made of
red sandstone.

It was like a factory punctured by windows, riddled by
walkways, braided by battlements. An uneasy jumble of

towers and blocks, it was difficult to work out where the entrance was.

And, flying above it, dark, spiky shapes, jerkily dipping and wheeling. Winged lizards, the dark Fosca angels and their putrescent riders.

And then she saw that the people from the caravan, now doubly burdened after the crocodile creatures had gone, were all winding towards a small, dark hole at the bottom of the main block. Would they be going underground, too? She had not noticed them at first, because everyone was stained red by dust. It lay on every surface, disguising every feature, clogging in every breath. Soon, she too would be covered in dust.

It might even be an improvement on the bruises.

As they left the edge of the cliff, moving towards the Palace, guards closed in all around them. The same faces she remembered from those night-time stops, the men with knives and swords. Lean, muscular men, tanned a deep brown under the red dust, with long, dark, straight hair held back from their faces with strips of rag. They wore only bleached cotton breeches, cut off and hanging loose below the knee.

Not one of them looked at her. They never had, during the journey. It was not that they were avoiding her eyes, more that there was no point in relating to her as a person. Just as juries never look at a condemned man.

She looked over her shoulder and saw another group of guards surrounding someone else behind them. She could not see who it was. Comyn? Timon? Whoever had been held in the other crate?

'Hilde? What is this place? Who built it?'

'No one remembers now. It's very old, like the underground city beneath Smintha. Sometimes people try to live here, in the Sun's own country. Mystics, hermits, fanatics. To live in the Sun, and die, burned and cleansed in the furnace of the Lord . . . '

Her voice was dry. It was impossible to tell whether she approved of such extreme practices.

'Who lives here now?' Eleanor said.

'Didn't Timon tell you? The Fosca. They are well suited to the conditions here . . . '

'Why have we been brought here?'

'The Fosca King commanded it.' Her voice was flat and passionless. Eleanor stumbled, her legs feeble and aching. Hilde looked at her, distantly.

'Not far now,' she said.

It was no comfort.

Laughter in a huge, echoing hall. There was the scent of roses everywhere. Matthias's mouth was choking and dry. He recognised the voice, although it had changed. In a way he was glad that his eyes were still covered and that he could not see the thing that Lefevre had become. The sound of the laughter was more than enough.

The Fosca King was talking to someone, someone he had learnt to know as Weard during the interminable journey with the caravan.

'So you lost your toy! Too bad, you should have been more careful . . . You didn't realise about the baby? Well, who did you think it was? Don't come whining to me because you're too stupid to understand what's going on.'

The voice was high with mockery and cruelty. It was enjoying Weard's discomfiture.

'Get on with your unpacking, man. Where's my prisoner?'

A kick in the ribs. Matthias rolled over, feigning unconsciousness. But there was no point in that, he remembered, not with Lefevre. He sat up, awkwardly, his hands still bound behind him.

'Oh, Matthias, Matthias, how I've waited for this!' The voice was closer now, almost lustful in its eagerness.

He was only half concentrating on what Lefevre said. He forced himself to acknowledge that there was someone else in the hall, someone utterly terrifying.

But he could still speak, although his mouth was so dry. 'Whatever for, Lefevre? Aren't the Fosca company enough?'

'Ah, there you have it.' The voice was sad. 'No conversational skills, you see. After all, I did invent them. They only know the things I have told them, no surprises with them, none at all. Unlike you, Matthias, who know so much.'

'More than you?' It was difficult to keep his voice even when he could smell the thing that had been Lefevre so close.

It was not an unpleasant smell, in a way. The smell of rotting roses, of rose petals staining the water in a rose-bowl, of petals falling amongst grass and melting into its substance.

'No, Matthias, you do not know more than I, no, how could that be? But different things, perhaps. News of the Lady, for example. I would be glad –'

'No.'

But it was not wise to show his refusal so plainly. The voice came nearer, whispering in his ear.

'Matthias, my dear, wise friend. You are in no position to refuse anything. You never have been. Now, shall I take off your blindfold? Would you like to see who my companions are?'

'I know who they are.' Three figures surrounding Eleanor, glimpsed in a vision late one night . . .

'Name them!'

'Your own wraith. My friend, my dear friend. And the Lord Lycias, in human form.'

'But can you identify them?'

He stayed silent. Not without his staff. Not without a fire, and glass to cast over it. The friend of his childhood, yes, of course he knew who that was. But the other two could be any shape, any form: man, woman, old, young.

Both treacherous, both malicious and mischievous. But the Sun King was infinitely the more dangerous, a power not lightly to be named.

He was in the room with them.

Matthias had known it from the first, had felt the overwhelming, terrifying power of the God, somehow reined in, somehow confined within human form.

'Look!' hissed the thing in his ear.

The blindfold was whisked from his head and for one instant he stared full into the face of the Sun God, seated on a raised throne at the end of the hall.

The God smiled.

Matthias had seen that smile before. Lycias had smiled like that at Nerissa. Calmly, cruelly. And then He had kissed her, burning her eyes to ashes.

'His eyes,' said the Sun God, gently. 'You are so slow. Have you learnt nothing, Fosca King?'

Matthias could not turn his head, could not look away from

the infinitely cruel gaze of the God. But he heard the hiss of iron in fire, smelt the scorching of metal.

His hands were tied, his ankles in chains.

An arm round his neck, jamming his head back against the rose-petal breast of the Fosca King.

And then burning iron, the tip white hot, burning agony and eternal darkness into first one eye and then the other.

Chapter Twenty-eight
The Forest of Flowers

There was a banquet that night to celebrate the arrival of the caravan.

In the Palace of Blood, the Fosca King dined only on flowers. An ivory lily stained rose-red at its centre was its chalice; the wide flung petals of clematis its plate. It sipped at honey and dew and the small insects trapped rotting in the orchid's maw.

The King lay on a couch of rose petals, soft and gentle against its own hybrid flesh.

It was not of the same nature as the Fosca, angels or riders. It had been human, at one stage, and there were still eyes, and mouth, small and thin-lipped. But its face was now part of the petals of a flower, a creeping, exotic plant with a thousand tendrils, reaching out around it, running through the rose petals, disturbing their lie, letting them fall through the warm air. Its skin shifted as colour pulsed over it. It was inseparable from the silken flesh of a rose, swelling and expanding and breaking into folds of petals. Its limbs budded in sprays of blossom, dividing and multiplying, spreading wide. It lived in a drift of flowers, breathing their scent, existing in a curve of peony grace.

It was wild, like flowers, preying on wind and water and light and earth; predatory, like convolvulus and ivy and mistletoe and orchids. Intelligent, and gifted with the unseen arts of magic and Synchronicity. Tendrils supplied its immediate needs, but with its mind it controlled the Fosca riders and their mounts, and created wraiths of every shape, every motion.

It was bored. In its previous incarnation, as High Priest

to Lycias, it had balanced the Stasis, maintaining the difficult equilibrium of life and death so that its God might love a mortal, eternally. It was used to power, and judgment, and devious device.

It surveyed the banqueting hall through the drifting rose petals, and anticipated events of interest.

To its right, the Sun God's throne was empty. Soon it would be filled, it knew, and then the play would begin.

Dark angels lined the red corridors, black wings folded behind them in uneven points, attended by their riders.

Eleanor avoided their faces, the eager eyes and lascivious mouths. She looked only at Hilde, her eyes fastened firmly on the upright, thin figure and old, scraped-back, grey hair. She wanted Timon, or Comyn, or anyone else familiar in this place. She wanted people to pretend to be her friends. Pretence would be enough, so long as it was consistent. She was past caring about sincerity. Truth was for the fortunate. It was a luxury, reserved for those who were not desperate. Lies were all she looked for here, in the Palace of Blood.

They were all she found.

The doors far ahead were flung wide and the scent of flowers reeked down the corridor.

Light glowed from the distant hall, a shimmering, golden brilliance. She recognised the Sun of Lycias, the light that had destroyed so much.

Walking down a blood-red corridor, lit only by frail torches, she wanted to run screaming from golden light, but where could she go? A figure opened a door at the side of the corridor and fell into step beside her.

Timon. She was almost sobbing, reaching for his hand. 'Where have you been?'

'Oh, Lady, Eleanor, what have we got into here?' His voice was high with tension, and she saw sweat on his brow. The bright red hair was damp with it, clustering in tight curls. Green eyes flickered from face to face of the dark angels, returning with relief to Eleanor.

'I thought *you* knew what was going on!'

'He's certainly the one for that.' Another grim voice, cold with hate, stepping out of the shadows on her other side.

Comyn. Tall, dark, hidden as usual. She stared at him,

expecting to see the bruises and cuts that covered Timon and herself.

He was unmarked. Dressed in a golden silk, moving with grace beside her. He smiled at her, and she looked away.

The smile concealed so much.

They were almost at the doors. In panic, she turned to Timon. He put his arm around her, warm and comforting, and then they stepped into light.

Into the hall of the Fosca King and his God.

Eleanor stopped on the threshold, overwhelmed by colour and light and perfume. Timon stood with her, his arm still about her shoulders.

Comyn walked steadily forward, tall, straight and graceful. He walked forward through drifting flowers, brushed by petals and leaves, to the throne at the far end.

Set in the bower of roses it was, twined from leaves and stems, a place of subtle grace and scented peace.

He sat down, and smiled.

'Welcome,' the God said. 'Welcome to My servant's home.'

It was wrong, all wrong. She felt the ground cut away beneath her feet, the world turned upside down in distress and deceit.

It could not be Comyn, so quiet, so serious.

But the God can do anything. Can become dark-haired, intense and serious. Can explain to her gently where she is, where she is going, offering his shirt in friendship. She was wearing his shirt! How could he be the God?

Timon, at her side, had clenched his fists in fury.

A fight, against Lycias? She laid her hand over his and smiled at him, but this smile went all wrong too, and she could see his face drain of colour, looking at her.

To the left of the figure on the throne, a flower stirred amidst its foliage.

She did not notice at first, watching the colour of Timon's eyes deepen with fury.

'Traitor!' he yelled, foolish beyond belief, leaping across the flower-strewn floor towards the Sun God's throne.

Creeping tendrils ran from the stirring flower and clasped his ankles and legs in twining green. He fell, crashing to the ground, and leaves and flowers sprouted from the stems, breaking into bud and flower in an instant, blooming over bright curls and white skin.

Her hands were over her mouth in soundless horror. He was covered in flowers, he had disappeared from sight. And the flower to the left of the Sun God's throne was laughing, laughing.

'Eleanor,' said a voice that sent her soul writhing into hiding. A voice from the heart of the flower, sweet as a Siren song, cloying like honey, whispering her name with love.

It caused a curtain of petals to fall aside, and she saw Matthias standing free there, his face empty and blind like the Benu Bird.

'Eleanor – ' He could hardly speak, bereft of power and sight. 'Don't – for Lady's sake, don't believe – '

The creature that was Hilde moved towards him, hands raised like claws, and Eleanor screamed, 'Matthias! Matthias! Matthias!' and hardly heard his last few words.

' – what you see here . . . '

She began to run, avoiding the green, flowing tendrils disguising Timon's body, but long, long before she got there, they had caught her too, dragging her to the floor, twining and constricting and binding.

With whiplash strength flowers wound round her neck and tightened.

She gasped and struggled, the world turning blood-red in her eyes, rose-red and throbbing as she gasped for breath. There was none, no breath to sweeten the scent of roses, no breath to hold back the overwhelming tide of blood in her heart.

The struggles died away and at last she lay still.

And the God, wreathed in flowers, laughed.

It had begun.

Chapter Twenty-nine
Lycias

She was adrift on flowers, borne on a sea of petals, scented all around with roses and jasmine and orange-blossom.

Stroked gently back to life by soft, urgent fingers.

'Oh, my love, my love . . .'

A litany of desire filtered through the air.

Reluctantly she opened her eyes. Timon was there, pale and trembling, gazing at her with wide eyes. At once he took her in his arms, and his lips were on hers, breathing life into her.

She clung to him in relief, gasping in the sweet air, the sweet taste of him. Tender as silk he was, touching her breast, stroking, warm and light, a clear focus of perception and sensation.

Emerald eyes shone with passion and she was drowning in the waves of his desire. She sighed, not knowing where she was or what she was doing. Glad only to be alive and wanted and loved, she opened herself to him.

She had no defence against him. She put aside everything that had happened to her. Her head was flung back against a cloud of petals, her eyes half closed, living only in this moment of intensity as he pushed aside gentle folds of flesh, moving with grace.

Through the heat haze of moving delight she knew that his green eyes were devouring her, driving deep into her soul, smoothing away all her memories and fears.

She was content to let it happen, seized by sensuality.

There was only the moment, the act, the desire.

His face above her was ringed in a halo of fire.

Smiling.

And the fire spread, flaming through the petals of her body, flaming through her veins and her arteries, along nerves and over her skin. Flames kindled the flowers about them, scorching and burning and destroying.

The fire of the Sun God, searing down her limbs, through her life, leaving as ashes every innocent joy.

Branding her, forever, as faithless.

The Gods lie.

For Lady's sake, don't believe what you see here.

A game of revenge, bitter and cruel, more cruel than a cat with a sparrow. More cruel than anything she could conceive. Leading her from depth to depth, defiling everything she had thought inviolate. Anything good and clear and real was destroyed and at every step of the way she had been given a choice.

He laughed at her, Timon/Lycias, but His laughter was touched with such anger.

'Was this the great love that broke the Stasis? The love that cost Me My beloved?'

She moaned, in the ash of burnt flowers.

'I gave you every chance, every way out. You need not have assented to everything that happened to you. Even – I gave you My son. Foolish, empty woman. At every turn, I gave you the child. In honour, to see if you were worthy. My son – is unknown, even to Me. A gift of chance, a being of possibilities and potentials   And yet, you turned aside, and passed Him to others, lost in selfish dreams, in stupid memory.

'And the one memory which could have kept you safe, the memory of love, you let fall.

'As rose petals fall, discarded and useless.'

Eleanor said, 'But Lukas is dead! What fidelity do the dead require?'

'He is not dead.'

There were ashes around her, in her hair, the ashes of mourning, in her mouth, the ashes of the past.

His voice continued. 'You never even checked, did you? You never even asked if the people at that original party saw you return that night. Saw you, beautiful, with snow in you hair, and a dream in your eyes. I invented that pretty scene,

showed you a construction, a lie. You could have found it
out. But you didn't even try. And you never questioned that
Lukas was dead.

'It's easy to mourn. But to fight, to take responsibility, to
keep going, that is the hard thing.

'Lukas is not dead. And you are faithless, and guilty. I warn
you again; I shall have My revenge. You cannot escape it.'
Brilliant emerald eyes plumbed the depths of her being.

'I have only just begun.'

PART TWO

Chapter One
Jolin Rosco

In Shelt, there were days of nightmare.

Rosco helped them move, his face totally withdrawn, the blue eyes dark and shadowed. He left the precise arrangements to Olwyn Mittelson, disappearing for long periods, leaving the Mage to care for the two women.

Mittelson negotiated with friends and family. They stayed no more than a night at each resting place, moving on, leaving no address, no message. He chose well, and no one ever refused them a bed, but there was tension in every face they approached.

And all the time, the soldiers in scarlet swept through the streets, arresting anyone who looked them in the eye, anyone meeting in groups of more than three, anyone who did not look ordinary and unthreatening.

Six men were arrested, hung, drawn and quartered in the square outside the vast temple to Astret at the city's centre.

An example, said the pamphlet. Circulated by the Sea Lords, hastily produced on good paper, threats and fury combined.

Give up the Lady Felicia, or more will die.

Return her to her family, and there will be no more deaths.

Think. First your menfolk. Then your women. Then your children.

That was the unbearable thing. No one knew whether this was an idle threat. The death of the six men had been a savage shock to the people of Shelt. One of them had been the only trained doctor still working in the harbour area. There seemed to be no constraints on the Sea Lords' revenge, no tempering

of justice or mercy. It was as if violence were being pushed
to its ultimate extent, cutting down the helpless and innocent
together with the guilty. A wild force had been unleashed
in Shelt, and all their previous troubles – the unemployment,
poverty and hardship – seemed trivial in comparison.
Nowhere was safe, no one was safe. People watched over their
shoulders and bolted the doors at night. It didn't help. There
was nowhere else to go.

Was it worth it?

Olwyn Mittelson's face was contemptuous as he read the
threats. But Rosco was angry, angrier than Olwyn had ever
seen him before.

'Bastards,' he said quietly and viciously. 'I knew someone
once who warned against heresy. Who said that the Mages
were a potential force for evil, but I didn't understand
then. . . .'

'Not all Mage-lore is warped.' Mittelson was undisturbed.

'So you say – but yes, I agree. I have known good
Mages . . .' Rosco was pacing the floor of a back room of
a run-down laundry, their temporary lodging.

Mangles stood at one side of the room, heavy copper kettles
on the floor, wide porcelain sinks along the other side. The
room still smelt of steam and soap powder, although the day's
work had been long finished. Felicia and Annis were asleep
in the room upstairs. Rain pounded against the window, a
steady pattering of water, dreary and unceasing.

'But what good comes of it?' Rosco stopped pacing and
looked at the other man, sitting with his knees drawn up on
a bench against the wall.

Mittelson's eyes did not flinch.

'What good comes of it?' Rosco's voice was low, almost
empty of feeling. 'Of all this struggle and fighting? What good
has ever come of it?'

'The Stasis broke . . .'

The words hung heavily between them.

'But the price . . .' He could hardly speak.

'What price, "Jolin Rosco"? What price have you paid?'
Mittelson stood up, matching the other in height, though not
in presence.

'Where do you come from, Rosco? Who are you, so
passionate to restore justice here?'

'Are you doubting me?' He sounded only academically interested in the answer.

'No, not that. Everything I've ever known leads me to trust you. And the Lady, on the shore, two nights ago . . .But I need to know your past, now. There should be no secrets between us. Were do you come from? Who are you?'

The vivid face barely glanced at him.

'It doesn't matter,' he said. 'Not now.' Then he went to the door and clattered off down the stairs, slamming the door to the street, not to return that night.

And Mittelson sat on a bench, listening first to the footsteps moving rapidly away through the drenched streets and then to the sound of rain alone. He watched his own face staring back at him, reflected in the curved copper kettles, the pale eyes so wise, so knowing.

He sighed. He had no answer, no answer at all.

Months ago, Olwyn Mittelson had walked on the sea-shore far south of Shelt. It was winter, and a light dusting of snow lay on the sand. It was deeply cold, with a wet, raw cold that made the bones ache.

The sea was far out, a pale line of grey, very quiet, sluggishly turning and returning. He paid no attention to it, scanning the heavy skies above.

That morning, he had watched the Sea Lords use their power. From the top of the cliff over the bay of Marqun, he had lain flat, peering over the edge while they held a Marqun ceremony. Through the scrubby, wind-flattened grass he had observed the course of it.

Twelve Sea Lords, Gawne closest to the pool, Dederic at his side. Dressed in subtle silks, warm furs, heavy cloaks. Each holding a spiral staff, concentrating on the carving at the top.

The tide, crashing on the rocks below the pool, was almost spilling over into it, pounding in a foam of white up against the slippery black rim.

And then the moment of terrifying power, when the first wave surged into the pool. Mittelson almost found himself impelled to lean over the edge, towards the raging ferment below, as the whirlpool formed.

He had to know, he had to find out just what the stakes

were. Why it was worth destroying the livelihood of the fishermen of Shelt.

He had been offered the choice of remaining a Sea Lord. He might have been standing there with them, dressed in silk and fur, holding a spiral staff. If he had taken the oath of allegiance.

Remembering again, he went further back. The scene was clear in his memory, although it had happened long ago. A meeting after dinner one evening, in the Sea Lords' private quarters within the Castle.

This was before Torold had come to Shelt. The old Earl was already ailing at this stage, at the start of his losing battle against cancer. He kept to his own apartments, and the Sea Lords were undisturbed.

The wine had been good, the food excellent, but Mittelson had been aware of tension round the table. And then Gawne had beckoned him aside, leading him out onto the balcony.

Mittelson suddenly understood the reason for the uneasy gathering. His fellow Sea Lords were now silent, waiting for the outcome of this meeting between Gawne and Mittelson.

No preliminaries. An unadorned proposition.

'We have been offered power,' Gawne had said. 'Unimaginable power. All that is needed in return is a pledge of loyalty. Only that.'

'To whom?' Mittelson was uncomfortable. He disliked secret conferences.

Gawne had smiled. 'Trust is the main thing,' he said. 'The secret will only be revealed to those who trust. You must take the oath first, and then you will be told the identity of our master.'

'Intolerable.' Mittelson frowned. 'To take an oath, a serious oath, and not know the issues involved? Have you lost your mind, Gawne?'

He had always known Gawne for an ambitious man, but never a stupid one.

'Everyone else has agreed.' He gestured to the men still seated at the table. 'They have recognised the way forward.'

He paused, and Mittelson knew that the colourless eyes were watching him closely. Gawne cared about this. He wanted Mittelson with him. His voice was low. 'There will be power in it. Healing and long life for us all, for our beloved Earl. That I can promise you.'

He had this quality of conviction, thought Mittelson. The stillness of his unblinking eyes, the high hunched shoulders, the large, capable hands. He was credible, somehow. It would be easy to trust him.

But an oath of allegiance to an unknown force?

Not tolerable. He had refused.

It was taken as unreliability. They had not thrown him out right away, but his tasks became menial and insignificant. Curing the butler's backache. Tending the various accidents and injuries to the Guard.

He was excluded from most of the Sea Lord ceremonies. He watched the fanatic, clever Brice Lammon being coached to take his place.

And then, during the last stages of the Earl's illness, the decree banning fishing had been issued. It was an incredible, incomprehensible decision that disinherited the very men who had brought the Sea Lords to power in the first place. Mittelson had felt impelled to work amongst the stricken, desperate families. He had not forgotten the past.

They had taken his spiral staff away then. But Olwyn Mittelson had seen it coming, had been prepared. Peraldonian Mages rarely used staffs, he knew. It ought to be possible . . . He had evolved methods and procedures that needed no artificial aids.

Only expressive hands. Strength of will, directed through pale eyes. And imagination.

He had practised for a long time to be sure of safely attending a Marqun. He knew the forces involved, the kind of power that would be exerted. Twelve Mages, with their staffs, and their unknown master.

He would have to be careful, very careful, or he would be drawn in too.

So, one winter's morning, he lay on a cliff-top while snow clouds gathered above and watched as the tide swirled into a tide-pool. He saw the whirlpool began to spin below him, and concentrated hard on remaining inviolate. He held fast to a counter shape spun between his mind and hands.

He had been prepared for power, but even so the strength of the Marqun took him by surprise. The vortex in the pool was very nearly irresistible. He could see the twelve Sea Lords all swaying where they stood, all leaning towards the spiral, prevented only by their staffs from tumbling down into it.

And from the depths of the spiral, something arose. Unwinding, unwreathing, rearing up out of the hollow maelstrom of water.

A foam of froth revealed eyes, mouth and teeth, changing, moving . . . Water continued to fall, running over and through a sinuous shape. Thin and subtle he was, with cascading claws of leaping sea-spray. He shone in pale winter light, transparently grey, mimicking solid shape and form. He shifted and moved under the wash of water, unstill, unceasing. Weed, caught up in the curving wave of his being, was dark like entrails.

Mittelson's concentration almost broke. He had not thought such a thing possible, such an abomination.

The sea dragon curled forward, and flickering tongues of water tasted the lips of the Sea Lords.

They did not flinch, did not move. Paralysed, they stood motionless while he breathed salt into their mouths, whispering in their ears, wavering and dancing before their eyes.

Mittelson had turned away, burying his face in the thick woollen sleeve of his jumper, his heart thudding uncontrollably.

Ladon. The monstrous snake of old legend. Avid, licentious, jealous son of an ancient sea-god.

He understood it now. Shelt could not be allowed to fish in the eastern sea, because Ladon would not share.

The pattern became clear as he considered it. The power Ladon gave to the Lords would be immense; wealth would be the least part of it. The power to heal, to prolong life. That was the essence of it. That was the power that Gawne craved, that Gawne had used as the ultimate temptation.

There were many paths open to each Mage, of course, paths varied and potent. In the south, the Great Mage Lefevre had perfected extraordinary skills; Mittelson had heard rumours of creatures called scurries, of a race named Parid. Wraiths. The skills of a Mage often leant in the direction of the alteration of form. As the least of his own skills, Mittelson could disguise appearance.

It could not rival the power to prolong life. No one in Stromsall knew that Lefevre had effectively banished death for the length of the Stasis. No one knew that he had shared the same ambition as Gawne. Living forever. The ultimate temptation.

Yet there was one other area of skill open to the Mage. The perilous path of prophecy. Usually it was the gift of Lycias, but sometimes, when men became Mages and used the power of the Moon, then, sometimes, they knew the future.

Mittelson himself had occasional flashes of fore-knowledge that originated in no experience, no conscious act or thought.

As he lay on the cliff-top, his eyes turned away from the Marqun below, he had one such intuition. It led him, that very afternoon, cold and tired, to a rocky cove far south of Shelt. Someone would meet him there.

He was watching the movement of gulls, resting on the wind, slowly wheeling above the grey water.

Late that afternoon, after two hours' cold pacing the length of the beach, he saw far away on the horizon a moving shape that drew his eyes.

The distances and perspectives were all wrong.

It was far away, too far to see markings, and yet much, much larger than any gull. A vast shape, huge wings beating rhythmically through the air, pushing aside the clouds, coming in low over water. He held his breath, watching the approach of a great hawk.

He had heard of them, and of the people who rode them. Dedicated to Astret, Lady of the Moon. Telepathically linked, he knew. Bonded for life, a unique and extraordinary relationship. He had never seen one before, was not in the least prepared for its presence.

As it came closer, he saw that it was exhausted, the heavy wings labouring against the cold air, its head dipping with effort.

It was a soft grey in colour, its eyes dark and liquid, an alien creature of grace and power. Its beak was fiercely hooked, its claws wickedly curved and pointed. On its back was slumped the unconscious figure of a man.

The hawk settled at the water's edge and looked at him.

Mittelson took one step, and then stopped. He used every wavelength of his mind, questioning, testing.

Nothing aggressive, nothing threatening. But his probes were blocked, thoroughly and efficiently, and the dark eyes of the Arrarat blinked with contempt.

There was blood all over the unconscious man. He had stayed on the hawk's back only by means of the leather strap around its shoulders. His hands and arms were woven into and around it. He lay lengthways along the bird's back, his arms stretched wide, his head twisted to one side, long legs hanging free.

Taking a deep breath, Mittelson walked forward across the snowy sand to where the Arrarat waited.

The hawk watched him incuriously. Nervously, he raised one hand to touch it. Its feathers were wet with snow. He ran his hand over their smooth surface and then touched that of the man lying there. It was cold as stone.

Quickly, paying no attention to the hawk, only aware that the man there would die, if he were not dead already, Mittelson pulled his hands free from the strap.

The man slid off into the shallow waves. He was long-limbed, wet black hair falling over a white face, blood staining his clothes front and back.

But he was not dead.

Then began a strange period. The stranger could not be moved far, for there was a terrible injury in his back, close to both spine and lung. A deep wound, not clean like a sword, but jagged and curved. There was another through his shoulder from the front. Claw wounds, thought Mittelson, wondering what creature had claws of that size.

He should have died. Something had made him live, something had put him on the Arrarat hawk, weaving bloody arms in and out of the leather strap. Something that was not human. Mittelson put the knowledge aside; the time for questions would come when – if – the man recovered.

Mittelson was adept at healing, knowing conventional and magical methods, but even so, this nearly defeated him.

The Arrarat hawk helped. It brought dry wood for Mittelson to build fires, fish, rabbits – enough food to eat.

Once it arrived with woollen blankets clutched in its claws, stolen from some woman's washing line.

There was a freshwater spring a little way up the cliff. Mittelson kept the fire burning, wrapped the unconscious man in blankets and spells, and waited.

In his delirium he murmured many things, many names. A woman's name, over and over. Eleanor. Other things Mittelson made no effort to understand. There would be time enough for that.

He returned one day, his head full of the herbs and roots he needed, to find intense blue eyes waiting for him in the shadowy cave, clear at last.

'Who are you?' The man spoke with the least possible expense of energy. He was lying on his side, his head resting on a bent arm. There was a curious hunger in his eyes – for knowledge, company? It was impossible to tell.

Mittelson told him his name, his occupation (physician, he said). There was no reaction. He paused, disconcerted by the brilliance of those blue eyes.

'Where am I?' The voice was light, pleasant, with an accent Mittelson could not place. He told him about Shelt, and the region, and found himself, perhaps unwisely, naming its ruler, its varied and unusual troubles.

He could not tell if the man was listening, for his face had dropped down onto his arm, withdrawn and hidden. But he felt impelled to keep talking, trying to keep this man diverted from his own thoughts.

They were nightmares. Mittelson saw grief in the bright eyes, sorrow the man could not easily hide in his weakness.

When at last he stopped, sure that the stranger was sleeping, he looked up to find the Arrarat hawk standing far along the seashore, watching the cave. Waiting.

Some days later, returning after fetching fresh water, Mittelson found the cave empty.

There were tracks on the sand. The stranger could not possibly have gone far. Quickly, Mittelson followed the uneven prints towards the sea.

Hawk and man stood at the water's edge, not touching. The man was swaying, but his eyes were steady, locked on those of the bird.

There was complete silence, the silence of intimate communication. Mittelson stood in the shadow of the cliff, watching.

And then the man took one step backwards, his head thrown up, and a great cry split the silence.

'*Why*? Astrella, *why*?'

The hawk tossed its head, as if shaking off the connection. Mittelson saw it bunch its muscles together, ready for the leap into the sky.

The man saw it, too. He started to run, but the hawk was off, up and away, the heavy wings beating on the air.

'Come back!' The cry was anguished. 'Astrella!'

His strength gave out. He stumbled, falling to his knees and collapsed face down in the surf. Mittelson started running.

The hawk, high above, circled the cove, making sure that the man was safe.

Then, every wing-beat the throb of destiny, it left Lukas Marling alone in a strange land, to make of it what he could.

He refused to tell Mittelson anything, anything at all. But Mittelson observed much, and put together an imprecise picture from what he remembered of the Arrarat hawks, and what he had heard from the man's ramblings during his illness.

A follower of Astret, intimately concerned in the breaking of the Stasis. A warrior, accustomed to violence, but loyal, warm with friends and lovers.

He was used to Mage-lore, had known Mages, and effortlessly recognised Mittelson's own power. He was not in the least overawed by it.

'What is your name?' Mittelson asked, early on.

'You can call me – Rosco, if you like. Jolin Rosco.'

It was an ancient, obscure name, only vaguely familiar to Mittelson from the time before the Stasis. The man smiled slightly, acknowledging that it was an alias, and that Mittelson recognised it as such.

'You can disguise me too. It might be wise, if you want help,' he said. And it was true that his black hair would mark him out in Shelt, where most were fair.

Mittelson had explained about the fishermen, and the Sea

Lords of Shelt. There was something about this man which drew confidences, and Mittelson was prepared to take a chance on trusting him.

He said he would help. That he had some experience of guerrilla warfare, of leading men. He left it to Mittelson to decide, pushing nothing, showing no emotion one way or the other. He clearly did not care at all what happened.

With some men, it would be a risk. But Mittelson watched and waited, trusting to the strange combination of intuition and foreknowledge that had led him to the cove that wintry afternoon.

So he healed the man who called himself Jolin Rosco, and introduced him to the fisherpeople of Shelt.

And as events gathered momentum, from the careful instruction of the fisherpeople in the arts of war, the skilful use of propaganda and politics, to the attack on the armoury and stables, Mittelson wove a pattern of events to involve Jolin Rosco.

Leading him away from the shadows of memory. From the chains of the past.

Chapter Two
Fisherpeople

When the man who called himself Rosco was at last capable of travelling, Mittelson took him back to the city, through dingy streets to the squalid cottage he shared with two men near the Fisher Temple. It was not easy.

Alex and Ferant Aldrich were brothers, distant cousins to Mittelson. Fishermen, deprived of their living by the Sea Lords of Shelt. They were both younger than Mittelson, small, intense men with leathery, weather-beaten skin and frowning, narrow eyes. But there the resemblance ended. Alex Aldrich was a fanatic. The frown in his eyes was powered by fury and obsession. He flung himself round the cramped rooms as if caged, restlessly tramping the bare boards, swinging his arms as if to wipe every unnecessary object from his path.

He had blocked the door when Mittelson first returned with Rosco.

'Where the bloody hell have you been?' There was anxiety and anger in equal proportions in his voice. 'You were needed *here*, man.' His eyes darted to the tall stranger leaning tiredly against the wall to the cottage. 'And who the fuck is this?'

A plainsman, Mittelson said. Found abandoned south of Shelt, seriously injured. It was not all that unlikely; the plainsmen were in no position to carry passengers. Frosty silence greeted the news. Mittelson elaborated: Rosco seemed to have lost his memory, but had certain skills . . .

Alex exploded. 'What does *that* matter? You were needed *here*, Mittelson! There's no one else –'

'What about Pelham?' Mittelson frowned.

'Arrested a week ago. Sedition, they said. Stirring up trouble, as of course he was –'

'Bastards . . .' Quietly, viciously spoken.

'Mittelson, there's fever down by the Temple, and it looks like Mullen has got it too. We'll be lucky to contain it without fresh supplies of touraic. And Agatha *died* – '

'She was over eighty . . .' Mittelson spoke automatically, his curious pale eyes abstracted.

'She died of a putrid sore throat which you could have cured in two days. We didn't have any fucking fallow-root and *you* never told us where to find it!' The stream of accusations ran on.

Lukas watched with a kind of dismayed fascination. There was a struggle between Mittelson and Alex, but it was clear where the authority lay. For all his bluster and bad language, Alex Aldrich was like a child, with reason complaining of neglect. Mittelson reacted with patience and calm, but Lukas could see that he acknowledged the responsibility. Alex was right. Mittelson should not have spent so much time away from Shelt. Time spent healing Lukas Marling.

Ferant said nothing. He sat poring over his books and barely acknowledged the stranger, his thin fingers drumming on the table with impatience as Lukas was introduced.

It was an unpromising beginning. It was not easily improved, either, for no sooner were Mittelson and Rosco (as everyone called him) installed in the back room of the cottage, than a stream of people began to arrive.

Children with rickets, pale women with crying babies and swollen ankles, old men crippled with rheumatism, young men with racking coughs and blood-stained handkerchiefs. Everyone too thin, everyone depressed or angry or sullen or exhausted. Shivering in the cold winds of Shelt, clutching at flimsy layers of clothing. The fire smoked in the small front room, giving inadequate heat, but the door was solid and the window glass unbroken, and the narrow hallway known as the waiting-room was always crowded.

They came to Mittelson for healing. Rosco watched from the back room as the Mage measured out pills and potions, bound up wounds, gave advice and consolation and, when time allowed, listened to what they had to say. If they were too ill to move he would go to them, drifting black-cloaked through the filthy, slushy streets to sit at the bedside of the fevered man, the woman in labour, the child failing . . .

Olwyn Mittelson rarely rested. He had indeed been away too long. At every spare moment he pounded powders and measured liquids. He sent Alex Aldrich on long, exhausting expeditions, searching through the snow for herbs and minerals.

Occasionally, late at night, he barred the doors and Lukas knew that he was teaching the Aldrich brothers more than healing. They were learning how to fight using magic, the dark and dangerous arts of violent distortion. Most Mages disdained such practices; Mittelson was teaching them only a bare minimum, and Lukas knew that even that was risky. But one day they would be needed to help Mittelson against the Sea Lords. One day . . .

Mittelson worked ceaselessly, preoccupied from dawn to midnight and beyond. And all the time, as the Mage worked, Lukas Marling watched and observed, waiting for his strength to return.

He could not sleep. The cramped back room where he lay was dank with the left-over smells of cooking and sickness and strange herbs. His eyes were wide open against the darkness. He was conscious of small sounds from the front room, of the scrabbling of mice or rats in the eaves. He could see, although it was dark, the rows of bottles and jars on the shelves by the door. Greasy, well-thumbed books lay in piles on every horizontal surface.

The constant activity in the small house, the people who streamed through every day, the vivid, distressed faces and low murmured voices seemed like so many shadows to him. His thoughts ran along other paths, plumbed other depths.

He knew what had happened. He was not alone in Shelt. Astrella had not left for good; her thoughts still met his. He knew she was nearby, hiding in the wind-strewn cloud above, or racing the moon shadows in the dark.

At night she sent him pictures, strange moving tableaux of thoughts, feelings and memories. A mountain top, a cruel decision forced on Eleanor . . .

She had left him for dead, and had broken the Stasis.

He could not quite assimilate this one. His mind returned to it again and again, trying to understand what had happened. He had not yet found a way to weave it into the texture of his past experiences. It dominated his thoughts, hard and sharp as a bizarre, dark crystal.

He heard movements in the front room where Mittelson worked, the kind of sound made by someone trying to be quiet. Noiselessly he stood up and moved across the room to the door. He always moved without hesitation in the dark.

He pushed the door aside and saw a frail, wavering light held between eloquent hands.

'Couldn't you sleep? You ought to try.' Mittelson raised his eyes from the spinning web of light caught between his fingers. Under his hands a small pyramid of grains wavered in shape.

'Don't let me interrupt you.'

'I've almost finished . . .' The light from his hands seemed to drip downwards onto the pile of grains. A few of them spilt sideways, running over the table.

The light disappeared. Mittelson leant back in the chair, a faint sheen of sweat on his forehead.

'Augmenting the stocks?'

'A hundred grains. Enough for one dose.' His hands were trembling, pushing the grains back into a small glass jar. Lukas went to the sink in the corner and poured him some water.

Mittelson drank it without comment.

'Is it worth it? For one dose?'

Mittelson shrugged. 'The difference between success and failure, that's all.'

'A risk, surely. One should not squander such skills . . .'

'I could mix the medicines with sea-water, of course.' His tone was heavily sarcastic.

'Would that help?' This was obscure.

'How do you think you survived, Jolin Rosco? I had no potions or drugs on that sea-shore. I soaked your bandages in sea-water, and let the dragon claim you.' His voice was reckless with tiredness.

'*What?*'

There was a silence. Mittelson stood up, gathering into his arms the assorted glass jars and weights and measures. 'It's late,' he said. 'And I certainly need sleep, even if you don't.'

'Dragon, Olwyn? What "dragon"?'

He sighed. 'The waters of Shelt are famed for their healing, are they not? The fishermen are forbidden their trade so that the Sea Lords may have exclusive use of the sea. The trouble is, they operate courtesy of a dragon . . .'

'Fire-breathing? Winged? I know, it guards a crock of gold –'

'There's no fire under the waves, and not much use for wings either.' Mittelson was wholly serious. 'But there's gold sure enough. The gold this dragon guards is the gift of healing, of prolonging life. You owe your life to a sea-worm shaped from foam and spray.'

'And I thought it was all down to you . . .' But his eyes were abstracted, his thoughts in chaos. He went to the window and looked out at the dingy street, the litter blowing in the onshore wind. 'You said "claim", Olwyn. What claim?'

He shrugged. 'There has to be a price, of course. As you are well aware, with your intimate knowledge of magic and its practitioners, there is always a price. I don't know what it will be, however . . .'

'Is this supposed to help me sleep?'

'No. But it will give you something different to think about.'

'Yes. Well, thanks. Next time I'll take a walk.'

Mittelson looked at him suddenly, severely. 'You are here for a reason, you know. The Arrarat would not have brought you else. There is something for you to do here.'

'Perhaps. But I should like to decide what.'

'Few people are allowed to decide their own fates. It may be forced on you.'

'Threat, Olwyn? Or prediction?'

'Whichever you'll accept.'

'Neither. This is my life.' But it had been held forfeit, sacrificed in order to break the Stasis. What could he call his own now?

Ferant and Alex were useful to Mittelson if Rosco was not. He was teaching them occult spells, sharing what knowledge he had. Almost as if he knew that there would be other calls on his time, other demands. Rosco, still recovering, saw them wrestle with unfamiliar names, lists of remedies, details of formulae and compounds. Ferant was the quicker – too quick sometimes, leaping to inaccurate conclusions – and it was Alex who pedantically insisted on every point being exhaustively explained.

Mittelson had authority over them and endless patience. Ferant and Alex were in debt to him on two counts. He was teaching them arcane arts: healing and a little of the darker aspects of Magecraft. And, in the short term, providing them with food and a roof. Resentfully they tolerated the presence of the tall stranger called Rosco, and grudgingly shared out the food brought by the more affluent of Mittelson's patients.

For some time, Rosco endured their suspicion and dislike in silence, content to absorb what was going on, what was happening to the fisherpeople of Shelt. He watched and waited, and thought.

Then he began to walk. As his strength returned, he wound his way through the narrow alleys and tumbled, cramped cottages of the harbour area. Many faces were by now familiar to him though he knew few of their names. He nodded to them; sometimes it was acknowledged, usually not.

Mittleson's strange friend, he was. The story had circulated throughout the community. A plainsman, with no knowledge of his past, no role to play in the present. It was accepted only because of Mittelson himself, the tireless benefactor of the disenfranchised populace of Shelt.

It was a hard winter, with bitter winds and frequent snow, slippery and slushy by day, hard and brittle at night. The wind from the sea whipped the snow into grey, clinging drifts, disturbing the outlines of walls and buildings.

Tramping the streets for the brief daylight hours, Rosco saw rats rifling through the mounting piles of rubbish, starving dogs and cats fighting over what few scraps there were. He heard children grizzling and men shouting. These people were wronged. Deeply. Cruelly deprived of their livelihood. He hunched his shoulders against the drifting falls of snow and wondered what to do about it. Whether he should do anything at all.

The boat was called *Futility*. The letters were carefully traced over the bows in firm lines of black. Some other name in chipped scarlet was not quite legible beneath the fresh paint. Rosco stared at it for a moment, frowning. Then he turned to look at the other hulls drawn up on the dry sand.

He was in the wide, shallow bay sheltered between the two arms of the north and south briggs. It was largely empty now, apart from the ruins of fishing boats which lay beached well above the high-tide mark. Any boat found in the sea was immediately destroyed by the Sea Lords' patrol. Only a few were left now, some thirty or so out of a fishing fleet that had been numbered by the hundred.

They were rotting there, their paint peeling, their fittings rusty. In the cold late afternoon light, he wandered between the abandoned boats, running his hand over the splintering planks, considering them.

Graceful lines, clinker-built, the overlapping timbers flowing into generous curves. Not large, right for perhaps three or four men, light enough to be towed on pairs of wheels by horses or teams of men across the sand to the water . . .

Labour-intensive, perhaps, but the only way to launch boats in a shallow bay, sheltered between two vicious outcrops of rock.

There was no other harbour for over a hundred miles on this stretch of coast. Uneven rock formations, precipitous, crumbling cliffs, heavy and violent tides. The bay of Shelt was the only possible place for a boat to put in.

The great ships had to anchor further out, beyond the briggs, sending their goods and passengers ashore in smaller boats. Cobles, they were called, sturdy and dependable. Only three were in use now, painted the Castle colours of scarlet and grey. Staffed by the coastguard's men, purely in order to service the schooners and clippers from far away.

No boats were now permitted to cull the harvests of the sea for the working people of Shelt. The fishermen's cobles had been abandoned, neglected out of lethargy and despair, and then forgotten. But not by everyone. The lettering on this boat was obsessively neat.

Rosco wondered who had taken the trouble. No one in the Castle Guard would have cared enough, and surely no fisherman would rename his boat in such a way, not unless they had lost all hope, all volition. Were they content to accept whatever the Sea Lords threw at them?

Content. He had never been content in his past life. Only once, on a calm island, for a few brief days . . .

'Well, well. Mittelson's mysterious friend. What are you doing here?'

A man he recognised as Philp Cammish, head of one of the fishing families, was standing there, hands dug deep into pockets, shoulders hunched against the wind. He was regarding Rosco dispassionately.

'Just looking. Do you have a boat here?'

'That one.' The man's mouth turned down as he pointed to one of the larger vessels. Pale blue paint and white trimmings were shabby and scratched, the damp wood showing through. *Cursed* read the name inscribed in pedantic black across the bows.

The other boats shared the same careful, incongruous lettering. The *Spite, Vanity, Storm, Mischief, Waste, Pitiful, Injurious, Foul, Trash* lay derelict on the sand, casting long shadows.

'What's her real name?'

There was a long silence. The man turned his back on Rosco, staring out at the flat line of grey water. The wind stirred the thin hair clinging to the top of his head.

'*Cursed.* It has no other now.'

'You're happy with that?'

'Happy?' The word was quiet, devoid of anger. Cammish was still watching the monotonous grey wash of the tide.

'What are you going to do about it?'

'Me?' He swung round and looked directly at the other. 'Learn another trade. Knitting, perhaps.' Only then did the bitterness break through.

'Much future in that, is there? A good return on time and investment? And who will buy, Philp Cammish? Torold and his friends? Or do you plan to supply the Sea Lords themselves?'

Another long pause. Rosco thought the older man would probably walk away.

'What are you doing to earn your keep then? What's your particular contribution to the economy of Shelt? What skills do you have?'

I can fight, he nearly said. Shoot an accurate arrow in the dark. Ride an Arrarat hawk. Throw a knife, wield a sword, run like hell. Dodge one, but not two, dark angels . . .

'I can teach,' he said. 'Archery, fencing. Do you know anyone who wants lessons?'

Silently Cammish looked at him. Then he shrugged.

'What do you charge?' he said with heavy irony, and walked away.

Nonetheless, that was how it started. In a number of changing venues – deserted barns, old warehouses, hidden rocky coves – he held daily classes for anyone who wanted them. The time and location of each class was passed round by word of mouth. Much energy and thought was devoted to keeping the classes secret; it was essential that the Sea Lords should not discover such illegal activity.

But anyone could go. Anyone with time on their hands. Fishermen, the unemployed, young lads, young women. There was no bar to age or sex. Everyone was welcome.

It was better than knitting. They came in ones and twos at first, but as his reputation spread, so the barn became crowded with sweaty people blundering round with swords, sticks, boathooks, and anything that would make an impact.

There were never enough real weapons. The blacksmiths were all in the pay of the Castle and too apprehensive of losing their licences to undertake illegal work.

He showed them how to make the short, double-curved bows that the Cavers had preferred to use. A laminate of horn, sinew and wood, small and neat but very powerful. Some of the older men wanted to wear helmets after the prevailing fashion of the Castle, but Rosco pointed out that helmets made soldiers blind and deaf for the sake of safety. Did they want to be handicapped in that way?

They muttered together in doubt, and in the end came round. Gradually he got to know the people of Shelt.

Not all of them came, of course. There were some who felt they didn't need lessons, men and women confident of their skills and suspicious of strangers. And there were others who thought the whole exercise futile.

They were the more dangerous. Their spokesman was Philp Cammish's son Hobard. He was aided by Ferant Aldrich, one of the two brothers who shared Mittelson's house. It had been Ferant who had renamed the cobles.

*   *   *

They were drinking one night at the Fish and Net. The bar was crowded, thick with smoke, sour with the smell of beer.

Rosco had spent the day showing them the technique of sword-fighting using a cloak partly as a shield and partly to disguise what was going on. They were already used to knives, good at throwing them, getting better at the quick slice, the unexpected side-step.

He taught them to use a swathe of material as a smoke-screen, to flick it into an assailant's eyes, to dodge behind it one moment, and then how to wind it quickly round the left forearm as an impromptu shield the next.

It had been fun. They were drinking and laughing with a kind of relief, buoyed up with hope and enthusiasm.

It was Jarry who began it, Jarry Lindel, a young, fair-haired woman with glittering, passionate eyes. She was a skilful fighter, moving with energy and agility.

'Well, what next?' she said, leaning across the table towards Rosco.

'Tomorrow we try again. Your left turn was out of balance —'

'No, not that!'

Rosco knew what she meant, but this was something he wanted to avoid.

'All this training, all this expertise! What do we do with it, Rosco? Give side-shows?'

He said nothing, lifting his glass for another drink, and it was Mittelson who spoke.

'You know the answer to that, don't you Jarry? Fight, that's what we're going to do. Fight for our rights, our lives, our trades. For the Lady Astret, if you like.'

There was a sudden silence amongst the men and women all around them, a silence that spread throughout the Fish and Net. Many eyes turned towards them.

'There's no chance.' Alex Aldrich, bitter anger showing through his lowered voice. 'There are almost six thousand men in Castle pay —'

'Not all are loyal to the Sea Lords.'

'Not enough to make any difference. And the dammed Sea Lords themselves with their spirals and spells! What could we do?'

'We need arms first.' Rosco spoke slowly, unwillingly. His face was still in shadow. 'We'll need to raid the armoury – '

A murmur of disbelief round the room. He ignored it.

'First the armoury. Boathooks won't win the day. And after that, or possibly at the same time, we'll have to release their horses – '

'Horses? Why? We don't ride!' Jarry stared at him.

'But the plainsmen do, don't they? You have ready-made allies waiting for you out there. All they need is fresh mounts.'

'Your connections?' Jarry looked at Rosco with new respect.

Again it was Mittelson who answered for him. 'You could put it like that . . .And there are other factors.'

Calmly, unhurriedly, he began to outline the bare bones of an idea. A way of catching Torold's attention, of bringing pressure to bear on the Sea Lords . . .

And so the twin plans evolved. The scheme to abduct Torold's niece, and the other, to draw in the plainsmen.

And when Mittelson, late one night, weaving spirals of light into potent energy for his medicines, stopped to rest for a moment, he found his thoughts disturbed by strange visions.

Images hung in his mind and refused to go away. He tried to concentrate on something else, went walking, tried to read, to sleep, but they kept returning, sharp and indisputable.

The image of a ship, wrecked on the south brigg. Of a woman, framed in moonlight. And of a marriage.

The Fisher Temple lay close to the harbour, down an undistinguished backstreet. From the outside it looked like a small warehouse, unmarked double doors at its front, long, sloping wooden roof and no windows.

Oaths were taken there, ceremonies celebrated, prayers had been offered there to Astret for the safe return of ships. The Sea Lords, if they had known that it was still so potent in the lives of the fisherpeople, would certainly have closed it down, for it was attended by women in their traditional role as priestesses to Astret.

In Shelt the Sea Lords had usurped that role, had started to perform the Rites themselves. The vast Temple to Astret near the Castle was the home of dark priests, and none of the fisherpeople ever went there.

Here, at the Fisher Temple, Jarry Lindel's sister Rosa shared the office of priestess with three other women, Ellen and Githa Lavran, cousins, and Graya Fosse.

Two of them were always present, alternating the duties of meditative prayer and tending the temple.

It was Ellen Lavran, a worn, middle-aged woman with thin grey hair and high shoulders, who greeted Jolin Rosco there one cold morning.

'We have been waiting,' she said, opening the door. For what, he wondered? She had already moved away into the dark recesses of the Temple.

It smelt pleasantly of furniture polish and juniper with hints of rosemary. Grey-green branches of evergreen drooped softly from pewter bowls and vases, cascading like falls of water beneath the murals of sea-swept cobles and windswept men, sails and ropes, nets and lines, fish, shells and seaweed, which covered the walls in washes of subtle, subdued colour.

Candles were burning on the plain, white-draped altar, highlighting the icon of Astret that hung there. Her face was silver and gold, shining with clear, cold light.

The other priestess on duty, Rosa Lindel, was praying there, kneeling, her hands clasped together, her head flung back, looking up into the flawless eyes of Astret.

He stood still for a moment, far down the aisle, not wanting to interrupt the intensity of the woman's prayer. He was unsure exactly why he had come. To reaffirm something, perhaps. To clarify where he stood, what he was.

The woman by the altar suddenly stood up, her hands dropping to her side. She turned round, slowly.

Her eyes shone with the light of Astret, repeating the expression of the icon, repeating the cold clarity of the Moon.

The voice was unknown to him, quite unlike the comfortable brogue of Jarry's pretty sister. It spoke only three words, but it was enough to send the other priestess running through the streets, spreading the news.

Earl of Shelt.

Chapter Three
Escape

A dream drifted through the Palace of Blood that night.

It had no ears, no eyes, no voice. No physical presence at all. It hovered anxiously over the bed of ashes where Eleanor lay, unconscious amidst the ruins of love. It tried to send her a moment of peace, a wisp of hope, but failed. There was still so far to go, so much to endure.

Trembling, although the dream had no flesh, it turned aside from the shifting ashes in the centre of the Fosca King's Palace and looked for relief. It passed quickly by the dead man still sitting on the Sun God's throne. It had known Comyn Shreeve once, and didn't want to dwell on what had since happened. Possessed by the God. An empty husk, used as a decoy. The dream shuddered. It left the Hall, searching for hope in the stifling, lonely passages.

It found instead a wraith, fleeing, screaming down the corridors, the reason for its existence annihilated by the God's act. Scattering grey hair, skirts falling away, arthritic limbs given crazed agility, it staggered and jerked in an uneven gait of bizarre speed, casting absurd shadows.

A flower sprouted rapidly from the wall of the corridor and tendrils reached out, imprisoning the wraith, feeding from its frail essence.

The dream that was Nerissa passed by, longing for a different role.

In a high tower of the Palace of Blood it found an ambitious, violent man. Weard, monotonously pulling petals from a rose, tearing it apart, crushing its stamen and calyx, hardly noticing as the thorns drew blood from his large, thick hands.

Swearing suddenly under his breath, he stood up. He had

had enough. The farce he had seen played out in the Hall had been a lot more than enough. He let the crushed flower fall, and threw back the door to his room so that it slammed against the wall.

'Right,' he said softly. 'Now it's my turn.'

He had been patient for a long time. But now he wanted more than promises, more than crumbs. He left his tower and went to find the creature that had been Lefevre, the creature who had taught him almost everything he knew.

And the dream, impelled by horrified curiosity, followed.

The Fosca King was in love. In love with the Sun God, almost fainting with desire, with eager anticipation. It was enchanted and delighted by the patterns of Lycias's revenge, and gratified, for the God had acted within a stage set by the King of the Fosca.

It had watched the events of that evening with thrilled excitement. Surely now the Lord would restore His High Priest. Now that He had accomplished such a spectacular revenge, surely He would reward His loyal servant.

It sat in a forest of flowers at the heart of the Palace of Blood, waiting. Soon, soon, the Lord would come. And the banished priest would be reinstated as the trusted, adored, respected voice of God on earth. Granted power over more than the Kingdom of Blood. With gentle tendrils, Lucian Lefevre touched the coloured flesh of the petals tumbling through the air, and waited.

And as the dream realised where Weard was going, it turned aside. In fear, it passed swiftly by the Forest of Flowers, avoiding the creature that sat at its centre. It remembered too clearly an encounter long ago, between the High Priest of the Sun and the Priestess of the Moon. It wanted no repetition of that.

At last, in a chamber not far from the Fosca King's lair, it stopped searching, resting in the curve of a sheet, on the unobserved light from a feeble lamp.

It found Matthias, lying unmoving on a narrow pallet. Waiting.

Waiting for a dream.

'How did you bear it, Nerissa? Being blind?'

Voiceless, she sent love through the air.

'I never really tried to imagine what it was like, for you or for Blaise. But imagining would not have been enough, would it? An imagination trained to magic, to ancient lore and arcane rite, could not have coped with this. It would have fallen far short, inadequate and limited. But now I know, or rather, am beginning to know, just why imagination fails . . .'

The dream flickered palely at the edge of his blindness and he understood what she wanted to say.

'And is knowing the future any kind of help? You did not find it so, leaping to your death at Cliokest. As I speak now, the Sun is burning through the mists around the future. I want to hold them in place, to disguise and hide this foreknowledge.

'I don't want to know, Nerissa! There is so much guilt already. Must I be responsible for the future as well? Can't I refuse this one? Is there no escape?'

She had no voice, no breath, no physical presence, but he understood her answer, sadly drifting through some other medium.

No escape. No alternative. No relief.

Not while the Gods lie, and humanity is less than perfect.

The Father said farewell to His son. In dreams of light and love He lifted the child high, and danced over the world.

As babies do, it chuckled and laughed. But when Lycias drew the dance to a close and bent to kiss the child's brow, its dark, dark eyes were briefly severe.

It was beginning to understand.

The Sun God was already off and away, creating dimensions in the trilling of a song, celebrating the first triumph in His great game of revenge.

Giving little thought to what He had left behind at the Palace of Blood. And no thought at all to the Fosca King, waiting in trembling anticipation.

'Where's my reward?'

'What had you in mind, Weard?' Later yet that night, just before dawn, the Fosca King was diverted from its avid expectation. It turned to face its servant, its flower-face rank with frustration.

'Knowledge. The staff would have done, but –'

'But you lost it through your own carelessness. I see no reason for an additional prize.'

'Teach me about wraiths—how I may make and use them . . .'

Weard's hands, huge and heavy, were sweating in the greenhouse heat of the Forest of Flowers. He stood solid as iron, crushing foliage and petals beneath his boots. Long, curling brown hair tumbled over his shoulders, lank with sweat and grease. His leather jerkin, patterned and sewn with many-coloured thread, was hanging open, revealing brown skin and powerful muscles.

His eyes shone with intelligence, with ambition and greed. The Fosca King looked at him with distaste. The High Priest to the Sun God should have companions wiser than this.

'No,' it said, distantly. 'I have another lieutenant now. A real Mage, someone of power . . .'

Its attention was flickering, darting to something behind Weard, something quiet in the dense foliage. He turned round. A slight figure stood there, with ruined eyes and grim mouth. Matthias. Listening and waiting to speak.

He stood absolutely still, his hand resting lightly on the stem of a twisted tree. Ignoring Weard, he spoke only to the Fosca King.

'Lefevre, flower of the desert . . . You don't need me. Not really. You wait only for the Sun God to return, don't you? To be reinstated, to get it all back. All that power, all that influence. Poor Lefevre, poor Fosca King, waiting for Your God. He has gone, you know. Can't you tell? The Lord Lycias has left the Kingdom of Blood. And I don't think He will be coming back.'

His voice, quiet though it was, carried absolute conviction.

Weard began to laugh, but it sounded crude and forced. 'So this is your great lieutenant? Your real Mage, someone of power?'

A green tendril sprang for his throat but he was ready for it, stepping to the side, slashing with his sword at the writhing stem.

The Fosca King took no notice. It looked only at Matthias. 'How do you know?' Its voice breathed in anguish.

A slight pause. Then—'There is a power in blindness. If you weren't lost in this obsession, you'd have remembered.

The blind man, if he is truly cursed, knows the future. Are you willing to listen?'

'The future? You? You have that gift?' An edge to the anguish now, a colouring of violence.

'Would you call it a gift?' said Matthias slowly. His words came with difficulty, as if he was finding it hard to speak in this new role. 'Not all of it is clear, of course. There is that much relief. But I do know, for sure, that the God will never return to you.'

Blind, he did not see the changing shape of the monstrous flower in front of him, did not see it shudder, beginning to swell and spread.

But Weard had been ready for it. In a split second of decision he took Matthias's arm, dragging him away through the stirring forest, out into the dry corridors, rushing and hustling him far away from the Fosca King.

'No!' Matthias skidded to a halt, pulling back against the impetus of Weard's flight. 'Eleanor. And the baby.'

'No time for that, you've not seen what that thing can do . . .' Weard was pulling him along, hands like hams on his arms and shoulders.

'We must get them out!' He could hardly stand against the other's strength, but this was imperative.

'What the hell for? It's over!'

'No. It can't be, not yet. Weard, for Lady's sake, wait!' He was yelling now, sweating and trembling. Desperate. 'What will it take, Weard? Anything. Knowledge, power – what do you want?'

At last the man stopped, standing suddenly still in the foetid corridor while the scent of roses choked in the air around them.

'Teach me to be a full Mage,' he said. 'With my own staff, my own power. You can do it. I've watched you . . .'

Matthias leant against the wall, trying to use his newly acquired gift. This one was unclear, still lost in mists. He would have to chance it. He would not abandon Eleanor again.

'All right,' he said. 'Get them out, and I'll make you into a Mage.'

A choice not lightly taken. What else could he do?

*   *   *

Eleanor lay discarded on a bed of ashes. Weard plucked her up, slinging her casually over one shoulder. With the other hand he propelled Matthias forward, not allowing him to stop by Comyn's body, not allowing him to discover what had happened to Lycias's pawn.

As they ran from the Hall, its walls began to crack. Green fronds pushed the stones apart. The bower that enclosed the Sun God's throne grew fleshy shoots, hectic blossom, buds and leaves and branches, swarming over the floor and wall and ceiling.

A chandelier crashed to the ground just as they left the Hall, strangled by the weight of greenery. Dark angels fled chattering in front of them, paying no attention at all. Leaves brushed their faces, tendrils snagged their ankles, thorns caught their clothes.

But Weard was used to action, strong and determined. Impelled, now, by unassailable ambition. He knew the Palace well, and could hazard what the Fosca King would do next.

He knew where the baby was, too. He had made it his business. He had appropriated the child just as soon as he discovered who it was. The son of Lycias had to be of overwhelming significance, and that was enough for Weard. He had no plan, no vision of the baby's potential. But it was Lycias's son, and Lefevre wanted it, and so Weard had hidden it.

It was with the refugees from Smintha, the caravan people who had settled in ragged disarray around the outskirts of the Palace. There was a rabble of them there now. They had been joined by others along the route, the outcasts from the desert tribes, thieves, murderers, beggars, losers. They had seen the promise of something fine in the action of those monstrous creatures who moved at Weard's command. Such power was not negligible; they had been drawn to find the Fosca King.

Matthias and Weard ran down long corridors, Eleanor still unconscious over Weard's shoulder. They passed through dusty halls and deserted galleries, and a thread of green pursued and overtook them, breaking up stone paving, running over the walls, holding doors closed ahead of them.

Time and time again Weard demanded Mage-power from

Matthias. Without his staff, without his sight, it was near impossible. The simplest trick, opening doors, became an ordeal. But Weard was quick to learn, quick to understand, and was already partly a Mage, and the doors sprang open under his heavy hands.

The corridors became more narrow, more winding, plunging down to ground level. And then they were out in the open, the blast of heat from the morning sun an overwhelming physical presence around them. Surrounded by a burning, blood-red, dusty plain, a ramshackle shanty-town of tents and shacks clustered around the back of the Palace.

The only sound, as they approached, was of a baby crying in the distance. And as they passed through the silent, squalid jumble of tents and sheds, Matthias at least was surprised to find that it was not deserted.

Sitting in lonely apathy, slouching against walls, watching incuriously, were the remnants of the caravan that had left Smintha. A murmur of drab conversation only occasionally disturbed the air. Even the men who had held weapons, who had acted as guards during that long trek, seemed to have lost volition.

'They all know,' muttered Weard. 'They ought to get out while the going's good. Did you hear?' He raised his voice at them. 'Get out of here. It's over, there's nothing for you here –'

But no one registered his words. No one tried to stop them as they pushed into the shack from which the sound was coming. In the claustrophobic gloom of one of the tents they found the baby, lying squalling in an open basket, wrapped round in stinking rags.

Matthias lifted it, carefully, cradling the downy head to his uncomfortably beating heart. It stopped crying immediately, and Matthias sighed with relief.

And Eleanor, still unconscious over Weard's shoulder, gave a small moan, settling into a more natural sleep.

The baby nestled against Matthias and began to suck its thumb.

Chapter Four
Sunflower

Alive. Lukas was alive.

But the Gods lie.

'Matthias!' She came screaming back to consciousness, shouting, flailing against the crushing weight of sunlight. 'Matthias! Where are you, where are you?'

'Hush!' Her wild hands blundered against him, were caught in his light clasp. She swung round to face him. She had forgotten his face, his eyes.

'Oh, Matthias, how can you bear it!' And then she remembered the things that she could not bear, and gasped, ripping her hands away, trying not to wail, not to start screaming again.

He did not touch her, did not try to offer comfort. It would have been no good if he had. She would have shuddered, remembering that other touch, that leaping fire. She ached everywhere, the memory of burning still deep in her bones, still regnant over her skin.

'He said, Lukas is alive. Matthias, Lukas is alive!'

'Do you trust Him?' This was from Weard, his voice grating and loud.

They were near the top of a cliff of red sandstone, crouched on a wide ledge, overlooking the plain and rocks where the Palace of Blood stood.

She had no idea how they had got there, knew nothing of the effort, Matthias carrying the baby, Weard holding her over one shoulder, guiding Matthias with the other hand. They had run from the Palace, kicking up sand and dust, flying across the empty plain.

In panic she looked around from their high ledge, trying

to work out where she was. Dark angels were circling the sky above, but were too interested in what was happening at the Palace to pay much attention to the four figures below.

They had crept and scrambled their way over dunes and rocks, gradually getting higher and higher, until they stood at the top of a dry, baked, sandstone cliff, overlooking the plain below.

Eleanor would have answered Weard: no, she did not trust Lycias; but the sight below was too much.

Beneath them, on the plain, the Palace was breaking up. Leaves sprang from windows and doors, tendrils pushed apart stone and mortar. Doors were thrown from their hinges, ceilings from their supporting walls. As the roofs caved in, she saw roots disturbing the lie of foundations. Floors heaved like the sea.

And the monstrous flower at the centre grew vast, ripping through every constraint, hurling down the halls of its Palace, letting it all fall to rubble.

It spread itself, tendrils and fronds, leaves and boughs, and red stone gave way to green foliage, and hard lines of brick and block became soft and fluid, blurred by the growth of florescence.

Tendrils, running, avid, over the sand and rock, reached into the shanty tents and sheds, and plucked from them anyone who had not run fast enough, far enough.

The white heart of the flower was gaping wide, supported on a framework of branches and shoots. It held its few prisoners fast, wrapped in green, trapped high on the trellis of its limbs, nourishment for its great quest.

It was faithful in its desire. As ever, the being who had been both Lefevre and the Fosca King wanted to reach the Sun. To be united with the God. It held its white head up, yearning, and followed the Sun's movement slowly across the heavens.

Girasole. Heliotrope.

Sunflower.

Weard described it to Matthias, in words flat and dull, for Eleanor was silent with too much emotion, too much fear. She found herself clutching the baby, holding it to her heart as the Desert Rose revealed itself.

'We had better move on,' Matthias said at last. 'The flower will need food. And the angels, the dark angels – '

'Are flying high, on the look-out.' Weard squinted up at the sky. 'Scavengers.'

'But where to?' cried Eleanor. She could find words, so long as they did not refer to what had happened. The future at least was bearable. 'Where do we go from here?'

Matthias turned to face her. He looked as if he would never smile again.

'To find Lukas, of course. Where else?'

'But was He lying? How do we know?'

'Oh, Eleanor, don't you understand, even now?' He was very gentle with her, but overwrought tears were streaming down her face. 'Lycias would not have bothered, would not have set it all up, except to test you. To hurt you. And it would have been no test if Lukas were really dead.'

'But I thought he was! He *was* really dead to me. I saw it happen. I have mourned him, have cried . . .' She stopped. What use was it?

'But not for long. How long did it take, Eleanor? Does time pass the same in your world as here? Here a few months have passed, no more. It did not take you long to learn to rely on someone else.'

'What are you getting at? Do you mean I shouldn't have trusted Timon? – Lycias? What else could I do, Matthias? He's a *God*! What chance did I have? You brought me here, abandoning me to this desert and to Lycias. I had to trust someone, there was no one else . . . I would have died without Timon!' The confusion in her thoughts was absolute.

'There was the baby. The baby would have helped.'

This was beyond belief. 'How could I know that? I didn't realise it was Lycias's son until He said so. The baby was just another part of the nightmare – '

He was silent, frowning, his mouth compressed.

'I thought you were my friend, Matthias! Lukas's brother and all that. How could you do such a thing?'

He started talking again, and she wondered if he had even taken in what she had said. His hands were gently stroking the head of the baby in his lap.

'But the greater mistake, the real error of judgment, was that you did not make sure. You did not, in your own

world, try to find if it had happened as Lycias had shown
you.'

'Matthias, you have done a terrible thing. I ought to hate
you. I don't need a *lecture*!'

He was grey-white, his mouth compressed. He swept on
as if she had not spoken.

'He showed you a series of visions. Those visions hold the
same status in reality. Lycias showed you a return to that
original party. You thought that it had really happened, that
you had encountered people there. Well, did you speak to
them? Did anyone see you or comment on your appearance?
They would have remembered. You could have found it out
for the lie it was. If the God had shown you one lie, might there
not have been others? You might then, with good reason, have
doubted that other vision, the vision of Lukas's death.

'It's not enough to accept what the Gods throw at us. To
wail and beat the breast, and stop thinking. You should not
assent.'

'Stop it, Matthias.' This was all too much. Why was
Matthias saying this? Did she have to hear these words? Her
voice was ragged now, torn this way and that by conflicting
hurt and hope.

Still he continued. 'You must understand what is
happening. This is important. You must not make such a
mistake again.'

'What about you?' She turned on him now, agonised
bewilderment finding expression in fury. 'Don't *you* make
mistakes?'

He paused, brows drawn together over burnt eyes. 'I make
the worst ones of all, Eleanor. Far worse than yours, because
I know, supposedly, what I'm doing . . .'

'What else have you done?'

He said nothing, but put the baby down, turning towards
Weard, opening his empty hands hopelessly.

Weard was crouched on the rock, building a small fire. Dry
wood crackled in the quiet, hot air. Arranged at his side was
a velvet cloth, and lying on it was a number of unusual glass
shapes: moons, globes, hexagons.

He looked up at them in the brief silence.

'Lesson number one, Matthias,' he said. 'Glass over fire.
How to be a Mage in three easy stages.'

'Three things, Weard.' Matthias spoke evenly but Eleanor could see that his hands were clenched at his side.

'One. As you must know, it takes infinitely more than three stages. Two. Glass over fire is towards the end of the course, not the start. Three. To be any kind of effective Mage, according to the tradition of Astret, a spiral staff is generally needed. I no longer have one.'

'We'll make one then.'

'A living tree is needed. Rowan is the best. The nearest suitable tree is – oh, about five hundred miles from here.'

'What about that?' Weard's huge hand was gesturing down to the plain. 'The Desert Rose. That's living wood, if ever there was such a thing.'

Matthias almost smiled. 'Go and cut yourself a staff then, Weard. Your first task as trainee Mage.'

For a moment the big man looked down at the seething, heaving tangle of flower and branch. At the struggling figures held fast by tendrils all around it, at the voracious action of the creeping runners, searching the wide plain.

'Sod it.' He swung round in a sudden violent movement, taking Matthias by the throat, wedging him hard against rock. 'Think again, ruined Mage. I'm not that stupid.' He raised his fist, ready to smash it down into the reddening face under his hand.

A shriek through the air. A darting, screaming slash of flame-coloured fury, and Weard was falling back against the rock, bright blood steaming from his lacerated forearm.

An Arrarat hawk, winging in wide circles over the plain below, settled into a slow glide on a billowing thermal.

'Arrarat, Arrarat!' Eleanor ran to Matthias, helping him sit up, not even bothering to look at Weard so astonished was she by this miraculous deliverance. 'Is it yours? Chestnut, gold-coloured – no, I remember – '

'Adila,' said Matthias. 'She was Comyn's. Poor Comyn . . .I must ask you about Comyn some time, but now – '

'Now we get the fuck out of here!' Weard muttered savagely through his teeth as he pulled the knot tight on the rag round his forearm. 'Call that damn hawk.' This to Matthias.

'She won't come.'

'Why not? Call her!' He was shouting now.

Matthias shrugged and cupped his hands together over his mouth. The ornate warbling cry seemed to echo round the wide empty spaces of the plain below them.

The Arrarat took no notice, held between wind and air, flaming through the cerulean sky.

'Try it again! Again!' Weard's voice was blustering with uncontrolled violence. Eleanor remembered the fury on his face when the baby broke the staff, the madness in his eyes when he hit her. What on earth were they going to do in the company of this wild creature?

Matthias felt it too. He sighed. 'Weard.' His voice was calm. 'The Arrarat only obey their own, their chosen rider. They may come to someone else if they think the cause is right – but not otherwise. Adila is not ours to order.'

'What about your own hawk? You've got one, haven't you?'

'Asta died. When the Stasis broke –'

This time the Arrarat did not intervene. Weard's fist crashed down onto the blind man's face, sending him spinning back against the rock, almost falling on top of the baby lying quietly in the sand.

'Fool!' The shout was now hysterical with rage and fury. 'You have another! I know all about you, Mage, I know you rode one when you brought the girl here.'

'Alta.' Matthias spoke through swollen, bloody lips. 'Not mine. Borrowed for the task. Far away, now.'

There was the sudden silence of potential danger. Eleanor thought Weard would explode, his face suffused with passion, his huge hands bunched into trembling fists. She bent over the baby, picking it up with some vague idea of shielding it, getting it out of the way.

And then they all heard it, the huge shaking of the ground as massive creatures moved across it. The crocodile monsters were leaving the dark cavern under the mountain of rocks. Their mouths were hanging open in wide grins.

All along the edge of the rocks, far away from the running, voracious tendrils, stood the remnants of the caravan people, the men on horseback, the women laden with bags and bundles. Somehow they had preserved belongings and weapons from the wreck of the Palace; somehow they had got themselves together.

Another trek. The caravan was on the move again.

Weard didn't even bother to speak. He strode over to Eleanor, reaching for the baby in her arms.

'No!' She whirled away from him, the baby clasped to her breast.

'I'll take that child. You're no good to me, a Mage who can't even open doors, a stupid little slut. But the baby, Lycias's son – give it to me.'

His left hand grasped her shoulder, the right already swinging, ready for the blow. Her head was turned away, bent low over the child, and she didn't see what happened.

Didn't see his face change from anger to bewilderment. Didn't see the colour drain away, leaving him blank and expressionless. Didn't hear the ringing of bells, or feel the breath of cool, soft air which wrapped itself round the man and washed all the violence away.

When she looked again, he was already far away from them, scrambling down the cliff side, slithering over rock and sand.

Incredulously she watched him reach the plain and begin to run, pounding with an even, powerful step across the wide space to the caravan, skirting the tendrils of the Desert Rose in a wide arc.

'He's gone!' she breathed. 'He just – changed. And left us . . .'

Matthias was leaning over her, helping her to her feet. His hands gently stroked the top of the baby's head.

'What are you called, little child?' he said softly. 'And what else are you going to surprise us with?'

But the baby had closed its dark eyes, distant once more in sleep.

Chapter Five
Decision

'Where's he going?'

Matthias's voice was quiet and unstressed at Eleanor's side.

'He's running across the plain. Joining the caravan or something. I don't believe it, Matthias!'

'Unlooked-for good fortune, certainly.' He stepped backwards, feeling behind him with cautious hands until he found a ledge to sit on. He was sheet white, a sheen of sweat on his forehead. The wounds across his face were red and raw.

For the first time she really noticed him, really understood what had happened. And although she was still raw with fury and resentment at his words and actions, a rush of compassion took her by surprise.

'Matthias – can I do anything? Anything to help?' she looked around the bare rock face, the dusty cliff and plain. 'There's no water even. What are we going to do?'

'Eleanor.' His voice was flat with exhaustion. 'I don't deserve your kindness. There is so much to explain, so many alternatives to discuss – but not now. There's a way out, I think. But now . . .' He was slipping sideways against the rock.

As she watched, his thin body relaxed and his head dropped. Under the heat of the noon-day sun he slept, and Eleanor sat on the edge of the cliff, her feet dangling over the edge, and watched the marvellous flight of the Arrarat hawk, steady over the plain.

She had so much to think about, so much to remember.

And hope. Amidst all the horror, she had hope; for Lukas was not dead.

* * *

She found herself watching the baby. It was sleeping in the shadow of a rock. Lycias's son. Part human, part divine. A worker of miracles – for why else should Weard have suddenly abandoned them, running away to rejoin the caravan? And there were other things too. The shattering of the spiral staff, the way the baby appeared and disappeared. It never seemed to need feeding, was never cross through hunger or thirst.

Lucky thing, she thought, and wondered what to call it. Odd, how it was always 'it' rather than 'he'. Not quite human, of course. She eyed it with misgiving. She hoped, passionately, that it was not going to turn out like its father.

Her skin was beginning to tingle. The sun was relentlessly, viciously hot, and she would burn. Her nose would be bright red, her legs and arms sore and itching. She moved back against the rock, trying to get within the small area of shade near the baby.

She hated the sun, always had. She had never, in her old life, wanted to go on fashionable holidays to the south. It struck her as ironically apt that she should find herself a protagonist in a feud with the Sun God.

Timon, red-haired like herself. Lycias, vengeful and cruel. Her mind was already beginning to glance away from what had happened in the Palace of Blood. She did not believe herself guilty of anything. She had thought Lukas dead, and there had been no reason to doubt his death. She had been desperate, not knowing what she was doing.

It had been rape, nothing less than that. The deepest violation of trust. She had not for one moment forgotten Lukas.

But there was now a steady weight of misery and nightmare clouding the edge of the knowledge that Lukas lived. Nothing was easy, nothing straightforward. She wondered if she would ever be able to put aside that red-hot fire running over skin, flaming along every nerve to her very essence. The overwhelming power of it, the desecration.

Not while the Sun repeated and reinforced the violation, burning viciously in a cloudless sky. There was no defence from it, no protection or relief. She closed her eyes, leaning back against the rock next to Matthias, and tried to sleep.

* * *

When she awoke, she thought for one desperate moment that she was alone, that she had been abandoned in the desert again. She sprang to her feet, wildly calling, 'Matthias, Matthias, where are you?'

'Eleanor.' His voice, calm and steady from a little further along the ledge, out of sight. She scrambled along to him, and then stopped.

The ledge broadened out on the other side of the cliff to a wide expanse of dark red, dusty rock. Standing at the centre of it was the golden Arrarat, Adila, waiting for her. And Matthias, holding the baby, half sitting, half leaning against a rock at its side. He had torn a strip from his shirt, binding it around the wounds in his face. It was a relief not to look at the raw, suppurating flesh.

'We have a choice, Eleanor,' he said when she was closer. 'Adila will take us wherever you want to go – '

'To Lukas!' she cried. 'Let's go and find him!'

'Yes, of course . . .But, there is something we could do first.' He paused, absently stroking the dark hair on the baby's head. 'I think – I know, rather, that we were followed on that caravan journey from Smintha. I still had some powers on that journey. I knew there were shadows behind us. We were being followed by Phinian Blythe.'

'Phin, poor Phin . . .Comyn told me about him.'

'You will understand then what I am asking of you. The baby – the baby could perhaps release him. I don't at all understand everything it can do, Lycias's son, but I don't know any other way to help Blythe.'

'Why didn't you try before? You had the baby when I first got here.' It wasn't that she didn't want to help Phin, it was just that she was avid, eager to find Lukas again. She had to justify what had happened. She had to see him again, to know that he trusted her still.

'I did not know then the exact nature of this child. I do not really, now. But it had another role then.'

'What role?'

He was silent for a moment, and she suddenly knew that he was embarrassed to tell her. 'Matthias, why did you give me that baby? Why did you bring me back?'

'Lycias – was burning the land. A drought of epic

proportions over all Peraldon. Forest fires, cattle dying, the failure of crops. Disease, famine . . . It was a punishment, revenge, for ending the Stasis. For the decision you made.'

'I thought it was the right decision.' It cost so much, she thought, it had to be right. It cost Lukas's life, and I mourned him for so long . . .

But the Gods lie, and Lukas is alive.

'It was right. And courageous. Don't think I don't understand, and honour you for it.' Again, another difficult pause. She saw the Arrarat cock its head, golden eyes glowing with interest and pity.

'But Lycias is vengeful. He afflicted our land – and it was decided that your life would not be too high a price to pay if it would appease the Sun King.'

'*Who* decided?' This was outrageous, beyond belief.

'The idea came from the Emperor originally. He claimed to have received a vision from Lycias Himself. His Mage, Imbert Cupere, reinforced the idea. Everyone believed him; they needed to because it offered hope, a possible way out. So the Emperor's plan was taken up, by Aylmer – Thibaud, de Mowbray. Thurstan.'

Thurstan? 'What about you?'

'There was a consensus, Eleanor. One life against so many. I – went along with it.'

'You did more than that! You *worked* with them. You set up the Rite together –'

'Eleanor. Everything I have done since the Stasis began was directed towards improving the life of the followers of Astret on Peraldon. Bringing you back appeared to be the only way of easing a terrible situation –'

'You take too much on yourself, Matthias!' She was furious. 'Do you see yourself as some kind of God, then, responsible for other people, for a whole race? Just who do you think you are?'

'I – tried to do the right thing in an impossible situation –'

'And Phin? Did he "go along" with it too?' Her voice was hard and bitter. How could she ever trust Matthias again? And Thurstan she had believed to be at least neutral.

Why hadn't they been *grateful*? She broke their bloody Stasis for them.

'Phin alone said we should not do it. And he, in many ways,

had the most reason of all to wish for a scapegoat to divert
Lycias . . .'

'The Children?' She was putting it all together, working
out what had happened. It was almost incredible.

'They are obscenities, Eleanor. You would not wish them
on your worst enemy. He suffers – more than anyone I have
ever seen.'

'But *he* didn't want me back.' She was clinging to this,
to some proof that they weren't all using her.

'No. And for that reason alone, I think we should make
this effort to rid him of the Children of the Night.'

'You sound like some prissy schoolmistress.' It was petty
and hurtful, but she couldn't help it. He made no reply,
seeming to wait for something. 'You haven't explained why
I was given the baby. Who was its mother anyway?'

So Matthias told her then a story, the terrible story of
Coronis's pregnancy and marriage. Of how his friend Haddon
had loved her, loved her so much that he was willing to act
as father to someone else's child.

'Lycias killed Coronis,' he said quietly, 'because of that
marriage. She was not faithful to Him, you see. He struck
her down one day when she was near term. And as the funeral
fires burnt around her body, the flames charring the dead
flesh, He ripped the child from her womb. I saw it happen.
This child.'

'Haddon?' Her voice was small now. She had lost her
petulance.

'Cursed, like Phin. Pursued by storm, never allowed to
rest, he roams the plains, searching for the Child he loves.'

'Although he was not its father?'

'No. But he so loved Coronis that his heart overflows with
love for her son. One day, I hope, he will find the child
again . . .'

She stared at the baby on his knee, its dark, deep eyes
containing extraordinary mysteries. 'How did you get hold
of him?'

'I was sent to Stromsall by the Emperor Xanthon, just at
the start of the drought. It was a complicated situation on
Peraldon, you see. The Cavers were in negotiation with the
Peraldonians, trying to find some political structure that
would give them safety within the southern continent.

'There was huge resentment, you see. People don't want to grow old and die. It takes – maturity to understand that ageing is not necessarily an evil. The Cavers were loathed for their part in ending the Stasis. And you, of course.'

Of course. No one wanted to grow old, it was only natural. It had taken Eleanor herself a long time to realise just what the issues were.

Matthias went on. 'There were two courses open to the Cavers. Either leave Peraldon and go north to Stromstall, to the lands where Astret is freely acknowledged. Or stay in Peraldon and try to make the people there understand the value of life in the shadow of death.

'The Emperor sent me to Stromsall to discover what had been going on there. He had no aggressive intentions. He genuinely wanted peace, as we did. I also wanted to see if there would be a home for us there if it didn't work out in Peraldon. But on my visit to Stromsall I found only horror. And Bilith was a city devastated by shock . . .

'Bilith was the home of Coronis. Her funeral pyre was burning when I arrived. Haddon had disappeared and Coronis's father Lapith lost his life when searching for him. Only one other person realised what had happened to the baby, and he was an *eloish* plainsman . . .' Matthias's fingers traced a spiral in the dust by his side. 'The *eloish* are not really trustworthy, of course. They have no regard for the lives of city-dwellers, no understanding of the ties that bind people. Their word is generally held to be of little account, but there was something about Jerr Morrelow.' He paused. 'He knew who the baby was, I'm sure, although he wasn't telling. And there was no sense to be had from anyone else in Bilith. I travelled to the south of Stromsall, to the Lake of Lallon, a place sacred to the Lady Astret. It was where I'd first found Coronis.

'I hoped to find knowledge, an explanation of some kind. Instead I found the baby, fast asleep, wrapped in a blanket.'

He shrugged. 'I have no idea how it got there. I can only assume that the Lady Astret managed to wrest it from the Sun King. Coronis, after all, was vowed to Her service, and Stromsall is dedicated to the Lady. No doubt there was some kind of fight over it . . .

'I brought the baby back with me to Peraldon. During that

journey, flying on Alta, I recognised that there was
something – unusual – about the child. It was powerful, as
might be expected from the child of a god. But more than
that, it seemed to me that its power was a force for good,
for healing. I did not tell anyone else of this; I wanted no
other battles over it. And when the Emperor Xanthon made
the decision to bring you back, as the Lord Lycias had
instructed him, I said I would only assist in this if I could
give you the baby. I hoped, you see, that it would help. That
it might deflect some of the anger of its Father.'

'If the Emperor wanted me to be a scapegoat, why did he
allow this?'

'He did not know there was anything special about the
child. I led him to believe that I had a plan. I said that it
was to involve you. I made him believe that caring for a baby,
for this particular baby, would make you vulnerable in the
God's eyes. There was an element of truth in it. The Gods
hurt us most through what we love. You know that now.'

'So you and the Emperor thought that I would love it, just
because I'm female? You're all so bloody simple!'

'Give us our due, Eleanor,' he said mildly. 'Every woman
I've known since the beginning of the Stasis has longed for
children. Perhaps we were not sufficiently imaginative. And,
of us all, it may console you to know that Thurstan didn't
believe you'd automatically care for the baby, just like that.
He said you weren't at all that kind of woman.'

'Well, he was right!' But she was enraged. How dare
Thurstan Merauld make such a judgment about her?

'Shall we go then?' His face was turned towards her, as
if he could read her expression with blind eyes.

'What do you know, Matthias? What's the great secret?'
Suddenly she was sure that there was one. 'What are you
hiding from me?'

'Everything I have told you has been the truth.'

'Perhaps. But what have you left out?' There was
something, she was sure.

'Nothing.' He was calm, undisturbed. Was she imagining
it?

'Where are we going, Eleanor? It's your decision.' He
sounded totally neutral. He was standing up, the baby
comfortable against his shoulder.

'I don't like decisions . . .' She looked at the golden eyes of the hawk and sighed. 'All right, then,' she said. 'Let's go and find Phin first. Then we'll go to Lukas.'

She climbed up first, forgetting what it felt like; the warm, dry feathers, the muscles bunching together ready for the leap upwards, the musky scent of the Arrarat.

Matthias handed her the baby and then climbed up behind. He had taken off his shirt, looping it into a sling around her neck. The baby fitted it comfortably enough, leaving her hands free to hold the leather strap.

She felt a sudden, extraordinary flood of happiness, to be riding an Arrarat hawk again.

Lukas was alive, and she was flying through the sky, and she was going to meet an old friend. She almost laughed with the joy of it.

She forgot the strange timbre of Matthias's voice. She did not see the frown on his face. After all, she did not even know that he could see the future.

She didn't know that he understood, fully, what this decision entailed.

Chapter Six
Astrella

Felicia drew Rosco, not surprisingly, as a hawk.

He was furiously angry.

Until the night of Ismay's death, he had been both kind and friendly to her, bringing books, paper and pencils to amuse her, gently mocking – undemanding.

But after that night, about which she remembered little, he avoided her whenever possible. He refused to meet her eyes, no longer visited her room, was cold and distant when contact was unavoidable. His face was gaunt, his eyes hard and fierce.

So, she drew him as a hawk, and he found it on her bed one day as they were packing for yet another move.

'Hell,' he said softly, still not looking at her. Long fingers crumpled it up, dropping it onto the fire. 'What do you know, Lady Felicia? What has Olwyn told you?'

She lifted her chin, forcing him to meet her eyes.

'Nothing,' she said neutrally. 'Olwyn, like you and my father and uncle and Gawne and Fessil and every other man in my life, has told me nothing. But that doesn't mean that I *know* nothing.'

She stopped suddenly, taken aback by his expression.

'Go on,' he invited quietly. He was towering over the bed, staring down at her, blocking the light from the window.

'You think, because I am ill and weak, that I know nothing. To be kept in bed, like a child or a doll. And it is true that of the extraordinary things that have happened to me – the shipwreck, the Marqun, the other night – I remember little.

'But I watch and wait, and I have learnt that you – ' She paused. Did she dare say it? 'You – do not belong here. You

are not part of this.' She had watched him every time they
met, fascinated by the detached way he spoke, the energy
and passion in his eyes.

He let his breath out on a sigh, and a sudden, ironical smile
flickered over the mobile features.

'You can say that again . . .'

She waited.

He turned away from her, moving across the narrow room
to the window. It was raining again, a steady, cold drizzle
dripping on the window-sill, puddling the dark, dirty streets
outside. It was mid-morning, but the light in the room was
more like twilight. She could not see him clearly.

'And how about you, Felicia? Why do you let men like
Olwyn Mittelson and Torold and your father – and me, for
Lady's sake, treat you in this way?'

She smiled, turning her hands up on the sheets.

He was frowning. 'No, it's not just a question of physical
weakness. You're playing games, too. You don't have to let
this happen.'

'What do you suggest? What else could I do?' She was no
longer smiling.

'Don't take *my* advice, for a start!' A long, cold pause.
'Or – tell us to go to hell, dear Felicia. Each and every one
of us. Think. What could we do? You are the Lady Felicia
Westray, heiress of Eldin – and Shelt, too, I shouldn't
wonder. You don't have to allow us to push you around.'

She was about to answer, and then she realised what he
was doing. 'But we weren't talking about me, were we?
Diversionary tactics, it's called. What are you doing here,
fighting for the fishermen of Shelt, "Jolin Rosco"? I've read
the history books too. You're a stranger with an assumed
name. What happens in Shelt is nothing to do with you. So
why are you here?'

He moved away from the window and for once she saw
his face unselfconsciously revealed. He smiled gently at her,
and she saw the ruin of hope in his eyes.

'That, my dear, is what we would all like to know.'

Next day, on her way to the baker's, Annis picked up a leaflet
dropped in the street. Kester's face stared back at her.
Her hands were shaking so much she almost dropped it.

She felt dizzy, stupid, almost unable to comprehend the words. They were simple enough.

'This man is being held hostage against the return of the Lady Felicia. Her kidnappers are hereby warned that for every day she is held, this man will receive fifty lashes.

'If the Lady Felicia is not released, unharmed, within the week, he will lose his right hand.

'It will not end there.'

It was signed 'Gawne of Aquile, First Sea Lord'.

Olwyn Mittelson remarked on her pallor that evening.

'You'll be rivalling Felicia if you're not careful . . .What's wrong, Annis?'

He was a Mage, like Gawne. He had helped Felicia, but to what purpose? She didn't trust him, with those pale eyes.

'Serethrun,' she said, fastening on an excuse.'What's happened to him? Why isn't he back yet?'

'He has a long way to go,' said Mittelson. 'I don't expect him for at least a week.'

'Where has he gone?' Annis wondered vaguely why it had not occurred to her before.

Mittelson leant back in his chair. These rooms were rather more comfortable than most they had used. Carpeted floors, heavy wooden furniture, fine china in carved cabinets, books on every available shelf.

This was their second night in the large house in one of the more affluent areas of the city. It was owned by Vere Holtby's family. He was an unlikely supporter of the fishermen's cause, a romantic who had wanted to join the fishing families as a boy. His dismayed parents had sought to steer him to safer harbours, but had failed. Vere had left home to become friends with the fishermen. He had in the end been disinherited.

Mittelson had known Vere Holtby for a long time, often amused by his enthusiasm. Short and tubby, Vere was passionate and committed, and not very wise. He viewed it all as a heroic adventure.

'Serethrun has gone to get his kinsfolk. He has taken the Castle horses to the *eloish*. They will be – valuable allies.'

She barely registered the reference to the *eloish*. 'A week? He'll take a week?'

'What's bothering you, Annis? What's the problem?'

Mittelson was watching her with those strange eyes. She would have to be careful. 'I'm – worried about him. He's very young . . .'

'There is nothing young about the *eloish*.' Mittelson sat back, returning to the book on his lap, apparently satisfied. 'Serethrun can look after himself.'

Felicia said, 'You must tell me what's wrong.'

Later that night, Annis was sitting by the fire in Felicia's room, staring blankly.

She had seen a man flogged once before. Thirty lashes, and his back had been in ribbons. Blood everywhere. He had screamed and fainted and they had thrown water over him to revive him. Again and again.

Fifty lashes, every day. Kes wouldn't last a week.

You've probably killed your precious Kester. Rosco's acid words, after the horses had been freed. Was it her fault?

'Should we return?'

Annis looked sharply at the patient figure on the bed.

'What do you mean?'

'Leave these people. Mittelson and Rosco. Take our chance back at the Castle. I'm much stronger now.'

'What about Gawne?' But as she spoke, Annis's mind was daring to imagine it; the triumphant return to the Castle, the welcome; Kes, free.

'Look.' Felicia had thrown back the bedclothes and swung her legs over the side, sliding onto the floor.

She walked slowly and steadily across the room to the fire, and if every step was difficult for her, it did not show in her face.

Her eyes were bright, sea-green, her cheeks flushed with pleasure and triumph.

Annis watched her thinking, We could do it, we could run away, could make our own way across the city back to the Castle. And this time Felicia would refuse to be bullied, would be strong enough to resist Gawne and Fessil. She had changed, there was strength and purpose there.

And Kester would be free.

'Tonight?' she said.

*   *   *

They reached the end of the road before Rosco caught up with them. They had not heard his approach, hurrying along the dark, greasy pavements.

'Going far, ladies?'

Annis swung round. 'We're not prisoners! You can't keep us locked up forever!'

'No one's imprisoning you. I thought you understood. But neither you nor the Lady Felicia would be safe back at the Castle.'

He spoke in measured, fair tones. Seriously, as if he knew what was in Annis's mind.

'Felicia, are you all right?' A quick glance to the girl at her side, standing in shadow.

'Yes, quite all right. Taking your advice, in fact.'

'A bit soon for that, I would have thought. One needs practice in these things. It's no fun for a beginner. You could start by telling Olwyn to shut the door whenever he leaves a room. Or Vere to eat fewer lardy cakes. Gradually work up to telling Gawne where to get off. That sort of thing.'

And although he was speaking to Felicia, his eyes never left Annis's face. The agreeable voice ran on.

'Seen any good pamphlets lately, Annis?'

She felt herself flush. And then the tears sprang to her eyes and she sagged against the wall, letting them fall unheeded down her face.

'What is it, Annis?' Felicia was watching her, pale once more.

Rosco came towards them, bringing from his jeans' pocket a crumpled piece of paper.

'This, I think,' he said, giving it to Felicia.

She scanned it quickly and then spoke rapidly, urgently, to the weeping girl.

'This is Kes – your Kester?'

Annis nodded. She put her hand on Felicia's arm.

'Please, can't we go back?'

'To the Castle?' She was speaking automatically, but she looked beyond Annis to Rosco.

He was regarding them thoughtfully. A slight pause. Then, 'I'll get him out if you like,' he said.

'You know it's a trap, of course.' Felicia spoke without heat.

He shrugged. 'I'll get him out,' he repeated.

'They'll take you too.' Calmly.

'No they won't.'

'How can you be sure?' Annis, anything but calm.

'Because – I know what's going to happen. Some of it.'

'How can you? How can you?' Annis was shouting, too frightened to believe him.

'Because, in all this – I've been given a role. On the sea-shore, remember? There's no easy way out of this.'

Felicia stared. 'Death in the Castle would be easy?'

He ignored her, raising an eyebrow at Annis. 'I'll get your Kes out, don't worry. Go back to Olwyn now. He'll explain.'

Olwyn Mittelson did nothing of the kind. All he did was to build up the fire in the grate.

'Watch,' he said, and threw a handful of powder into the fire.

It blazed suddenly, illuminating four faces. Annis, on the edge of hysteria, fear and hope all mixed into one. Vere Holtby, his eyes almost starting from his pale, pasty face, a more than willing participant.

Mittelson, withdrawn and secret.

Felicia, calm as the ebb-tide.

In the flickering, golden glow, they saw Rosco, as in a dream, standing alone on the cliff north of the Castle.

His hands were cupped over his mouth, calling. And then, from the deep indigo sky, came the scything sweep of wings, and an Arrarat hawk to light on the rocks beside him.

There was an audible gasp from Annis, a half-voiced curse from Vere. Felicia's eyes filled with inexplicable tears. Only Mittelson knew what to expect, and even he could not have spoken.

For a moment Rosco stood there with his arms round the hawk's neck.

'Is he leaving?' Felicia, her voice suddenly high and anxious in the dark, cluttered room.

'No, not yet.' Mittelson spoke slowly, regretfully.

Then the man they knew as Jolin Rosco swung lightly up onto the bird's back, and it took off, arcing high up towards the Castle.

They saw it land on one of the high towers over Torold's

private quarters – and then the fire died down, back to its usual quiet glow, and they were left looking at each other.

Astrella had chosen well. The tower was deserted, a roof garden of unlikely coniferous shrubs and trees, one of Torold's more eccentric enthusiasms. Quietly Rosco pushed through the branches to the top of the stairs.

A door there, firmly locked. He had acquired much strange knowledge over the years, both from his brother and from Mittelson. It was not necessary to use Mage-lore here, however.

From his pocket he took an oddly shaped key, surrounded by a fringe of flexible wire. A moment's concentration, a slight adjustment, and the door was open.

If only it were all going to be that easy . . .

His only chance lay in being unobserved for as long as possible. He had to get through the Castle, down to the cells, and then back again to where Astrella would be waiting.

As he reached the bottom of the stairs he heard a door slam further along the corridor. Heavy, uneven footsteps. He slipped noiselessly into the shadow of an alcoved doorway, praying that whoever it was would not want to go that way . . .

Another door opened, another set of footsteps on the stone floor. An explosion of anger rang through the corridor.

'Esmond, for Lady's sake! Out of my way! I've got enough to worry about without you.'

The other man spoke, soft words Rosco could not catch.

The first voice continued, abruptly losing its bluster. 'Oh, to hell with it. What am I going to do?'

'Leave it to Gawne, my gentle lord . . .' The other, a light, musical tenor. Pressing back into the shadows, Rosco watched the two men as they passed.

Torold, he assumed, richly dressed in a loose, heavy velvet robe, soft leather boots, full silken sleeves showing beneath emerald cloth. His face was flushed, dark hair damp with perspiration, his step unsteady. An almost empty goblet hung from his right hand, the last drops of dark wine slopping onto the floor.

The other man was of a more delicate build, short golden curls framing a finely modelled head. There was a neatly defined moustache on his upper lip. His shirt was of blue silk, soft and full, his breeches of light tan leather. A sapphire ring glinted on his left hand.

As they passed Rosco, he saw Torold's arm wind around the other's waist, his head drooping against the smaller man's hair.

They were gone.

Rosco turned down the corridor and slipped into the room Torold had just left.

A serving-man, folding clothes left on the bed, only had time to look round as the blow dropped him where he stood. He lay, quietly breathing, amidst the scatter of scarlet and ivory cloth.

Quickly Rosco flung open the wardrobes, hastily choosing, but not at random, an outfit for himself. Jeans and jersey were unknown within the Castle. State clothes might be recognised. He took a light grey riding cloak, dark grey breeches, a deep gold shirt, black leather sword belt and scabbard. They were a little loose, but fitted well enough. He paused, glancing at himself in the mirror.

The apparent confidence of the fair-haired stranger reflected there was disconcerting. A perfect gentleman, perfectly at home, elegant in every way. Flamboyant even. He looked as if he belonged there, among the velvet hangings and rich furnishing. With impatience he turned away and left the apartment of the Earl of Shelt.

As he moved through the Castle it became more crowded. There was a party on: the aristocracy of Shelt were out in force, all a-glitter with silks and satins and gleaming jet jewellery. The main staircase was crowded with careless revellers. They had settled on the russet carpet like so many exotic butterflies, holding glasses of amber wine, as if waiting for the entertainment to begin.

Rosco needed to find his way to the Castle basements, where the dungeons were. He was prepared to murmur apologies, to thread his way down the stairs through the spreading silken skirts, but in the Great Hall below he saw a tall figure in drifting, watery grey.

Gawne. He was standing quite still, coolly surveying the crowds. No one approached him; no one distracted him. He was watching everyone, as if trying to discover their secret.

Trying to pass him by would be a foolish, unnecessary risk.

There were other ways down. Mittelson had drawn maps and plans. It depended on his getting outside once more, crossing the gardens through to the kitchen block.

He turned back along one of the long galleries, passing a group of people listening to a small band of musicians. Flute, harpsichord . . . He walked quickly through increasingly deserted rooms until he found one empty on the west side of the Castle. There was a balcony, and steps leading from it down to the gardens.

There were people there, too. Lanterns and musicians, and waiters bearing trays. He saw two other Sea Lords, in their distinctive grey silk, mingling with the crowds.

Keeping well to the shadows, he moved swiftly down the stone staircase. Pots of hyacinths scented the warm spring night. He could see, far over on the other side of the lawns, a door in a high wall. He knew it led to the kitchen garden. There were soldiers along the wall, armed and ready.

Well, he knew this was a trap, just as Felicia had said. He had come prepared. Astrella was not far away, circling the Castle high above.

He was good at the dark, had spent the Stasis in a condition of night. He waited in shadows, drifted with the wind from cover to cover, watching the crowds, watching the Castle, searching for a diversion.

He saw, high above the gardens, one of the Castle towers alight with candles. Conifer trees and shrubs blocked the scene from below, but Astrella was showing him pictures.

Yes, it would do. Torold in a panic, looking for Esmond . . .

Astrella. His mind spoke gently, lovingly. *Catch me a bird of paradise, a little lovebird . . .*

An impression of conifer-scented luxury swam through the air to him. Silken pillows, laid out on a high tower beneath the stars, a tender and ardent bower for desire.

Yes, he breathed. *Bring me the little one, golden curls and sweet of voice. Gently, though, my love. Not a scratch now . . .*

A sudden scream through the sky, a scream of pure and dreadful panic. And then Torold's voice, high with fear and shock.

And Astrella, gliding down towards the new-mown grass,

depositing the pale, naked body of a golden-haired lover at
the far end of the garden.

With his clear night vision, Rosco saw Esmond tumble out
of the grip of ferocious claws without a mark on him, moaning
with terror. He was staggering, in a daze, feebly trying to
run. Astrella had taken off immediately, was already no more
than a shadow in the sky.

Rosco walked away as the hysterical screams began. The
soldiers were running towards Esmond, doors were flung
open from the Castle. Torold would be thundering down the
stairs from the tower, creating every disturbance.

Unobserved, he pushed open the door to the kitchen
garden. He skirted the wall, crushing thyme and rosemary
under his feet, until he found a path through the neat rows
of plants and bushes. It led direct to the kitchen door.

It was unguarded and deserted. His adaptable key opened
it without trouble.

He passed through, back into the Castle.

Chapter Seven
Questions

It was late. The kitchens were deserted, the main catering events of the evening having finished long ago. He slipped between scrubbed tables and huge ovens, carefully avoiding the annexe where coffee and cakes were being prepared. He heard the chink of china and subdued voices.

His luck held. No one saw him, and there was no one in the corridor outside the kitchens. And in the passage leading down to the lower levels, the only soldiers he saw were crowded round one of the grills, watching the pantomime in the garden.

He knew where to go. Mittelson had shown him the layout of the Castle long ago, when they were planning the attack on the stables and armoury.

He had assumed that there would be guards at every juncture, locked doors, barred gateways. He had come prepared with weapons, incendiary devices, tricks and disguises.

But there was no need for anything of the sort. The bare passages were silent and deserted. There were doors and gates, but none of them was bolted. All he noticed was the growing stench of something rotting.

Parid. His step slowed. He should have brought Mittelson. He tried to remember what he'd learnt of the Parid and their shifting shapes.

Failed Gods, Phin had once said. With God-like powers, created by Lefevre. He remembered a golden woman, who became monstrous in a moment. A web stretched wide between trees. Teeth, biting. And a great shark leaping from the waters round Cliokest.

He had never defeated them alone before. Always it had taken the skills of a Mage, or the intervention of the Arrarat to help.

Was it worth it, to save one man?

Bright light glowed ahead round a bend in the passageway. He went more cautiously, moving soundlessly over the warm, dry stone.

He heard singing, light and easy, a gentle crooning. It sounded as if it were coming from a great distance.

He pressed back against the wall and edged forward, looking round the corner. The corridor widened into a low ceilinged hall. A torch burned in a bracket on the wall. At first he thought there was no one there, but then the flickering light caught on a glint of blood. A man was lying face down on a pallet against the wall. His back was a red pulp. There were no bars, no chains; he could not possibly move unaided.

The singing stopped. 'Well met, Lukas Marling.' The cool voice behind him was well remembered from both past events and from nightmares.

Sharrak, gold staining and corrupting the outline of feminine grace, smiling at him. He took a deep breath.

'You're far from home,' he said, watching, wary.

'So are you. Poor little Caver. You lost your lady, didn't you? In more ways than one . . .'

'What do you mean?' He had to ask, although he knew better than to believe anything it said.

'She left you to die, you know. Refused to give you a chance. Scared by the Lord Lycias, she was. You were the price of her freedom.'

He said nothing. Astrella had given him pictures, dreadful knowledge. The snowy mountainside, and Eleanor's decision. She had chosen to break the Stasis at the cost of his life . . .

It was knowledge that left him free now to throw away that life if he wished.

He stood in the dungeons of Shelt, looking at the parody of a God in the flickering torchlight, and shrugged. His death had been the price of the breaking of the Stasis. He knew it well. The dark crystal, reflecting through his thoughts every hour of every day since arriving in Shelt . . .

Yet he had lived. It filled him with horror, with foreboding. Every act of ritual magic required a price; he had died to break the Stasis, and that price had not been too high. But then there had been a resurrection. Perhaps the Stasis was waiting to slide back into place, perhaps that death was still owed, still required.

Perhaps it would be called for now. He didn't really mind, because Eleanor had been whisked back to her own world, beyond any possible reach. She thought him dead, and would never return.

It didn't matter what he did, where he went, how he lived. He had thrown in his lot with Olwyn Mittelson for want of anything better to do. He was waiting for death.

But still, he disliked coercion.

'What do you want?' he said to the golden vision, lowering his sword. It was never any good against the Parid. 'The usual?'

Its lip curled at him and for a moment the shape wavered between the insect/spider form and spun gold. He looked away, considering the dusty stone arches of the ceiling.

'Power,' he said, answering his own question. 'That's what the Parid want, isn't it? Real Gods demand other things. Morality, sometimes – integrity. Love, faith, loyalty.

'But you, the Parid, pretend Gods, thirst only for power.'

'Why not?' it said, silkily. 'It makes life – intriguing.'

'It makes you just a little less than us. Sometime even humanity can aspire to other ideals. But nothing can desire power as much as man. Lefevre, Gawne, Torold. All of them.'

'And you?' It was close to him, no longer smiling.

'I – want freedom. Not to be used by anyone or anything else.'

'Why align yourself to causes, then? Astret, the fishermen of Shelt, what are they doing but using you?'

'But I have chosen those paths.' Why was he telling it this?

It seemed to withdraw into itself. The gold stains curled and contracted. And then – 'Take your friend,' it said suddenly. 'Take him and go.'

He stared at it. There was a strange expression on its face, something he did not understand. He thought it would live in his nightmares, that expression. But Sharrak stood aside, letting him pass.

Unbelieving, he went to the figure on the pallet and

crouched down. He touched the unknowing hand softly. 'If I help you up, can you walk?' he asked.

Kester Robard opened heavy eyes clouded with pain, and nodded. He had no energy for speech.

Gently Lukas pulled him to his feet, taking care to avoid the raw wounds on his back. Somehow the sick man managed to get his arm round Lukas's shoulders. Half dragging, half supporting him, Lukas started back down the silent corridors.

No longer did the Parid croon its strange lullaby. He heard only two words from the light sweet voice, following them down the passageways.

'Remember me . . .'

Astrella was waiting for him in the shadows of the kitchen garden wall. As he helped Kester, half fainting, onto the bird's back, and climbed up behind him, there was a frown on his face.

Yet again. Why?

The next day, while Mittelson dressed Kester's wounds and Annis watched fearfully; while Felicia practised walking around the house, and Vere Holtby prattled foolishly, question after question, Lukas Marling paced the cliffs north of the city of Shelt.

He had not slept again.

Astrella had come to him, soaring high over the swollen sea, swooping down to the wind-blown cliff-top. She knew more than she would tell. He could not make her give him the information he wanted.

What was happening in Peraldon. What the Cavers were doing now. What had happened to Phin, to Matthias, to Thurstan and Stefan, all his family and friends. She would not take him home. With loving regret, firmly and mysteriously, she had refused to take him away from Shelt.

He was in exile, living in a limbo, waiting to pay the death he knew was owed.

And Felicia. There was a compulsion there. Compelled by Astret. Commanded. Forced.

But what did it matter? Eleanor was gone. His family and friends, to all intent and purpose, were also gone.

What else could he do?

Chapter Eight
Flying

Eleanor had forgotten how wild it felt. How unsteady, how uneven. The dizzying scoops and swerves, the seemingly casual catching at thermals. And then the wide sweep of a glide, smoothly powerful, casting a deep shadow on the endless red desert beneath them.

The air was hot and dry around them, burning blue. A faint haze hung over the horizon, disguising the shapes of sand-clouded rocks. In minutes they were far away from the plain and the Desert Rose, travelling in the opposite direction to the trail of the caravan.

She did not know Adila. Her mind could not easily mix with that of Comyn's hawk. It was frustrating to her, not to know the warm delight, the loyalty and courage of the Arrarat at first hand. She wondered if Matthias, with his greater experience of Arrarat, was managing any better. She flung a question over her shoulder.

'Yes, I understand Adila. Not completely, we're not bonded of course, but yes, I do know his intentions, his will.'

'Does he know where we could get water?' She could not remember the last time she had had enough to drink. Soaring through the air it felt even worse, the hot, drying wind whipping over her skin. Her tongue was swollen and sore, her throat parched. 'I'm so thirsty, Matthias!'

There was silence for a moment while he communicated with the hawk. 'Yes,' he said. 'We'll put down in an hour or two. There's a spring. It might still be flowing . . .'

It was, but only just. A thin patch of scrubby grass fringed the edge of a stratified rock. A weak trickle of water ran over its surface, disappearing into the sand beneath.

Eleanor almost fell off Adila, casually dumping the baby in the shade of the rock. She flung herself on to her knees in the red dust and tried to catch some of the water in her hands. There was barely enough to cover her palm.

She sighed. 'We need a cup or dish to gather it. There's very little.'

Matthias was holding something out to her. A flake of rock, with a hollow in one side. She took it and held it beneath the thin trickle. It took a long time to fill.

She put it in Matthias's hands.

'Eleanor.' Matthias was mildly reproving. 'What about the baby?'

She glanced at it, quiet in the shade. 'It'll be all right. It's divine, or something. I've never seen it eat or drink anything.'

'That's no reason not to offer it. You can't have it both ways. If he's human, he needs to drink. If he's divine, he should at least command respect.'

She looked back at the baby, lying peacefully on the sand. It was cooing softly, waving pudgy hands in the air. Its black eyes were abstracted. She picked it up, guiding the stone fragment to the baby's lips. It drank delicately, without fuss, all of it.

Then Matthias. He was looking desperate again, she thought. It must hurt, that wound in his face. He drank the water she put in his hands without comment.

'Do you want me . . . Shall I take a look at your face now?' she suggested doubtfully. 'It ought to be cleaned, perhaps.'

'It's all right, Eleanor,' he said, with a faint grin. 'I can manage. Just see if you can get any more water from the spring, will you?'

She held the rock-dish steady and he cleaned the wounds with another strip torn from the rags of his shirt. It didn't look as bad as she had anticipated.

'Matthias, it seems to be healing quite fast,' she said, puzzled.

'Yes. It's the baby, I think. A focus for harmony and peace. As if evil and sickness cannot coexist with it.'

She remembered something then. 'It broke your staff, you know. At least, I suppose it was your staff. Weard had it when the caravan left Smintha. Just before we were taken prisoner.'

'A spiral staff in the wrong hands is dangerous. I'm not sorry it was destroyed.'

'But what about you? Don't you need it?'

'I'll find another, one day. Or something else. I'm just glad that Weard no longer has it.'

'Was it you in the crate on that creature behind us? Did you realise that I was there?'

'I'd been in that crate for days before we picked you up. Yes, I knew it was you. Comyn was put in with me, you see. He told me what had happened.'

'I don't understand about Comyn. Surely he wasn't possessed by Lycias all the time?'

'No, I think it was intermittent. He said that he kept blacking out, that he had no memory of certain conversations or events. He was deeply worried by it, but neither of us realised what was going on. Lycias can do whatever He likes . . .'

'How can anyone ever trust *anything*?'

'I don't know that one can. It's lies all the way . . .' This revealed a depth of cynicism and depression she was unwilling to contemplate. Not while the baby slept calmly in the sun, and Lukas was alive.

They decided to remain where they were that night, for the sky was rapidly darkening and neither of them wanted to leave the spring.

It became very cold after the rapid nightfall. Eleanor shivered and cuddled the baby again. It laughed softly. She sat on the sand next to Adila, leaning back against the smooth feathers for warmth.

'Let's call him Coron,' she said 'After his mother.'

'Yes. She should not be forgotten.' He reached out to where he thought she was. She moved, and took his hand in her own.

'I'm sorry, Eleanor, that I brought you back to this. It should not be necessary to ask someone else to bear the responsibility.'

No, indeed, she thought. And yet – 'Don't. If I hadn't come back, I would still be thinking Lukas dead. Don't regret.'

He said nothing more, sitting down beside her close to Acelet, and because it was now pitch dark, she missed the expression on his blind face.

She didn't know the half of it, yet. His prescience was by no means consistent. He was aware that vast areas were shrouded still in mist, and for that he was grateful. But still pictures lanced through his blindness, illuminating the dark. And constantly, however hard he tried to avoid it, he saw the setting for a wedding, a cold and windy city by the sea . . .

There was a long way to go before she would meet Lukas again, and that meeting would not go as she expected.

He wished he did not know what was going to happen in that northern city. It was no comfort at all.

The next day, the endless miles of sand were punctuated only once. A familiar chunky black shape squatted on smooth undulations.

The taxi. There was no sign of life.

'Let's take a look at it,' she said to Matthias. 'There might be something useful in it.'

Food, she meant. Water.

Acelet put them down next to it, and Eleanor ran over, hauling on the door handle. It was burning to the touch, but swung open with a screech. A blast of hot air hit her like a wall.

Empty. Leather seats smelling musty, sweltering in the heat. A few sweet papers on the floor, sand clogging round the pedals. There was still a key in the ignition.

She turned it. A splutter, a painful grating noise, and then silence.

'What is it? Is it broken?' Matthias was standing beside the car.

She sat back in the seat against the burning leather. 'Damn cars. They always do this. It's out of petrol.'

She opened the glove compartment. A bag of chocolate eclair toffees, sticky with heat. 'Wow, a find, Matthias! Sweeties!'

'Not much use to us without water,' he said. 'Shall we move on? Blythe may have supplies.'

'Probably not enough for us too, though.' She was silent for a moment, sitting familiarly behind the driving wheel.

'Matthias, who were those people? The man with all those blond curls, that girl? The ones who turned up in a pub in London and brought me here.'

'Ah, yes. Imbert Cupere and Edine Malreaux. Clever, aren't they?'

'That's not what I meant. Are they Cavers?'

'No.' He was concealing things again. She became angry. 'Matthias, you *owe* me an explanation. Who are they?'

He sighed. 'All right. Imbert is advisor and counsellor to the Emperor Xanthon. He trained under Lefevre at the Peraldonian College. And when Xanthon decided to set up the Seventh Rite again, to bring you back, he insisted that I work with Imbert. I was not entirely trusted, unlike Imbert.'

'Where did you train?'

'On Peraldon. With Lefevre, and Imbert, and Blaise, Thibaud, Aylmer . . . We all did, all the Mages.'

'What about Edine?'

'She is not a qualified Mage, and can never be one, because she is a woman. Women are of course barred from the Mages' College, although they can contribute useful skills – '

'Matthias, just a minute. I don't believe this. Your people worship Astret, a woman. Your religion depends on female priests. The Sun Emperor and Moon Empress have equal power. Are you seriously saying that women are barred from *everything* to do with magic?'

He shrugged. 'It is forbidden by that very religion. The Cabbala – the secret traditions known only to Mages and priests – is very clear on this.'

'*Why?*'

He paused before answering. 'Men and women – are different. At essence, they will never understand each other. Our life reflects this, the rigid division – '

'Biology as destiny. I don't think it's as simple as that, Matthias, it's not clear-cut. Individuals are always going to be a mix of masculine and feminine elements. Just think, men can be intuitive, women aggressive. Women become scientists and men nurses: no one has to be confined in any one role.'

'Our world is dominated by a Sun God and a Moon Goddess. There has never been any possibility that the two poles can blend together.'

'I think you're missing the point. Male and female together, loving each other, can create something that goes beyond rigid divisions. We are part of each other. We need one another, in every way, everywhere . . .'

'Perhaps. You may be right. No doubt things are different in your world. There may be better ways of organising things. I'm not trying to justify it, it's just how it is.' He was content to let it rest there.

'Edine is Imbert's constant companion, and he has taught her much. Edine's particular skill is one of flexibility. She practises the arts of disguise, of camouflage. She and Imbert make a formidable team, don't you think?'

'What do you mean?'

'Well, in your world, did they stand out as strangers? Or did they seem just ordinary, at home there?'

'Yes . . . yes, they did.' Laughing in a pub, driving through traffic jams, swearing when the lights changed. 'So it was a joint project, setting up the Rite. You and Imbert, with Edine as skivvy.'

He passed over this. 'It certainly needed more than one Mage to direct the Rite, and the Emperor didn't trust the Mages aligned to Astret. Imbert was the most powerful of his own Mages. And even so, it wasn't easy. I had thought the Synchronicity of finding your world would be too difficult, impossible, in fact –'

'That's what you told me.'

'It's what I believed at the time. But Imbert has areas of knowledge unknown to me, and I – I found that I had access to unusual powers when the Benu was released. It was as if that one act had opened up a whole series of potential significances. It was not easy,' he repeated, 'but it was possible to find you. We worked together, Imbert, Edine and I, to discover how to reach you. On the instructions of the Emperor.'

'How did the Fosca King become involved in all this?' Her voice was becoming hard again. So many plans, so many conflicting hopes all hanging on her return. She didn't understand the bond with the creature that lived in the centre of the Palace of Blood.

'The Fosca King, you must remember, is the incarnation of the Great Mage and High Priest to the Sun, Lefevre. He – it – wanted to ingratiate itself with Lycias. It hoped to please the Sun God, to win for itself a place of favour once more.'

She sat silently for a moment, remembering that monstrous

flower, obsessively following the sun across the heavens. In
love, yearning, wanting.

She knew all about that.

Oh, Lukas. A deep hollow pain within her. When will I
see you again?

It was far too hot in the car, even with the windows open.
She got out, not looking at Matthias.

'Come on,' she said. 'Let's go and find Phin and get this
over with.' She turned back to the Arrarat, standing patiently
on the sand, the baby in the shadow of its wing.

She picked the baby up and held it briefly against her
shoulder. Cool waves of comfort flowed from it. There were
tears in her eyes once more. It was a relief to drop her face
against Coron's soft head, to enfold arms round someone
loving and trusting.

There was little enough love and trust here.

The tears helped. And the flight on the Arrarat hawk.

The baby was growing in ways unknown to the world. For
the moment it was content to exist in the confines of a weak,
soft body. It enjoyed the feel of protective arms, the sound
of a heart beating, voices talking over its head. Sometimes
it was puzzled by the anger and hurt in the voices around
it. It abhorred all violence.

It would have nothing to do with distortion. With untruths,
or perverted magic. It was beginning to wonder about the
nature of its Father. As yet, of course, it could only love and
delight in that ultimate glory of light and fire.

But when tears fell on its head, it began to know something
else. Compassion. It remembered the healing of water. The
sound of its mother's voice, soft as rain. The movement of
water over the skin, the rhythm of waves. The movement
of tides, Moon-given, Moon-inspired. Its mother was not
negligible, or forgotten.

And when it flew high over the desert on the back of a great
hawk, it began to know power.

To fly was to live. To soar high over the world was the
essence. It delighted, dancing further through the dimensions
with every beat of the wings, along paths known and
unknown to its Father. The baby thrilled through the air,
breathless with astonishment.

That night, while Eleanor and Matthias slept wearily on the sand next to the hawk, hungry, thirsty, lonely and cold, it decided that the time was right.

Phinian Blythe reached Smintha at dusk. His vision was clouded both with shadows and with weakness. He had stopped trying to eat days ago, thinking it might be a way out. But the Children frolicked around him, lending him their own febrile energy. They would move his limbs, forcing him to restless action, while he had any awareness at all.

From the top of a dune he looked down on the city. The long shadows of evening lay in bands over the grid pattern of suburban roads. The dark pools glimmered faintly in the diminishing light. He saw the ruined buildings lining several of the central avenues, but failed to recognise the path of the Storm-bearer. He had no thoughts to spare for anyone else.

Thurstan was now trailing him at a distance of some miles. Gradually the shadows had worn Thurstan down, and he had dropped further and further behind. Blythe did not mind. It was a relief to shudder unobserved.

He could not stand this much longer. His mind was beginning to retreat into the lost labyrinths of madness. He forgot who he was and where he was going most of the time now. He remembered something about a storm, and a child, but it was clouded by horrors and soon that too, he knew, would fade into the web of nightmare about him.

He found himself stumbling down the side of the dune towards the city, slipping sometimes on the still hot sand. Thurstan would follow his tracks until he stopped. They would exchange a few words, and Thurstan would leave food and water out for him before moving away to settle for the night.

He passed along the quiet road lined with empty houses, not bothering to explore. There would be no comfort for him there. Though he supposed Thurstan might be glad of a bed, a chair.

The night fell with chilling rapidity. Usually he had halted by this stage, attempting to sleep for a while. Sometimes it worked. But not now. He could envisage no welcome oblivion in Lycias's city. He should stop and give Thurstan a chance to catch up with him. Exchange a few words, reassure him that he was still surviving.

He couldn't face it. He could give no such reassurance that night.

Karis's face was telling him farewell, making him live again and again the pain of losing her. He wished he had never loved her, that he had never known her, that she had never been born. He watched, yet again, as worms crawled from her eyes, filth from her lips, as she leant to kiss him.

He walked on. It was a long way to the centre of the city and it was completely dark now. The streets became more narrow, turning and winding between the tall buildings as he left the residential areas.

Marial was crying just behind his shoulders, begging him to wait. It was always thus; the agonised cries, the tug of cold fingers at his hair, his clothes, tearing at his flesh, pulling him back, clutching, wailing.

He wished that he had turned back, that he had waited for Marial. Then he too would have died, and he would not be here now.

Empty eyes drew him onwards. Idas was waiting to swallow his soul, to rake with agony a mind already dizzy with horrors. He wished that it had happened, long ago, before he had left Peraldon. He wished that he had been stripped of humanity, emptied of warmth, before he had set out on that quest, so dreadful, so futile.

Anything would be better than this, anything at all.

The narrow street abruptly opened out into a large arena surrounded by a ring of colonnades. Although there were stars clear and bright far away, he did not look up. He was spared the sight of Lycias's face gazing down over the city.

He was walking onwards, blindly, uncaring, out across the wide stretch of stone. As he moved, weighted by shadows, it seemed that the circumference of the arena was blurred, lost. As if he might walk forever over hard stones, through wide-flung spaces shrouded by the dark.

His step faltered as his strength failed. He stumbled and then fell to his knees, his head bent, his hands hanging loose at his side. He could go no further.

There was no need.

A golden Arrarat hawk glided down to settle by the Temple gates. Lost in shadows, Blythe did not notice.

The rider slid to the ground. As he touched the mosaic

floor, there was the faintest sound of bells. Blythe did not hear them, his heart in hiding.

Then silence. Deep quiet, flecked by stars.

Phinian . . .

Such a soft voice, sounding in his soul. It was calm with the healing of water. But as Blythe dragged his eyes upwards, the golden Arrarat suddenly spread its wings, rearing up behind the slim figure standing there.

Angel-like, he was framed by golden wings, defined by the power of flight.

This is enough, said the silent voice, but Blythe could not see clearly who it was. There was a face, but all he knew was that dark eyes were frowning. The wings of the hawk folded behind the child, the bird gentled once more.

The figure raised small hands, quiet and graceful, fingers spread wide. The shadows flinched, flickering around Blythe's shoulders as if preparing for flight.

Blythe looked into dark eyes. The shadows had left him once before, but only to mutilate and murder.

This was different.

Phinian . . . shall I take them from you? Shall I carry them for you? The words grew from silence, deep with understanding.

He was weeping. He could not speak.

This was a child, an innocent child. Black hair and black eyes, living in golden, beautiful light. Wide eyes, a gentle voice. Open hands, offering peace. An offer of perfection, made in perfect love.

To be wreathed in shadows? Hung round with horrors? Stained with evil and agony?

'They are not yours to bear,' he said at last. There was something of him left, after all.

Nor yours now, replied the child and, as Blythe watched, the dark shapes at the ends of his fingers changed into ravens and lifted, flying away through the black night.

There were no words. Nothing he could say, no possible way to express it.

There was no need. He found himself falling, drifting through the air, light as a feather, free as a bird.

Long before he touched the cold stone, he was asleep.

Chapter Nine
Enchantment

At first she thought it was a mirage.

The cold and hunger had awakened her just before dawn. She stretched stiff, uncomfortable limbs and stood up, clutching the remains of Comyn's shirt together.

The baby was gone again, and the hawk. Was Coron riding Adila? A delightful thought this, but how could he? Surely he would not be strong enough to stay on the back of an Arrarat. But where were they?

Although she was no longer frightened for the baby, trusting its ability to survive, she felt suddenly bereft. What use are arms with no one to hold?

She wandered away from the dark shape made by Matthias, still huddled in sleep. They had travelled a long way from the Palace of Blood and the Desert Rose, covering distance much more quickly than the caravan.

They might almost be at Smintha, she thought, looking at the patterns of dunes around them. Smintha had been set amidst soft sand hills. She decided to climb to the top of the nearest one to see if there was any sign of the city, or of her missing companions.

The sun rose rapidly, burning through the icy air as she trudged up the side of the dune. By the time she reached the top she was beginning to feel warm, partly through exertion, partly because the strengthening rays of heat were beginning to break through.

In the west, towers sprang from mist.

They wavered and shimmered, and light sparkled between them, glinting, glistening.

She held her hand over her eyes, squinting against the

brightness, and watched the mist clear. It ought to be Smintha, but the shining made her wonder.

A city floated there. Its foundations were still lost in mist and it seemed as if it were all suspended above the surface of the desert. White towers and arches glinted palely in the bright air. Bridges were flung high in leaping parabola and, falling from them, water tumbled in shining cascades.

Water!

It was beautiful, but the water meant much more than that. Cool and rippling, ready for drinking, for bathing, for splashing. She had to get there, quickly. And as the thought formed, she saw the great golden hawk leap into the air from the city, sweeping through the air towards them. Adila, coming to take them to the city . . .

She ran back down the dune, slipping and sliding, just as the hawk alighted on the sand by their camp.

'Matthias, Matthias! There's the most amazing thing, quick, there's *water*!'

He was only just waking up, moving slowly, with difficulty, like she had. His hands went to his head, to the rough bandage, and then dropped again.

'What is it, Eleanor? What do you mean, water?'

'Over the dunes, in the west. A city, a whole city. It ought to be Smintha, but it can't be because it's built on water! It looks like it's floating or something. Oh, Matthias, I wish you could see!'

'So do I.' His voice was grim. 'I don't like to spoil anything, Eleanor, but you must surely have heard of mirages? I've rather lost track, but I'd have thought that Smintha would be miles away still, and there's no human habitation between there and the Kingdom of Blood. It has to be an illusion.'

'It's *not*! I know it's not! Quick, let's get Adila to take us there! Matthias, it's *magic*!'

'Some things at least are clear to me. There is no water in Smintha. And mirages are common in the desert.'

'Let's go and see!' She had him by the arm, dragging him over to the hawk. It was watching them quizzically, its head to one side. She could have sworn that it was laughing at them.

He hung back. 'Where's the baby?' he asked. 'Have you got him?' She felt his fury with his own condition.

'No, Adila will show you, Matthias, there's no need to worry. The baby will be in the city, you'll see!'

Where else would it be? How else to explain such an extraordinary transformation?

They soared high over the dunes towards the shining city, golden sand dry and arid beneath them.

He said nothing at first, and then she heard him laugh softly. 'Okay, Eleanor. You win. It's no mirage . . .'

Adila had shown him, she thought. He could see through Adila's eyes.

For pure pleasure, pure delight, the Arrarat hawk glided slowly over the city before putting them down. She saw the roads full of sparkling, rushing water. A river encircled the city boundaries. The city was not floating, but cut off from the desert by the impetuous moat of moving water.

Water from it overflowed though every street, every avenue and square. A gleaming wash of clear ripples covered all the ground, inches deep. Just as the glass panels on the roofs sparkled in the sunlight, so did each street and alley, square and terrace. She could see the pattern of mosaic tiles, cobblestones, marble pavements, herring-bone bricks through it.

And flashes of sudden, brilliant colour, darting along paths and empty roads.

Adila put them down by a fountain outside one of the larger buildings. It was a baroque construction of marble and brass, and water overflowed at every level, falling down over leaping dolphins and mermaids, running to join the streams and rivers pouring through the city.

Alight with laughter, she jumped down from Adila, pulling on Matthias's arm, dragging him along.

Cool water. To tread, to dance, to run and skip and leap on cool water after a month in the desert. As much as she could drink, as much as she wanted, and more. Enough to wash away misery and memory along with the dust and sand. She was singing, laughing, kicking up clouds of spray, delighting.

Matthias was sitting at the edge of the fountain, listening to her, his hands upturned, catching at the soft falls of water around him. He had not foreseen this, did not understand its significance. Only gradually did he realise that there was someone else there watching them. His head turned, up towards the sun, and the man standing there.

'Hello, Matthias.' A light hand on his shoulder, a familiar voice.

'Thurstan.' He sighed in relief. For a moment he held his hand over the other's. The questions could come later.

Eleanor had seen him too. She came towards them, kicking up rainbow sprays. 'Where's Phin? Is he here too?'

'And of course it's a great pleasure to meet you again, Eleanor Knight. It's been a long time.'

She had always found him difficult. But he was smiling, so she forgot her momentary irritation. 'Sorry,' she said. 'But – is Phin with you?'

He shrugged. 'Somewhere here, I think. We – rather lost touch.'

'I'll go and look . . .' And before they could stop her, she was off, running along the cool, bright-threaded streams.

It *was* Smintha. She recognised the pattern of streets, the shapes of the buildings. A tired, deserted city, eaten away by sand and heat, metamorphosed into a playground for fishes.

It was because of Coron, it had to be. No one else would be capable of such a miracle. He would be here somewhere, living in rainbow showers, catching at the jewelled fishes. But extraordinary though the child was, Eleanor was not looking for him now. She wanted only to find Phin.

She knew where he would be. She was looking for the Temple of Lycias, with its vast, colonnaded arena. The well where she had first met Comyn and Timon.

The memory had lost its sting. This was a place of transformation, of renewal. Rebirth. No one could come to harm here.

In the end she found it, drawn by a subtle, water-borne scent.

The arena was a field of lilies. Creamy white, pale pink, gentle gold, deep green circular leaves spread generously over its surface. A dragonfly hovered overhead.

She began to walk through lilies, through water. Until she found him.

He was sitting on the steps at the edge of the lotus field, holding out his hand to the fishes, idly waving it through the water. They were bobbing curiously at it, tentative, but not frightened.

She stood still for a moment, watching the play of reflected light on dark circled eyes, severe lines, the deep scars on his unmoving left hand.

He became aware of her gaze and looked up.

His eyes, black as velvet, were quiet and welcoming. Free from shadows.

She ran the last few steps, and was caught in his arms, held tight in an embrace of warmth and relief. The look on his face and the sheer comfort of it made her cry again. It had been so long, and they had both travelled so far.

'So, where *is* Lukas?'

It was much later. Thurstan still had supplies from the journey. They shared dried meat and fruit, and it felt like a feast, washed down by sweet, sparkling water. They had talked most of the day, although there were many silences and not a little disbelief, mainly from Thurstan.

Eleanor hadn't been able to bear all of it, wandering away at one point when Matthias was describing what happened in the Palace of Blood. That event had no place here, in this paradise. She was intent on cutting it out of her life.

She found, back where they had left Adila, lying content in the hawk's shadow, the baby.

He was naked, little Coron. She picked him up, nuzzling the top of his head. He smelt so sweet, so cool and fresh.

She sat on the edge of the fountain with him, splashing water over his chubby legs, laughing as he squealed and banged his hands together.

'How did you do it, Coron?' she whispered, holding him close. 'How did you ride Adila and change the city?'

She looked into his eyes, and found laughter there, a memory that flickered and danced in mischief. He revealed glimpses of a multiplicity of secrets, an extraordinary character. He was beyond normal categorisation, she realised, privileged and enchanted by the knowledge.

For convenience, and to conserve energy, Coron would chose to remain for most of the time in this original guise, his primary incarnation. It held no monopoly, however. His essential nature was of one of childlike innocence, but Coron was confined to no particular age or degree of maturity. He could be anything, anyone. All things to all people . . .

And, as she learned this, Eleanor recognised the possibility of hope. With Coron to help, she might escape the threat of vengeance. For a moment the memory returned, the green eyes flashing, the cold voice mocking: I have only just begun . . .

But the baby was laughing again, wriggling free, reaching out to catch the bubbles in the sparkling cascade.

She watched him, and the sound of his laughter made her smile once more. This was a time of extraordinary privilege for her. She would never forget it.

When at last she returned to the others, they had moved on. Phin was asking after Lukas.

'Astrella took him north, a long way to the north . . .'

Matthias was leaning back against a wall, in shadow.

'Why?' The obvious question, but one she had not asked before. 'Do you know, Matthias?' She was sitting next to Phin, the baby on her lap, almost unable to believe her extraordinary good fortune.

To be in a sparkling paradise with old friends, with Phin and the baby, talking about going to find Lukas. And yet Matthias was still concealing things. She could see that he didn't want to tell them anything more.

He spoke unwillingly. 'I think that the Lady Astret has some role in mind for Lukas . . .'

'Better that he should have died, then,' said Blythe, almost under his breath. But Eleanor heard him.

'What do you mean?' She swung round to stare at him.

'You know perfectly well, Eleanor. Better than most. It's not much fun acting out divine schemes, is it?'

She opened her mouth to agree, but then fell silent.

'Not fun, no. But I don't know . . .' she said slowly. 'It feels as if I were hardly alive before coming here. At least this is real.'

Matthias's blind face was turned away and she did not see the pain written plain there. Phin was still watching her, frowning.

'And there's Coron, too. He can work miracles, even if he

is Lycias's son. How else do you think Smintha has become a paradise? It was surely Coron who lifted Phin's shadows, no one else has that kind of power. He just – changes everything, everywhere. Who knows what else he might do? How can we know that everything is going to go wrong?'

Thurstan stood up, holding out a hand to her. 'One thing I have learnt during a somewhat stormy acquaintance with you, Eleanor, is that you have your own defences. And there's no point in worrying about the future, is there? There's nothing we can do about it, after all.'

Matthias moved uncontrollably, and Eleanor looked at him. 'What do you know, Matthias? What's wrong?'

'Don't – be too optimistic, Eleanor. It's all very well, hope, when we're resting in the child's divine playground. It even seems reasonable.

'But this is *not* reality, however it may feel. Fish don't swim in the streets of desert cities. It's not really like this. And it won't last – '

'The future, Matthias? What are you seeing?' Blythe spoke quietly, prompted by water-borne intuitions.

'Nothing clearly. Nothing precisely. I can't tell you anything, don't ask me . . .' He was sweating, his hands clenched.

Eleanor turned away, looking out over the sunset-stained water. Matthias was lying, and she knew it. He had knowledge of the future, knowledge he was not willing to discuss.

But Thurstan was right. She did have her own defences, and one of the most useful of them was the ability to put aside uncomfortable thoughts. If Matthias saw horrors ahead of them, she didn't want to know about them. She was not going to be a victim this time, anyway. Neither would she accept any predestined role, no matter what Matthias's nightmares were. Holding the baby, she felt sure that everything would be all right.

Thurstan smiled, shrugging. 'So, perhaps we should consider what to do next. I for one would like to return to Cliokest and see how they're getting on with the Well.'

'Let's go north! Thurstan, come with us!' Eleanor was being generous, good humour overflowing to embrace even the equivocal Thurstan. He too was in a better temper than she had ever known before, his gold hair gleaming in the sun, his skin bronzed, eyes flashing blue and clear in the bright light.

She turned to Matthias for support but he had moved away without her noticing, slowly following the stream that led through to the water-lily square. Here his blindness was not the disability she had begun to expect. It was as if running water lent its own clarity to the people who lived within the fast-flowing moat.

'I think Thurstan should indeed go back to Cliokest,' said Blythe. 'He's been a splendid nursemaid, and I don't know what I would have done without him . . .' A quick glance which spoke of a debt too great to mention easily. 'God knows what they'll be up to back at the Citadel. At each other's throats, I shouldn't wonder.'

It was not a joke. They were all aware of the difficulty of reconciling Cavers and Peraldonians. The Jerenites held a unique role in that conflict, aligned neither to Sun nor Moon.

'And I too would be glad to see Lukas again.' Blythe smiled at Eleanor. 'I could help carry the baby.'

And this was not a joke either, for if he was grateful to Thurstan, what he felt for the child was of a different order.

So it was agreed. Thurstan would return to Cliokest and the others would travel north.

They stayed that night in the enchanted place that the child had created for them, and slept, soothed by the murmur of softly flowing water.

Chapter Ten
Fosca

Towards dawn, while the others slept, Phinian Blythe met the child again. Now that he was able to sleep free from torment, it was a joy to lie awake, lulled by cascades of water, watching the unclouded stars.

He had chosen to rest some way from the others, in a small paved garden behind one of the grand houses. He was not yet entirely accustomed to the company of friends, and it was in a curious way a relief to be alone.

Water was flowing over the edge of an oval pool and fish danced freely over marble and old stone. Statues of Lycias, of warriors and children and beautiful maidens, gleamed palely in the soft moonlight.

He sat on a stone bench against the wall, content simply to observe the play of silver light on rippling water, over smooth stone.

One of the statues moved. A child crossed the running streams of water, holding out his arms to Blythe.

Coron had been lost that day. The transformed city was beautiful, and he wandered through the maze of streets shot through with moon-silver fish. But there were other layers of reality, other paths he could take. The multi-dimensioned realms beckoned, where his Father and others waited.

He was so young, so newly awakened to power, that he did not know what to do, or where his allegiance lay.

He came to Blythe as a small naked boy, brown-skinned, ebony-haired, and Blythe took him in his arms, stroking back the glossy curls, delighting in this trust.

'What shall I do? What can I do?'

His eyes were no longer quite innocent. Understanding was beginning to exact a price. Knowledge of shadows could not lightly be brushed away.

'There is so much grief . . .'

Blythe almost wept for the child. Lost innocence should not be the price of the lifting of shadows.

And yet Coron had the power to put things right, to heal and save. Where should he begin? With such a Father, such a birth. Ripped from the burning body of his mother by the Lord of Flames, the Sun King.

It would be easy for this child to go wrong. Perhaps Blythe, childless, wifeless, should try to help Coron. As Coron had saved him. It would be a delight to care for this child. Perhaps that was what he should do . . .

But then he remembered someone with a greater claim than his own.

'The Storm-bearer – Haddon.' He looked into the deep, dark eyes, breathing the words slowly, fearfully. 'The Storm-bearer needs healing. And he loved your mother; he would know what to do.'

Coron stared at him, wide-eyed. Blythe tried to explain.

'He brought me hope when there was none. Like you, he wanted to help. But your Father. . . It will not be easy.' The words were inadequate.

The child nodded, satisfied. He wriggled down from Blythe's lap and started to hum, a light gentle noise.

All around the water slowly stopped rushing, tumbling, and subsided to a trickle. The wells stopped overflowing, the river stopped running. Coron looked back at him for a moment and then nodded.

With the movement he disappeared.

And Blythe was left in the ordinary, desert-bound city of Smintha, and the only water falling was salt, over his face.

Matthias was woken by the sudden silence. In a moment of black despair, a despair he could not now afford to allow himself, he realised that the enchantment had gone. That Coron had left.

They were alone once more. Under the sun of Lycias, enduring the pattern of revenge. Thurstan would return to Cliokest, and perhaps things might be better there. But

Eleanor was frivolous with foolish hope, Blythe drained and
exhausted. Himself weighted by guilt, locked in a blindness
illuminated only by appalling glimpses of the future.

As he sat under the arches of one of the colonnades round
the mosaic arena, cold and uncomfortable in the dark hour
before dawn, a dream hovered once more on the edge of his
understanding.

She had waited outside the city while the water flowed, not
daring to intrude. But now that the child had left, Nerissa
was free to offer the one small comfort she possessed.

It was an item of knowledge outside the weight of future
events. A subtle pointer to a different path.

Underground, they would be beyond Sun and Moon.

Underground they would be in a different realm, and
different priorities would prevail. They might even find a way
to halt the marriage . . .

He spoke in the end, acknowledging her presence.

'So, you see it too, do you, Nerissa? Even death offers no
relief from that particular vision . . .'

No relief, no. But she had done her best, had faithfully
given what little hope she possessed. And in so doing, she
faded away into the last of the water, drifting in a gentle
stream back into the river as it subsided back into the sand.

Matthias was alone.

They didn't believe him at first.

Later that morning, Thurstan had come running from the
Temple of Lycias, shouting of an extraordinary find.

A great chasm, beneath the arena itself, mirroring the
circular shape above. There were two staircases there, he said,
spiral stairs going in opposite directions. They followed the
contour of curving walls. It seemed bottomless, he heard
nothing when he dropped a stone into it. It reminded him,
bizarrely, of Sharrak's Well.

But if there were stairs, they had to lead somewhere.

He had started loading the two horses with the remaining
supplies. They had decided together that Thurstan should
take one back to Cliokest, and the others could use a
combination of horse, foot and Arrarat in their trek
northwards.

There was some food left but not much. Thurstan decided

to augment it with things from the city. He found flour, rice, dried fruit and meat. And curiosity had sent him to the Temple of Lycias at the end of the mosaic arena.

There were no water-lilies now, no bright coloured fish flashing over fragments of stone. The mosaic surface showed merely a flat pattern of pale golden flowers set in dark foliage. Curiously lifeless, dull and formal. The sand was beginning to blow in again, a light film of grains skidding over the newly washed stone and marble.

No one was looking forward to a journey of many hundreds of miles through desert and other unknown regions. But the alternative, down one of those endless staircases to the underground passages Matthias assured them existed, was far worse.

'It's a hell of a risk, Matthias.' Thurstan glanced at him. They were all together in the arena, Eleanor having refused point-blank to enter the Temple. 'It's bound to be more difficult. Just think. No one knows how far the passages run, if they exist at all. You'll get lost. There'll be rockfalls, dead ends . . .'

'Have you thought what we might meet down there?' Eleanor spoke warily. 'I mean, those crocodile creatures go underground, don't they? And – well, it does sound very like Sharrak's Well. What if other Parid live there too?'

She did not voice the real reason for dreading the underground world. Herself, twined round in flowers, burning to ash. Her confidence had been badly shaken by the disappearance of the baby. 'I'd rather see where we're going.'

'I don't think you – any of you – understand what the alternatives are.' Matthias deliberately kept his voice steady and reasonable. He could sense the dread in Eleanor's voice, but not the reason for it. He was inclined to dismiss it. She had suffered such traumas recently, it was not surprising that she should be nervous and unstable.

'It's not just a question of light and dark. Overground we will be prey to every disaster the Sun King can throw at us. The dark angels, wraiths, fire, disease and drought. The Desert Rose should by no means be discounted either. Weard's caravan is on the move, somewhere between here and the north, and will be looking for us. And I know, I absolutely know, that we have no chance of getting to Lukas travelling overground.'

'How do you know?' Thurstan said.

'The future I see, if we travel overground, reveals a useless journey, beset with dangers and threat. Weard will find us, lives will be lost . . .' This was pure invention, of course. He only saw pictures of what was going to happen, not the alternatives. He saw them all underground, a sequence of images that made him shudder.

He could not tell them. Especially not Eleanor, because he needed her to be strong, not despairing, and she was close enough to the edge as it was.

'How do you know?' Thurstan repeated coldly and clearly, ignoring Matthias's unwillingness.

'It goes with blindness, didn't you know?' His voice was acid and unpleasant even to his own ears. 'Blaise saw the future sometimes. Nerissa too, just before she died. I can't help it if you don't believe me, but it's true all the same, like it or not.'

'Can we clarify this, Matthias?' Blythe spoke calmly. 'Do you genuinely think we should go underground because it is the best way of travelling, or are you advocating that route because that is what you see happening?'

'All right. We're going underground because that's what happens. That's where we go, that's what we do. Do you want to be forced into it?'

'What happens down there? You have to tell us, Matthias.' Thurstan spoke clearly.

'I don't know. Really. All I know is that our route lies that way . . . The future I see arises from the world as controlled by Sun and Moon. Different conditions, different modes of existence obtain when Sun and Moon are no longer experienced.'

Below ground, he thought, I may not have to know what will happen. I might be free of this burden, and there might even be a chance . . .

A chance that the delay in finding Blythe would not cost them too dear.

They were still arguing, still trying to understand, when Matthias suddenly shouted. 'There's no time! Now! Fosca!'

As prophecy, it might more usefully have come a little earlier.

For a moment they all stared up into the burning sky, the sun glaring back at them. Then, without any further warning, dark swinging shadows blotted the hard, gold disk. The air whistled under the strength of vast, leathery wings, and the clear air began to stink.

A razor-sharp claw scythed through the air, narrowly missing Eleanor's face as she was pushed aside by Blythe. He grabbed her wrist, pulling her to the side of the arena.

Thurstan had Matthias by the arm, pushing him towards the nearest cover, the Temple. The two horses were beginning to rear and stamp in panic.

Matthias was inside the Temple doors, but the three winged creatures were circling the air over the arena, and Eleanor and Blythe were at its further side.

Thurstan ran for the horses, leaping the reins, but a long, hooked tentacle swept down from above, just beyond his eyes, ripping into the horse's neck.

The hook wedged in flesh, half lifting the agonised animal from the ground, before it tore itself free in a fountain of blood. Thurstan rolled in the dust, only just avoiding the threshing hooves, trying to reach the weapons still tied to the horse's back.

It was almost impossible. The horse had stopped moving, expiring on the red-stained mosaic, and the swords were almost within his reach, but the Fosca was wheeling round, the jagged claws and hooks tearing through the air towards him.

'Run!' Blythe was shouting to Eleanor. 'Now, quickly! Go to Matthias!'

He pushed her out along the colonnade, hardly waiting to see whether she was doing as he said. Then out into the arena where Thurstan had a sword free, braced against the creatures wheeling above.

One of them darted at Blythe as he ran, and he felt a claw rake across his back, another swinging towards his face. He put up his useless left hand, and blocked the swinging claw, the force of it jarring all along his arm.

Pale lidless eyes gleamed at him. Rotting rags of skin hung like petals round the grey, avid face. A supra-audible squeal

split the air as he reached Thurstan and grasped the other
sword.

The Fosca were putting their riders down.

'Matthias! Can't you do something?' Eleanor had reached
him, was clasping his arm, shouting at the blind face turned
towards the centre of the fight.

'How brave are you, Eleanor?'

'Oh, Christ, no!'

'You can do it,' he said, meaning, you will do it.

He knew what would happen here, too. And so he let her
run out into the arena again, and she shouted, over and over,
into the stench of blood and the swirl of violence, 'Fosca!
Fosca!'

They turned, briefly distracted by the high thin sound, and
began to weave across the mosaic floor towards her.

It was always the way. Scapegoat again, and no Moon to
help.

Blythe and Thurstan were faster. Racing round the
colonnades, abandoning the last horse, they cannoned into
her, hustling her into the Temple, out of the reach of hooks
and claws.

The Fosca riders were not far behind, following with that
half dancing, uneven gait. It made no difference: she would
not go down those stairs again. Eleanor hung back, furious
with panic.

'Not down there!'

They were at one of the bolted doors by the altar.

'Come on!' Thurstan had her by the arm, dragging her
towards the door.

Phin and Matthias were already out of sight. She pulled
free of his grip, starting to run back out to the Temple.

She saw a hooked limb sweep round the corner, the knife
tentacle reaching and stabbing, and would have preferred it,
would have fallen on it, rather that go down those stairs again.

'Shit!' Thurstan's hand on her shoulder, a fist swinging,
and then she knew no more.

They drew the bolt behind them and started down. Matthias
said there was no rush. The Fosca riders, ungainly as they
were on foot, would not follow them into this place. In pitch-
black darkness, Matthias led the way. Thurstan was carrying

Eleanor, Blythe their swords. They had nothing else.

At first they could see nothing at all. It was a nightmare descent. Their footsteps echoed in a vast space, their voices were dwarfed by emptiness. They kept close to the outer wall, feeling cautiously with their hands the contour of the dry stone.

'There's something here – a door . . .' Matthias's voice from lower down. They paused on the stairs as he wrestled with the catch. It swung open, and immediately the darkness lifted. A strange, drab light crept into the well from the empty corridor beyond the door.

They looked around. The chasm was as wide as the combined area of the Temple of Lycias and the mosaic arena above. A wide, darkening space stretched below them as far as they could see and beyond.

No one wanted to look into the chasm for long. The stairs they stood on were made of slabs of dull black stone, curving through a wide, shallow arc. They were supported by elaborate curls of wrought iron, which rose on each side to form banisters. As their eyes became accustomed to this different light, they could see another staircase winding down the other side of the chasm. Further below them they saw the two staircases cross, but at that point the curls of wrought iron rose up to enclose each staircase completely. There was no possible way to move from one to the other. Indeed, there seemed to be no possible reason to do so. The staircases were identical. Doors led onto them at various points below them. They were quite deserted.

Thurstan looked along the corridor and saw a featureless passageway. 'Oh well,' he said. 'If we get tired of going down, we can always take a chance on one of the doors.' It was a relief to think that they could get off the staircase at any point.

'I'd still rather get further from the surface,' said Matthias. 'Let's continue down.'

It was at this point that Eleanor recovered consciousness, dazed and querulous. When she realised where they were, Thurstan had to threaten violence again to stop her returning to the surface.

Phin took her hand, pulling her close. She was shaking continuously. He asked her why.

'When I was here before, I only came part of the way down

these stairs – not far, but . . . Oh, Phin, this is a terrible place!'

'Not necessarily.' Matthias had overheard.

'What about the Parid?' Blythe asked him. 'They prefer to live underground, I know. Failed Gods can't compete with the real thing, after all. Underground or underwater, they're beyond the reach of Sun or Moon. But they're still dangerous . . . All right for Mages with staffs and spells. But, with all due respect, Matthias, we're not going to be much good against one now.'

'They're far away.' He spoke distantly, bleakly. Lies now. They would multiply underground, the lies and deceptions. It was why the Parid always preferred the Underworld, Phin was right. Lacking either the brilliance of the sun or the clarity of the moon, it would be easy to blur the truth here. He was beginning to lie already. 'Whatever we meet down here, it won't be Sharrak.' His voice was certain and sure; they would probably believe him.

Thurstan was stubborn. 'There's more than one Parid.'

Matthias shrugged. 'There's more than one way for a Mage to operate. I don't have to depend on a piece of twisted wood.' But it helps, he thought, it helps. What I would give for a spiral staff now . . .

The steps were wide and even, smooth, slightly dusty. They all kept close together and spoke rarely. The atmosphere was oppressive, hot and stuffy.

Eleanor's jaw ached where Thurstan had hit her. He hadn't apologised. And her legs were unsteady. True, going up would be worse, but she knew this descent was a terrible mistake. She remembered Sharrak's Well only too clearly, and the appalling vision that had almost deprived her of hope when she fell . . . She was out of breath, sweating with exertion and apprehension.

Phin's presence at her side was some comfort. It was the only thing keeping her from running back up again. He moved smoothly, unworried and confident. She had forgotten his dogged endurance. He had survived the shadows, and kept going. Nightmares or strange moments of prevision would not cripple him . . .

Although it was hot and airless their voices echoed in the grey light. The noises they made, their steps and speed, slowly reverberated across wide distances. The space around was immense. The curve of the staircase was gentle, the tread of the steps shallow.

'How much further?' she asked Matthias. They all still habitually asked Matthias to explain everything.

'I've no idea.' He seemed unworried. 'But have you noticed that the air is becoming fresher? There must be some source of ventilation down here. Perhaps other doors are open . . .'

He was right. It was still hot, a humid, enervating heat, but the air was by no means stagnant.

Another twenty minutes' weary descent and then Matthias stopped. 'There – can you smell anything?'

They paused on the stairs. It was only faint, the lightest scent of summer. Eleanor couldn't believe it.

'Cut grass,' she said, wondering. 'New-mown grass.'

It was completely unexpected, unfairly undermining her precarious control. It was almost enough to make her cry again. One of her favourite smells, recalling rounders at school, making daisy chains out at fourth deep; strawberries for tea, tennis shoes grazed with green.

'No, it's water, salt water. Fishing at Peraldon . . .' Blythe remembered boyhood days, a dog at his side, the friend who had shared everything. Long gone, almost forgotten.

'Candles,' said Thurstan. 'Grease-paint. Gas lamps at the old theatre – before the Stasis, you remember, Matthias – the theatre at Sarant. Those dancing girls!'

Matthias was silent. To him, the scent was musky. The smell of Arrarat Isle, its huge fire burning below, and the Arrarat hawks winging in lazy spirals through the air. He was waiting at the cave edge to be chosen.

Waiting for Asta to alight next to him and lay her quiet, gentle head against his shoulder.

He murmured, almost against his will, 'Oh, Asta . . .'

For a moment they were all caught off-guard.

And when the stairs began to dissolve beneath their feet, wavering, losing solidity like melting jelly, they were too far apart to catch hold of each other.

A scream from Eleanor, a curse from Thurstan, as they fell, down into the empty depths.

Chapter Eleven
Promises

'You're drinking too much.'

'It's nothing to do with you.'

A hand drifted across over Torold's hair, pushing back curls damp with sweat. The room was too hot, the fire roaring in the stone fireplace, built up with logs and dry branches.

Torold liked the heat. It was as if he were trying to create a world separate from the cold sea outside the Castle, from the cold resentment of the unemployed men in his city. Stifling, golden, glowing heat bounced off embroidered tapestries from deep pile rugs.

'It's everything to do with me. What am I without you? You are my soul, my centre, my only peace, my only pleasure.' Esmond's breath was sweet against his face, the lips soft and gentle on his skin.

'Oh hell, Esmond, what am I to do?' He leant back in his chair, looking up at the slim figure standing beside him.

It was a familiar refrain. But this time Esmond offered more than sympathy and physical comfort. He took the wine glass from Torold's hand and put it down on the table, out of reach.

'What is the problem, exactly?'

'You *know* what the problem is!' Torold snapped, his eye on the wine glass, avoiding the graceful figure standing at his side.

'It's nothing to do with Felicia.'

'Rubbish! Of course it's Felicia, or rather the lack of Felicia! What about Javon –?'

'The problem is that you have no heir.'

His voice was light and elegant, composed and graceful, cutting through the oppressive heat of the room.

Torold closed his eyes, dropping his head into his hands.
'I know . . .' His voice was muffled.

'Nor likely to have . . .'

'Not while I have you.' Torold reached out for the delicate
hand of his lover.

'I would not mind, you know. A marriage of convenience,
you could have. Keep the farce going long enough to beget
a child. I would wait –'

'I know, I know. Do you think I haven't considered it?
I nearly sent an ambassador to Chan six months ago. It
wouldn't work.' His voice was low, difficult to catch over
the crackle of the flames. 'I could not – bear – anyone else.
A woman!'

There was silence. The wind was whipping round the
Castle, the rain splattering against the windows, driving hard
against the glass. The heavy brocade curtains lifted slightly
as the loose-fitting windows rattled, and Torold kissed the
fine hand lying in his own clasp.

'Why are you so worried about having an heir? You won't
be here, after all, when the problem arises.' Esmond's voice
was still quiet, still reasonable.

'It contributes to the unrest in the city. Unsettles the
populace. Gawne says –'

'Gawne! There you have it!' Esmond had moved round,
was sitting now on the carpet at Torold's knees, gazing at
him with those heavenly eyes, the delicate nose and sensual
lips. He was flushed with heat, and anger.

'There would be no unrest in the city – none that you could
not control – if the fishermen were allowed their trade.'

'But the wealth of Shelt depends on the Sea Lords' freedom
to use the sea as they wish. You know that!'

'But what are the Sea Lords to you? To me, even? What
is all this wealth worth if there is no peace? What good have
they ever done for *us*?'

They have kept me safe, thought Torold. Because of them,
I've shown Javon that I can rule a city. The Sea Lords have
given me a reason for staying in the north, the freedom to
let me pursue my own life, my own love, and Javon doesn't
know . . .

His eyes ran over the golden hair of his lover.

'Things have changed. You are worried now, not sleeping,

drinking too much.' Esmond was reading his thoughts, understanding his heart as so often before. 'Your peace has gone. Javon will find out soon enough when he gets no word from his daughter. The Sea Lords require too much from you, and from the people here.'

'So what do I do? What can I do?'

'Get rid of them!' Esmond was almost whispering now, moving closer to him, unable to resist looking over his shoulder. 'Overpower the Sea Lords. It shouldn't be too difficult. Your own troops, the rebels – that hawk . . .' He shuddered elaborately, but his eyes were gleaming with excitement. '*They* are the ones with the power, the real power. There are rumours that the *eloish* –' He paused, but Torold did not take him up on it. 'To kidnap Felicia, to *keep* her; to use that hawk to abduct your hostage, that guard, what was his name?'

'Kester Robart . . .' Torold spoke absently, staring blankly into the flames

'Kester. . . They are led by a Mage, you know. Olwyn Mittelson, remember him?'

'I remember.'

'A powerful Mage. The Sea Lords have not been able even to find the rebels. What use are they? The rebels are holding Javon's *daughter*! Think what will happen when he discovers this!

'It's because of Olwyn Mittelson. Could Mittelson have greater, stranger, powers even than Gawne?'

The question hung in the overheated air. Torold moved his gaze away from the fire and looked at Esmond.

'What shall we do?' he said.

'A lovebird, a little bird of paradise, golden-haired, slim of limb and line . . .' Brilliant, heavy eyes of extraordinary intensity regarded Esmond coolly.

The man had either been drinking, or was reckless with something more than drink. . . Esmond looked uneasily from Rosco to Vere Holtby, the soldiers' minstrel.

It had taken courage to arrange this meeting. It had taken nerve to approach Holtby, for all his mild manner and plump figure. But Esmond had watched him before, had known his background, intrigued by something in the way he moved, some lilt in the music he played.

Preoccupied by people, by relationships, Esmond had noticed more in the Castle than anyone credited. The Sea Lords were wrapped in with magic, Torold in a haze of wine, the Guard in their duties. Esmond Crinnion was a courtier with no particular role, enjoying a unique and privileged position, free to move here and there. He had found in Vere Holtby a mystery of intriguing proportions.

It happened easily, so easily that Esmond suspected that they had been waiting for just such an approach.

Which, of course, they had.

There were three of them sitting round the table in an alcove of the Fish and Net. Vere Holtby he knew, of course. He also remembered Olwyn Mittelson from the days when he had been one of the Sea Lords and, more recently, by repute. The third man, the one who had introduced himself as Jolin Rosco, was a stranger.

And difficult. Eyes glittering, tongue acid, he brought a flush to Esmond's cheeks and set things off on quite the wrong foot.

He decided to ignore Rosco and concentrate instead on Olwyn Mittelson.

'I have a message,' he began, diffidently.

'From the noble Lord Torold, no doubt?' Still Rosco was mocking.

'Rosco.' Mittelson's voice was equable. Patient, even. 'Give it a rest. You agreed to this.'

'I don't have to like it, though.'

'You're not making things easy.'

'I'll leave it to you, then.' He pushed the chair away from the table, nodded to Holtby, and was on the point of pushing through the crowds to the door. He turned back. A curious smile on the long mouth. 'You were not hurt, I trust, in your experience of flight?'

'Was it your bloody hawk, then?' Esmond raised his chin, looking him straight in the eye.

'Yes, my bloody hawk.' There was a pause while they stared at each other. Then Rosco shrugged. He sighed, sitting down once more.

'All right, Olwyn, I'll behave. Get on with it.'

It took more than one meeting in the end and never once did Esmond see Felicia or her serving-maid. He had to take them on trust, just as they had to risk trusting him.

He had no idea whether it was wise or not. He only wanted his lover to sleep easy at night, resting his head quietly on Esmond's shoulder.

He liked the idea of Rosco, tossing and turning under the worries of state. Rosco, married to that pale little rag doll, duty bound to provide an heir for Shelt. Rosco, dealing with Gawne and Dederic and the rest of them, once their main sphere of influence was finished.

A fine nest of thorns that would be.

He smiled, and reported back to Torold.

The storms that hit Shelt that spring brought flooding and mudslip. Several houses in the shanty town were caught in an avalanche of liquid dirt washed down from the Castle gardens, and were crushed to matchsticks by the weight of it. The areas near the river became uninhabitable as the water level rose, flushing out the tramps and druggies, the thieves and the leprous. Rats began to swarm, even through the better parts of the city, deprived of their natural habitat by rising water.

One wild night, several of the fishermen's neglected boats were swept out of the harbour on the back of a raging wave, right out to sea before anyone knew what was happening. Their owners inspected the splintered remains the next day and shrugged. What use were they anyway?

The rain fell ceaselessly. It was like one of the worst periods of the Stasis, when monsoon conditions had prevailed for what seemed like years. As then, the storms were broken by wind, by thunder and lightning. The few plants that ventured into bud and bloom were pushed flat by the force of the gale, the young leaves stripped from bending trees. And in houses and shops, people raised their voices, irritated by the trivial, driven to fury by the unrest in the air.

Perhaps the Stasis was returning, they said. Perhaps the violence would start all over again, the continual warfare, the sieges and raids . . .

The resentment and anxiety in the city found expression in flaring aggression. A Castle guard was found dead one night, knifed in an alley, blood mingling with water in the rushing gutter.

On the instructions of Gawne, six fishermen were hanged. It was always the way, always the method. Let the punishment outweigh the crime. Never mind about innocence and guilt, scapegoats will do. Rosco was out every night, discussing tactics, attending meetings. In the deserted barns, on farms south of the city, the training classes were no longer merely for fun. Archery, sword-fighting, the use of dagger and cloak. All these meetings were illegal, all subject to discovery and betrayal.

There were many close escapes. The venues were invariably changed at the last minute, false information circulated, passwords and codes in constant use. And for Mittelson and the women, for Kester slowly recovering, the strain of always moving, always packing and drifting on was beginning to tell.

Felicia awoke screaming one night. In moments, Annis was at her side, arms wide and comforting.

'Oh, there, my lady, only a dream, nothing but a dream . . .' The useless words which fail even to comfort children. Felicia was sitting bolt upright in bed, her eyes wide and staring, hands making small fluttering movements as if trying to ward off something.

'Ah, no, no, no . . .' Her voice was high and wild, still in the dream.

The door banged suddenly, and Mittelson was there, carrying a lantern. Annis had drawn her hand back, ready for the light slap to wake Felicia, but Mittelson grasped her wrist, halting the action.

'No!' he hissed. 'Be quiet!'

Felicia was trembling, apparently listening to some unheard song.

She fell back on the pillows, suddenly released from the grip of nightmare.

Mittelson was standing over the bed, staring down at the girl with his strange, pale gaze. Annis took a step forward, looking at him with distrust.

His voice was quiet and compelling. 'Felicia, Lady Felicia, wake up.'

She stirred, and then her wide eyes opened once more, and this time she looked directly at them, her brow creased in bewilderment.

'Olwyn – you're here? Oh, I've had such a dream!'

'Draw it.' Mittelson put the pad from her bedside table into her hands. 'Draw it now, while it's still clear.'

She stared at him, still half asleep. Then, almost automatically, her pencil began to trace an outline on the paper.

A dragon with a curving head of spray, a thousand claws curving in a wave, a winding, sinuous body disappearing into a whirlpool.

'Yes . . .' breathed Mittelson. 'What happened, Felicia? What happened at the Marqun?'

She was staring at the picture under her hands as if mesmerised.

'They asked, Gawne asked, if Ladon would accept a bride, a human consort . . .' Her voice was so quiet that it was almost lost in the wind outside.

'I was their offering. A pledge of good faith, in return for – the continuation of their power. The gift of healing, of long life . . .' She looked at Mittelson, her face blank.

'And Ladon?' He was speaking gently, very gently, and yet Annis could see the excitement in those pale eyes, the anticipation of knowledge.

She shook her head. 'No, I can't, don't ask me –' All at once her hands were covering her face, and she was shuddering, soundlessly.

'Felicia! Tell me!' He was shouting, dragging her hands away from her eyes. 'Felicia, I must know! How can we fight, how can we get anywhere if we don't know?'

'It – tasted – me. Those mouths, those lips, like hands – running over me . . .' She began to retch, and Annis ran for a bowl.

She fled past Rosco, standing by the door. He had heard it all. Waiting until the girl was a little calmer, a little quieter, he spoke without any apparent emotion at all.

'Never mind, Felicia. You'll not be left for Ladon. Olwyn here and Our Lady Astret have something else in mind. You and I, dear Felicia, are fated for the gentle binding, the net of marriage, noble and inescapable.'

She looked up at him, and it was as if there were no one else in the room.

'Would that be so very terrible?' Her voice sounded strange in the sudden quiet.

'I – really – don't know at all.'

Watching her, Rosco hardly noticed that Mittelson had left the room.

'Would you, purely academically speaking of course, marry me, dear Felicia, if the occasion arose?'

'Unfair.' Her voice was cool, although it was not what she felt. 'There is no way of answering that question "academically", as you well know. Anything I say is a give-away.' You'll have to do better, was the unspoken criticism. 'Besides,' she added. 'I don't know who you are.'

He sat on the end of her bed, as far away as possible. He was looking straight out of the uncurtained window to the blister of rain distorting the glass.

His profile was severe, unsmiling. A straight nose, firm chin. Faint, complicated lines of laughter and anger around those bright eyes. Deeper lines between nose and mouth. Dark stubble beginning to show through. He should be more careful, she thought. There were spies everywhere.

'My real name is Lukas Marling. I was born far south of here, near the city of Peraldon, into a community of people who later became known as Cavers. On the other side of the Boundary, we tried to abide by the Lady's Rule, purely and simply. Without heresy. We fought to end the Stasis, so abhorred by Our Lady. We succeeded.'

A long pause. Then, 'I am not free, Felicia. I cannot love you.'

'Someone else?'

'She – is from another world, another dimension. I don't know if you can understand that. I'm not sure that I do, even. . . Her return here is out of the question. She was instrumental in breaking the Stasis, you see. The God is vengeful. She must never return.'

'So surely you are free?'

'She is alive. And there is always a chance . . .'

'A chance she'll come back?'

'I can only hope – and pray – that she never does. But she lives, and breathes, and exists, somewhere, somehow.'

Another long pause. He had turned his face away, and she could no longer see the soft fall of dark lashes against the cheek.

'I am not free, Felicia. But if this marriage between you

and me is the price of peace in Shelt, then I am prepared to go ahead with it. But you should at least know what you're taking on.'

She said nothing, pleating the sheet obsessively in trembling fingers. Her mind was a chaos of conflicting thoughts and emotions. And then she heard herself speak, as if from a far distance.

'I am prepared to take the chance, you know. That she does not return. I would marry you, though you are not free.'

She had said it, had given it all away, had laid herself open to more than Ladon had ever threatened.

He stood up, his face still in shadow, and took her hand from the sheet. His touch was icy cold, but steady, steady as iron, while she was still quivering, a constant tremor that had stayed with her since the dream.

He bent and brushed her hand with his lips. 'I hope, Felicia, you will have no reason to regret this.'

But the rain still hurled against the window, and suddenly it sprang open, slamming back against the wall, cold, bitter air swirling round the shadowy room.

He shut it, quietly, not pausing to look at the sea heaving beyond.

'Goodnight, Felicia. Sleep well.'

And he was gone, and she was left staring at the hand he had kissed.

And, by the side of the bed, a dragon named Ladon, sketched in pencil, living in more than nightmares.

Chapter Twelve
Dreaming

It was grass. Short cut, starred by only a few daisies. It was cool and dewy beneath her bare feet.

Eleanor was walking through a dark garden. There were no moon or stars and yet she could see her hands and feet, glowing palely in the twilight. All around her, empty air stretched away into nothing. There was only the grass under her feet, scenting her steps with sweetness, and the rhythm of her walking.

She was calm and at ease. She was so unworried about her friends that she might almost have forgotten their existence. They would be all right, she knew. Phin fishing at the ocean's edge. Thurstan in an old theatre. Matthias with his Ararat hawk once more.

These small scraps of knowledge had drifted into her mind with the scent of grass. She felt that she could walk forever over cool grass, secure in the knowledge of safety. Her friends were safe, and Lukas was alive.

She stopped. That thought changed everything. Her mind still glanced away from the horror of the last time she had accepted appearances. She had found herself making love to Lycias, thinking Lukas dead. How could she be so foolish as to believe this? Had she learnt nothing?

Don't believe what you see here. Don't assent. The Gods lie.

No Gods here. Neither Sun nor Moon nor laughing baby.

It made it worse, somehow. There was nothing solid on which to rely.

The scent of grass was artificially sweet. Cloying and too strong. She noticed, for the first time, that the grass beneath her feet did not go on forever; a line of dark trees, cypresses she thought, bordered its edge. A mist hung over the trees, sending silently drifting fingers towards them. The scent and appearance of grass all seemed to be emanating from the attenuated wisps of cloud.

Under her feet, the grass felt like plastic. She looked down. It had vanished. She was standing now on yellow flowers, pale and fragile. Their starry shapes filled a vast plain, edged only by the line of tall and ancient trees. The mist that came from behind the trees was spreading towards her, blanketing out the branches and flowers. There was no sound, and no possibility of sound.

This was a counterfeit world, and she would have nothing to do with it. She turned away from the clouds of darkness and began to run.

Phinian Blythe watched the waves break on the shore and doubted. It was the coastline outside Peraldon. He recognised the sweep of the bay, the shape of the headland far away. But there was no blue sky above, no city to his left, no context for this vision.

Instead, quiet air led away into darkness on all sides. He could not tell from where the light was coming. His hand glimmered at his side, the crest of white on the incoming waves bubbled and splashed.

A dog was nuzzling his hand.

Triss. Without thinking he stroked the smooth head, the silky ears.

He looked down, letting his hand drop. It looked and felt just like Triss. But he had lived with shadows for a long time, and knew what the differences were.

It was not reasonable that this should be Triss, who had died long ago. Just as the shadows had not shown him the true Karis, the real Marial and Idas. He had had enough of lies and distortions. He wondered if there were ever any alternative.

Someone was running towards him along the beach.

Eleanor.

'Phin!' She was shouting. 'This isn't real, don't believe it!'

'I know.' He held his arms wide for her, smiling with relief. Held against his heart, she was warm and living and real.

Like him, she had come a long way. And had learnt enough to recognise the lies around them.

'Look, it's coming from over there.' She pointed, and he saw the darkness deepen into a swirl of creeping mist. There was something about it which repelled observation. He found his eyes travelling past it, glancing over Eleanor's head down at the creature pretending to be Triss.

It grinned foolishly at him, and the grin stretched wider and wider, splitting the skull, splitting through the body and fur, so that dim twilight showed through the widening spaces. Rags of its substance drifted away like vapour and mingled with the tumbling foam at the water's edge, becoming lost in it. A wave broke all along the shore, folding inwards, and the sea rolled up in the curving spiral of the arc, instantly disappearing into a vanishing vortex.

'This is a terrible place,' said Eleanor again, as they stood on the wide plain of frail flowers. The billows of drifting smoke seemed suddenly much closer.

He felt something by his feet. He bent down and, from the crushed petals, picked up one of the swords dropped in the fall.

'Come on,' he said. 'Let's find the others.'

Matthias stood on the edge of a cave while the Arrarat circled all around him.

He could see, here. He could see rows of caves set into the rock of Arrarat Isle, the fire burning far below on the wide, dusty floor. But he knew that the rock was false, that the bright fire was imaginary. He had no eyes, and therefore anything that presented itself as vision was a lie.

The Arrarat were different. They were not part of the lies of the underworld, not part of anyone's deluded day-dreams. They could only be true, to themselves and to their chosen riders. He could not see them, and because of that he knew that they were really there.

One of them was going to choose him.

His heart was full of hope and longing. To be chosen twice was unknown. He was uniquely honoured.

He was not worthy. Humility; but now the taste was no longer bitter. He felt the rush of air, heard the beat of heavy wings and a hawk stood beside him. Blindly he reached out his arms and found the soft feathers, the rippling strength.

The hawk inclined its head against him, and he listened to the alien, familiar heartbeat. Amery, her name was. He was trembling with joy and relief.

The false cavern with its gaudy fire had disappeared. The illusions and lies, for the moment, had ceased. He stood alone with his true hawk Amery, communing once more with that other intelligence. He found a mind that soared lightly over blindness and stupid visions, answering lies with boundless love.

Amery would take him to find the others. And then they would travel with her to find Lukas, and it would all be all right.

The theatre was dark all around Thurstan. He was sitting high up, wedged tightly between an enormous woman and a pillar. He was not in the least worried. He knew the others would be all right. He remembered the descriptions each had given of the wafting scent on the staircase. There was nothing there to frighten anyone. And although Thurstan was not naturally credulous, there was something about the theatre which conquered all his reservations.

Wherever this place was, whatever was happening, it would soon be over. A play, by definition, is finite. All too soon the curtain would fall, and there you'd be, back in boring, dangerous old reality. It was Thurstan's only weakness.

So when he found himself squashed into the upper circle, gazing down to a brightly lit stage, he momentarily suspended disbelief and settled back to enjoy himself.

He knew this play, he'd seen it before. It was a farce, one of those old-fashioned ones, with people getting mixed up and falling in love with the wrong person.

After what they had all just been through, he was more than ready for some light relief. An idea occurred to him. Perhaps they were all here, in other parts of the theatre. He leant forward to look, but it was too dark and he could see nothing in the velvety blackness.

It had only just started. The overture was threadbare and the scenery creaked. He didn't mind. He watched a shipwrecked sailor look for his companions on a storm-blown island with palm trees. Artificial thunder rattled from a sheet of metal. The sailor was bemused, teased by an airy spirit . . .

There was a magician, a crook, a monster, some clowns and a beautiful girl. Well, he supposed she was meant to be beautiful (golden hair, blue eyeshadow), but he was unimpressed. She squealed shrilly, running from the monster into the arms of the shipwrecked sailor. The monster stumped across the stage and stood at the footlights, glaring out at the audience.

It was wearing a mask, green, with a bulbous nose. A wig of black hair, back-combed and frizzy. Dressed in sacking, wreathed with leaves and creepers. It spoke in a carefully roughened alto voice words of great beauty. Beneath the sacking, Thurstan saw the shadows of ankle and calf, a fluid movement, a graceful line.

There were songs and several fights. The lovers played chess, the magician gave up magic and returned to court life.

All very satisfactory. Thurstan watched them come forward for the curtain call, and the monster removed its mask.

Heavy, dark, languorous eyes. Dusky, golden skin. Long, long eyelashes, and black hair tumbling half-way down her back.

He threw her a rose, a pale yellow bloom he found in his buttonhole, and she looked up at him. She did not smile, but it was enough.

The theatre slowly emptied. He was alone.

The lights were dimming. He sat in his seat next to the pillar and waited. There were voices backstage and then the curtain was lifted and a wizened old man worked his way across the stage, sweeping dust and rose petals, replacing the palms and wave machine. Then he too was gone, a door slamming far away, the sound of a bolt.

Thurstan sat alone in the warm silence and waited. He felt strangely relaxed, strangely reluctant to question his situation.

He was aware of darkness deepening all around him. It was scented with the usual smells of the theatre: gas-lamps, polish, paint, powder, tobacco, perfume, oranges, sawdust. He liked the elaborate black caverns leading away into nothing, the boxes. The potential of it. The hidden secrets of the dark, promising mystery and enchantment.

A shaft of light from a skylight at the back of the stage showed it to be littered with props. A throne, the uneven dips of the cardboard waves, a vase of artificial flowers, the back half of a horse, miscellaneous masks, a coffin, a mountain of shiny-covered cushions.

He stood up slowly, and moved to the door leading down to the stage.

The theatre was completely soundless. He was quite alone. The door swung shut silently behind him, caught in a slowing hinge. He moved downstairs in the pitch black. It seemed much further than he remembered, curving round and round. Surely he had passed the stage door?

At length he saw it, faintly illumined in some unknown light. He pushed it open. He always moved neatly. Backstage. The light from the skylight was yellowy-red, from a street-lamp outside he assumed. On a shelf by the pulley for the curtain he found the stub of a candle set in a saucer, matches at its side.

He lit the candle, and then found others in its soft glow. He took the matches from one to another, lighting odd corners, the pantomime horse, the vase of flowers.

The street-lamp outside went out. For a moment he was confused. The candlelight was unsteady. As it flickered he moved carelessly against the spray of artificial flowers.

They fell, and the glass vase shattered, scattering shards over and around the candle.

'Damn.' His voice, after the crash of glass, did not sound so much strange as rather weak. Insubstantial.

He looked around for the broom that the old man had used, but the stage was in a much heavier blackness now and he could see nothing. It was very still.

He knelt down and began to pick flowers from the mess of glass. In the black silence, his hands moved swiftly. They did not shake. They kept moving, and he refused to acknowledge that anything was happening.

He concentrated. Clear up the mess and tidy away. Then it would be all right.

The floor was dusty and dry. A red paper flower, and then a white one, taken first in his right hand, passed to his left. His boot, scuffed and dirty, treading on the wooden boards. His eyes obsessively tracking every movement, every object.

He could not look up, could not stop this examination of

paper flowers: the floor, his hands, boots, broken glass. He could not look up because there was someone there.

In the deeper shadows at the side of the stage, someone stood, and Thurstan's hands slowed in their action, slowed until they stopped.

He knelt on wooden boards, and dared not look up.

Whoever it was moved slightly, and took a mask from the pile, putting it on.

No. Not this.

Are you a child, Thurstan? To hide behind such frail refusals? The voice behind the moon mask rang in silence round the theatre.

'I will not.' He spoke aloud.

You are the lesser because of it.

'I will not be used.'

Another voice behind him, familiar, regretful.

'Thurstan. My only child. So hard, hard and rigid. Such limitations!'

'Mother!' He stood up, swinging round, turning his back on the masked figure.

She was there in the wings, the laughter-lines of intelligence round her eyes, the sad mouth, her hair piled high, her hands calm.

'You were not kind,' Martitia said.

'I could not afford to be! There was no room for kindness!'

You diminish yourself.

At every step of the way, you become smaller

'Leave me alone!' He had his hands over his ears, his eyes tight shut. This was not anything real, anything true. It had nothing to do with him. It was a dream, only a dream.

Another dizzying alteration. The unheard voice was joined by another, and that was when he thought he would die. From fear. Only that.

Wearing masks They stepped out onto the stage. They ignored him. He was too small.

It was dark all around him, but the darkness was dazzling against his closed eyes, dazzling everywhere.

The two masked figures echoed down the corridors of reality and dream. Their hatred reverberated over aeons, spanned universes.

He thought that one of them almost raised a hand in

friendship to the other, but it must have been an illusion.
They were enemies, these two.

Sun and Moon. Male and Female. Light and Dark.

Their battleground was humanity, under the Sun, under
the Moon. They were only actors here, underground. They
could only meet, masked, on a stage.

It was more than enough.

The explosion of light knocked Thurstan to the floor.

The bitterness of the hatred, the cutting edge of vengeance,
the wild plunges of resentment and fury whipped his mind
into dark retreat.

It was too much.

Something brushed his face. He stirred indistinctly. A sound,
a light mocking sound. A slow handclap.

He opened his eyes and got to his feet in one movement,
quickly as a cat.

Someone had thrown a rose at him.

He was still on stage. Alone. Not caring who was watching
out there in the auditorium, he walked calmly to the side of
the stage and was sick.

Afterwards, he stood still for a while, facing the wall,
leaning his sweating head against his forearm. The acid-sweet
smell of vomit filled the theatre. The caretaker would be
cross.

It didn't matter.

The girl had stopped clapping. She was walking down the
centre aisle towards the stage, the full cream linen skirt
swinging with every step.

'Why. . .?' His voice was dry and harsh. What could he
say? 'Why did you throw that rose at me?'

'The monster rarely receives flowers.'

And then he remembered who she was, the pretty actress
in the ugly mask in the play he'd watched. Long ago.

'Come with me,' she said, holding out her hand.

It didn't matter. So he went with her and left the theatre.

Chapter Thirteen
Return

Serethrun returned to Shelt next morning, just before dawn.

From the wide sloping plain to the west of Shelt, he could smell the city on the air, the smells of cooking and woodsmoke, of sewers and the sea. As he drew nearer, he heard the sounds of Shelt, the noisy tradesmen, chattering crowds, the rumble of carts and carriages. As his senses became filled with the sights, sounds and smells of the city, he knew himself to be one of them once more. *Mereth*. City-dweller. He felt equivocal about it now. He was torn between two states of being, and no longer knew which he preferred.

Returning to the *eloish* had been a revelation. They were not as he remembered them.

Three days hard riding west from Shelt had brought him to the edge of Barent's Forest. He had chosen well: the horses followed his chestnut stallion without hesitation. The black-brown herd spread across the plains like an uneven flood.

On the eve of the third day, he halted on the edge of the forest and dismounted. The chestnut stamped and tossed its head. Absently, Serethrun stroked the creature's mane. 'Hush, my dear,' he said softly. 'Wait here and you will be safe . . .'

The *eloish* would be here somewhere, deep in the hidden glades, the distant avenues. Since the theft of their own horses, they had needed the forest, the firewood, its store of fruit and nuts, to survive. They lived in the shelter of huge trees, concealed by dense undergrowth. They trespassed on no one's land in the forest. The empty plains were no use to them without horses.

No one ever found them within the forest; but then hardly

anyone tried. The *eloish* were beyond the concerns of the city-bred. Their priorities were different. They were not even worth robbing, for they possessed nothing considered valuable.

Ancient trees separated the forest from the plain, a line of oak, beech and ash rising from a thick tangle of brambles.

Serethrun trusted that he would find them, that he was still *eloish* enough to recognise and follow the signs, but it took much longer than he had anticipated. In the end they found him.

As night fell, he pushed through clinging thorns, waded over rapid streams, following the faint paths left by deer. The *eloish* never used anything else. It was a clear, bright evening. The network of branches overhead framed a silvery half-moon, a thousand stars.

The forest was very quiet. It did not occur to him to call out, for nothing would be more likely to advertise that he was no longer *eloish*. He found himself walking more and more slowly as time went on. He took care to brush aside branches noiselessly. He avoided the small shoots pushing through the mud. He moved gently, smoothly, and felt old skills returning. We walk in silence through the forest, he remembered, and are not found by the unknowing . . .

He stopped in the shadow of a birch tree and laid his hand on its trunk. In that moment of stillness, he realised that he was no longer alone. He did not turn his head, made no sudden movement. As quietly as leaf fall, he breathed a few words.

'Greetings, my friends . . .'

A rustle of leaves betrayed their laughter. He could see them now, standing as still as he was amongst the trees, dressed in dull, mottled colours, shades of grey under the moon. Their faces were stained with wood-dyes, their hair plaited with leaves and grass.

They were indescribably alien, another species, another race. He saw dark slanted eyes watch him with derision.

'Irian?' He could not find her in the dim light. 'Irian, I must talk to you.'

'You come to tell me of the death of Renferell Maryn.' Her voice was cold and distant. She stepped out into the space between two young birches, and he saw that she was very thin, drawn and scrawny like a young bird.

'No. There is no need to tell you, you will know of that already. I have not forgotten what it is to be *eloish*.' He paused. 'No, this is something else. I have brought a gift for you all.'

'We need nothing from you.'

'Do you not?' He looked around, allowing his glance to rest momentarily on individuals. He could see them all now, his eyes had adjusted to the fine details. The forest was crowded with the *eloish*. Some sat high in the tree branches, others rested along the uneven contours of a tumbled tree trunk.

On a bank rising on the other side of a small stream, he saw Brianne leaning on one elbow, regarding him thoughtfully. She was twined together with Jerr Morrelow, their bodies half concealed beneath a drifting pile of leaves. She gazed steadily at him, and said something to Jerr. He was smiling, meeting Serethrun's eyes as he lazily stroked her narrow, dirt-streaked shoulders. He said nothing.

'What has happened to you?' Serethrun said. 'Are you truly one with the forest now; have you forgotten who you are?'

'It just – looks – like – that.' Jerr Morrelow spoke slowly. 'Can it be you who has forgotten? The city has clouded your vision, befogged your memory. We were always like this . . .' He stood up, breaking away from Brianne.

'Not in the north, we weren't. Riding the plains, riding the tundra, life was different, hard and sharp –' He could not analyse what had gone wrong, why they were so different.

'But that life is past,' said Brianne.

Irian still watched silently, waiting for him to tell them. 'I have brought horses. Enough for us all. We can ride again –'

'But what is the price, Serethrun?' Irian spoke calmly.

'One battle. A fight, to overturn the Sea Lords of Shelt. It is a worthy cause.' He heard a rustle of dissent from the *eloish*.

'A *mereth* cause. Nothing to do with us.'

'The horses I have brought belonged to the Guard of Shelt. They are creatures of the *mereth*. Will you disdain to ride them?'

'We don't need them.'

This was worse than he had imagined. He searched his mind for arguments.

'So, will you stay here? Wild and feral as the fox, forgetting the sun and snow –'

'There is sun here, and snow. Think again, Serethrun.' Irian crossed the forest floor towards him. He saw that the black paint still stained her body: was she speaking from within the trance?

Her eyes were steady but unfocused. 'No, *mereth* brother, the change lies in you. Is it the city? Or are there other forces. . .?' A long sigh, her eyes wide with secret visions. 'Perhaps you are no longer free, poor Serethrun, poor, lost brother, and it is nothing to do with the city. A double enchantment holds you . . .'

'Listen to me, Irian!' He did not want her pity, paid little attention to her words. He put his hands on her shoulders and all at once her eyes cleared. She sighed and he knew that she was back with them. 'We can be free, we can leave the forest, go anywhere, roam the wide world if we want!' He raised his voice so that they could all hear.

'Why must you live within the darkness of the forest? Have you forgotten the unbroken sky, the colours of the sunset over an empty horizon? How can you bear to be so confined here!'

They were all silent now, watching him. They were remembering now, the feel of wind in the hair, the space, the cold freedom . . .

'You said, a battle.' Irian spoke thoughtfully. 'Lives would be lost . . .'

'We would gain our freedom!'

'And you have brought us horses? Enough?' Lara Valde, Archon of the *eloish* was standing at his shoulder. He had not heard her approach.

Another voice from the high bank behind him: Enthor, his old friend. 'More than enough! There can be few horses left in Shelt now!' He was running down the bank, the leaves rising in a great cloud around him, a sudden force of energy and power.

'Serethrun, you have truly returned to us!' Enthor had taken Serethrun's hand, pulling him close in the traditional, loving embrace of the *eloish*. 'A thousand welcomes to our dear brother!'

Jerr had joined them. His eyes were glittering. 'Let's not rush things. We could of course just take the horses and leave. There is no need to join in a *mereth* squabble . . .' A ripple of interest stirred the waiting observers.

'And we would be followed, hunted down, entrapped and humiliated. Again. The Sea Lords have to be deposed. And I for one would like to take a part in that . . .' Serethrun was ready for this.

Jerr smiled in lazy agreement. 'Of course, revenge is sweet. I would not wish to pass up the opportunity of opening their eyes to various wrongs . . .'

In the end, they had accepted him – and his proposal. It was, he realised, to do with the advent of the horses. They had fired the *eloish* with memory, with the desire for speed. He had stayed, sharing their food, living in the forest for some time, planning and deciding.

He told them almost everything that had happened to him, everything that was happening in Shelt. His sister Irian watched him, but said little.

It was only later, on his way back to Shelt, that he remembered her strange words. A double enchantment. He did not know what she meant.

It didn't matter. They would all come. They would be ready, partnered by their new horses, ready for a battle to overthrow the Sea Lords. To overthrow the power that so wronged them. Their voices had sung through the forest, partnering the owl in stealth and savagery.

Mittelson had no idea what forces would be unleashed.

Serethrun slipped into the city with the morning traders from the southern farms, and pushed through the crowded streets, his cloak hood shadowing his face.

He didn't know if he would be recognised, whether the pamphlet using his face was still circulated. But everyone was hooded, for the rain was constant, the wind whipping at sodden cloaks, and he saw no one he knew.

He was making for the shanty town, for the shacks and sheds where the down-and-outs lived. There were people he trusted there, people who would tell him where Mittelson and Felicia and Rosco were.

But the shanty-town had gone. Instead brown, stinking,

swirling water lapped through streets he thought he knew, rubbish floating and rotting on its greasy surface. It spread through the city, through the homes and the lives of people who had always found a living from the sea. Now it meant only destruction to them.

Avoiding the flooded streets, he moved through crowded alleys and pathways towards the harbour. He saw the odd face he recognised, crouched in doorways, through the steamy windows of shops, but no one he dared trust. Lanterns were lit everywhere, although it was still mid-morning, for the sky was heavy and black with the promise of yet more rain.

There were soldiers everywhere, scarlet cloaks garish in the dim light, breaking up the small groups of people congregating on every corner, in every bar. He saw men frisked for weapons, asked for papers and identification. He took care to avoid the soldiers' eyes, to slouch and drift, to look purposeless. Like everyone else.

He had been away only a few weeks, but everything had changed. It was partly that the memory of his life as an *eloish* was now very vivid, that only a few hours ago he had raced the wind as it flew over the plain. The city seemed to him an aberration, a place of stinking, earth-bound stone, of colourless, cloddish people. Drab and dirty, it enclosed him, and he almost forgot why he was there.

The harbour was barely recognisable, a vast lake of swollen, filthy sea-water, crashing against buildings, the boats bobbing like toys, dragged down at one end by their moorings. Several had come adrift and had been crushed in the violence of the storms, leaving only a wreckage of driftwood.

'Our friends the Sea Lords seem to be falling down on the job,' said a cool voice behind him.

Mittelson. He turned to face him, his hands in his pockets.

'Well, Olwyn? What's been going on here?'

'Greetings, Serethrun Maryn.' The pale eyes gleamed briefly. 'See for yourself. The Sea Lords no longer concern themselves with weather-control.' He waited.

'They're here,' Serethrun said without elaboration. 'All the *eloish*. Ten miles to the east. Ready and waiting.'

'Good. Very well done, Serethrun.' Olwyn Mittelson said nothing more, turning back towards the city, and Serethrun followed at a distance.

I hope you know what you're doing, thought Serethrun. And although it was raining and desperate here in the city of Shelt, he was glad to be back. There was something to achieve here. And Felicia, of course. He was looking forward to meeting Felicia again.

He met instead Kester Robard, pacing a narrow room over some stables in one of the better areas of the city. He was moving restlessly, shifting his shoulders uncomfortably against his shirt. Serethrun watched him for a moment, unobserved. Mittelson had told him of Kester's rescue, and the reason for it.

He had never liked Kester Robard.

He had been one of the men Serethrun had originally wanted as a friend. In those early days at the barracks, when Serethrun had first tried to find a place for himself in the Guard, Kester Robard had proved a considerable barrier.

Not because he was unfriendly, or a bully, or unkind, or a joker, like so many others. But because he took no notice. He laughed among his own friends, triumphed in all the exercises, had friends amongst the Castle administration. There was any number of women ready to languish over him.

He was tall and well-built with light brown, curling hair. He moved with a confident tread, with deliberate, sensual ease. He spoke slowly, laconically. His hazel eyes had run impartially over Serethrun, one of the crowd. They never paused, never noticed. And so, for a long time, no one even bothered to learn who Serethrun Maryn was, and what kind of friend he could be.

This time, however, Kester stopped dead in the middle of his pacing, and regarded Serethrun with interest.

'Well, well,' he said calmly. 'Wrecker Maryn, as I live.'

Serethrun's first impulse was to leave the room, leave Shelt, get out of it all and back to the *eloish*. But he saw that the man was moving awkwardly, and remembered Mittelson's words. Flogged. Badly injured, within spitting distance of permanent disability. Because of Annis, and Felicia.

'I am no wrecker,' he said, equally calm. 'I was framed.'

'Oh yes?'

Serethrun said nothing, moving into the room, pouring himself coffee from the pot on the stove in the corner. His

boots left damp marks on the bare wooden boards. His clothes
were beginning to steam.

'I've come a long way,' he remarked. 'Tell me the news.'
Where was Mittelson? Serethrun had assumed that he was
following. And what about Rosco? The women?

He heard a door slam downstairs. Through the window
he saw the tall, untidy figure of Mittelson striding away
through the rain.

'What are you doing with these people?' Kester Robard
had stopped pacing, had hitched one hip onto the rough
wooden table by the window. He was watching Serethrun
with something like contempt.

'Much the same as you, I imagine.' He drank coffee, almost
choking on the bitter heat of it. '*I* was discredited as a
wrecker, *you* because of your connection with Annis. We have
neither of us been treated with justice.'

'Do you think you'll get justice from Mittelson? From
Rosco?' It was impossible to tell what Robard was getting
at, for his voice was cool, unemotional and distant.

'There was no justice at the Castle.' Serethrun stared
moodily at the steaming liquid in his mug. 'And they were
killing Felicia.'

'Or healing her. . . Lady, you should have heard her
scream last night!'

'What?' Serethrun looked up sharply.

'The queen of nightmares, the Lady Felicia. I don't think
Mittelson is doing much for her.'

'Gawne was worse –'

'And what do you make of this?' Robard had moved across
the room, had drawn a bundle of bright cloth from a cupboard
there.

A scarlet cloak, such as the Guard wore.

'Your cloak, of course.' Serethrun stared at him,
uncomprehending.

'No. Not mine, or yours. Someone else's.' For a moment
there was silence in the narrow, dusty room. 'Serethrun. . .
I was at the inquiry. With Niall, remember? I heard your
story, and Lambard's. You were both telling the truth.'

'No. Lambard lied. He had to be lying.'

'Perhaps someone else, looking like Lambard, rode past
you on the cliff path that night. Someone tall, straight blond

hair, in a scarlet cloak, intent on discrediting you. Did you never suspect Rosco?'

'*Rosco*? Why? Why should he set that up?' It was unthinkable.

'They needed you. Think, Maryn. A plainsman, one of the *eloish*. Someone acquainted with dubious powers, with unusual modes of existence. What a coup for insurrectionists! An *eloish* who knew the Castle, knew the cliffs! A horseman. Someone vulnerable, whom it would be easy to discredit, suborn. You've been used, man. A parcel of loony magicians and fishermen. Riff-raff. Enchantments, spirals, betrayals, Lady knows what else. Playing on your insecurities – '

There was a sound from the room next door, the sound of a window slamming. And then Felicia's voice, high and panicky. 'Annis! Olwyn!'

In moments, Serethrun and Kester were both in her room, Kester struggling with the wildly swinging window, and Serethrun at her bedside, reaching for her hands.

'Felicia, Lady Felicia, what's wrong?'

The window was fastened at last, and Robard turned to face them.

'Nightmares again, my Lady?'

'I was not asleep . . .' She drew herself up, away from Serethrun, brushing the hair back from her face. 'But Serethrun, you've been away so long! Where have you been?'

He thought he saw a genuine welcome in her face, but she quickly turned away, watching the door. 'Where's Olwyn? I must talk to him.'

Serethrun glanced at Kester, who shrugged. 'What's wrong, my Lady? What frightened you? It was only the wind, making the window bang.'

'A storm . . .' Her voice was only a whisper. 'You – both worked with the coastguard, didn't you? When do the high spring tides start?'

Serethrun looked away from her, over to the window. Through the shiny roof-tops he could see the swirl of brown water down by the harbour, where there should have been cobbles and paving stones.

'Soon . . .' he said slowly. 'And the snow on the high moor has only just begun to thaw. Shelt is in for a hard time.'

But neither of them noticed that there was more than

anxiety in Felicia's face. The panic was deep-seated now, a destructive, violent force.

'Where's Olwyn?' she asked again, a small, thin voice against the storm.

He arrived only minutes later, before Serethrun and Kester had a chance to continue their absorbing discussion. He was carrying a pile of pamphlets.

'There, Felicia,' he said. 'How do you like your handiwork?'

The sinuous shape of Ladon, sketched in lurid colour on a black background, glared at her.

'THE SEA LORDS' ALLY' was the heading. The text, on the other side, was simple and immediate.

'The dragon Ladon rules our sea. Takes our fish, our livelihood, our power. He gives the Sea Lords gifts of healing and prolonged life, and in return demands sole rights to the sea. For the sake of this unholy alliance, we are dispossessed. Disinherited. So that the Sea Lords may benefit.

'So that the Sea Lords should live forever.

'At the spring tides, the power of the dragon will be clear to all. But we are not alone. The Lady Astret is with us. Her Will works in us all.

'The Lady will triumph.'

And at the bottom, sketched amidst a pattern of lines and spirals, Felicia's own face was linked to Jolin Rosco's.

She had not drawn that. She looked up at Mittelson.

'There's no point in all this,' she said tiredly, pointing to the two faces. 'There will be no time for that.'

'Trust me, Felicia.' He was unprepossessing, with his narrow, triangular face and long greasy hair, but his voice carried complete conviction.

Serethrun had picked up the pamphlet, was turning it over in his hands. From his pocket he produced another scrap of paper, torn and crumpled. The sketch of his own face, the text, 'Wrecker Maryn', the lies and calumny that had ruined his life. The typeface was the same, the weight of paper identical. The phrasing, grammar and style the same.

Saying nothing, he spread the two pamphlets flat on the bed in front of Felicia. Then he looked up.

'Trust you, Mittelson? I'd as soon rot.'

He was deadly cold, his face pale with anger. He stepped to one side suddenly, his sword drawn, ready to run the thin man through.

'If you want to know whether we set you up, then the answer is yes.' Mittelson's voice was undisturbed. 'Whether we framed you, lost you your job, drew you into illegal conspiracies, then again the answer is yes. We wanted you vulnerable and angry and dispossessed.'

'For fuck's sake!' He was on the edge of extreme violence, but the soft voice kept going.

'There was no other way to get Felicia out. I saw – I knew that the ship from Eldin would be wrecked. There is a traitor in the Castle, no friend to us or Torold and Javon. Lammon is his name, a Mage only recently inaugurated. It was his storm that raged that night. It was his plan to murder Javon's heiress. Someone had to be there to save Felicia. Someone who was riding the central stretch of the cliff path.'

'We drew straws for it! It was pure chance!' This was impossible, incomprehensible. A re-run of the enquiry.

'I held the straws.' A new voice, equally calm. 'And as you picked the southern stretch, I suggested, if you remember, that it was a bad night for the old and lonely. You asked Lambard Bowen to swap then.' The flautist, Vere Holtby, who had played for them in the barracks that afternoon. He was standing in the doorway with Rosco. The room seemed suddenly very small, dominated by powerful men.

But Felicia sat still and silent in the centre of it all, and let them argue.

'Why me?' Serethrun's voice was very quiet. 'Why did you pick on me?' But he knew the answer as he spoke. Kester had told him already. Plainsman contacts, someone who knew both Castle and cliffs, someone skilled with horses, someone it would be easy to discredit, to use. *Eloish.*

He dragged his eyes away from the Mage and looked instead at Rosco, leaning against the doorpost.

'*Was* it you, that night on the cliff?'

'Yes.'

'Why did you *lie* to me?'

'You never asked.'

'Stop it!' Felicia, strongly now, cutting through the anger

and resentment. 'Stop it, all of you! Serethrun, I would be *dead* without you. Twice you saved my life –'

'And in the Fish that night, there were spirals . . .' He swept on, disregarding her words. No one denied it.

'An enchantment, a trick. That was all it ever was.'

A silence. And then he was pushing through the men at the doorway, clattering down the stairs, out into the rain-sodden streets.

'Where's he going?' Felicia, wide-eyed to Mittelson.

'To send the *eloish* away, I assume.' His pale gaze was unblinking, unexcited.

'I'd better stop him then.' Rosco was gone before anyone else had moved.

As the street door banged and the footsteps faded away, Mittelson looked at Kester Robard, standing silent by the window.

'Well, that was a good morning's work, wasn't it? A nice recompense for getting you out.'

'I would not have been held, if you had not abducted the Lady Felicia in the first place.'

'She would not have survived in the Castle, not with Lammon as a Sea Lord.'

'It always comes back to me, doesn't it?' Felicia still spoke quietly, and neither of them noticed the look in her eyes. 'Kester, I would have died if they'd left me there. Olwyn is right.'

'Is your situation so much better now?'

She said nothing more. She looked tired, so soon they left her.

Not much better now. Not with the tide rising and the dragon waiting.

Chapter Fourteen
Underground

All the roads in Smintha led to one place. All the streets, avenues, terraces and crescents radiated in more or less regular patterns outwards from a central pivot. That pivot was the Temple of Lycias, and it extended on many levels, deep into the earth. By implication, all the roads led downwards too. It could be said that all of Smintha ran towards the centre.

All lifelines run in one direction.

The houses of Smintha had cellars, the municipal buildings their vaults and dungeons. But below those there were stairs and wells and lift-shafts and ladders. Tunnels and passageways and subways and burrows. An entire underground city existed there. Only the smallest part of Smintha lay naked beneath the sun. Distance was not measured only in length but also in depth.

Sixth level, they used to say. Where the grain was stored and the herbs hung drying. Where the wine barrels waited for the appropriate date . . . They were still there, waiting, but there was no one to drink their contents.

Fourth level. The galleries. A thousand statues, and many more pictures and portraits. Scenes from life and the imagination, splashes of colour, here shielded from the sun. Pale watercolours hinted at memories of a more vivid world. And puzzles and toys, stuffed animals and trays of pinned butterflies. Mechanical dolls and distorting mirrors, musical boxes and calliope organs. Dust-clouds muffled them all.

The light was refracted, caught in the deep wells by slanting mirrors and sent hurling down long corridors. In addition, the walls were faintly luminous, lined with some potent excretion from the ancient worms who originally dug the shell for the catacomb City of Stairs.

At another level the servants lived. Cramped houses, narrow roads, but their own world, busy with music halls and bars and markets.

Higher up there were grander dwellings, with carved, arching ceilings and marble-lined hallways, where the wealthy lived. The cool halls echoed now, long deserted.

On the first level, just below the city buildings, the priests lived, tending the sun-burnt temples above. The desert Smintha was a counterfeit city. We live here, said its citizens, to honour the Lord of the Sun. We bathe in the light of His love, and adore His brilliant face . . .

But it was too difficult. Too harsh and too hot. Gradually, with regret, they explored the caves beneath the sand. They found halls and passageways, sweet springs of water, a natural architecture waiting for inhabitation. With relief, they moved underground.

Deepest of all, the gates are barred.

All roads lead to one place, all stairs approach the centre. All life has but one end.

Two people stood on a sweeping, curved staircase, looking down onto an iron-encircled vestibule. The iron was a continuation of the elaborate structure of the staircase, flowing out on level ground to enclose an empty area like a cage.

At one side of the enclosed area, opposite the stairs, the ornamental iron rose into gates shaped like the wings of a bird. Beyond the cage of wrought iron, the staircase and the gates, everything was masked in twilight.

In dim light, here filtered through so many mirrors, down so many luminous wells that it had almost lost volition, the people on the staircase could almost be mistaken for statues, unmoving as they were. But the silken drapes of their robes fluttered constantly, as if brushed by an invisible wind. The woman's hand, resting lightly on the man's shoulder, was trembling, and her breath came in faint gasps.

There was no other movement there, no proof that the world tilted on its axis, that time passed, that day followed night, summer followed winter. There was a vast weight of earth above them, a huge stupefying mass of levels and buildings and roads and sand, all beaten down by the pressure of the vengeful sun. But here it was almost possible to forget the sun, so far underground as they were.

And yet the folds of silk moved in a rippling wind.

They had brought a torch with them, a flaming brand, which they had thrust into a bracket on the wall of the stairwell. It crackled as it burnt, a small and feeble noise. There was one other sound: a brief, irrelevant prayer, repeated over and over again by Imbert Cupere. 'Lord protect us, Lord have mercy, Lord protect us . . .'

It seemed an unconscious act, a reflex almost, for his eyes were calm and watchful, regarding the shadowy realm beyond the gates. Edine moved closer to him.

'We will have to get them out of there.'

'Yes, indeed . . . But there is a curious elegance in these fragmenting dreams, you must admit. Memories are so evocative. I begin to understand why Lefevre spent so much time here. Don't you think it would be interesting to find out what would happen if we left them there?'

'You know what would happen. But we have a task to accomplish, and time passes . . .'

'How right you are.' Imbert turned to regard her, and lightly touched her cheek with his hand. 'Wait here then,' he said.

'No.' She caught his hand and held it briefly. 'Let me. They will find a woman less threatening.'

For a moment he studied her, his eyes tracing every contour of her face, as though he might forget her. Then he nodded. 'Be very careful, my love . . .'

Eleanor Knight and Phinian Blythe were standing close together in a field of flowers, in a strangely vaulting silence, and in the distance the darkness deepened. They stared through the twilight, trying to make sense of it. They had been entirely unaware of Imbert and Edine's presence, unaware of the iron-enclosed vestibule. The faint noise of the key in the lock made them look round. They saw Edine in the distance within a cage of iron. It was illuminated by the frail, flickering light of the torch. She looked as helpless as a tiny trapped animal held within bars, but as they watched she pushed the massive winged gate open.

Quickly she stepped back into the caged vestibule. Even at that distance they could tell how nervous she was by the swift untidiness of her movements.

Phin shivered suddenly. 'If that's a way out, I think we should take it. I don't trust this place, not at all.' His voice was quiet.

They were surrounded by a carpet of flowers, pale yellow, star-shaped, set in fragile thin leaves, scenting the air with sweetness. Calm dark air stretched away in all directions.

There was no obvious threat. And Eleanor didn't like Edine, she didn't trust her at all. She and Imbert had brought Eleanor from her own world, deliberately abandoning her to Lycias's revenge. She was no friend, and never would be.

But they could not stay there. Eleanor did not know what the threat was, why it was so dangerous, but she had learnt to distrust illusions. This was the home of illusion, of fantasy and dream. They had to get out of it.

She glanced at Phin, and found he was looking at her, a brief, reassuring smile on his lips. He took her hand, and together they began to walk towards the gate.

The flowers did not hold them back, nothing caught at their clothes, there was no hindrance to their movement. And yet it was like walking through mud, pushing through resistant, viscous density. The flowers were unwilling to let them go.

It was a relief to look away from the blank twilight to the woman standing there. She moved aside to let them pass through, but Eleanor had halted on the threshold.

'Edine.' Her voice was cool and unfriendly. She looked beyond Edine and saw the man still standing on the stairs. 'And Imbert, too. You do get around, don't you?' She turned to Blythe. 'They brought me here, they're the ones I told you about. They drove the taxi –'

'So inefficient, cars. You come from an impoverished society, Miss Knight. To rely on machinery for transport!' Edine's voice belied the lightness of the words. It was low and uneven, on the edge of failing altogether. She was frightened, deadly frightened. She came no closer. Eleanor raised her eyebrows.

'You were glad enough of it in the desert.'

There was a small silence. Eleanor saw that Imbert was looking over the endless plain of flowers.

'What do you want? Why are you here?' Blythe's voice was very severe. Imbert glanced at him.

'Perhaps you should consider instead why *you* are here.'

'There is a reason for everything,' said Edine. She stepped forward onto the Field of Flowers, taking hold of the gate. She was breathing quickly. 'You really must leave this place. Trust me. You've been here too long already.' Like Imbert, she was looking past them into the darkness beyond. Eleanor and Blythe turned and saw the winged clouds of deeper blackness, reaching out to them through the dark cypresses. The pale yellow flowers were all turned towards the brooding wings, rippling gently, although there was no wind.

A river mist hung heavy in the air. But as they watched, it shifted and twisted, although there was no breeze there, no breath to move it.

It was curiously fascinating, almost attractive, wreathing through the air towards them. It swayed with such grace. Surely there was the echo of a face, a hand? Something familiar . . . Eleanor took one step back towards it, trying to trace the vague outline. She thought that she might find someone she knew, held there in smoke. It was obsessive.

Phin caught her hand, pulling her back. A flutter of panic, of dreadful fear as he looked at her. His eyes seemed to reflect nightmares.

'No! Don't go near it!'

'Phin, what is it, what's wrong?'

'If I might make a suggestion – perhaps you should come away from there . . .' Imbert was talking to them, a light patter of sound. He had left the staircase and was now standing in the centre of the vestibule, so that the circle of light created by the torch shone around him.

They saw his face, pure and chiselled like a statue's. His eyes were a clear, cold grey, his hair flowing in soft and beautiful curls. He was calm, proud and powerful; almost, but not quite, relaxed. A soft fall of dark red silk concealed his body, but Eleanor could see the veins of his neck clear against the pale skin.

He looked fresh and almost innocent in the uneven, difficult light.

'Where is this place? And where are Matthias and
Thurstan?' Blythe said, unmoving.

'Matthias will soon enjoy a reunion with an old
acquaintance.' It was Edine who answered, her voice now
ironic, as if the mere presence of Imbert at her side was a
reassurance. 'And Thurstan Merauld, he's busy too. I
shouldn't worry about them if I were you . . .'

'An old acquaintance? Who do you mean?' Eleanor
resented the irony, the amused smiles.

Imbert glanced over his shoulder, up at the dim sweep of
stairs behind him. High above them a figure stood, brash and
ugly against the complicated iron-work. He had probably
been there all the time. Slowly he came downstairs, through
the enclosing iron arches. Unhesitating, he crossed the
encircled vestibule, straight to the gate, as if proving his
courage. Pausing there, he regarded them, a wide smile on
his unpleasant face. Eleanor had no trouble at all in
recognising him.

Weard. He bowed to her, a crude, ironic flourish. 'Shall
I show you your quarters, lady? You don't want to stay here.'
She did not answer, for she had noticed something else.

In his left hand Weard carried a spiral staff.

Imbert and Edine were watching them. There was
something predatory about the stillness of their gaze.

Eleanor lifted her chin. 'What do you want?' she said to
them. 'What is going on here?'

They glanced at each other, smiling faintly. Their eyes
shared secrets.

'You'll find out,' said Edine.

Weard took them out through the tall double gates and across
the empty vestibule. They began to climb the enwrought
staircase. Gradually the unsteadying twilight of the yellow-
flowered park disappeared. It was a relief, hard to analyse.
Instead the light became soft and sickly, flowing along a rough
earthen wall. Edine and Imbert led the way, taking with them
the torch.

Their robes still fluttered in the unknown breeze. Still it
seemed that an invisible multitude washed past them, down
to the Field of Flowers.

There was writing etched in the stone of each of the shallow steps, a ceaseless jumble of words, cramped and crowded hard upon each other. It was no script Eleanor or Phin recognised.

The stairs wound up through many levels, always masked by the writhing iron-work. There were gates at regular intervals, gates of iron wrought with unreadable words and symbols. Some were locked, some opened at a touch. Edine held keys, and went ahead. As they climbed upwards, the pressure of the movement going in the other direction lessened, until it died altogether.

At each level there were other wrought-iron gates and doors opening off the stairwell. Phin and Eleanor saw wide streets leading away. Doors and windows pock-marked the rough-hewn walls. A thousand dwelling places stretched away into the depths of the earth.

They left the staircase at the junction with one of the wide avenues. A group of dark-skinned men joined them there, falling into place around them. They were dressed in rags and carried knives. Eleanor did not recognise their faces, but the style was familiar. Caravan people, she thought bleakly. It was no comfort. There was no ambiguity about it; they were prisoners.

Empty corridors, deserted buildings. The men with them were silent, and Weard had never been loquacious. At length Imbert and Edine turned aside at the elegant facade of a palazzo. Standing together at the inlaid marble doorway, they looked back at Eleanor and Blythe. There was a clinical detachment in their glance, a kind of cool curiosity. They did not speak, but continued watching as Weard shepherded them down the wide avenue of ornate façades and blank windows.

Weard walked beside them, attended by two guards. There were columns at intervals, reaching up to the arched ceiling. They were set with angled mirrors, reflecting what little light there was.

'What is this place?' At last Eleanor found words to break the silence. She was finding it hard to keep calm. It was a relief to have left the golden plain and winding staircase behind, but now they were Weard's prisoners, and Weard carried a spiral staff . . .

'Smintha is two cities,' said Weard, disposed to show off knowledge. 'That bloody, baking grid above ground, where the fanatics tried to live. And this, where everyone else kept out of the sun. Dedicated to Lycias, is Smintha. The trouble is, no one could stand the sun. And that was before the heatwave!' He laughed.

'Where are they all now?' It was clear that no one had lived in these echoing corridors for some time.

'The water went sour. There was a plague. Those who survived were shit-scared. They packed up, formed a caravan. Didn't they, Krell?'

The man to Eleanor's right, a wiry figure with a strip of cloth tied round his forehead, grunted in response.

Weard halted for a moment and looked at him. An expression crossed his face, an expression Eleanor found hard to identify.

'Krell,' he said softly. 'Tell the lady what happened to the caravan. You'd like to know, wouldn't you, slut?' he shot at her. 'You'll be remembering your time with the caravan, won't you?'

'The caravan's gone,' said Krell, his voice slow and even, heavily accented. 'There's no one left now. Except us . . .'

'What happened to it?' She had to ask.

The man's face lost all colour. She could see his hand clench on the knife at his waist. 'You don't want to know, lady –'

A crack of laughter from Weard. 'No, perhaps she doesn't. Perhaps we'll leave you to find out, Eleanor Knight.' He turned away from her then, and the guards prodded Eleanor and Phin forward.

'Where are you taking us? What's going on down here now?'

Weard smiled, the fleshy lips drawn wide. 'Ah, that's interesting, that is. There's something here, you see. Hidden away, deep down at the centre. In the Field of Flowers, beneath the Temple of Lycias. Couldn't you tell? The priests never let anyone down the second staircase, the one that goes direct . . . But of course, there's no one here now. No priests, no soldiers, no servants or doxies – except Imbert Cupere and pretty Edine . . . Imbert's interested in that place at the centre. A place where things are transformed, or so it seems. Something waits there . . .'

She could well believe it. There was something unknown deep in the Field of Flowers, something held in a shifting smoky cloud of darkness. The darkness that seemed to reach out towards them, carrying so many promises.

She didn't want to think about it. 'Who made all this? All these vast tunnels?' They were passing through a wide gallery dwarfed by soaring arches. The walls vanished upwards, curving slightly inwards to meet far above them. Rows of tall black windows stared at them.

Weard laughed. 'You know them, slut. You've ridden on them. The lizards of Lycias. The caravan creatures.'

Looking closely at the surface of the tunnel, Eleanor could see ancient scars made by digging claws. 'But the columns?'

'Put in later, by the people of Smintha. They reflect what light there is against the walls. The earth here is mixed with worm saliva: it's slightly luminous. This was a private, self-sufficient world. There are shops, offices, theatres, galleries . . . And this' – he halted and pushed open the heavy door of a faceless building – 'is where they kept their prisoners.'

And before they really realised what was happening, he had thrust them across a narrow hall into a dimly lit room, and slammed the door shut behind them.

Chapter Fifteen
Matthias

Far above the dark Field of Flowers, many levels above that final destination, in the deserted dwelling of some rich nobleman, Matthias leant back against soft, silk-covered cushions and spoke to Weard.

'How did you get it?'

It was not easy addressing questions to someone half drunk with power and victory. Matthias could not see that Weard's large sweating face kept breaking into inane grins, but he was more than disconcerted by the uneven soaring of Weard's voice as he tried to contain his triumph.

'Oh, it was *easy*! And you, Mage Matthias, told me yourself what to do. Keeping the bargain, aren't you? Teaching me your skills . . .'

There was something very different about Weard, and it was not due to the power of the staff.

A haunted quality. He had always been brutal and ruthless, but now there was a tinge of fear in the loud blustering voice.

'How did you get it, Weard? What did you have to do?'

'The Desert Rose . . . Remember, Matthias? "Go cut yourself a staff," you said. "Living wood is needed." So I did.'

'What was the price?' Always the crucial point.

'Price? None whatever!' But beneath the triumph, there was something terrible. Matthias did not want to know – lack of knowledge was always such a relief – but he had no alternative.

Things were beginning to fall into place. He knew where he was and who was in control. If the overworld is governed by Sun and Moon, then the underworld is available to anyone

with ambition and skill. Mages. Parid. It was like a blank sheet
of paper, waiting for someone to make his or her mark on it.

How had they lived here, the citizens of Smintha, deprived
of their God? What had filled the vacuum? Deep in the back
of his mind, a memory stirred. Perhaps this was not simply
a blank sheet. There was something else here. He cast his
mind over the secrets in the hidden diaries of Blaise. He had
memorised them all, long ago, and then he had hidden them
well away from curious eyes. He was not prepared to risk
sharing such knowledge with anyone else.

There had been a note about Smintha, little more than a
tentative suggestion, as if Blaise had not been able quite to
believe it. It was a portal, Smintha. Smintha stood over one
of the ways through, one of the last thresholds . . .

They had all, already, experienced vivid and misleading
hallucinations. Amery had shown him that the Field of
Flowers was bordered by dark cypresses and sterile willows.
A cloud of mist billowed within its twilight shadows . . . That
was where the fascination lay, the enchantment that replaced
Sun and Moon in the lives of those who chose to live
underground.

It was deeply disturbing to him. He did not fully
understand the significance of such a place, how the
hallucinations arose from the thoughts and memories of the
people who stood within the field of scented flowers.

But he recognised the massive, arcane power of that place,
wreathing restlessly at its centre. He sensed its deadly activity,
smelt in its mistiness something dark and avid. Was it death?
The final dissolution, the end of every road, every life? There
was an answer there, a deep and powerful secret, almost
within his grasp.

One thing was certain. Imbert and Edine knew little more
than he did about the realm beyond the gates. They usually
remained on the upper levels, Weard had said, investigating
the libraries and workshops.

What were they looking for, Matthias wondered? What did
they hope to find here, beyond the reach of Sun and Moon?

There were so many unanswered questions. Weard had told
him that Eleanor and Phinian were safe, not far away. They
would be needed, he had said, but had not explained why.
This was only one of the many mysteries below Smintha.

Matthias didn't know where Thurstan was, for another, and this was worrying. He trusted Thurstan to look after himself, but there were too many unknowns here, too much that was occult. Thurstan was in essence a practical man of action, someone who acknowledged no God. The City of Stairs with its empty palaces, and the Field of Flowers with its creeping illusions, would be baffling mysteries to him.

Amery, his new-found and beautiful Arrarat hawk, had left him. He had asked her to take him to the others, and she had put him down in one of the wide echoing tunnels lined with the faded façades of elegant palaces. But then she had left him, soaring away down the empty avenues, and Weard's guards had found him. Matthias trusted that Amery would return if he needed her, but he had no idea where she had gone. Neither could he understand how Weard fitted in to Imbert and Edine's world, nor what they wanted with him.

But Weard's possession of a spiral staff was in some ways the most immediately worrying aspect of it all. Matthias found that his hands were clenched hard on the ornately carved arms of his chair.

'The Desert Rose would not just – give you a staff.'

'I fed it.' The bluster was all gone. Weard's voice was very quiet, almost muffled by the heavy hangings of the room.

'On what?'

A long pause. 'Ah, Matthias,' said Weard at last. 'If only you could see the Kingdom of Blood now! You would not recognise what it has become. No barren, arid desert now. A leafy, living jungle it is. The Desert Rose covers many miles now, spreading wide its tentacles over the dry sand – '

'What did you feed it?'

'The caravan . . .' It was almost whispered. 'I led them into range. Lizards and all. I kept back only a few men. And then I cut a living branch.'

His voice ran on. He had stripped its leaves, chanting and reciting. He had held it over a fire, torturing the living wood into the vanishing spiral of power, while beyond the smoke the Rose entrapped creatures and men and women within its flowery embrace. He had barely noticed the noise, he said, although the screaming had gone on for a long time. There was a rustle of leaves moving, of tendrils darting across the sand, but he was well out of reach. It had not distracted him.

Matthias thought of the caravan, those desperate, wrecked losers, the drained old men, the drab, trailing figures of the women. They were the last remnants of the civilisation of Smintha. They had owned the fine furnishings on which Matthias now rested, had moved through its varied levels, singing, working, playing. Perhaps they had even dared to walk in the Field of Flowers. Perhaps they had dared the drifting mist . . .

The huge lizards, the creatures whose ancestors had burrowed out the tunnels of the underworld, had died. They had been devoured by the Desert Rose, absorbed into a forest of wild, voracious appetite and savagery.

For the sake of a spiral staff. Matthias could sense its presence, leaning against the wall of the room close to Weard. Where his own staff had provided a focus for dreams, for the Mage's trained imagination, this staff would only amplify nightmares, and worse.

'Whom do you command now, Weard?' He tried to sound undisturbed.

'The City of Stairs is *very* interesting.' Weard would not answer him directly.

'No Sun God to placate? No Moon Goddess to fear?'

Again, he would not answer.

Matthias tried again. 'What are you doing with Imbert and Edine?'

'We have a project on, we Mages.'

Imbert and Weard? It seemed an unlikely combination.

'What project? What on earth would ever bring you and Imbert together?'

Weard was unoffended. 'They came to Smintha looking for something, although they didn't know what. I was here already. Where else should I have gone? This is my home, the Sminthans were my people – '

'And yet you led them to the Rose?'

'And found a staff.' His voice was low. 'It was a fair bargain,' he said. 'Imbert said it was well worth it . . .'

'And that makes it all right?'

'Oh yes. The project is going to succeed, you see, with us working together. Imbert Cupere never had a staff, he's Peraldonian, after all; but he does know a lot. And *I* hold a staff so powerful that it could blast all of Smintha to smithereens – if I only knew how. Imbert's going to show me. You were no fucking use . . . But even so, Mage, we require your help.'

'What can you possibly need from me, Weard? Now that you've got your staff, and Imbert to tell you how to use it? What is the aim of all this unlikely cooperation?'

He laughed. 'Why, the Stasis, of course. The Stasis back again, so that we may live forever.'

Matthias shivered, although the room was hot and stuffy. He had half known it would be this.

'The Benu is free,' he said patiently. 'There's no way of capturing it again.'

'If it was done once, it can be done again. And there is power to be used . . .'

'Where? What power?'

But even as he asked, Matthias knew the answer.

Imbert, brilliant and ruthless. Edine, clever, unknown. Weard himself, a half-trained Mage of brutal violence and uneven force.

A spiral staff. Not just any spiral staff, won through long years of study, but a staff made of the very substance of the greatest Mage of them all. The Desert Rose Lefevre, High Priest to the Sun. The original architect of the Stasis. That will, imagination and skill, caught in a length of tortured wood. It would be an instrument of inconceivable potency.

Weard was silent and Matthias knew that he was under observation. He suddenly realised why he was here, why they were holding him separate from the others.

He was a source of power, too. He held all the accumulated wisdom of Blaise's diaries and much else. The man who engineered the end of the Stasis would have much to offer those who wanted to reinstate that condition.

He felt sick, in that stuffy room, wondering how far he would be able to resist. Wondering what he would have to endure to stop himself joining his former colleagues and his self-appointed pupil in this task.

There was something else too. The realm at the end of the spiral staircases, at the end of every journey to the interior. It lay at the centre of Smintha, the portal. If he was right, the dark plain marked the start of the true underworld, the final destination.

He wondered if they would attempt to harness the power of that twisting mist deep below, with its disintegrating array of hallucinations. They could not be so foolish, he thought, surely not. Matthias felt his breath catch in his lungs. To release that power into the world would be worse than any reinstatement of the Stasis.

Eternal death rather than eternal life.

Amery, I'm going to need you. Stay close, please stay close.

But she had gone, and Matthias was alone with Weard.

Thurstan rolled over on the bed, reaching for the pliant shape of the woman he loved.

This overwhelming passion had developed swiftly. He had abandoned himself to it because she was so beautiful, so exquisite with husky voice, long limbs and wild raven curls. It had been a very long time since he had had a woman.

That explained the sexual urgency. But he had thrown away all caution, all reason, because he could not bear the thought of what had happened in the theatre. He needed diversion.

Anything to stop him thinking. He did not know where he was or what he was doing. He just wanted to blot out the memory of that infinite hatred.

She was soft and enticing, her voice expressing the sweetest music he had ever heard. And her body was slim and supple, and welded itself to him in velvet-smooth patterns of grace.

Just remembering the previous night made his breathing quicken. He ran his hand down the length of her spine, from nape of neck to the soft dip before the swell of the buttocks, and she stirred in her sleep, rolling over onto her back.

In the shabby back bedroom of a boarding house he began to make love to her again, mindlessly surrendering to the wave of lust. Memory slipped further from him.

Chapter Sixteen
The Sea Lords

Blundering through the wet streets, dodging through crowds, for a time Serethrun managed to lose Rosco. He was furious, more angry than he had ever been before in his life. Even the inquiry after the wreck had been nothing to this.

What had he done in allying himself to these men? He had been out of his mind to trust Mittelson and Rosco. Literally. Tricked and deceived by a swirling spiral. And later, why had he continued to go along with them when he hardly even knew them?

Why couldn't they have told him what was going on? That was the root of it. The feeling of betrayal, by men he had grown to like and trust. They should have been open with him.

But he knew, deep down, that any approach from the fishermen of Shelt, when he was working with the Guard, would have been dismissed as irrelevant, dangerous, nonsense. He was so glad to have won acceptance, so relieved to be part of the great machinery of the Guard, that he almost forgot who he was.

Eloish. By definition, outsiders. He could no longer separate himself from them, the people who disdained the usual preoccupations of humanity. Owning no houses, no wealth, few possessions. Uncluttered by the usual patterns of family ties. We have other priorities, he thought: roaming the plains, following the wind, storm, the herds of deer and the flight of the birds. We carry no passengers, and make no concessions.

It was not that Serethrun distrusted all magic. There was always magic, everywhere. Before the Stasis, the *eloish* had followed the herds like any other nomad tribe. But during the wild storms, many of the herds of eldeer and all the wild horses were rounded up. They were kept in corrals near Shelt and the other cities, protected by city guards. The *eloish* used their shaman women to find other prey for them. They began to assess the wind, to use the storm. Under cover of thunder, they raided the city corrals.

It was no wonder that the *eloish* were hated. It was no wonder that it had been hard for Serethrun to be accepted within Shelt. It had taken so long to build up that frail degree of acceptance. And Mittelson and Rosco had casually, brutally, destroyed it all. Why should he help them? What were the fisherpeople to him?

But it was all connected. The injustice that condemned the plainspeople to scratching the hardest of existences, the corralling of the herds, the theft of the horses, was the responsibility of the Sea Lords and their counterparts in the other cities. The *eloish* had been pushed ever further to the north and west by the raiding parties. With reason they feared and hated the Sea Lords of Shelt and their high-handed disregard for the life of others.

That was why Mittelson had acted as he did, why they had destroyed Serethrun's position in the Guard. It was not a wanton act. They were fighting for the rights of ordinary people to pursue their ordinary lives. Serethrun could not deny the justice of the fishermen's cause.

Rosco and Mittelson were obsessed with altering the balance of power in Shelt, an issue which he could hardly ignore.

He had risked all his past for them. The *eloish*, in the end, had trusted him. Had left the shelter of the dense forest to stand, awaiting his message outside Shelt. They had forgiven him his rejection of their way of life. They had forgiven him for trying to save his father's life, because they too recognised the injustice that soured all their lives.

There were other things, too. He remembered the sailor's face on the sinking ship. And the body of the woman, washed by the waves, an offering on the altar of men's ambition.

Felicia. The other enchantment, one he did not wish to escape. At last he knew what Irian had meant. He remembered hiding behind the hangings in the bedroom when Gawne had threatened to hold another Marqun. The

Sea Lords were using Felicia for unthinkable ends, ends that, he had to acknowledge it, made Mittelson and Rosco look like novices.

He was skirting the edge of the floodwaters, moving west through the city, back towards the plains gate. Somehow he was not surprised to feel a light hand on his shoulder.

'Serethrun.' Rosco's voice was unusually gentle.

He stopped, not turning round, and dug his hands in his pockets. 'All right,' he said, bitterly, angrily. 'All right! Perhaps, only just perhaps, it might be worth it.'

'That's more than we deserve.' Rosco's voice was wholly serious. Serethrun turned round to face him, and there was a long silence.

Then Rosco said, slowly, 'I would not have blamed you, you know, if you'd run out.'

'Why? Do you want to?' It was a flash of intuition, unexpected and certain.

They were walking back through the hurrying crowds, back towards the rising tidewaters of river and sea.

'Yes. Oh, yes. But I have discovered, like you, that there is more at stake here than personal pride. At least, that is the sop, the only consolation.'

'Let's have a drink,' Serethrun said abruptly. He turned aside, pushing across the pavement to the tavern at the roadside without looking to see if Rosco was following.

Which he was. Appropriately enough.

In the depths a dragon stirred. It spread itself luxuriously over the sands and rocks, carelessly snapping at the unwise fish. Its appetites were not of the same order as those of the frail men who tried to placate it. It hungered, yes; but not only for food and power.

Its many mouths had tasted flesh: the sweet, soft line of it. And now it wanted more. Not just anyone, not the foolish swimmers or pleasure-boat owners who occasionally tumbled into the untrustworthy depths.

But the cool white limbs of a girl. It had encountered her first during a storm when, tempted by the Sea Lords, it had wrecked a ship. Then Ladon had only seen her, a flickering glimmering shape in the distance, before someone had pulled her from the water.

The same woman had been offered again, later, as a bribe during one of their foolish ceremonies.

It had accepted, for it recognised something strange in this girl (running multitudinous lips along the smooth limbs, the delicate lines). Tasting her breath, watching her hair drifting in water, it recognised the touch of a greater God than itself.

The Moon shone from her being, white and cool and clear. Something fine, something of clarity and power.

It would have her. Take her from the city to live in the sea, a sea child, a sea mate. It would enwrap her in wave and salt and a hundred mouths would worship, the long limbs intertwine. It would hold the Moon child fast to itself, drifting in sea-water, a perfect match of light and motion; and what strange progeny would then result?

The time was nearly right. At each high tide it reached further into the city, searching, searching.

Loving. Wanting. Needing. And nothing, nothing, would be able to stop it.

That afternoon the tide rose higher than anyone had predicted. Even the great houses on the hill around the Castle found their basements flooded with stinking mud and water.

Rats ran openly through dingy streets towards the plains gates, joining the steady stream of people leaving the city. With belongings crammed into barrows and carts, bundles under arms, men and women prepared to camp out on the high ground north of the city.

'Olwyn, can't we leave too?' Annis, standing by the window, watched the straggling crowds pushing through the narrow streets to the plain gates. 'It's dangerous, surely? We're being pushed closer to the Castle all the time. We could camp on the hill for a week, just until the spring tides go down . . .'

'No, not yet. We can't leave the city. Everyone going through those gates is searched, their papers examined. We'd never get through.'

'What about Rosco's hawk? Couldn't it get us out of this?'

'The Arrarat will only carry strangers if the cause if right. Astrella will take no one from the city.'

'Why not?' There was more than petulance in her voice.

'You must ask Rosco, not me. He'll be here later.'

Olwyn Mittelson looked up from the pamphlet he was drafting. Another view of Ladon, and Gawne and Dederic, all the Sea Lords, standing round the edge of a tide-pool. Felicia had sketched it, but Gawne no longer looked like a goat. A death's head, he was, communing with a dragon.

Felicia was also standing by the window, close to Annis, as if mere physical proximity could give her strength.

It was unthinkable, now, that she should walk through streets, stand up against her uncle and his ministers, strive for independence. She was in the grip of a nightmare now, a nightmare that drew her to stand by the window, again and again, watching the tide rise.

She tried not to sleep, for Ladon lived in her dreams. She could eat nothing without vomiting. A cold knot of panic and discomfort cramped in her stomach, sending clammy waves of weakness through all her body. She was sea-sick on land, because the sea was now encroaching into the city itself. She felt frail strength and courage ebb away, and even the small trust that lay between Rosco and herself began to drown in the steady wash of waves.

She was waiting for the sea to reclaim her.

She was not without courage. Trying not to think, trying not to hear the wash of the sea through the city streets, she drew pictures for Mittelson, somehow trusting that he knew what he was doing and that he meant her no harm.

As the flooding river and high tides flowed through the city, so the constant stream of propaganda littered the shops, bars, public places. Thrust through the doors of private houses, nailed to noticeboards and hoardings. Pernicious litter, ever-present, ever-nagging. Vivid, garish and incendiary. They fell into puddles, blew into the sea, were torn and crushed underfoot, swept up and burnt.

But some were read, some were noticed.

In a high tower Torold and Esmond sat, looking through rain-splattered windows to a roof-top garden of conifers and evergreens, blown ragged by wind. Esmond held a sheaf of papers in his hands. He had gathered them from roofs, floors, litter bins and gutters. They were stained and torn, muddy

and damp. But their message was clear. The Sea Lords were
in thrall to a monster.

Torold had read the pamphlets, holding them in trembling
hands. The wine flask at his side was almost empty. 'How
much longer, Esmond? Is there long to wait now?'

'Mittelson – the Mage – said it would be decided, all of
it, at the spring tide.'

'How can he know?' It was almost a shout. 'I can't keep
this up much longer, I'm sure Gawne suspects something,
I'm no good at acting – '

'Hush, my dear. Only two days now, only two days . . .'

'And this man – Rosco – how can we trust him?'

'He rides an Arrarat hawk.'

'What of it? The *eloish* ride the storm itself. They are not
our friends . . .'

'They could be, perhaps. In other circumstances. But
anyway, Torold, look to your own past. Remember when you
were a child, the nursery rhymes, the old legends and stories?
The golden hawks that belonged to the Benu Bird, the pace
of the Universe. They were always good, splendid and strong.
I cannot find it in myself to distrust the rider of an Arrarat
hawk.'

Perhaps one day Torold would discover how deeply
Esmond lied. But by then, Esmond hoped and prayed, he
would have his lover safe, wandering together through forests
of pines and larches, the snow crisp under their boots, their
breath warm in the air. Away from the wearisome business
of government and politics, away from the pressures of state,
away from the influence of brother Javon.

'Gawne has called a meeting this afternoon. Emergency
measures for the city, or something. I suppose I'll have to
be there.' Torold passed a sweating hand over his brow,
sighing tiredly.

Esmond watched him with compassion. If Torold had even
once showed a real desire to help the citizens of Shelt and
its surrounds, he might have thought twice about engineering
this abdication from power. But Torold was not in the least
interested in the authority his brother had won for him.
Gratified for a while by pomp and ceremony, enjoying good
food and fine wine, it had seemed at first a pleasant honour
to be Earl of Shelt. He was free of Javon's influence in Shelt.

But the Sea Lords had destroyed that. First the boundaries to the west were to be secured. A series of raids against the plainspeople who roamed those regions. Shelt was to be held inviolate from *eloish* influences. The Sea Lords did not want their strange abilities investigated by black shaman women: they had no desire to share their secrets.

Shelt's military power was without compare, and the plainspeople had fled further west and north, leaving the plains near Shelt clear and empty.

At first Torold had rather enjoyed the campaigns. He was a good soldier, a fine swordsman, an excellent horseman. He had the gift of command. Men were glad to follow him. He had not bothered to think what these actions cost in terms of the lives of the plainspeople.

In the end he had returned to Shelt, trailing strings of horses stolen from the plainspeople. Torold had celebrated, happy to be home, happy in the arms of his new lover.

But then there had been more strange demands from the Sea Lords. Nothing to do with boundaries; something that seemed at first only a benefit for everyone.

The Sea Lords began to market their powers of healing. Those injured in battle regained the use of limbs and muscles they had thought wasted. Plagues and fevers lost their virulence, and spread no further. Those terminally ill with cancers and palsy were baptised in the tide-pool at Marqun and were miraculously restored. The elderly regained vigour. If they could pay.

The wealthy from all around sent their sickly friends and relatives to Shelt. They brought with them money and gifts, treaties and promises. Shelt, and Torold Westray, became rich and admired. He relaxed happily into a life of luxury and ease.

The price of all this healing was the destruction of the fishing industry. 'They'll find other work,' Gawne had said confidently. 'The farms in the south and west could be more intensively worked. They'll move on, don't worry. No one will starve.'

False confidence. Men bound to the sea for countless generations did not easily adjust to land work. They were the people of Shelt, followers of the Lady in more than word. Shelt would not have existed at all but for the fishermen.

They had established their harbour and watched the tides and prayed to the Lady to watch over the rhythm of their lives. And until the Sea Lords usurped Her power, that was exactly what She did.

Why should they move on, so that foreign princes might be free of arthritis? No one left. Some starved. And insurrection was rife throughout the city.

Torold found his nights disturbed by rioting fishermen, by raids and brawls. His days were dogged by petitions and deputations, worrying him for justice and freedom. He flung himself into training the Guard, expanding it, honing it to a fine, sharp, cutting edge. It was the only answer he knew. And, deep down, he knew that civil war was in the air.

And then Felicia had arrived, and the situation had rapidly deteriorated. If he was in awe of Gawne, and worried by the unrest in Shelt, he was terrified of his brother. Letting him down in this way. Failing his daughter, and his trust.

He was brave on the battlefield, splendid on horseback, commanding and credible. But scared to death of his elder brother's vicious tongue, his iron will. Nervous of the kind of responsibility that could not be easily answered with a sword or an arrow.

He wanted to give it all up, return to being a captain in his brother's Guard, or better still to live in quiet seclusion with Esmond and a small party of friends. They could hunt and wrestle and carouse in a remote forest somewhere, far away from the sea, far away from the cares of state; and then his love for Esmond would be evergreen as the surrounding trees.

He crumpled up the damp scraps of paper on the table and tossed them into the fire, where they smoked unpleasantly before falling into ash. He leant across the table and took Esmond's hand.

He was not looking forward to the afternoon's meeting.

Gawne, Dederic, Quass, Manton, Lammon: the whole collection of them were ranged round the large oval table by the window. Even Fessil, the doctor, was there, brought in to add layman's support to whatever the Sea Lords wanted.

Torold swept into the council room, squaring his shoulders, wishing he hadn't had so much to drink at lunchtime.

Esmond had not been there to divert him: laid low with migraine, said the message. It was not unusual, and Torold had thought little of it.

The council chamber was hot, as he liked it, the windows securely fastened against the wind and rain. Through the casements the sky was iron grey, heavy with rain. Torches were lit round the walls, although it was still early afternoon.

The Sea Lords stood up as Torold entered, grey-green silks shimmering in the torchlight. They were always so silent, so thin and bloodless. Impatiently he slumped into his massively carved chair, and waved for them all to sit. Gawne, First Lord of Aquile, remained standing.

'Well, Gawne?' he said brusquely. 'What's it about this time?'

The rotas, said Gawne. The lists of patients ready for the Marqun ceremonies. The disposition of their households, how to organise extra visitors when the tide was rising and so much of Shelt uninhabitable.

He droned on, lists and rates, by-laws and taxes. Torold's suspicion subsided. And then, at the end of one particularly long-winded item (provisions from Hoel) it began.

'My Lord Torold, a deeply distressing rumour has reached our ears.' He paused.

Torold could feel his pulse-rate quicken.

'We would be most interested to discover whether it is with your knowledge and consent that Esmond Crinnion has been meeting the renegade Mage Mittelson and his confederates.'

'Nonsense! Of course not, he is utterly loyal to me – '

'His loyalty to you is not in question. It is his loyalty to the Sea Lords that is the issue.'

'By implication, you accuse me.' He was not a stupid man, he had been prepared for this. He had half a dozen of his personal Guard stationed outside the door. The scabbard at his side was not only for show. These were old men, untrained in battle, unused to aggression. They would not prevail.

He disliked the small Mage, Lammon. He was known to have opposed the takeover by Javon and Torold. Torold even remembered Esmond warning him that Brice Lammon was dangerous. He only pretended loyalty, Esmond had said. Really he was planning something else . . . Lammon's eyes were difficult to catch, flickering here and there. In a fight, he alone of the men in the room would be worth watching.

Gawne was staring at Torold with those curiously hooded eyes. His shoulders seemed to be hunched higher than ever. 'My Lord Torold, there is no doubt that Crinnion is involved in conspiracy. Perhaps you have listened to unwise advice. If you were to abjure him, we might overlook your – lack of judgment.'

'What – exactly – do you mean by "abjure"?' Were they daring to threaten him?

'He is a traitor. You know the penalty.'

'I make my own decisions, Gawne.' This was not just bluster, his sword hilt was steady in his hand.

'Then are you, too, involved in treachery?'

The room was quiet, so quiet that the rain outside sounded like a thousand drums ceaselessly pattering.

'Have you lost your mind, Gawne? What treachery? *I* am Earl of Shelt! I make my own decisions, make my own friends!'

Gawne was smiling. It did not reach his eyes. Irrelevant thoughts sped through Torold's mind as he watched him. Gawne never really smiled, eyes and all. Ice-cold, he was, dressed in dreary grey, tall and thin and bloodless.

Dederic was standing now, and Quass, a short, elderly man with wispy hair.

Torold pushed his chair back suddenly, on his feet and sword out in one smooth movement.

Gawne remained motionless. 'You err, Torold Westray. The real Earl of Shelt rules the sea beyond these windows – '

'That *dragon*!' Torold was shouting with incredulity. 'Ruling Shelt! Balls! Stories to frighten children!'

'Not so, my Lord.' Dederic, worried, uneasy in the tension.

'What does it matter to you, Lord Torold? You were never interested in your citizens.' This from the little weaselly Mage, Lammon, bitterly, angrily.

'We will hold a Marqun tonight. At the first of the spring tides. You may see for yourself who rules Shelt. You will attend, Lord Torold.' Gawne's voice was still calm, devoid of any feeling.

'I will not! I – '

'It will be a ceremony of healing.'

'Healing? What do you mean, healing? For whom?'

There was a sudden stillness in the room. Then, in answer, Gawne struck his spiral staff on the floor, and the wide doors to the corridor opened.

At first Torold did not recognise the strange figure standing there. The look in the man's eyes was so bizarre, so alien, that all trace of personality was lost. A slight, fair-haired figure, familiar in every way but in this expression, standing apart and uncomprehending.

'Esmond!' The cry came from his heart, he could not disguise it. He began to stumble towards the doors, but the unresisting figure started to fall back into the shadows.

His head lolled with the movement, the mouth slackly open and dribbling. His eyes, a clear and beautiful blue, were open but empty. And then, suddenly, standing between Torold and his lover, there was the shifting insectoid shape of a spider or a mantis or a woman, with gold hair and clasping claws, dressed in light or in brittle carapace, shimmering between forms.

'Esmond!' He was on his knees, transfixed by horrors.

A hand on his shoulder.

'Come,' said Gawne. 'Only the Marqun can restore him.'

'What have you done? What has happened? What is *that*?' He shook the hand off, still staring at the hideous shape as the double doors closed.

'We are joined by one skilled in transformation. A creature of the Parid from the far south. It has helped us to find out many things from Esmond. We have discovered, Torold, where the rebels hide. What their plans are, and what yours are. He was indeed loyal to you, little Esmond. You have seen the result. But perhaps a Marqun can heal him — and you.'

'Me? What are you talking about?'

'You are involved in dangerous heresy, Torold, not trusting your own council of Sea Lords. We wish to prove to you that we are worthy of your trust. Only the sea can heal such a breach of faith.'

'What about Esmond?' It was all he could think about, all that mattered.

Gawne shrugged. 'If you had denied Crinnion, agreed that

he should pay the penalty for treason, we would have been assured of your good faith. There would have been no necessity for a Marqun.'

Gawne hunched his shoulders yet higher. His eyes gleamed. 'Now we have no choice.'

Chapter Seventeen
The Hidden Rite

'The Rite requires that a number of different conditions should be met. We can fulfil most of them. We need you, Matthias, to help us with the others.'

Their voices were so reasonable, so clear and civilised. Matthias remembered the difficult conferences with Imbert and Edine, gathering the knowledge and power to set up the Seventh Rite again, the Rite that brought Eleanor back to them.

And further back, before the Stasis, he had worked with them at the college on Peraldon. Imbert had been the star then, brilliant and imaginative, singled out and adopted by the Mage Lefevre. Armed with Lefevre's support, Imbert had persuaded the College of Mages to tolerate Edine's presence as his companion.

It was not purely selfish, he maintained. She released in him ideas and theories unusual to the main body of magic philosophy. He would closely observe the effect; he promised that none of the Cabbalic secrets would be revealed to her.

They formed a natural partnership: cool and elegant, with an unexpected, mischievous passion for theatrical display and device. Imbert had decided to work mainly within the fields of disguise and shape-shifting, and Edine became essential to his experiments. Matthias knew that they would be more than capable of creating and using wraiths. They would be able to control any Parid, order the scurries with a flicker of thought.

They were not mystics or sages. They were Peraldonians, through and through. The spiral staff of Astret's followers, its shape echoing the waxing and waning of the moon, was unknown to them. Even more limiting, they had little knowledge of Synchronicity. They used their magic for purely practical, immediately gratifying purposes. But what could be more practical then wanting to live forever?

They would require much from Matthias, and although their knowledge was not complete, he knew that he had few defences against them.

He could not see what kind of place they were in, but there were carved wooden chairs and tables, a smooth stone floor beneath the carpets under his feet. The house of a wealthy man. A priest, possibly, for it was near to the surface. It was hot and stuffy. The sun felt very close. With foreboding, he wondered whether he would ever feel fresh, cool air against his skin again.

They gave him wine to drink, but he refused, fearing that it might be drugged.

Imbert had laughed. 'Matthias, we have no need of you befuddled or senseless! Quite the opposite.'

Still he refused it, asking for water. He would need all his wits sharp and clear to deal with these two.

Weard was different, neither subtle nor sophisticated. But Matthias had experienced his violence before, and knew better than to underestimate it.

There was also the bargain. He had promised to instruct Weard in Mage-lore as the price of getting Eleanor and the baby out of the Palace of Blood.

They were holding Eleanor and Blythe not far away, Imbert had said. Matthias should perhaps consider their position, imprisoned here.

He sighed. They were right. They had no need to give him drugs: there were a number of levers around to extract the information they required for the Hidden Rite.

'Let us tell you what we know already, Matthias.' Imbert's voice was kind and considerate. 'And then we won't have to waste time covering old ground.'

Their voices droned on, listing ceremonies, scriptures, spells and incantations. They knew far more than he would have believed possible. Had he underrated them?

'A fire, of course. A great fire,' said Edine.

'A fire to match the sun, to blaze through the ordinary world, to entice and delight — '

'And destroy,' Matthias finished for Imbert, his voice grim.

'The Benu is the destroyer. It brings death, death to every one of us – '

'And rebirth to humanity as a whole.'

'But what use is that to *me*? To Edine? Will we ever find ourselves incarnate – with eyes to see and skin to feel and hearts to love – at the same time, in the same place? Would I even *know* my love, in some other life, some other guise?' His voice was dark, hollow with passion. 'We will burn through the cycle of being and non-being. We will scorch it to nothing, cleanse it of impurity, cauterise the curse of death – '

'We will build a fire.'

'The greatest fire of all.'

'It will call the Bird to its fated path.'

'It will not escape . . .'

'What will you burn, to make such a fire?' He broke into the pattern of chiming voices.

The sound ceased. They looked at him. He held his breath, suddenly aware of the direction of their thoughts.

'The Desert Rose, Matthias. We are going to burn the Desert Rose.'

'The peripheral roots dry out underground. Only the central stems are green and fleshy. The rest will burn.'

They explained in cool tones, in reasoned words, as if this were a logical and feasible course. He listened with incredulity and growing horror.

This was impossible, beyond mere danger, beyond imagination. He fought for words. 'You have surely lost your senses. Remember what the Desert Rose is, remember which mind controls it. Are you seriously planning to make a bonfire of the Great Mage?'

'Whatever the Rose is now, there is very little left of Lucian Lefevre. It can only contribute to the success of the Rite.' Imbert sounded entirely confident.

Edine broke in, 'And if there is anything of Lefevre left, just think what it will add! The essence of the Great Mage, released in smoke and flame! How could we fail?'

'After all, it was Lefevre who had trapped the Benu in the first place.'

Their voices blended together once more. He heard the obsessiveness, the will-directed ambition. He knew then that their judgment had been irretrievably distorted. What had happened to make them so overreach themselves?

'We've spent a long time preparing the glass, the herbs, the offering – ' Edine continued.

'Offering? Who?' How did they know about the offering? He could no longer disguise his anxiety. Perhaps it no longer mattered.

'Ah, you'll have to wait to find out about that one. But rest assured, Matthias, our chosen offering will not be without significance within the shape of the Rite.'

Who would they chose, he wondered, dismayed. Eleanor, Blythe? Either of them would contribute a degree of symmetry to the thing. Coron? But he had to be far away by now . . . Thurstan, wherever he was? Himself?

How did the offering go? An aware, passive victim. Eleanor would never lend herself to such a cause, nor Blythe, he was sure. Coron was unknown, but it was impossible that he should contribute to evil. Thurstan was surely out of the question too.

And as for himself, he would only give his life to prevent such a thing happening.

And when the fire was burning, on the pyre formed by the body of the Rose, the offering would die . . .

He became aware that the room had fallen silent. They were watching him. He shifted uncomfortably against the plump cushions. 'Go on,' he said, his voice tired and distant. 'What else?'

'It's your turn, Matthias. You tell us. What else?'

No. He had no need to speak his refusal aloud. They knew he would not willingly give them help in trapping the Benu. Re-establishing the Stasis. Betraying Astret.

There was an academic interest in finding out what methods of persuasion they would try. He was relying on the likelihood that they would at least be subtle about it.

He was wrong.

'Come with me.' Imbert took his hand, and pulled him to his feet. 'Find out what is at stake, Matthias. Come and see why it is necessary – for us all – to reinstate the Stasis.'

'Don't imagine that you're doing this for anyone else, Imbert. I know you. This is a private act, to further a private obsession.'

'You misjudge me, Matthias. You always have.'

They were walking through one of the upper avenues. Imbert spoke gently, thoughtfully. 'After all, you have never known love, have you? Astret's Mages don't love. Neither do they admit women to their company. And so their view is distorted, cut off from the essential human concerns.'

'Uncluttered by human concerns . . . That is the theory of it.'

'Theory!' Imbert stopped for a moment, and Matthias heard a gate swing open. 'Stairs here, Matthias. Take care.'

They started to descend a narrow staircase. Imbert had removed his guiding hand, and Matthias discovered instead a smooth rail. 'No experience of love is a limitation, a distorting factor. Edine and I – '

'Yes?' Matthias suddenly felt Imbert's hand on his arm once more.

'Here we are. Just a little further, and then the spiral stairs . . .'

'The Field of Flowers. Is that where we're going?' he said. Another pause, another gate clanging against its support, echoing in vast spaces.

The sudden, appalling knowledge that air had opened up all around them, above and below, quiet and undisturbed.

'Yes. The spiral stairs now. I think, Matthias, that you did not fully appreciate their significance when first you fell into those depths . . .'

Matthias said nothing. He heard a huge tension in Imbert's voice, as if he were suppressing a dreadful secret. It had not been there when they worked together to bring Eleanor back. Imbert had changed.

Or something had changed him.

'Imbert. We need go no further. There is nothing down there which could possibly make me change my mind. I know what lies there.'

'Frightened, Matthias? Worried that the mists will find something – attractive in your thoughts? That they might fasten on to the mysterious essence that holds a Mage of power together?'

'You find it amusing?'

The descent continued. It was difficult to estimate how far they had come. Other gates clanged, barrier after barrier. Every now and then Matthias felt a breath of foetid air from the curving wall to his left as various passages led back into the City of Stairs.

At length there were no more junctions, no more escapes from the staircase. They tramped on in silence.

Matthias heard the gate clang once more, and felt Imbert's hand on his sleeve. 'There, Matthias. Can you sense it? Can you feel it waiting, wanting? The stairs still protect us, the iron cage is some reassurance. But the Field of Flowers is stirring, and the shadows acknowledge us . . .'

Two Mages, two flickering consciousnesses of dubious, varying potency. Thinking to chance, to trespass on the lonely plains, the territory of the Unseen, Unseeing God.

I wait, assessing their slow approach. One is reluctant, the other avid. My wings spread wide, reaching towards them, drawn by warmth. The bars of black trees still contain me, but my flowers are turning, fed by the presence of the living.

What do they wish for here? Some taste of forgetting, some release from elaboration? My wings lift and fall, soft and heavy as breathing, darker than oblivion.

Their thoughts do not call. Their words fall, empty. One of them is nearly mine, but not yet. They are not ready for dissolution, and I settle, back among the trees.

Why are they here? Do they want dreams? Memories? Visions? All are mine to offer, should I so choose. They have nothing to give, and are nothing . . .

One of them is afflicted, guilt-driven. My Children are about me, are mine once more. Perhaps I should release them . . .

The dark ravens rustle beneath my wings. I turn away from the trespassers, but the Children fret still.

I let them go. Find your prey, I say. He is not far away.

Standing just beyond the iron gates, his feet crushing the scented flowers, Matthias was shaking. 'Out of here, Imbert, we must get away from here –' His face was white, sweat glistening at his temples. Imbert watched with curiosity.

'Visions of the future, Matthias? The curse of the blind Mage, of course. But I thought you would be exempt from pre-knowledge underground.'

'So did I.' He began to walk, pushing his way through the clouds of yellow flowers, back towards where he thought the gates were. He held out his hands, seeking the comfort of cold iron. Imbert caught up with him, grasping his shoulder.

'*Now* do you understand? It's not just that I want to love Edine forever, it's not that I want to *live* forever . . . But what waits here – is intolerable –'

'*Out* of here, quickly, before it starts – '

'Starts? What? It is not our turn yet!'

'Death is not the only option here. What dreams have you seen here, Imbert? Why do you keep coming back?'

Matthias had passed through the gates, was standing on hard, unflowered earth. Passionately, he longed for his ordinary, earth-bound vision once more. He needed to see what lurked behind Imbert's eyes. His voice gave hints at it, but only the eyes gave it all away.

He wondered if Imbert was in thrall. Whether he had surrendered to the dark wings of the unseen being who ruled the underworld. Whether his desire to reinstate the Stasis was really an attempt to escape a fate already decided.

'Tell me, Imbert! What is the draw?' Matthias only had voices to go on now. He needed to keep Imbert talking. They were climbing the spiral stairs once more, retreating from the centre.

'At first – I didn't know what it was. I just wanted to find out . . . I had a suspicion, of course. I too studied the Cabbala, Matthias, I did not waste my time at Peraldon. And Lefevre told me much. He told me once that he came here in order to create Parid. Did you know that? The Parid are constructed from rags. The rags of personality snatched from the mists before their final dissolution. Lefevre used the scurries to give form and substance, and imprinted them with whatever he managed to salvage from those dark wings.'

'A bargain with the Unseen One? Or a theft? No wonder . . .' He paused. 'Can you do this too? Have you made a Parid?'

'It's not easy.' He would not answer directly. 'I think that was why Lefevre used animal forms so often. Simpler, more direct to work with, to mould.'

'What do you use?'

'Whatever I find.'

'Imbert.' Matthias stood still on the stairs. 'This is inconceivably dangerous. You *cannot* expect to cheat the Unseen One of Its due and get away with it – '

'Lefevre did.'

'And what is Lefevre now? A sprawling wilderness of thwarted desire . . . Do you aspire to that condition?'

'No. I am in love with no God, I love only – Edine. I aspire to eternal life, so that we may live together eternally.'

'But you are chancing death here, not life!'

'Perhaps we need you, Matthias. To show us how it can be done without disturbing the underworld. You know the details, you know how the Rite should go – '

'It is perilously difficult! A massive gathering of power and force! There could not be a worse place than this for such an occurrence.'

'We will need you to show us how to conduct the Rite in safety. For take place it assuredly will. Here. Below the Temple of Lycias.'

He could not believe the foolhardiness of this. The arrogance, the wilful disregard of reason.

'Are you completely out of your mind? *Why*? Why here?'

'Oh, Matthias! So you don't know everything, after all. It's perfectly simple, perfectly logical. We will perform the Rite here because we are following in the footsteps of the Master. Didn't you know? This is where Lefevre conducted the original Rite. This is where it all happened before, where the Benu was captured so that Lycias might love Mariana eternally.

'It took place here, at the Temple of Lycias. Over the portal. Where we stand now.'

Chapter Eighteen
Coercion

Imbert and Edine had taken him back to the ornate room with its soft carpets and antique furniture. They brought him food and wine and water and locked the door.

He sat at the table, unmoving.

Think about it. They were playing with fire in every possible way, thoughtless as children. Except that they knew so much, and were genuinely clever. Using the Fosca, they had managed to gather together in one place Eleanor, Phin, himself, and the staff of the Desert Rose. The Rose itself, to be sacrificed in flames. It might even work, if they were careful enough . . . It might even release the underworld, if they were reckless enough.

The billowing clouds hid the winged being, the Unseen One. The final victor who took the remnants of life and teased apart the various strands. As a weaver spins wool into workable threads, so the clouds envelope each individual and unravel the muddle of memory, thought and emotion into – nothing.

It was the final dissolution in the dim realm of all forgetting, under the aegis of an unknown God. There was no way through to the Unseen One, no rite or priesthood, no prayer or ceremony, no possible way at all to approach such a being. Its nature was hidden, from all people, for all time. The priests of the Sun, the priestesses of the Moon were united on this one point.

Think about it. Imbert was powerful, but his knowledge of the Cabbalic Rites was not complete. He and Edine had needed Matthias to bring Eleanor back. And it was by no means certain that Imbert had yet achieved a Parid of his own making. He had dodged that question. Only Lefevre had ever been able to construct Parid, only Lefevre had ever negotiated the Fields of Flowers unscarred . . .

Only Lefevre had performed the Hidden Rite.

Imbert and Edine were voraciously ambitious. Clever, learned, tricksy, all of those. But they had never sought out the depths of mystic lore, had never surrendered everything for the love of the God, the love of the Goddess. How could they, loving each other? There was no single-minded austerity of purpose.

Matthias found himself in a double-edged dilemma. They didn't know everything; they had needed Matthias to bring Eleanor back from her own world. But because they didn't know everything, they would need Matthias again to capture the Benu. Without Matthias, there was a good chance that they would distort the whole thing, that they might release the power that waited beyond the plains of asphodel. He could hear that possibility in Imbert's voice. Imbert was half in love with the idea . . .

They might release the Unseen One into the world. If the Rite failed, in the wrong way, that is what would happen.

He was not prepared for Weard that night. The door flew open with a crash against the wall. He heard a table topple, the china and glass break.

'Damn you, Mage, you'll do it! The Rite, it's up to you – ' Huge hands had lifted him from his bed, wrapped with violence around his throat. He smelt spirits on Weard's breath, heard the words slur. He was viciously out of control.

Matthias tried to defuse the aggression, struggling to speak calmly. His words were soft and conciliatory. Death is not the worst that can happen; you are young yet, it is far away; the dangers of the Rite are far greater than any reward . . . There was nothing he could say that would make any difference.

'I've been down there, I've seen what waits.' Weard's voice was more than brutal and aggressive. There was something haunted there, something full of fear and guilt. 'You're going to get me out of this, I'm not going to face that thing down there. You'll make this Rite happen, and let me live forever!'

His voice rose. Matthias tried to keep talking, his words

calm and unhurried, but what could he offer against the desire
for immortality, the fear of dissolution? He had finished up,
back to the wall, braced and foolishly trembling, waiting for
Weard to begin.

Matthias knew what would happen. Weard was not subtle.
He heard a faint crackle in the air. Light would be spinning
around the spiral staff, gathering strength. Weard was muttering constantly, familiar, dangerous words under his breath.

Matthias stood completely still, his hands loose at his side.
He was concentrating, driving his mind to some refuge far
away from the potent words, the malevolent hiss of power
from the staff. This was an irrelevance, this was not
important.

He could feel but not see the green glow spring out from
the spiral, leaping across the air towards him, wrapping itself
around him.

He shivered, but made no sound. The staff was powerful,
a weapon of brute force, but Weard's mind was neither
trained nor skilful in its use. Matthias could handle this. He
felt the spiral of light begin to waver, to lose its shape, to
dissolve and disappear.

Weard's voice was low and savage. 'How dare you resist,
Mage Matthias? Why refuse now? You've fallen in with
everything else so far. You brought the girl back, didn't you?
None of this would be happening if she were not here. You
are implicated from start to finish. You will have to pay . . .'

All at once Matthias felt his control slipping.

Unerringly, Weard had articulated the bitter centre of
Matthias's every thought. He was marked by guilt, forever
and irretrievably, because he had acquiesced in bringing
Eleanor back. He was eternally at fault.

Dark shadows whispered beyond his hearing. We come,
they said.

He understood why Weard's voice was edged with horror
now. Weard had destroyed the caravan. Weard knew all about
guilt, too. He had discovered Matthias's own guilt with
deadly accuracy.

The shadows were flickering, preparing to settle. A spiral
of light drilled its way into his body, was scorching down
the nerves and sinews in patterns of nauseating fire. It
mattered not at all, for the Children were so close. But still

his body shuddered violently, arching against the strength of the spiral, a long, low moan from his lips.

Weard's voice ran on. 'You know what you've brought her back to, don't you? They're going to use her as the offering, of course, and it'll draw the Benu. It will have to come, if the Rite offers Eleanor Knight, because she released it once before. It owes her − '

A shout, a shriek. 'Everyone *pays*, there's no way out, it's a closed trap! If you act, whatever you do, you *pay*!'

It felt as if the spiral were contorting Matthias's limbs into strange shapes. He tried to summon his fragmenting wits, to remember defences and meditations, to find some sanctuary, some safe viewpoint whence his mind could observe, untouched, the body's agony.

But he had no staff and no eyes. No power, influence, wisdom or skill. The Children awaited him. In the end, he was defeated by his own sense of vulnerability, his own guilt. He had brought Eleanor back to this. And he had seen the future.

What could he do to prevent this? Was there any way out at all?

A closed trap. He remembered what he had seen, above ground, in that promise for the future, the desperate misery of Eleanor's face, the hawk falling into flame, the reversal of all his hopes. And the avid shadows rising, fastening their grip around the living, waiting for him . . .

In blackest sorrow, he found his will to resist failing. What was the point of it?

'Where are we?' Some time later, after they had made love again in the drab, characterless room on the lumpy bed that squeaked, Thurstan stood up and crossed the dusty, uncarpeted floor to the window.

A dull city backstreet met his eyes. The street was empty, although he could see a few small shops down one end of it, a butcher's, a cobbler, bakery, apothecary . . . But there was no one there. The shelves were empty, the doors hung open, gaping onto dusty streets. There was litter everywhere, torn paper, scraps of colour on drab earth.

He turned back to the woman stretched out on the bed. She was watching him.

'I don't even know your name,' he said.

She smiled at him. 'A little late for introductions, wouldn't you say?'

He sat down beside her, stroking the dark hair back from her face. 'Perhaps . . . My name is Thurstan Merauld. I do not know what this place is.'

There was a strange half-light outside. Nothing like sunlight or moonlight, or twilight. More like a feeble artificial light, diffused, flat and dull over everything.

'We are far underground,' she said, stroking the skin of his outstretched hand. 'There are many different levels, and each has its own quality, its own structure.'

She paused, looking into his hard, clear eyes. 'I am called Lily Herrys. You know my profession. What else do you need to find out?'

Staring at her wide dark eyes, her mouth slightly open, small even teeth glinting in the dreary light, he couldn't imagine what she meant.

'I – I was with some friends,' he said at last. It was a struggle to remember. 'Where are they?'

'I don't know. Who are they, your friends?'

But as he listed their names, trying to describe who they were, where they were from, they seemed to slip away from him, fading into an insignificant past.

She brought him coffee as he talked, and he sipped it automatically. It was hot and pungent, from a kettle set on a primitive stove near the dressing-table.

It wiped away the last shreds of memory, and all knowledge of identity. Sipping coffee, sitting on a rumpled bed in an unknown building, in a strange street, a foreign city, he was deeply content.

She was beautiful and warm and loving.

He decided to stay. There was nowhere else to go.

Chapter Nineteen
Betrayal

The figure lying on the pallet bed was motionless. Only the faint movement of the chest betrayed that Matthias Marling still lived and breathed.

'It depends on the sequence. The Synchronicity of it. You need to keep your minds uncluttered, so that you may recognise the structures. That is where the chants come in. They are not prayers or incantations as such, but a technique for clearing the mind.'

Matthias spoke with difficulty, against a huge weight of exhaustion. His voice was very faint. Weard was avid at his side, straining to catch every word.

'Once started it will not be interrupted. It may fail – '

'It won't.'

'But it will not cease before the end. Such power gathered at one point will have to follow its own course. It cannot be defused. It can only be contained, according to the Rite.'

The voice faded once more and Imbert, standing across the room, cursed.

'Damn it Weard, you've nearly killed him! You and that bloody staff have nearly put paid to it all – '

'And the offering – Eleanor . . .' Matthias stopped. How could he do this? What had he come to?

'Go on, Matthias. You know what's involved.' Imbert's voice was gentle.

'She need only be passive, not necessarily willing. There's no need to hurt her. Drugs would do it, so long as there's no struggle; for that could distract, destroy the rhythm –'

Still the tired voice whispered on, giving instructions,

explaining, outlining a plan for leading his brother's lover into deadly peril.

Betrayals and treachery, framed in the fluttering shadows that waited just behind his shoulders. Among the ruins of despair, all that was left to Matthias Marling now.

Later, Weard laughed softly, standing at the open door to Eleanor and Phin's cell.

'So you see,' he said, 'Matthias is being extremely helpful. It won't take long now . . .'

Still laughing, he bowed ironically, and a swarm of scurries rippled into their prison, holding the door shut while a key was turned on the other side.

The scurries were constant attendants, bringing unpleasant little meals of dried biscuits and sour cheese. There was always water to drink: clear, cold and fresh. At intervals, Phin and Eleanor were taken down the corridor to some kind of public wash-house. Surprisingly, the water there was also pure. The legacy of the baby, Phin had suggested: Smintha had floated on enchanted streams not so long ago. They were not ill-treated.

They had started building the fire, Weard had said, gloating. A great conflagration to be sparked by smaller fires set all round the perimeter of the Desert Rose. They were rehearsing the Hidden Rite, with all its complexities, under Matthias's direction. An offering was being prepared. They could not lose: the Benu would be trapped once more and then they would all be free to live forever.

Eternal life, eternal power.

After he had gone, Eleanor turned to Phin. 'I don't believe this is happening! He's Lukas's brother! How could Matthias do this? Work with that brute, try to trap the Benu again, all of that, how dare he even *attempt* it?'

'We have to trust that Matthias knows what he's doing.'

'But he's not well! There's something about being blind and knowing the future: he's not the same. He hasn't even got a staff any more!'

'Matthias's power has nothing to do with sight or staff. He's beyond such props. He has resources that neither of us understand. We have to trust him.' Blythe sounded completely confident. He moved away from her, his eyes idly considering the graffiti on the walls. 'Matthias is acting, pretending – I am sure of it. He would not help them set up a new Stasis. Think what he did in breaking the Stasis in the first place.'

'You did more.'

'It wasn't a competition.' He paused. 'Listen, Eleanor, Matthias is immensely powerful, immensely knowledgeable. I'm sure he has some plan.'

'Why do you think that?' She watched him curiously. Although they had both been through so much, so far apart, she invariably found herself trusting his judgment.

'It's not easy to describe. You'd think that a Mage, blinded, without a staff, would just fall apart, become worse than useless. Matthias has spent a lifetime relying on his vision and on his staff, and yet, think what he's like now – '

'Difficult and miserable,' she said sourly.

'But not crushed. Not without ideas and plans – '

'It doesn't sound like it. And he knows the future, and he won't tell me what it holds . . .'

'There are probably good reasons for it; I get the impression that he doesn't always trust this prevision. It might not be accurate, for a start.'

It was like a breath of fresh air, talking to Phin now. She felt her doubts and fears subside. It was impossible not to feel encouraged by him.

He has changed, she thought. In every way. Physically he might look dreadful, exhausted by the weight of the shadows, crippled by the scars on his left hand. But the deepest change was nothing to do with appearance. There was a certainty about him, a strength that went far beyond ordinary courage. As if the experience of the shadows had purified all that guilt and fear into something rare, something she did not understand. She could not define it. There was a clarity in the way he looked, a lightness in the way he spoke. He was no longer cluttered by ordinary preoccupations.

Whereas she felt as if all her emotions were up for grabs. Rocketing around through grief and joy, guilt and anger and love and fear. She was obsessed by the need to find Lukas and at the same time pathetically nervous of what she might find. Matthias had given so many half-concealed hints that it would not go well that she was existing in a state of raw anxiety.

'Phin, do you think – do you think Lukas will wait for me?' Their present predicament – even the shifting shapes of the scurries around the walls – faded into insignificance.

Blythe's eyes were considering. 'When Lukas thought you were dead, on that mountainside just before the end, I recognised what he was experiencing. It was what I felt when Karis died. Not something easily put aside or forgotten. So yes, Eleanor, I think he'll wait for you . . .'

She wanted to believe this; she knew he was sensible and perceptive. But her mind was full of clouds. What if Lukas thinks I'm dead too? What if, like me, he is tricked into something else?

Although their prison was not cold, and Phin was speaking with confidence, she shivered.

Revenge, said Lycias. I will have My revenge.

Had it run its course? How much more would be required? (I have just begun, said the small voice in her memory. I have only just begun . . .)

Phin put his arm round her. Obscurely, it made her want to cry. 'You know, don't you, that there's only one thing which really matters in all this? That the child Coron is free, flying on an Arrarat hawk. There is no reason to give up now. The child is free. The Benu is free. There is hope.' She leant her head against his shoulder, laid her hand over the scars on his left wrist.

But her mind still ran on well-worn rails. Matthias can see the future, and he's saying nothing.

'We'll have to know how big it is. How far the Desert Rose extends.'

Matthias's voice was only slightly stronger. Edine had given him medicines and drugs, but they had done little good. His strength and hope had drained away at the same rate. He no longer asked where Eleanor and Blythe were, what had happened to Thurstan. Amidst so many lies and betrayals, it was easier to keep his mind on what they required. He did not want to have to remember the future again. He answered all their questions, listened to their ideas, corrected their theories, instructed them every inch of the way in the Hidden Rite.

The Children had passed him by. They were waiting for

someone else, some other soul weighted with sin and guilt. He did not know who it would be. He had no energy left to speculate.

Obsessed with the Rite, Imbert did not notice the recklessness of Matthias's voice. He merely glanced at the slight figure still lying motionless on the ornate couch and shrugged.

'Difficult to say. Miles of it: ten, twenty, who knows?'

'It has to be completely surrounded by fire. Cut off from water. We must know its extent. Weard or someone. They'll have to go above ground and take a look.'

'Not Weard. The Desert Rose would not easily forgive the loss of one of its limbs. There is no one else. The Rose can control scurries and Fosca above ground. What about that Arrarat of yours?'

'She won't fly with anyone else.'

Matthias felt suddenly cold, gripped with fear. He would be sent above ground, and once more he would know what was going to happen.

'You'll have to do it, then.' Edine spoke prosaically.

'Don't be ridiculous. What could I see?'

'You will have the Arrarat's eyes. You'll do it,' she repeated. They knew so much. How did they understand about the bond with the Arrarat?

'I can't go above ground.' He was not acting now, and sweat was beading his forehead. He clenched his fists, searching for an argument they might accept. 'The Fosca would make straight for us.'

'You'll have to be careful, then.' Imbert was unmoved. 'Matthias, I don't think you quite appreciate that the Rite is *going to happen*. The Rite will take place, and it will succeed. This I know, just as you in your heart know it.'

So do you too have visions of the future, Imbert? thought Matthias. And yet you are not blinded, not imprisoned in a barrier of unseeing flesh. How can *your* vision be trusted? Or is it just bluff?

Imbert continued. 'I'm very much afraid that Miss Knight will have to stand surety to your cooperation in this matter.'

Visionary or charlatan, there was no reason to doubt him. Matthias exaggerated his weakness, tried to bargain, but

Imbert was adamant. And if they were going to perform any of the Rite at all, they did need to know.

The fire had to engulf all of the Rose. Anything less would be worse than useless. They could not afford only to injure the Desert Rose, the Great Mage Lefevre. It had to be destroyed.

On the third day after they had first fallen to the realm of the Unseen God, Matthias rode Amery, his new hawk, out in the open. They soared high over the desert, high over the lush jungle.

Amery showed him writhing tendrils, weaving stems, thorns and suckers. Deep shade at the heart of the jungle sheltered no animals, no butterflies or silent snakes. No birds sang in the verdant branches, no mosquitoes danced in the trapped sunlight.

There were flowers, small blossoms of white and scarlet, open to the air, dotted all over its vast expanse. He recognised them as eyes, fringed with silk, watching out for prey. But in the centre, rising high over the rest of the forest, one huge flower of shining petals followed the sun relentlessly over the heavens.

There were eyes here too, pale and wild, deep in its centre, just above the gaping hole that was the mouth. Busy tendrils fed that wide maw, passing the careless bodies of small lizards and desert rats miles through the echoing, empty glades. It was growing all the time, spreading wide over the desert, encroaching on the barren sand.

As it roamed the desert, large areas of it dried out under the force of the scorching sun. There was never enough water to support a plant that size. It left behind it a trail of dead wood. Acres within the living plant were dry and brittle, and branches snapped under their own weight, littering the silent avenues. Where the wood had died, bonfires would be lit from beneath.

Skimming high above its surface, the Fosca searched for food, venturing far afield. Nomad camps were raided, their inhabitants scooped up in claws and talons, brought wailing through the hot air to the centre of the Rose.

Amery flew higher yet, taking care to avoid the eyes of Fosca and flower. With ordinary sight, Matthias would not have been able to distinguish details, but now his only vision was that of an Arrarat hawk, the predator who can see a mouse move in a field far away.

Imbert had been correct. Twenty miles in diameter, he had said. Twenty miles of carnivorous, ravening jungle, broken up by large areas of dead wood. Matthias wondered how far the Desert Rose retained the skills of a Mage. Whether it could still produce wraiths, and govern the Parid. Certainly it remained in control of the Fosca. Buzzing like flies, rushing to feed their master . . .

Matthias concentrated on Amery's vision, on the patterns of flying Fosca. He was trying to block from his mind the knowledge of the future that made life above ground so agonising for him.

Nevertheless he saw scenes of distress and death, fragments of dreadful tension, clearer now he was above ground once more. Choices, lives lost and in thrall.

A raging fire, and a hawk falling towards it . . .

What he did not know was whether it was fixed. Whether what he saw was like a memory, running the other way, unalterable and indisputable.

Amery dipped and swerved and the hot desert wind blew through Matthias's hair. Her action was strong, sure and steady. She glided through generous sweeps, smooth and light. The Rose beneath them was like a moving stain on the surface of the desert. Soaring flight enlightened his thoughts, releasing his mind into the open clearings of imagination.

In what way are memories accurate? What truth is there that is not coloured by emotion and circumstance? Very little, he thought, with a glimmer of hope. Perhaps there were ways out of it, perhaps what he saw was only a probability, a possibility. He did not have to be circumscribed by it.

In this way Matthias tried to shut his mind to the pictures of the future that so disturbed him. On the whole, he failed.

He ran his hands over the warm feathers, and noted the extent of the monstrous, moving forest on the desert below. He tried to remember the patterns of the running tendrils, the disposition of the dark angels over its boundaries, the areas of dry and dead wood.

And, in despair, staggering with weakness after each flight, he gave to Edine and Imbert the information they needed.

For three days he described charts and maps, and listened to them instruct the scurries and the few men remaining from the caravan. Nightly, while the Fosca rested, scurries ventured above ground and stripped the dead trees from the avenues of Smintha, the olive groves along the barren valley of the Whiterod. Underground, they ransacked houses, stripping them of wooden furniture, of paper and straw. Great piles of wood were assembled along the tunnels ready for ignition.

He searched his memory for the obscure details of the Hidden Rite, the Rite to entrap the Benu. He had to get it right. It had to be perfect, immaculate in every way. The fire would form the context for a delicately balanced sequence of events. He discussed it with Imbert and Edine, discussed every move, every calculation, every weaving of the great spiral.

There was something he kept to himself, but as time went on it seemed increasingly futile and trivial. It would probably make no difference at all . . .

He grew, grudgingly, to respect Weard's intelligence. His mind was not subtle, not elegant, but it held a brutal grasp of priorities, a frighteningly competent memory, a complete grip on the practicalities of trapping the Bird of Time.

It was going to work, Imbert was right. The Hidden Rite would take place, and the Benu would be trapped once more.

And it would all be Matthias's fault.

Chapter Twenty
High Tide

The first of the three highest tides took place that evening. Felicia watched it through the tall windows of a great house.

Mittelson was not there. He had gone to the Bay of Marqun with Serethrun. He was watching from the cliff-top, waiting for a ceremony to take place. He intended to discover just what the Sea Lords were planning, what Ladon would do at the highest tide next evening. He thought that it would all be decided then.

He was wrong.

Kester and Annis were dancing in the ballroom of their unlikely lodging. Vere Holtby played the flute for them, and two other men stood at the door watching. They each carried knives thrust into their belts. Reflections flickered along the mirrored walls, the two men impassive, the laughing, handsome couple, waltzing the length of a deserted ballroom. Their shoes moved softly over the parquet floor.

That night they were staying in one of the great houses, a house abandoned (temporarily, its owners thought) for the duration of the spring tides. The family, close friends of Torold, had gone to join him in the Castle, taking their servants with them.

The house was vast and empty. Large staterooms on the two lower floors overlooked the city and the sea. Ballroom and dining-room, gallery and hall. There were balconies, steps leading down to gardens that were now lost beneath the swirl of muddy water.

A roof garden, complete with conifers and shrubs, following the fashion set by Lord Torold, was still fragrant in the damp air. It was too early for flowers.

Felicia was pacing the long gallery. She had not much energy for activity, but waiting passively was more than she could contemplate. Vere Holtby's flute played light cascades of easy fluency behind closed doors. She was aware that Annis was laughing, the sound frivolous and carefree.

Felicia listened only to the lap of water, rising against the basement walls.

'Why don't you shut the window?' The man whose real name was Lukas Marling was watching her from a chair by the fire, turning over the pages of a book on his lap.

She stood still by the window, looking out into the night at the light of lamps shining on water. For once, the rain had stopped.

'I want to know how high the tide is.' How much time I have left, she meant.

'Olwyn said there would be no reason to worry tonight. And he'll have news, he'll find out what the Sea Lords are planning at the Marqun. We'll be prepared for the highest tide.'

But she knew there was no possible preparation, not against the rising tide, driving into the heart of the city – and what it carried in its greasy waves.

He came and stood beside her, looking out across the city. There was a pause.

'Felicia,' he said softly. 'Would you like to ride Astrella tonight?'

'Ride your Arrarat hawk? Could I?' She turned to look at him with unusual animation.

'She would like to fly with you.'

Felicia had forgotten the telepathic link. 'Why?' she asked, not understanding.

He shrugged, looking out of the window once more. 'It is the best of reassurances, you know, to have an Arrarat for a friend.'

He was right, of course. Her imagination was all caught up in the flight of the great hawk, soaring high above the clammy clutch of the sea. Astrella would carry her beyond the reach of danger, beyond the reach of Ladon.

'Now?' she said, her eyes wide.

He smiled slightly. 'Why not? Come with me, Lady Felicia.'

He led her through wide, echoing corridors, up the sweeping stairs to the roof garden. She fastened the clasp of her cloak firmly as they stepped out into the wind. It was cold, but she hardly noticed.

Waiting there, dark eyes warm with intelligence, welcoming, was Astrella.

Unhesitating, although she had never been close to such a creature before, she went up to the hawk and reached thin arms around its neck.

For a moment she felt an alien heart beat against her own, reiterating a rhythm she had lived by, unrecognised, all her life.

It was the pace of circling stars. The steady flow of the seasons, the calm ebb and flow which was the framework for all love, all imagination, all life. It had survived the Stasis. It would survive the Sea Lords, the fanatical, power-hungry games of men. This was something she had always known to be right.

It was the reason for her ill-health. Until she stood there, and felt the strength of the Arrarat hawk, she had never known what she had lacked, what had deprived her of health and will. What was wrong.

It was this sense of balance, distorted by the Stasis, distorted by the Sea Lords and their magic. A harmony subtle and undeniable. Unseen, unknown. Ever changing, ever fluid. The source of all strength, originating in the flight of a hawk greater than any Arrarat.

The Benu, living to soar through the sky. The Benu, dying in order to live again.

Her eyes, turning to meet Lukas, were full of stars.

'Shall we ride, Felicia?' he said.

He lifted her high onto the hawk's back, onto the warm, smooth feathers, pointing out the leather strap.

A swift movement and he was behind her, his arms around her waist.

'Don't clutch.' he said, his voice almost unrecognisable. 'She doesn't like it . . .'

Then they were up, up and away into the cold, clear, dark sky, and the stars in her eyes danced around them. She had never felt such power, never known such glory.

She saw beneath them the city of Shelt, lost in moving,

shimmering ribbons of water, the Castle tall and gaunt out of reach of the tide.

Beyond that, moonlight trod a path across the sea, an invitation to the night.

Vast wings moved with decision. They accepted the invitation, following the moon's path out over the sea, going beyond the headland, north of Shelt.

Towards the Bay of Marqun.

'Hell!' Lying on wet grass, peering over the top of a precipitous cliff, Serethrun Maryn drew in his breath sharply.

Mittelson, at his side, knew what to expect; but even so he looked away for relief, out to sea, out to the shining moon.

Below them, in the Bay of Marqun, Ladon was holding court. They were all there, all Mittelson's former colleagues. Including Lammon, Mittelson's replacement, his eyes bright and fascinated.

Ladon was undulating slowly in front of them, emerging in the shape of breaking waves. Spray was leaping from the roaring whirlpool womb all around the dragon, and its claws reached out in falling water. But still Mittelson and Serethrun could make out myriad heads and eyes, darting back and forth, spitting with fury. Voices shrieked; but gradually, unwilling though they were, the two watching men began to understand what it wanted. A hymn of desire bled into the air from a hundred voices, an uneven choir enwrapped in rage. There were no words, but the sense was clear.

My beloved, where is she? Soft of limb and light, moon dust in her hair, eyes green as the sea . . . where is she? Why have you not found her for me?

'Prince Ladon.' It was Gawne, stepping forward, not back. He never had been short of courage, thought Mittelson wearily, not where the desire for immortality was concerned. The old struggle, the old issues. It would not be easy. Gawne continued, his thin voice cutting sharply through the roaring whirlpool and the lascivious song of the dragon. 'We know where she is. She will be yours by the dawn tide.'

A sigh of air pushed between a thousand teeth. The waves reared up and back, poised over the spindly figure of the Mage.

Until then, came the unheard words. *What have you for me until then? The hours are long before dawn . . .*

For answer, Gawne lifted one hand. From the shadows beneath the cliff, out of sight of the two men watching above, a slight figure moved into view.

Not reluctantly, in no way frightened or appalled, Esmond stood there, eyes blank, hands slack at his side.

Gawne said nothing, bowing, stepping back into the circle of Mages. He left Esmond standing there, gold hair shining in the moonlight, sheathed in azure velvet.

'No!' A scream of desperate intensity from under the cliff. Another figure rushed forward into view, reaching out for Esmond.

Torold, violent and determined, his sword unsheathed, his courage untarnished.

'Serethrun,' Mittelson, between his teeth, suddenly, angrily. 'We've got to get him out of there. Now!'

He was on his feet, pulling Serethrun up beside him.

'You're mad! You can't do anything against that!'

'Torold has to survive! He has to acknowledge Rosco as his heir or we'll have Javon to reckon with!'

'We can do nothing from here.' Serethrun was still staring at the scene below as if transfixed, and didn't at first realise what Mittelson was doing.

His eyes were half-closed, while his hands unfolded, revealing a path of light.

The image of a hawk flew along it, between the arch of Mittelson's fingers. Serethrun found himself looking away from the dragon, beyond those infinitely powerful hands, following the path up into the sky. Clouds parted in an arch, framing the widening, moonlit path.

Flying through the clouds, through the arch, through the light, was a true hawk of wild power. It was carrying two riders.

For a moment the dragon was diverted. Myriad eyes turned away from Esmond and Torold, gazing out to the clear, moonlit night. Water cascaded like viridescent scales.

The hawk swooped from a great height.

It wheeled once, on the level of the cliff-top, and Serethrun, unbelieving, heard Rosco shouting, with laughter in his voice, 'Catch!' – thrusting something at him as the Arrarat flew past.

A flutter of cloth and, before he understood what was happening, there was a woman in his arms, a familiar figure of frail insubstantiality.

Felicia, wriggling free in a moment, gasping with shock. 'Where's Rosco going, what's he doing?' she was shouting at Mittelson, whose hands were now empty of light.

But the Mage was already on his way, letting himself over the edge of the cliff, climbing down to the pool as quickly as he could over sliding clay and scrubby tufts of grass, down to steep, damp rock.

'Go on, then!' Felicia was still shouting, at Serethrun now, stamping her foot on the soggy turf. 'Go and help!'

He was already on his way. 'Wait here!' he yelled back at her.

She watched just long enough to make sure he was out of sight. Then she bunched up her skirts and began to run.

At the tide-pool, Ladon was poised to strike. As the Arrarat swooped low, Lukas jumped to the ground, grabbing Esmond. In that moment of stunned amazement, Esmond was thrust unresisting up onto the hawk's back. And although Torold was still shouting defiance and aggression, he had seen Esmond's uncomprehending eyes, and without hesitation climbed up behind him.

The hawk swerved and jabbed, lashing out with beak and claws, and Ladon yowled with rage as great gashes tore through the patterns of falling water.

The Mages were all concentrating, weaving vibrant spirals around the pool, trying to imprison the hawk and its two riders.

But Mittelson, standing behind them, quiet in the shadows, spun counter-shapes in his hands, and the spirals lost shape and structure. The hawk banked up, away from the cliff, soaring high, high over the cliff, back towards Shelt.

Gawne turned, screaming, 'Mittelson! Traitor! Bastard son of heresy!'

They all turned, all the Mages, and raised spiral staffs high.

Mittelson was standing back to rock, and his hands opened helplessly.

Not against thirteen. Not without a staff.

'Get out of this,' he breathed to Serethrun Maryn.

'Gawne!' Another shout, and as Gawne looked round, his staff lifted high, Lukas Marling ran forward beneath the sparkling staff. A man used to Mages. Speed and surprise sometimes, only sometimes, carried the day.

Gawne had been diverted by Mittelson, and by the Arrarat. His concentration was not at its height. Lukas's whole weight was behind the sword, a slim razor of steel.

The spiral charge was befogging his senses, spinning light and sound into curious, distracting vortices. But the speed, the volition of the action was undeniable. The sword found its mark, deep in the belly of the old Mage. The First Sea Lord shuddered once, soundlessly.

He toppled slowly forward into the deep pool, black blood staining the turbulent water with night, and Lukas reeled under the force of undirected spirals.

And then the dragon struck.

Deprived of its desired prey, it took the nearest at hand. Winding, sinuous as ribbon, its mouths wide and open, it seized in its slimy embrace the dazed man alone at the pool's edge.

With a roar of triumph it subsided into the depths once more, dragging down the uselessly resistant figure of Lukas Marling.

There was a path down, not to the tide-pool, but down the south side of the headland to a small rocky bay. Felicia had seen it often before from her room in the east wing of the Castle. She thought that, if perhaps she could get down to the shore, to the sea, she might be able to help.

She had no idea why she should think in this way. Never before in her life had she thought to play a part, to take decisions. The frailty of her body had excused her from action.

The flight on Astrella had changed everything, awakening in her strength and knowledge. Flying in moonlight, over the sea, watching the waves below, she felt an echo deep within her own body.

She knew the tide, its pulse and rhythm. And if it was distorted, soured by the presence of Ladon, she knew that she could change it. Empowered by flight, she was prepared to challenge a dragon.

She heard shouting, and dreadful roaring, and the vortex of water spinning on the other side of the jutting wall of rock. Magic power fizzed and sparked against rocks as spirals clashed and Mages fought. She could not imagine what would be happening, what spirals would interweave and interlock.

Over it all there was the harsh cry of a hawk, cutting through all the chaos. She listened hard for that wild song, that particular clarity.

And then she knew that Ladon was gone. That appalling choir of hate-filled voices was silent, lost beneath the waves. She heard the whirlpool subside, the shouting and surges of electric power lessen. The crashing of the tide quietened.

Watching the sea, she wondered why the dragon had disappeared so suddenly. She could sense it, plunging deep into the valleys of the ocean, deep into the chilling black water, leaving the shore far behind. There was some reason.

It had taken someone. Some hostage or offering, she didn't know which. Stolen away to the ocean's cold heart as she had been. Intolerable.

She stepped forward into the tide. She remembered the power of flight, the light of the moon across the waves, the rhythm of the tide echoing in her own body.

Stepping further out into the waves, she began to watch the tide for patterns of light.

Chapter Twenty-one
Sharrak

In the chaos of Gawne's death, and the sudden disappearance
of Ladon with Rosco, instinct took over. Serethrun grabbed
Mittelson by the arm. He had noticed something in the
shadows under the overhanging cliff.

A cave. He had no idea whether it went anywhere. It was
all too likely that it was just a narrow crack in the cliff, a
treacherous dead-end.

But Torold had come from somewhere. It was probably
a route through to the Castle, hidden, out of the way of the
dangerous spinning spirals of untrustworthy magic. Without
hesitation, the two men plunged into the darkness of the cave,
and Serethrun began to run his hands over the rock surface,
searching for the way out.

Mittelson was not behind him. Instead he was standing still
by the narrow crack in the rock face, his hands winding
together in strange shapes.

'Do you want them to follow?' He turned to face Serethrun,
and for a moment Serethrun saw his strange pale eyes
reflecting nothing but light.

The crack in the rock behind them narrowed, its edges
blending subtly together, and then there was pitch dark.

'It's only appearance.' Mittelson's voice, soft and
compelling. 'Wait, Serethrun.' Another slight pause, and
then the light Serethrun had seen in Mittelson's eyes flowed
into the space between his fingers, and a golden spiral began
to gleam against the surrounding black rock.

In the soft glow, Serethrun saw that ahead of them the cave
extended into the shadows. The ceiling became much lower.
To move further, they would have to crawl.

Quickly the two men crouched down, moving awkwardly against the jagged rock, Mittelson handicapped by holding the light in his hands steady. An uncomfortable progress, crouching on sharp rock, painfully jarring knees and palms. They moved in silence, concentrating on the uneven surface beneath them, the irregular spars jutting from the ceiling and the walls. The passage seemed to move upwards for some distance, cold and slippery with damp.

Serethrun's heart was racing. He was in shock, in deep shock. He had never seen Mages fight before, and his mind was imprinted by the swirling patterns of spirals. But worse than that, far worse, was the memory of Ladon, with those weaving heads and cruel claws, clutching Rosco, vanishing into the depths of the whirlpool.

'Is Rosco dead?'

'I – think so.' Mittelson's voice was quiet.

Serethrun paused for a moment. He became angry. 'What now, Mittelson? What of all your plans and machinations, those splendid hopes and dreams?'

'It was an accurate vision. I'm sure . . .' Mittelson's voice trailed off. He had really believed it too: Rosco married to Felicia. He had seen their wedding as clearly as the vision that had taken him to the lonely bay where he had found Rosco. That vision had informed all his plans, all his schemes.

He could not believe that it was inaccurate. He could not adjust to disaster.

'If we're in luck, Serethrun, if we're in luck – ah, yes, there we are . . .' He tried to sound calm, letting the words run on inconsequently. As if nothing much had happened. As if his friend had not just been taken by a dragon and his hopes destroyed.

The ceiling of the passage ahead of them suddenly lifted until they were able to stand upright in a narrow, uneven, down-sloping corridor. It was a relief.

'We need to get out of here. Felicia's running loose somewhere on the cliff.' There were undercurrents in Serethrun's voice that Mittelson was not prepared to consider.

'We can do nothing for Felicia right now. Or Rosco . . .' He spoke coldly, bitterly. He tried to pull himself together. There was still so much to do. 'The main thing now is to get you over to the *eloish* –'

'You want them to attack? *Now?*'

'Why wait? Gawne is out of the running, the Mages are leaderless, and Torold has Esmond safe. It's as much as we can hope for. There will be no better chance.'

'And what about Lammon, Mittelson? He set up that original storm, you said. Won't he try to take advantage of the situation?'

'We'll take that one as it comes – '

'And the fishermen? They're all set to follow Rosco. They won't accept just anyone else.'

'We'll have to chance it. They'll trust me, I think. There's nothing else we can do. We have to make the best of it. All you need do, Serethrun, is to concentrate on getting your *eloish* here on time.'

'But what about Felicia?' He would not give up on this.

Mittelson sighed. 'What is this, Serethrun? She'll be all right, no one will harm Javon's daughter, she's far too important . . .'

'The dragon – '

'Has a different prey. She'll be fine. What we need to do is to get out of here.'

'You have a long way to go.'

A light voice, clear and unexpected. A whisper in the air, a strange, unpleasant smell. The light in Mittelson's hands flickered. He drew in a ragged breath. What now?

A shape of shifting shadows drifted apart from the rock wall and took on form as they watched. A beautiful woman, stained with gold, gold that dripped from her finger-ends, from her hair, blurring the shape of her mouth, masking the look in her eyes.

The air stank. Sickly, like rotting meat, it clogged their senses. Mittelson let the light in his hands fall away, for the creature standing before them had its own luminescence and he wanted his hands free. Serethrun had his sword out, but Mittelson knew that it would be useless.

'What do you want?' he whispered, his mouth dry. This was unforeseen, like Rosco's death.

'What do *you* want?' It mimicked his words. There was a brief silence as he studied the heart-shaped face, the hands clasped at its breast, the wisps of trailing light falling around it. The image struck an echo in his mind. He knew what it was.

'Parid, that's what you are. Shape-shifter, mistress of all disguise, in love with power. I know what you want.' Distant knowledge, stories once babbled in delirium on a cold sea-shore, fancies and rumours he had collected and researched.

He knew the Parid. Rather, he knew of them, from the unconscious nonsense blurted by the man called Rosco, to small details remembered from conversations with Gawne long ago.

The gold around it was shimmering, flickering, and its shape was losing definition, insubstantial, unformed. As he watched, fascinated and uneasy, it became first a young woman with tumbled red-gold hair, then a dark, thick-set man with a hooked nose.

Finally, while laughter filled the air, it stood in front of them in another form.

A tall man, black-haired, blue-eyed. A dark Jolin Rosco to the life.

'We dyed his hair,' Mittelson murmured and, as he watched, the straight, forward-flopping fall of hair lightened and briefly became pale gold.

It could not hold. The gold spread, running over the face, dissolving the fine nose and long mouth in a wash of acid, subverting the long, graceful lines of the body. 'Yes, that was it . . .' Mittelson spoke half to himself.

'Mage.' It spoke again, once more in the shimmering form of feminine beauty. 'It can be held steady with the power of a Mage.'

'We need him to lead – '

'I know. The form will be enough.'

'You will take Rosco's form to lead the uprising?'

'In return for – ' The voice was slow, corrosive as the golden acid dripping from the ends of its hair.

'For what? Power, influence?'

'Yes. Just that.'

Looking at its wide eyes, innocent of guile or humanity, Mittelson recognised the lust there. Lust for power, for ultimate and enduring authority.

He recognised it because he shared it. Not overtly, in the obvious ways, like Gawne or Javon. But influence, behind the scenes, unobserved, unremarked.

Kingmaker. That was the role he coveted.

He considered the parody of a god, and knew that power was still within his grasp.

At his side, Serethrun was staring at him.

'You'd trust *that*?' He was incredulous.

'It won't work otherwise.' He spoke softly, musingly.

'It's monstrous! Vile! We can't work with that!'

'The *eloish* will die. The fishermen, leaderless, will fail. The Mages will elect a new leader, probably Brice Lammon. Torold will be the same ineffective figure-head. Shelt will languish into impotent decadence, and Ladon will take Felicia and call the tune. Do you want that?'

'But you can't trust that – thing!' He would not look at it, shimmering just beyond the line of his vision. He was gagging with the stench of it, pale with shock and horror.

'I keep my bargains.' Its curious, clear voice was undisturbed. 'I do not lie.'

Mittelson nodded. 'Take us to the Castle,' he said.

It drifted to one side, and Serethrun saw the start of a wider, man-made passage leading deep into the cliff side. Once more, Mittelson created light within his hands to lead the way. Serethrun followed him, keeping as far away from the Parid as possible.

It laughed, gently, as he passed.

'My name is Sharrak,' it said.

'*I* do not lie,' it repeated.

It showed them through tunnels, long and winding, deep into the cliff. Underground caverns, cluttered by stalagmites and stalactites, dank streams and pools where strange pale fish lurked. They had to duck under overhangs, climb steep gradients, following a complicated path through many branched passages, impossible to remember.

Mittelson was silent, refusing to answer Serethrun's objections. There was so much to decide, so many new factors to take into account. This was a risk greater than any he had taken before. He could see no other way. It would all be for nothing without Rosco as a figure-head. He hoped they would not need more than that.

At last they reached the dungeons of the Castle itself, barred cells, oubliettes, unexpectedly bricked-in doorways concealing ancient agonies.

'That way, Serethrun,' said Mittelson, pointing. 'It leads to the cellars. You can get out that way.'

'And then what?' His voice was deeply hostile.

'It must be two or three hours short of dawn now. Get the *eloish* to move while it's still dark. Get them to wait just beyond the Castle gates, out of sight from the camps. Tell them the bells will ring when we need them. Tell them to lie low until then.'

'Then?' Again, the mistrust was almost tangible.

'We'll meet you at Castle Square at dawn.'

'Who's "we"?'

'The fishermen, of course. Who do you think we're doing this for?'

'And *that*?' He waved at the smear of gold light watching them from the shadows.

'If necessary. Don't argue, Serethrun, this is the only way.'

'Don't patronise me, Olwyn Mittelson. This is an error of judgment. You don't understand what you're doing.' Serethrun was moving away from him, backing along the corridor, instinctively increasing the space between them.

'No.' Mittelson was thinking fast. 'Listen, Serethrun. Wait. I know what's happening here. And if you trust me, if you let me play this my way, I'll give you what you want.'

'What? What do you think I want?'

'You want to know why your father died. That's the only unanswered question now, isn't it? I'll tell you that, Serethrun, if and when we overthrow the Mages.'

'Tell me now.'

'Get the *eloish* into the city. That was the bargain from the very first. That's why you're here, why you joined us in the first place. Keep your side of it and you'll find out.'

Why your father died. Why you are here now.

Serethrun Maryn stood silent, considering Mittelson. He desired that knowledge, and dreaded it. For a moment he was caught in the dilemma, fearful and avid. It was how he had been trapped all along. A fish on the hook of knowledge. Why you were framed, why your father died . . .

He had had enough. He turned and pushed past the tall, thin Mage standing there watching him.

'I'll send you the *eloish*. As promised, because of the fisherpeople and Felicia and the injustice of it all. But not because of you, Mittelson, or your bargains and secrets. I don't want to know. I'm getting out of here. You can deal with this – monster – on your own.'

He disappeared down the winding tunnel, leaving Olwyn Mittelson behind, silent for a long time. At last he turned to the Parid.

'Now,' he said softly. 'Let's try it again.'

The light flickered and glistened and then Jolin Rosco stood before him.

'Well, Olwyn,' the image said slowly. 'Will this do?'

The spiral in his hands held the form steady, the glint of the blue eyes, the generous curve of the mouth.

'Yes,' he breathed. 'Yes, I think that will do . . .'

Chapter Twenty-two
Rescue

Felicia stood on the edge of the sea and concentrated. This night, as the tide rose, she felt no terror. It was as if her fears and emotions were suspended, held out of time in a place of purity. Everything was required of her. There was no time or room for weakness or vulnerability or fear.

Ladon was far away, wrapped in the deep, still silence of the ocean, almost beyond the reach of the tide. She would have to venture far away, and further yet to force his return.

She knew that she ought to feel tired. But the flight on Astrella had been so extraordinary, so extreme, that all her usual responses were forgotten. They were out of place now.

It was a cold night, cold and bright with moonlight. As the tide swept at her feet, and her thoughts were still caught up in the flight of the Arrarat, she remembered another night on the sea shore. She remembered her hand, taken and guided by the Woman with blackened-silver eyes. The light of the Moon was leading her now. It shone in gleaming paths over the restless sea, and she gazed out over the rippling patterns of it, searching deep beneath its surface.

In this way she lost all idea of place. She did not even notice when the shouting and roaring from the Bay of Marqun died away. A boat rounded the headland, passing quite close to the little bay, but she was hidden by rocks, out of sight. No one saw her.

The boat returned soon after, laden with the Mages. Standing in the waves she did not even notice it. Her mind was plunging deep into the quiet depths, searching.

Water washed over her ankles at the edge of the shore. The

tide was still rising, not yet at its swollen height. She was standing at the water's edge, concentrating on rhythm.

She watched the waves rise and fall, rushing towards her; and each time the wave gathered strength, curving over and inwards, she drew in a deep breath. And as it tumbled, crashing in a cascade of white, she breathed out, echoing the rhythm of the tide, becoming one with it.

Although Ladon lived in the tide, drawing power from it, she was not frightened. Her hands, held out, were weightless with moonlight, shining through the shadowy depths.

She sensed the shoals of fishes, wary at the edge of the dying whirlpool. The gentle gardens of weed and anenome, the calm, slow movement of flatfish drifting over sand, the sudden scuttles of crabs and crayfish. There were rocks there, tumbled and shelved, covered with limpets and weed and the small soft bones of sea-creatures long dead.

She was fathoms deep, far beneath the waves, skimming along the paths of the Moon, tracking a sea dragon to its lair. And at last, further yet, she found Ladon running from her, dragging his prisoner away through the ocean.

She would make him relinquish that prisoner. She had no idea who it was, not caring if it were Mage or fisherman. Not for one moment did it occur to her that it might be Jolin Rosco, whom she imagined soaring safely far above on the wings of a hawk.

Her mind, carried in the tide, passed through frivolous shoals of silver and azure, through waving forests of weed. Anenomes opened beneath the movement of her passing and coral glowed under her touch. Shadows, hiding among the rocks, stirred slight tentacles and delicate fins.

Deeper yet, the dark grew into flat shapes, limned with violet and turquoise. She took the tide with her, and the creatures drifted under its breath, lifted for once by light and movement.

It was dark and cold, following Ladon under the sea. Deeply chilling, wounding to the movement of the blood, the movement of breath. But she was tide-borne, informed by flight.

She found Ladon at last, drawn by the ill-will of his greed. He lived in a dank cave, and the pale body of a man lay limp in his clutch.

Her mind soared in triumph. There was no denying her. She did not hesitate or hang back. She knew Ladon, knew his strength and his weakness. She too had lived under the ocean in his grip. She sent her Moon-wrought tide to fall upon him and then she turned it, turned the tide. He snarled and clutched, but the turning tide tore from his grasp the deathly cold human body. And as the tide retreats in the strong swell of its backwash, she leapt upwards, surging through the deeps, flying through water as a bird flies through air. The strength of the Arrarat and the light of the Moon empowered her every movement.

She was irresistible and victorious.

The pale girl at the water's edge abruptly staggered, her knees suddenly weak. She put her hand to her head, wondering if she were going mad, her thoughts all clouded by the drift of the sea. She looked around, trying to get her bearings.

In the pale half-light before dawn, she saw with terrible shock a body washed up by the turning tide. Long, familiar, graceful limbs lay discarded on sand, abandoned by the retreating waves of her own making.

She was running, her heart thudding painfully, across the sliding shale. On her knees, trembling, she turned him over. She saw who it was.

He was breathing, but only just. Blue with cold, water running from his hair, over his skin, hanging heavy in his clothes.

Struggling, she tried to drag him out of the reach of the waves, her hands under his arms, pulling and lifting. The beach was steep, a tumble of pebbles and rocks, and she had little strength. She kept sliding back against the stones, falling, losing her footing, slipping on weed and damp rock and harsh, grating sand.

She was appallingly tired, exhausted by effort. It took her too long to get him out of reach of the waves, up on the shingle near the cliff. She was breathing heavily, her arms feeble and aching. At least there was no wind, no rain.

He was so wet, so cold. A dead, pinched look on his face, grey-blue from the grip of the sea. Somehow she had to warm him.

There was no time to hesitate. She took off her own cloak

and shawl, skirt and blouse, everything. And then, with fumbling, nervous fingers, she dragged the soaking clothes off him, the hard denim and ragged shirt. He was covered in scars, shining white on near-blue skin.

He lay helpless and unmoving as she rolled him over onto the pile of dry clothes and began to rub the icy flesh with warm wool. After a while, she had him more or less dry, and she was flushed and breathless with exertion.

In the bitter cold before dawn, she lay down beside him, pulling her wide grey cloak over them both. She put her arms round him, trying to get as close as possible, for she was warm and living, and knew what was necessary.

She too had been caught in the ocean's depths by Ladon. She knew this deep cold, the feeling of water washing in the veins instead of blood. The chilling ice in one's centre, the clammy denial of life.

So when she felt him stir beside her, felt the first movement beneath her hands, she did not move away. Slack muscles became firm beneath her touch, and he sighed.

Quickly, she cast a glance at his face. The blue eyes were open, looking at her with an expression she did not understand.

All she knew was that it was not rejection. But suddenly she stopped, stopped breathing almost, and his hand reached out and caught her wrist.

'Felicia . . . Felicia. What are you?' He raised her hand to his lips, as he had once before, and then kissed the fine skin of her wrist. Her eyes were wide, innocent and trusting. Waiting.

He was drawn by her warmth. He stirred against her again, shifting on the hard shingle, and she recognised his need.

His arms were now round her, locking her close to him, his mouth on hers, breathing in her heat. Her legs were flung wide and he lay between them. Cold and hard between soft thighs, delicate folds. She gasped at the strangeness of it.

He was not gentle, not kind, for the cold had to be conquered in every way. This was the other battle. In relentless rhythm, he drove into her, quickly, forcefully, dropping his head against her shoulder; and she could no longer see those unfathomable eyes.

A great shudder, a pulsing that went beyond any bounds

she understood. For a moment he was held there, motionless against her, and she saw the early sun above the horizon over his shoulder, casting cold light around them. She saw that he was flushed all over with warmth.

A movement, then. He lowered himself onto the sand at her side. His arm was still under her shoulder, his hand lying on her breast. The tenderness of it, the long fingers calm and soft on her skin, would never leave her.

For a time they lay quietly together, drowsy and relaxed. She was half-asleep when she felt him shiver.

And then he had pushed himself away from her, springing to his feet, stumbling back towards the sea.

'Felicia!' He was shouting at her, bitter and furious.

Everything had changed, and she didn't understand.

'Why did you do it? Why didn't you – ?'

'What? Leave you there with Ladon? Leave you to die for the want of human warmth?' She was standing too now, clutching at the discarded cloak, shivering with reaction. She was angry, too, for this was not what she had expected.

He paused suddenly, his face curiously shuttered. 'Don't you know?' he said flatly.

'What?' she yelled, frightened, hurt. Searching round for reasons. 'What is there to know? That you love someone else, that you're not free? You told me that yourself!'

'Not that. At least, not only that. Felicia, don't you see? We're playing someone else's game here. Acting out some ritual for a purpose which is not our own. It isn't up to us at all!'

'It was my choice! No one *made* me do that!'

'How do you know? How can anyone ever know?'

She turned away from him, fumbling with the damp rags of her clothes, pulling them on with trembling hands. She could hardly see through the tears that were running ceaselessly over her face, falling on her hands, onto the crushed garments.

She was chilled to the bone.

In two steps he was beside her again, his hands clasping her wrists, swinging her round to face him. His voice was low and intense, his eyes burning bright.

'You are worth more than this; you don't have to put up with this.'

'You hawk is waiting for you.' She would not look at him, she rested her eyes on the pale sky, the grey beach.

Over his shoulder she had seen Astrella put down lightly on the damp rock. Numbly she stared into the deep golden eyes, waiting while he dressed, waiting for him to help her up onto the soft downy back.

His arms round her waist were distant and impersonal. As if they had never touched each other before.

As if they were strangers.

Chapter Twenty-three
Eleanor

How long had passed? Days and nights were not totally indistinguishable in the City of Stairs. The walls betrayed a slightly stronger luminescence for long periods. Somewhere sunlight was falling into dark chasms, caught on shining mirrors and sent, ever fading, along the avenues and down the levels. It was like a web, a network of light that reminded them that there was a reality out there, that the empty corridors and deserted galleries were an aberration. Something wrong, something unreal. Somewhere where people hid from their God, and never remembered the Moon at all.

She was getting to know Phin again. Or rather, he was getting to know her. In a leisurely way he drew from her stories of her other life, descriptions of the people who mattered to her there. He had asked once before, but in conditions of such stress that her answers had been virtually incoherent.

Now, although they were imprisoned by Weard for a purpose they did not understand, she felt able to consider more calmly where she came from and who she was.

'Do you want to go back?' he said, once. They were on their own. The scurries had left, set to more urgent tasks, Weard said.

'Not while Lukas is here.' Her answer was unhesitating.

'And if – just for the sake of argument, you understand – if Lukas is no longer free to love you, what then?'

'Don't say it, Phin, don't even think it!'

But he had said it, and she did think about it, all the time. 'Sometimes I know I wouldn't care where I was or what I did if Lukas were there. And at other times I just want to go home. To be back in London, bored perhaps, mildly irritated by – oh, I don't know – work, people, machines, the packaging on biscuits, that kind of thing.' Her memory glanced over her past life and wondered what it was worth.

'What about your parents, your friends? Don't you want to see them?'

'Yes, of course,' she said without thinking, and then stopped. Then, more slowly, 'My parents – don't really need me, never have. They're too wrapped up in each other – '

'They love each other so much . . .?'

'I wouldn't say it was *love*, exactly. They're obsessed with each other; they can't leave it alone. It's rather destructive, really.'

'What about your friends?'

'How much do one's friends really care? You can go months, years without seeing most of them and it doesn't seriously upset anything. It's lovely meeting up again, but hardly anyone gets depressed by not seeing their friends.'

But then she remembered how much she had needed them all when she had thought Lukas dead. And, looking at Phin, quietly spoken, calmly concerned about her, she knew that she might miss him almost as much as Lukas if she returned to her own world.

He was still studying her. 'But if you never saw *any* of your friends again, if you stayed here and *never* went back?'

'I don't know. I just don't know. But it's academic, surely.' She looked at him and sighed. 'If they manage to reinstate the Stasis and trap the Benu, it'll probably destroy Matthias, apart from everything else. And no one else is capable of sending me back.

'And anyway, Lukas is alive, and I'm going to find him. There's no other option. It won't arise.'

Phin turned away from her, pacing the narrow cell. He hoped she was right. He trusted Matthias; the Benu and Coron were both free . . .

He liked to think of Coron, flying high on an Arrarat hawk, searching for the Storm-bearer. He knew what it was like to suffer the God's curse.

But sometimes he wondered if the shadows had indeed been sent by Lycias. So much had changed. He was not the same man who had lived with thoughts of revenge and murder, for the shadows had released him from such dreadful coils. They had left him renewed, healed, stronger . . . It had almost been – he hesitated to frame the thought – an act of kindness.

But his imprisonment with Eleanor was no reassurance. In their brief trips to the wash-room down the passage, they had seen scurries flickering along the corridors, guards carrying great piles of wood.

A fire was in the making. The level of activity was increasing. The Rite would soon take place.

A chain rattled, a bolt was drawn. The door swung open: Imbert. He smiled. 'Miss Knight, will you accompany me? I have something to show you.'

'I have a choice?'

'Not really. but you will be perfectly safe. Believe me.'

In doubt she glanced at Blythe. 'I do not rate such promises highly,' he said.

'You are mistaken.' Imbert shrugged. He looked only at Eleanor. 'Don't you want to know what's happening to Matthias? I am proposing to take you to him, that's all. He's asking for you.'

'Is he all right?'

'Come and see . . .' He held out his hand to her.

Indecision. She saw that Blythe was regarding Imbert steadily. But before she could even begin to resist, she noticed that the folds of Imbert's dark red robe were shifting, spreading out into the prison, colours of blood and stone dissolving into each other. Scurries, again.

She could not bear their touch. She smiled uncertainly at Phin. 'See you later,' she said.

Back through the vast halls, along avenues of mirrored pillars. She saw other passages branching off, fractured by doors, windows and balconies. Whole streets of buildings were dimly revealed in the greying light.

'How far does it go?'

Imbert glanced at her. 'We've not had time to explore thoroughly. There are houses, temples, meeting places, theatres, stores – a whole city of dwellings, radiating out from the central stairs beneath the Temple. All quite deserted. One day, when there's time, I shall investigate it all. Even the lower levels. It will be a pleasant way to pass the millennia . . .'

'You'll never do it.'

'What? Capture the Benu, or study archaeology?' Impossibly, he was almost laughing.

'Restore the Stasis. It'll never work.' She spoke with a confidence she did not feel.

'You think not?' Imbert raised one pale eyebrow. 'Look . . .' He held open a door at one side and Eleanor saw Matthias, standing free, deep in conversation with Edine.

A map was spread out on the table in front of Edine. Eleanor saw Matthias raise his head towards the door, acknowledging their presence. He seemed composed and calm. Waiting.

'What are you doing, Matthias?' Her voice was tightly controlled. 'Why are you working with them?'

'I have no choice . . .' He was distant, distant as the day when she had first appeared in the desert outside Smintha. It was beyond belief.

'No choice? Rubbish! Of course you have a choice, you're responsible for your own decisions – '

'Not when the future is clear. There is no possible way out of this, because I have seen what will happen.'

'Why accept it? Why go along with it?' Now she was shouting at him, enraged by this passivity. 'You always said, you don't have to assent. Don't believe what you see. Appearances mislead, don't accept what the Gods throw at us – '

'There's nothing I can do, Eleanor.' He was holding out his hands, empty and open, towards her. 'It's too late. I should never have brought you back. It's all my fault. There's nothing I can do now.' He was so white, so thin, frail as glass, almost transparent with weakness.

'I don't believe you! You're wrong, you're wrong, it's not like that!'

It can't be like that, she meant, not with Lukas alive, and the child flying free, and Phin released from shadows.

'I'm sorry, Eleanor. I just wanted to say – sorry . . .' And he turned back to Edine, and the light voice ran on, listing incantations, substances, methods.

In shock, she looked at Imbert. His expression was perfectly neutral, watching her carefully. He inclined his head, gesturing with his hand to the corridor outside. Empty houses, wide pathways, dim light. They hadn't explored it yet . . .

Without a second thought, she pushed past him, careering wildly down the corridor, away from the antechamber.

In automatic response, scurries began to dart after her, too quick for the eye to catch. Imbert said one word, softly, and the rapid flow of shifting shapes halted. The scurries sank back towards him, losing themselves once more in the folds of his scarlet robe.

Imbert looked back into the room and smiled at Edine. 'So,' he said. 'Now we can begin.'

'What if she lets Blythe out?'

'What difference could it make? Where can they go?' He sat back in a chair, steepling his fingers together. 'Everything is assembled, everything complete. All the exits are blocked. The Rose is here, and will find her. The context is all in order. Even the emotional content is, I would estimate, pitched just right.' He smiled. 'Betrayal, anger, despair — despair, Matthias, would that be a fair description?'

Matthias sank back into the chair behind him. He was shaking, but he said nothing.

She was running hard, back the way they had come. She had to find Blythe and release him. Together they would find some way to stop the Rite, stop Matthias. They would look for Thurstan and get out of here . . .

There was no one following her. She was more than puzzled by this. Perhaps they were all too busy with their horrible Rite to look for her. It seemed unlikely, but she could think of no other answer. The tunnel branched in every direction, but she thought she could remember the way. There had been a row of red-shuttered windows, just like those on her left, not far from the prisons . . .

The grim door and its narrow passage were deserted.

'Eleanor? Are you all right?' Phin's voice, from behind the locked door. She sighed with relief.

'Phin, do you know how this catch works?'

'You're on your *own*?' He sounded amazed. 'How did you get away?'

'They just – let me go. I don't understand it . . . Look, the door's only bolted, but there's a metal catch like a child's puzzle holding it closed.' A rusting jumble of chains and bars.

'A sty-lock. It's quite simple, just push the small end of it backwards through the loop, and unwind the chain . . .'

He was right. In seconds he stood beside her.

'Matthias *is* helping them. He really is, he told me so himself. He said he was sorry!' She was still shocked.

'It was said for effect. He would not possibly do such a thing.' Phin sounded so certain that for a moment she almost believed him. He was standing in the doorway to the open corridor. There was no one there.

'You didn't see him. Phin, it was dreadful! We have to stop him – '

'Don't worry about Matthias, Eleanor, he won't let you down.' They were walking past the red shutters.

'But he has done so already. He brought me back . . .' She spoke quietly, her mind full of images. Used as a scapegoat, under a burning sun, twined in burning flowers . . .

'Well, either way, we need to find him.'

She tried to shrug off the black depression. 'Perhaps we could overpower one of the guards and get a weapon – '

He smiled. 'Unnecessary.'

'But we could – '

'No. I've been thinking. That's not the way.'

'How do you *know*?'

'Don't worry, Eleanor, it'll be all right. We're up against Mages here, not soldiers. I don't think there can be many guards anyway. Where are they? Why weren't you followed?'

'Scurries . . .?'

'I can't see any. It's difficult to tell, of course, but they're not trying to stop us, are they? I don't understand what's going on, but our priority must be to find Thurstan and Matthias.'

Well, yes. 'Where do we *begin*?' They were at the junction of four wide avenues. In the centre a tall pillar surfaced with glass panels augmented the pale light. It was over six feet in diameter, and at the top branched out like a tree in soaring arches to support the ceiling.

She saw their faces, bizarrely distorted in the angled glass. Their voices sounded hollow, their footsteps echoed. The avenues were all empty, bare channels of abandoned dwellings masked by dust.

'Eleanor.' Phin put his hand on her shoulder, looking steadily into her eyes. 'Don't give up on Matthias. It's important that you shouldn't give up. I refuse to believe that he's helping them – '

'Just wait till you see him.'

'Okay. But we still need to find him. Which way did Imbert take you? Can you remember?' She turned slowly round, looking down each avenue in turn.

'I think – yes, that way. I remember those empty window boxes. I wondered what flowers had bloomed there . . .'

She paused. She had seen something else. 'Phin, there's a theatre or something down that one – ' She pointed. Stone columns there were decorated by peeling posters, their colour faded, their script unknown. 'Don't you remember Thurstan talking about greasepaint when we fell?'

'And dancing girls . . .' He frowned. 'Certainly worth a try – '

'Hey!' A sudden shout, a whistle blown, and footsteps running. Some half-dozen of Weard's guards had seen them, were racing towards them.

They didn't even look at each other. They ran towards the theatre, dodging between pillars. The doors weren't locked. Eleanor pushed them open and found herself in a dusty foyer.

Phin wasn't with her. She heard a scuffle, shouts . . . Frantically, she looked round. An ornate double flight of stairs led upwards, and other insignificant-seeming doors led from the foyer.

There was a crash against the door from the avenue. It swung open. Without thinking, she moved back against the wall behind her and found it give.

Another door. Stairs, leading downwards. She could not help Phin on her own, she had to remain free so that she could find Thurstan. Alone, she ran downstairs.

Chapter Twenty-four
The City of Stairs

The stairs led down in darkness. They were built on a spiral, but the curve was tighter than the iron-enclosed staircases leading to the Field of Flowers. Eleanor opened the door at the bottom and found herself standing in the wings of a stage. A light shone dimly through a skylight. She looked out at the empty stage, the deserted theatre.

There was no one there, no sign that anyone had been there for a very long time. She glanced over the piles of props at the back of the stage and saw the discarded masks, the paper flowers. They meant nothing to her. She looked out into the dark theatre, the rows of empty seats, the velvet caverns of the boxes.

'Thurstan?' For some reason she needed to speak his name. There was no answer, no response at all. She crossed the stage and found a door there, a door to another empty corridor.

She was alone again in the City of Stairs. More theatres, concert halls, galleries. This was where they had come to be entertained. Out of curiosity, she walked through one of the long halls of an art gallery. She stared at portraits of strangers, at landscapes half-familiar from her journey through Peraldon. In another building, she found miles of bookshelves, millions of volumes neatly filed as far as the eye could see. The dust was thick.

'Thurstan?' But she knew she was on her own now. Her voice echoed.

In one hall there were musical instruments: pipes, wooden and brass, violins and guitars, harps and antique keyboards in painted wooden cases. She ran her fingers along the untuned strings of a harp, tapped lightly on a small drum.

Clouds of dust rose at the movement. There was no music to be had here, only dust. Some of the instruments had been broken, deliberately smashed. Perhaps they had had no time to make new songs after the Stasis; it was a pathetic place, she thought.

There had been a plague, she remembered. Most people had died. The others had packed up, forming the caravan. They had left their songs and amusements and their dead behind.

It would be too easy to conjure up visions here, even without the aid of the Field of Flowers. The abandoned musical instruments, the unknown portraits, the unread books and dim houses with their shuttered doors and windows were full of ghosts. If she allowed it, her imagination would all too easily clothe them in reality. Faces at windows. A door slamming, a ball bouncing, voices singing.

This was no good.

She found another staircase. Two levels down now. She paused, looking around. The tunnels here were narrow, more like alleys than streets. The paint on the doors and windows was peeling and blistered. Her bare feet were treading a dirty pavement. Blocks of harsh, uneven stone, littered with paper and broken glass, the untidy rubbish of a city long abandoned.

No one had bothered to clean up this level of the City of Stairs. Perhaps this was where the ordinary people lived, the artisans, servants and tradesmen who ensured the comfort of those who lived in the palaces above. It was like a slum district, unkempt, grubby and dark.

She paused for a minute, standing to one side against an uneven earthen wall which was covered with peeling notices she didn't understand. Her mind was racing. It was finished down here, all of it. No one lived here now, there was no one to visit the theatres or drink in the bars or buy bread or wine anywhere. It was a no man's land, empty and abandoned.

And she was beginning to understand why. The city was tainted, stained by the presence of the Field of Flowers. The plague had blown through the city because there was no strength to resist. The creeping mist had deprived the city of life. In lost dreams and vague delusions it had stolen energy and power from the people of Smintha. They had lived in fiction, in plays and books and art and pantomimes, far removed from the reality of the sun above.

Thurstan would be lost here, a man who gave no allegiance to Sun or Moon . . .

Neither did she. She remembered Jocasta, who had lost her life because the Moon Goddess had decreed that Lukas Marling should love Eleanor Knight . . .

Their lives took place on a stage no less real than the one she had just passed through. Puppets. The clichéd metaphor held good; the Gods pulled the strings. Perhaps she might just as well give up and let events take their course, as Matthias had done. In a way she would almost welcome being found. It was too lonely here, a desperate, forsaken place . . .

She was about to turn round, to retrace her steps back up the staircase to the other level, when sudden sound shattered the silence.

A sash-window lifted in the wall behind her. She leapt away from it, across the alley to the wall opposite, and looked up. There was a man standing there.

A huge flood of relief.

'Thurstan!' She was almost crying.

He looked down at her immediately, and for a moment their eyes met. She moved away from the wall, into the centre of the alley.

'It's me, Eleanor! What are you doing here? We've got to get back to Phin and Matthias – '

He stared at her blankly. 'Eleanor?' he said. 'Sorry. I don't know anyone called Eleanor.'

'Thurstan, for God's sake! Wake up, you're still in a dream! This is Smintha, the underworld – ' But the window was slammed down, and the shadow behind it moved away.

There was a door to one side. No knocker, no bell. She tried to turn the handle, but her hands were damp with sweat. She paused, rubbing her hands against the rags of Comyn's shirt.

Paper rustled at her feet, disturbed by an unusual wind. She hated this place, hated the tawdry untidiness of it, the depressing, drab light. But at least she had found Thurstan. If she could only get him to acknowledge her . . .

She tried the door again. It opened slowly, reluctantly, and she kicked at it with her foot, bruising her bare toes. Cross, and more than a little nervous, she ran up the stairs, over the threadbare carpet, to the dusty landing at the top.

Three doors faced her. She thumped on them all, shouting, 'Thurstan! Thurstan, where are you? Come out!'

One of the doors crashed back on its hinges, and there he stood, pale hair tousled, dressed only in jeans.

'What the hell do you think you're doing? Get out of here, you've no right to be here!'

He was rigid with fury, glaring at her.

'Thurstan, Matthias is helping them start the Stasis again! We must stop him!'

'What? I don't know what you're talking about.' He suddenly turned away from her, murmuring something over his shoulder to whoever it was in the room behind him.

Eleanor heard laughter, soft and cool. And then a figure appeared behind him, a white hand on his bare shoulder, a woman of dusky beauty.

'Dear me,' she said, running her eyes over Eleanor. Suddenly Eleanor was acutely conscious of her bare legs and the inadequate remains of Comyn's shirt. 'Friend of yours, my love? Where does she come from?'

'She's nothing to do with me. I've no idea who she is, making such a fuss.'

'Thurstan! Wake up! Think! Don't you remember who you are?' Eleanor was casting around for something to jolt him into awareness. 'Martitia's son. Leader of the Jeren. Friend to Phin, to Lukas. Don't you remember? You kept Phin company, with those shadows . . .' Her voice trailed off. He was turning back to the woman in the room, closing the door on Eleanor.

She leapt forward, painfully jamming her foot in the opening. 'Thurstan! Listen! This isn't a real place, it's only left over from the people who used to live here – '

He was standing next to the woman, running his hand over her perfect, pale shoulders. From the concentration on his face, she knew that he had forgotten her already.

She didn't hesitate. She walked up to him and swung back her hand, landing him a stinging blow across the face.

His head jerked round, his cold blue eyes contemptuous but no more than mildly irritated.

'Go away,' he said. 'You're not wanted here.'

'What is your name? Who were your parents? Where are you from, where are you going? Remember Powel, Jocasta, Lukas? Your old friend, Lukas? Don't you remember *anything*?'

For a moment she thought that she saw a flash of comprehension, of understanding in those hard eyes, but then he shrugged.

'It doesn't matter,' he said. 'There's no point in any of that. It's nothing to do with me.'

'It's *everything* to do with you! It's who you are, what you are . . .'

But he was running his lips over the woman's neck, stroking back the soft fall of her hair, winding one hand round to cup her breast. The woman stared at Eleanor, a faint smile on her curving lips.

Eleanor felt her bearings slip, her certainty drop away. What else could she say? The more she insisted, the more Thurstan turned to the woman. He didn't want to recognise her, or remember anything.

She stared at him helplessly. She didn't know what else to do. There was an odd smell in the room, a musty, foetid odour, only half concealed by the reek of cheap scent. Eleanor turned away, and then stopped.

It was too important. She could not leave Thurstan here, involved in some stupid affair, when there was so much at stake.

'Remember the Stasis, Thurstan, when people didn't die, and there were no children? Remember Jeren, with its trees, and people who had stopped singing, stopped making poems? They were your people, your care. Yours and Martitia's. Martitia, your mother . . .'

His head was bent towards the woman, but his hands were still. He was listening.

'Thurstan, you know me! It hasn't always been easy, but you've known me for a long time now – '

'Yes.' His voice was very low. He looked up into Eleanor's eyes for the first time, and she saw that all knowledge and remembrance had returned.

'But it's no good. It doesn't matter, Eleanor, what we do, say or think. There's never been any point to any of it. It's someone else's game, nothing to do with us. It doesn't matter.'

And with that, he turned back to the woman at his side, stroking her hair, tracing with one finger the line of her eyebrow, her cheek, her full mouth, slightly open at his touch.

Eleanor could not think what to do. This was a fatal error of Thurstan's, one she had nearly fallen into herself not so very long ago.

She turned away from him, and the door swung shut, firmly, behind her. And as she walked down the steep stairs covered by a threadbare carpet of faded scarlet and blue, she realised what the expression on the woman's face meant.

Triumph.

Outside, a light wind still disturbed the litter. And although there was no sky, no sun, moon or stars, she felt as if a storm were approaching. The air was heavy with threat.

She had to find Phin. She didn't know if he'd been recaptured or not, but she had to tell him about Thurstan. She should retrace her steps, back to where she had last seen him.

Thurstan had to be jolted out of it. She knew he was in the grip of a dangerous obsession. She couldn't do it alone. She began to run back the way she had come, looking for the theatre door, but before long the alleyway gave way to something else.

Under her feet, hard-packed earth became more dusty. She looked down. Not dust, sand. She saw leaves and branches, flowers, budding and full-blown. How bizarre, she thought. Was this some kind of garden, a greenhouse . . .? At least it wasn't the Field of Flowers: the blooms were white, large and many-petalled.

Intrigued by the silky gleam of the ivory petals, she leant forward to smell one. The tendril that twined swiftly around her leg pulled her off balance. She screamed, suddenly, the sound splitting the earth-laden air. Other tendrils leapt at her arms. She threshed around, trying to struggle free of the twining creeper.

This can't be happening, she tried to tell herself, not here in this dead, empty place, but the tendrils lifted her from the ground, and started to move her along, passing from leaf to twig to branch, through dark underground tunnels and silent glades. She found herself shuddering with panic.

The Desert Rose. And it had her caught, held fast, in a twining, tenacious grip. And the blossoms were eyes, watching and open, and their scent the sickly sweet stench of carrion.

Chapter Twenty-five
Rose

'She's gone! The slut's not there!' The door to the elegant room where Imbert and Edine habitually met banged back on its hinges. Matthias winced at the sound.

'You refer to Miss Knight?' Imbert's tone was cool but Matthias recognised the contempt in it. It would do nothing to calm Weard.

He heard Edine move towards her lover. He imagined the placatory hand on his arm, the way they would stand, not quite touching, but linked like twins, facing their volatile colleague.

Her voice was tranquil. 'Don't disturb yourself, Weard, it's all according to plan. She's slipped a level or two, but it makes no difference . . .'

'I don't understand this! How can you let her run wild? What *is* happening down there?' He was still shouting, angry at the exclusion, the implied slur. 'What if she escapes?'

'There's no way out now. The tunnels are all blocked by scurries or bonfires or by the Rose itself.' Imbert's voice was smooth and patient, but Matthias detected an undercurrent of excitement. 'Let me explain a little, Weard. The Hidden Rite is not just a sequence of incantations and ritual actions. No. It must reflect a wide spectrum of emotions, of actions, of feeling. It must feel as if the whole of humanity is involved in this act. For you must not think that the Gods – even the Benu – act independently of humanity, however it may seem. People are involved, implicated at every level. The Rite has been set up to take what it needs from the circumstances and individuals in the city.

'Everything is in place, everything is relevant. The city

itself provides an ideal background. Most of humanity's achievements are contained here, in the books of the libraries, the art galleries, the armouries and food stores. And here and there throughout the city we have organised things so that individuals, representatives of humanity, may take crucial decisions, may experience vital emotions.'

Matthias heard wine being poured. They put a glass in his hand. He put it down, untasted. Imbert understood so much. More than Matthias had ever dreamed.

Imbert continued. 'Has she released Blythe, too?'

'Yes. They lost my men near the theatres . . .' Weard's voice was no longer loud. The bluster had faded. He sounded puzzled, bemused. Matthias knew that he had not taken in the significance of Imbert's words. 'They escaped me . . .'

'Weard. Blythe is no danger to us or anyone else. Someone who has survived the Children is not going to start acting in any meaningful way. And certainly not violently. He will in fact add to the Rite. A man released from horrors; it's another path, another way in to the Rite.'

'He'll be tired,' confirmed Edine. 'He'll be drawn downwards . . .'

'And what about the other one? Merauld. How's that going?'

'That's progressing nicely. Better than expected, in fact.' Edine sounded pleased.

'Lilith?'

'Performing well, as she always does. Very rewarding to work with. So clever, my love, so clever you are, to make and rule a Parid . . . He'll be ready to decide when the time comes.'

Matthias slumped back in his chair, numb with shock, appalled. For the moment he forgot all about Eleanor. This was the ultimate blow. There really was nothing left now but despair.

So, it was to be Thurstan. The element of human choice, the essence of the Rite. There had to be someone, man or woman, willing to take responsibility when there was interaction between the Divine and humanity.

To decide, to choose. To create the world afresh with the force of a word, a hope, an emotion.

Matthias had relied on Imbert and Edine not understanding

this. He had explained everything else, honestly and completely, holding back only this one crucial fact. Someone had to take responsibility.

He had underrated them. They had been playing games with him all along. They knew all about the Hidden Rite, all the arcane significance, the dangerous areas where philosophy, magic and religion coexist. All about the human element. They had used him only to confirm their own knowledge, to ensure that they did not trespass too closely on the realm which waited below.

But Thurstan would not go along with it, surely? Not Martitia's son, not the leader of the Jeren. He would not deny his own past in such a cause . . .

Matthias turned his aching head to the wall, shivering with foreboding. Not prevision this time, but dread, pure and simple.

Soon afterwards, Matthias took his last flight on Amery. Imbert waited with him in the wide avenue between the dusty palaces for the approach of the Arrarat. There came the sound of wings, but Matthias felt no lift in the heart, no joy. As he climbed onto the powerful back, Imbert put out a hand and touched his shoulder.

'Don't think of escape, Matthias. Remember, your friends are all still here. Just a final check on the ignition points, that's all we need. We don't want to leave anything of the Rose to survive, do we?' Matthias could hear the smile in his voice.

For a moment he paused. Amery's sight showed him a man of great personal beauty, of fine, sculpted features, an elegant and graceful figure. His appearance was without flaw. His eyes were humorous and compassionate, his mouth sensual and sensitive. It was impossible to believe that he would act from anything but the most elevated of motives.

Indeed, he did not. The Rite would take place because Imbert loved Edine . . .

'You are a stupid man, Imbert,' Matthias said clearly. 'I find it hard to believe that Lefevre should have chosen you –'

'It's not without irony, I agree. And if it's any consolation, I sometimes wonder at it myself. And then I remember what I am doing and why, and how close to success I am. It seems to me then that Lefevre was quite right. And look what he has become, after all . . .'

Matthias looked at him with his borrowed sight. 'You should not have spent so long in the Field of Flowers. You are marked for death. You will not survive the Rite.' His voice was light-less, echo-less.

'Wrong again, Matthias. You're underground now, you can't see the truth about me.' He was entirely undisturbed. 'Go and mark the boundaries, Matthias. We haven't got long.' Suddenly, he hit Amery's back with his open palm. 'Go on, get out of here!'

There was no reason to delay, anyway. As Amery flew down the long tunnel, out through the hidden cave, north of Smintha, out into the hot blue skies and burning sun, Matthias considered his chances. The longer it was left, the deeper would Thurstan become embroiled in the Rite, the more chance there would be of his forgetting who he was, what he was. Matthias felt sick, riding his wondrous hawk, seeing the wild stretches of desert through Amery's eyes.

The monstrous Rose Lefevre stained the dry red surface with lush green leaves and gaping white flowers. It was reaching far into the ruins of Smintha, now swarming over the city like a virulent disease, pulling down masonry in its search for food.

Dark angels buzzed around it and over it, feeding, tending, obeying its least wish, like worker ants around their queen, fascinated and doomed. The bonfires were all below ground, ranged round the outer perimeter of the roots. There, in the hot, baked earth, the peripheral roots had dried out and became brittle and desiccated. Easy to burn, easy to destroy. Fire would seal the Rite away from the rest of the world. Encircled by flames, the decisions would be taken, lives lost, the Rite enacted.

Amery flew high in the midday sun, so high that the dark angels would be unlikely to sense her presence. Matthias hoped that Lefevre was using no other faculties to protect his flowery incarnation. Did he share the prevision that afflicted Matthias as soon as he left the underworld? Did Lefevre too see the fire writhing along the fluid stems, the petals crumpling like paper, the ash falling to mix with sand? Did Lefevre also see the great Hawk, hanging high on a

thermal, wheeling in wide arcs high over the fire, waiting to
fall?

He shuddered. What could he do? They knew so much.
All he could do was to trust that his prevision was inaccurate
or incomplete, or a lie like so much else.

But it was no lie. As he swooped in the wide perspective
of the Arrarat flight, he was sure of that one thing. No lie.
A hawk would fall into the fire, become entrapped in a
vanishing spiral. It would all start again, the grinding misery
of the Stasis, the distortion of life and love. Eternal sterility.

He remembered birds caught in the Boundary of
unchanging time he had crossed so long ago. Frozen in the
instant between one second and the next, aware, suffering,
with no relief, no alteration. What could he do, how could
he hold it off, how avert such an evil?

Only one possibility. The picture of the future was clear.
It left room for only one hope. His heart was near to breaking
at the prospect.

That night, back in the tunnels of the underworld, he sent
his wondrous Arrarat Amery from him.

Go from here, he said. Leave this city, where the Rite will
take place, escape the Great Fire and leave behind you the
knowledge of my betrayal. Find the people of the north
where Lukas lives, and be swift, my love, swift as the arrow
of desire. Or it will be too late. And as Amery, pale, creamy
Amery, took a loving farewell, Matthias thought once more
of the Moon.

Astret, You should play a part now. This matters to You
even more than to us. Help us, Lady, help us to do what
is right.

No answering gleam of comfort, no answer to Matthias'
prayer. How could there be, when the Gods pursue their own
ends, regardless of humanity?

Although Matthias did not know it, the hatred that had
rocketed around the theatre where Thurstan had been
destroyed was real. It was almost the only real thing
anywhere.

Hatred, fury, revenge. The edge of vengeance.

She was imprisoned in leaves, constrained by running
creepers, cushioned by petals. She was almost rigid with panic.

at first, and then fury took over. Eleanor resisted, struggling, hitting out, tearing, kicking.

The Desert Rose was too vast, too varied. Too knowing. It anticipated her movements and cradled threshing limbs with easy strength.

Firmly and inexorably, it passed her through the underground levels, along the silent pathways broken by its roots, slowly moving her up towards the Sun.

She was terrified. Her mind was full of the unbearable present, and of something else. A dream, a memory of a prevision, of herself burning up in a cellar, wreathed around in burning tendrils. She remembered what she had been shown under Lycias's temple during the storm.

Again and again the image repeated. In the Palace of Blood, twined in flowers, fire scorching along every nerve . . . Herself, burning to ash, wrapped round in leaves . . .

He had only just begun, He said. Again she hurled herself against the frail-looking runners that clasped her so closely. Sometimes they broke and gave way, but always others sprang at her, encasing her, defusing her movements.

The wild energy of panic could not be maintained for long. She was becoming exhausted with the useless struggle. Her hands were sticky with sweat, her arms and legs cut by the thorns and the sharp edges of leaves. She was aching all over with the stress of it. She tried to conserve her strength at one point, trying to think clearly what to do next. But it was impossible to stop herself pulling back, bracing herself in resistance against the grip of the Desert Rose. She knew what was going to happen.

She started to cry out, shouting for Phin, for Thurstan, for Matthias and Amery, for anyone to release her from this fatal path.

No one heard. Her voice died away. The Desert Rose allowed her to drop to the floor, waiting for her to recover a little. It wanted her conscious and sapient, for it knew that its God would relish awareness in His victim.

It drew back and waited.

She lay for a while in a daze. And then, experimentally, she stretched tired limbs and found them free of flowers. She was alone in an open glade. Filtering through the deep, dark canopy of leaves, sunlight dappled the air. Was she above ground? Was she going to escape the figure, burning up in a cellar?

Underfoot there was dry sand, broken up by sprouting shoots and observant flowers. She knew she should avoid the gaze of the watchful flowers, but they turned to follow her as she moved, just as the parent flower turned to follow the Sun.

So she remained quite still, catching her breath, catching at the moment of hope. She could see the sun, and patches of blue, but the Desert Rose existed all around her. She knew where she was and what was happening. She was encased in the prison of the Rose's own being, watched by its eyes, pricked into movement by its thorns and tendrils. Dark glades echoed about her.

'Lefevre, Desert Rose, let me go.' She tried to keep her voice even and reasonable, but it sounded light and insubstantial among the fleshy stems. Perhaps it would reply; it had been human, once.

No. Refusal turned the leaves away from her.

'Why do you hold me? What do you want? What am I to you?'

The branches overhead slowly rolled apart, peeling aside, and a flood of sunlight beamed down into the heart of the Desert Rose. It battered down on her head, the heaviness of light.

Knowledge of the Desert Rose's will floated through the air. An offering, she would be. An offering to the God, a scapegoat, a bribe, an enticement.

Love me, sang the Rose to its God. And take this offering as a proof of my love.

The being that was now the Rose had been the servant of Lycias for a very long time. The deposed High Priest to the Sun still retained some knowledge of its Master. It yearned constantly upwards, tracking the steady progress across the heavens, the blazing glory of light that burnt to ashes all hopes of reconciliation. It hoped to appease the Sun God with an offering, a small sop to the fanatic power that existed in dreams of revenge.

Eleanor understood the nature of the Rose's thoughts. The leaves around her shivered with longing and desire, the flowers trembled with hope. Familiar emotions.

She ran quickly to one side, dodging at the last moment the twining stem that leapt for her throat. She had seen, far down a leafy glade, the dull red of the sun-baked desert.

She preferred to meet the Sun God on her own terms. She would be no passive sacrifice on the altar of Lefevre's obsession; she had something far more urgent to accomplish. She had to find Lukas again before it was too late.

She ran again, swerving and ducking, but branches sprang towards her, twigs snagged and locked together, the flat fleshy parts of leaves grew into each other, and a solid wall of greenery blocked her path. It happened almost instantaneously, an automatic response to her movement.

No way out, no way through. And all the time, Lukas lived and existed somewhere else, unaware of her presence. She couldn't bear it. All her foolhardy confidence and courage drained away.

She sank to her knees and let the creepers take her, pulling her along on verdant paths with secret joy.

Chapter Twenty-six
The Levels

'Matthias, wake up! Quick, there isn't much time!' Blythe was breathless with running. He had managed to avoid the guards outside the theatre, had found himself lost in an endless maze of backstreets; the empty corridors and deserted houses, the bronze mirrors and the flat light.

At every junction he had found a drift of scurries, murmuring constantly, flowing in one direction. They took no notice of him. He did not exist for them. It had been like searching through a dream. He heard strange chants in unknown languages, whispering down every passage. The city was filled with sound: the scurries, he realised; a sibilant wash of esoteric communication that unsettled the nerves. Were they operating autonomously, or was Imbert running them?

He did not pause to find out, but he had followed them, hoping that they would lead him to the Mages. And at length, heart pounding, he had come to the row of ornate palazzos where he had last seen Imbert and Edine.

The scurries wafted on, causing the façades to waver and shift, as if seen through water or distorting glass. They were making for the central stairwell, Blythe realised. The palazzos were unattended, the doors unlocked. He had crashed through room after room, racing along hallways and up stairs. He had found Matthias in a marble-lined palace, close to the spiral stairs. He was in an upper gallery, a long room lined with doors. He was slumped in a huddle against a wall, frail and unconscious.

Blythe shook the unresisting shoulder of the sleeping Mage. He was shocked by the change in Matthias's appearance. He needed help, help even to sit up. Would he be capable of action?

Matthias passed a weary hand over his forehead, saying nothing.

'Matthias, what's happening? What are Imbert and Edine up to? And what the hell is happening to the scurries? They're chanting, and seem completely unaware . . . There was nothing to stop me coming here. What *is* going on?'

There were scurries there too, repeating their incomprehensible incantations. Like the others, they seemed totally unresponsive to his movements. It was as if they were existing in some other dimension, on some other plain. Or perhaps they just knew that he no longer mattered.

They could be right. Imbert, Edine and Weard had other things on their minds now. They presumably reckoned Blythe a cipher, someone of little significance. What could he do, with no special skills, no knowledge of Mage-lore, a crippled, unmoving left hand? He was irrelevant and unimportant.

Matthias was now standing, still silent. Blythe hardly recognised him, this withdrawn, despairing figure. He felt a sudden chill. Had he truly betrayed them all?

'Matthias. Tell me. What's happening?'

'The Stasis. The Stasis is going to be reinstated.'

'But they can't! Not possibly! How could they begin to know what's involved?' He remembered the Great Hawk, the golden Benu Bird with its blank eyes dancing among the stars. How could two smooth, self-confident Peraldonians with their brutal lieutenant entrap such a force?

'They knew it all. And I confirmed it for them, and now they'll go ahead . . .'

And in a low, flat monotone, he told Blythe the secret he had held fast to himself, the double bluff he had hoped to play until the end, the bluff which had been called.

He seemed driven to make Blythe understand just what had happened. Why he had made such a terrible mistake. How he had compounded his guilt in such a fashion. He could no longer bear the burden of it alone.

He said nothing about the shadows. He wondered if Blythe would sense them, waiting so close . . .

There was silence. Blythe did not withdraw his hand from Matthias's shoulder. The tired voice started again, driven to reveal every betrayal, every treachery. Matthias began to outline the Rite, the broad sweep of it, going over its major components.

'Once it's started it cannot be stopped. The fires around the Desert Rose must completely consume it, there's no way we could leave it running wild, half-destroyed. And besides that, there will be so much power gathered in one place, so many forces arrayed, that the Rite will have to run its course. It will, anyway. I've seen it. It's about to begin now. Can't you feel it? The sounds down every tunnel, the empty stairways, the deserted buildings? All just waiting for something to happen, something to give meaning to it all.'

He had subsided against the wall again, holding thin hands to his head as if trying physically to stop his thoughts breaking through. 'There will be an offering, of course. They're going to use Eleanor. That's why the Bird will come, they think. She will probably lose her life during the Rite . . .' His voice barely checked, running over the outline as if it no longer mattered. His thoughts had concentrated on every detail for so long now that it appeared automatic.

'And the fire, of course, will be raging by that time. There will be no way through it; it will surround the central well and a large part of the city. Everything will be contained with the fire, within the Rite, within the Rose. There will be no way out.

'And they'll ask Thurstan if he'd be willing to stop time for love, will he take the responsibility for it all? And if he is truly destroyed, truly at the mercy of some passion, he'll agree – '

'He never would!'

'I think he already has.'

'No, not Thurstan. No matter what the cost, he'd never go along – '

'Think of the deceptions here, Phin!' His quiet voice was desperate. 'They are masters of hallucination, they'll befog and befuddle the senses, disperse the intellect, use every trick in the book and a thousand more! Imbert has lived in the Field of Flowers, he knows what happens there, he *uses* it. There's a Parid on the loose somewhere, too. Imbert made it . . . Haven't you realised? And think, Phinian Blythe, what is the greatest hallucination of all, the deepest degree of self-deception?' Matthias seemed to be clutching at straws, searching for some answer Blythe knew didn't exist. He was watching Matthias all the time, trying to trace the remnants of integrity in that ruined face and thin, anguished body. Dark hair hung straight over his fraying collar, damp with sweat. And Blythe thought, has Matthias really given it away, really acted with foreknowledge and treachery? Is it madness still to trust him?

There was a long pause.

'Passion. . . love,' he said at last. 'The greatest hallucination, the worst of self-deceptions.'

Matthias nodded and, impossibly, smiled. It was terrifying. 'But love is no deception, not at heart, not if it's the real thing. We don't know what Thurstan is experiencing, how far it has gone – '

'We'll have to find out.' Blythe looked blankly at the Mage.

'But there is no role for you here this time.' Matthias reached out a hand towards him. 'This is no longer your struggle; you have paid your price.'

The shadows, Children of the Night. They were very close; Blythe did indeed recognise their presence. He remembered them, hanging so heavily on his shoulders, formed from the memory of actions and emotion. Love, guilt and fear. He did not want to act again.

They had not come for him this time. He spoke evenly. 'You forget, Matthias. These are my friends. Yours too. Remember friendship, Matthias? Remember loyalty? Thurstan is part of my life, Eleanor – also. I'm not going to desert them. And you, Matthias, have to stop the Rite – '

But as he spoke, he heard three human voices chanting in unison, moving along the corridor towards them.

'It's too late, Phin. It's already underway . . . There's nothing you can do.'

The voices were very close. Swiftly, Blythe moved back into an alcove at the far end of the gallery. He saw Imbert, Edine and Weard enter.

'Rilyni e'marsera, rilyni felaseara . . .'

They were dressed in cloth of gold. Even Weard had discarded his patterned leather jerkin. He looked strangely powerful, almost dignified in the unaccustomed robes.

There was a sound of whispering all around them. All at

once Blythe realised that the room had been full of scurries all the time, blending with chair and table, hidden against the wall.

Matthias showed no reluctance, no hesitation. Weard helped him to his feet. Unresisting, he was draped in gold.

He joined the chant, the patterns of words soft and rhythmic. Aghast, Blythe saw sparks of fire cradled between his long fingers. Shadows leapt in the room around them. Dark caverns opened up.

Then the fire was caught, entrapped in the spiral staff held by Weard. It became a white-hot furnace, held just within control by the contortions of the wood. They turned to leave the room: Weard first, holding the raging staff high above his head, followed by Matthias, moving slowly like a much older man, and finally Imbert and Edine, hand in hand.

They left the door open. Blythe stared after them and saw a glance pass between Imbert and Edine. A pledge it was, a promise of significance. They would not fail.

He could not follow them. There was a river of scurries attending them, flowing over the stone floor and walls, whispering ceaselessly. And crawling along the wall, flickering over the gilded pictures and painted panelling, other, darker, shadows followed the Mages. They were waiting their chance, waiting for the act to be accomplished. He could not bear to watch them.

He had to find Eleanor and Thurstan, to get them out of this. He turned his back on the shadowed Mages with their mantle of scurries and opened an unmarked door in the far wall.

He found himself in a stairwell.

The levels. Staircases, cellars, landings, wells and dungeons. In the mind, other layers: reality, memory, deception, illusion, prevision, hallucination. The blurring of distinctions in the underground realm, beyond the light of Sun and Moon.

Fiercely, he though of Lycias and Astret, making Their world intolerable for humanity. People should not have to live and act beyond the pace of the seasons, the changing times of day and night. They should not have to chance the mists from far below, or the attendance of shadows.

Stairs reached up and down from the small landing where

he stood. Blythe mistrusted the vast drops, the sudden chasms and deep wells. It originated, he supposed, from Sharrak's well, so long ago, when he had fallen and expected to die.

And the spiral staircase that vanished, hurling them into the Field of Flowers. Those lowering wings and creeping mists . . . He did not want to go downwards.

What were his priorities? To stop the Rite, or to find Eleanor and Thurstan? Any objective observer would find it easy. Without doubt, he should turn back and follow Matthias and the others, killing if necessary. Anything to prevent the recurrence of the Stasis. The Rite was already under way, he would have to act quickly.

The fire held raging in Weard's staff, the fire that sprang from Matthias's own fingers, would be put to the circle of bonfires ringing the roots of the Desert Rose, ringing the city itself.

Soon Lefevre would burn. Soon glass would spin high in the sky and clash and break. A choice would be made, a decision taken, an offering accepted. And the Bird of Time, of Life and Death would be caught, trapped, imprisoned in a cage set up by devious, dangerous, proud people. Reckless people.

The air was hot and acrid around him. Somewhere, fires were already burning. Every second the Rite progressed on its relentless path.

He forced himself to stand still on his narrow landing in the dreary half-light. He considered Matthias. Blindness is a powerful force, a state wherein all one's other senses are distorted into unusual pathways.

Matthias could see the future. What would that be like, thought Blythe, still unmoving, to know where all one's actions would lead? It would be a kind of paralysis, surely. If what one saw was terrible, if one knew that the shadows waited, then action would be impossible.

Matthias was still acting, still taking decisions, giving directions. What did he see then, in the next few hours, the next few days? He was helping to set up the Stasis, a condition wherein the future could not be altered.

To live under the Stasis and know the future exactly would be intolerable. Therefore Matthias must be banking on some cloudy vision of probabilities that the attempt to reinstate the

Stasis would fail. Blythe would have to trust that Matthias knew what he was doing, that his blindness had led, not to despair, but to knowledge of a way out, a way to escape the Stasis.

Blythe knew now that he could not trust what Matthias had said, for there had been scurries there. Matthias could have been lying, deliberately misleading him – or the scurries.

He sensed, through the depths of the stair, that he was no longer alone. Something waited further down. There was a strangely disturbing smell. Something flowery, and something rotting. He could hear nothing. He stood still, forcing himself to keep thinking.

The Benu was the essence of freedom. The element of chance in all their lives. While it flew, free as the air, nothing was irrevocable. The future was not unalterable, not set and inescapable.

Blythe would go downwards to the other levels, and meet who or whatever waited for him. He would go to find Eleanor and Thurstan.

Chapter Twenty-seven
Rejection

The dawn tide was at its height as they passed over Shelt, but Felicia was no longer frightened by it. She was a match for dragons. Something worse was now taking place.

His arms around her waist were cold and unfriendly. His eyes glanced over her, there was no easy companionship, none of the smiling laughter that had begun to sweeten the impossibilities of her life. And after what had happened on the beach, this seemed to her a worse distortion than Ladon's corruption of the tide.

Astrella put them down on the balcony of the great house. There was a scent of fresh-turned earth from the newly washed gardens below. Vere's flute was now quiet, the house silent in the pale early light. Rosco helped her down and then moved quickly through the double doors into the ballroom.

She stayed behind on the balcony, her hand lifted for comfort against the Arrarat's shoulder. For a moment the hawk waited, as if aware of her misery. But then, sadly, it stretched wide the vast wings and lifted off into the morning light.

'My lady, what's wrong?' Annis, emerging from the house to look for her. Sent by Rosco, she assumed. He would look after her, like a pet or a child. She would be an obligation, a duty to him. He would not neglect her, not in the unimportant ways.

'My lady, come in, you must rest now . . .'

She looked up at the fast vanishing hawk, but she could no longer see it. Astrella was gone, taking with her Felicia's last strength.

Her knees gave way, and she stumbled into Annis's arms.

*   *   *

In the cold depths Ladon waited for the ebb tide to bring him news and strength. He had one more chance, one more possibility of claiming the Moon maiden for his own. He had thrilled in the power of the tide that had dragged his captive from him. He had been enraged at the time, but now, remembering, he gloried in that extraordinary strength and purpose.

He would have it for his own. He would join together with it and the kingdom of the sea would quail beneath the power of their joint rule.

Using her strength, he would order the flight of fishes through the waves, harvest the gardens of pearls and coral, tend the forests of weed and anenome. He would dictate the resting place of ships on the sea bed, ordering the existence of the creatures who dwelt beneath the waves as his servants. He would use the tide to take what he needed from the land, and there would be no more bargains with foolish Mages, no more compromises, no more waiting for them to fulfil vain promises.

They had not succeeded in bringing him his prize. Gawne had said he should have the Moon maiden by the dawn tide, but he had lied.

Still, he was paying the price for that.

Gawne, under the waves, danced to the ocean's tune. In drifting grey silk, his wound unkindly mended in the healing power of water, he tossed here and there, discarded, irrelevant. While Ladon moved through the cold waters, he would live forever. His hunched shoulders were bitter and hopeless.

It was what he had always wanted.

In the end, Mittelson and Sharrak reached the cellars. Serethrun was now well on his way to the *eloish*. The other two took their time. With care and patience, although the situation was desperate, Olwyn Mittelson drilled the Parid until it knew exactly what was required.

Then, together, they crept through the unusually quiet Castle, avoiding the public rooms where the Sea Lords were still in conclave.

They had found Torold anxiously watching at Esmond's bedside.

*   *   *

'How much control have you over the Castle Guard?'

'The third company is loyal, my own men. And about half the Household Guard. I would not like to rely on the others.'

'The fourth company is ours. A high proportion of men from fishing families. They will follow me. That leaves three other companies loyal to the Sea Lords. Six thousand men.'

Torold regarded the tall fair man standing by the fire with doubt. He had not met him before, but he had seen his face on handbills. Esmond had described him as charismatic, difficult. A leader, reckless of personal safety, passionate in his desire for justice.

This man was not quite what he expected: smooth, cool and confident. Torold could not like those cold blue eyes and sneering mouth, although Esmond had spoken, often, grudgingly, of his integrity.

Esmond lay now in a deep sleep, a sleep Torold hoped would restore him. He was tended by the Mage Mittelson, the unprepossessing figure he remembered from the fight at the Marqun pool.

Torold and Jolin Rosco discussed strategies, and all the time Torold waited for the knock on the door, the return of the Sea Lords under their new leader.

There had been a conference, hurried and secret on their return from Marqun. The new leader was chosen. Dederic, as second in command under Gawne, became first Sea Lord, but Torold knew that Dederic's own deputy, the recently inaugurated Mage Lammon, was the more powerful.

He had never liked him. Sharp eyes had watched Torold attend Esmond, and had sent him Fessil with potions and scented candles. Lammon represented the old order of Shelt, the families who had resented Torold's election as Earl. And, in turn, Torold refused to trust him, or his puppet doctor, Fessil.

The candles burnt with a different scent now. Mittelson had recognised the fumes as a sleeping drug, and had replaced them with candles of his own. The room was wreathed in strongly smelling smoke, disguising some other scent.

No one disturbed them. There was no sign of the Sea Lords, still in conference. The crisis was approaching.

It did not matter to Torold.

'But will he recover? Will he be all right?' Torold had taken Mittelson's arm, searching the pale eyes in his anxiety.

'I hope so, my Lord. I hope so. Just keep him clear of the Sea Lords. If you trust me, there are only two things you must do. Place the third company under Rosco's command. You will have to instruct Feltham, your commander. Is he reliable?'

'Entirely. We trained together . . .'

'And then, when it's all over, when the rest of the Guard accepts defeat, then you must announce Rosco as your heir, married to Felicia.'

'Does she *want* to marry you?' He looked at the tall man standing negligently by the window. He had known of the plan for the succession for a long time, but this was the first time this aspect of it had occurred to him. He didn't dislike the girl. He hardly knew her, she had always been too ill to receive visitors.

The fair-haired man smiled. 'Oh yes,' he said coolly. 'We've spent some time encouraging her trust and dependency. Whom else could she turn to?'

Me, thought Torold Westray, troubled. She should have turned to me, her uncle, her family. She should have felt able to trust me.

He looked at the pale, unmoving figure on the bed. Esmond had trusted him, and what had come of it? Horrors and collapse and madness. For relief he went to the window to look out over his City of Shelt.

The tide was still high, almost up to the Castle itself. Thin ribbons of dirty brown water lapped against the walls of his friends' houses. He had expected Shelt to be quiet, deserted. It was very early in the morning. People would either be asleep, in the attics of their flooded houses, or camping outside the city on the high ground.

But he could see crowds pushing through the muddy water, men with dark hooded cloaks and high wading boots. They moved quietly through the narrow streets, causing eddies in the swirling water. Their silence was unnerving.

'Who are they?' he asked Mittelson, his heart racing uncomfortably. A bell was tolling, a deep bass note from one of the watch-towers.

'Fishermen. And look, over there – ' Mittelson pointed up towards the west gate.

A tide of horsemen were battling their way into the city. The alarm bell by the gate began to sound as they watched.

Immediately it was echoed down the corridors of the Castle. Torold heard men running, heard doors slam. There was a thunder of knocks at the door.

Mittelson caught his arm as he turned to face it. 'The third company,' he said. 'Feltham. Remember.'

Torold shook off his arm and took one more look at the pale figure on the bed. Then, as Rosco and Mittelson disappeared down the passageway to the gardens, he cleared his voice.

The door was shaking under the weight of the fists outside.

'Come,' he said, and the doors swung open.

Lukas Marling pushed through the streets of Shelt, through the men he had sworn to lead, with his cloak pulled down over his face. They were all making for the Castle. The attack was taking place. Mittelson was leading it without him, and it was a hell of a risk.

He remembered what they had planned, knew how it would go. Serethrun would bring the *eloish*. The fisherpeople would infiltrate the ranks of the Guard, some of whom would be ready to join them anyway. Torold's men would strip off their scarlet cloaks and join the ranks of the fishermen. The aim was to defeat the rest of the Guard, to force the Sea Lords to capitulate.

Their magic was concerned only with healing, or with controlling the storm. They depended on the Guard to maintain their position. The revolt would be mainly a matter of strength and battle skills. And although Lukas was not arrogant, Mittelson was no soldier. He ought to turn back, join the grim and determined fisherpeople he had made his own, and fight for their cause.

There was something he had to do first.

Water was washing around his ankles now as he went through flooded streets towards the lake that was the old harbour.

In the deserted backstreets surrounding the harbour, where the water was waist-high, tables and crates had been placed along one of the paths: a walkway leading to one building.

He had been there before; he was no stranger to the Fisher Temple.

Walking along the sodden, makeshift stepping-stones, jumping over the frequent gaps, Lukas had strange perspectives of the cottage interiors. Unlit, stripped of character and life, black water glinted darkly in cramped living-rooms, in small shops and workplaces.

The Temple stood on a small rise, just clear of the water. An old woman sat hunched on a chair tilted precariously against the shabby double door. The paint was peeling, the wood beneath beginning to rot. No stranger would have known it for a Temple.

She was wrapped in shawls, her skirt plump with petticoats. She was knitting, the needles ceaselessly clattering. It was the only sound that morning, apart from the wash of water against buildings.

She looked up as he approached, watching him steadily while the needles continued their busy motion. The smell of the sea was heady here, salt and iodine, tainted by fish.

He was desperately tired, still white and cold from the clutch of the dragon. His mind was glancing away from the look on Felicia's face. He had been cruel, thoughtlessly cruel in the face of a courage he did not understand.

He wished the old woman had not been there, that he could just have walked into the Temple and said his piece. However, some acknowledgment at least was due to her.

'In the Lady's name, salutations.' He used the formal, archaic greeting. Her lined face did not alter, black eyes unwavering, looking through him.

'You should not be here,' she said at last. 'Lukas Marling, there is work for you this day. Your men need you.'

He was too tired to question her use of his real name. 'I have something to do first.'

'There is nothing for you here now.'

'I will not be denied.' His voice was still quiet in the sour morning and there was no other sound.

'I shall not let you pass.'

'You cannot stop me.'

'What will you use? Swords, fists? A knife? Lukas Marling, noble warrior, what weapons would you use against an old woman?'

He was silent for a while. Then he spoke. 'No need for weapons. I'll just wait until you get tired of it.' He leant against the wall of the Temple at her side and folded his arms.

Above the quiet wash of water on the street below, he could hear the shouting begin in the distance. Then the bells started, all the city bells, loud and raucous, spreading out from the area around the Castle.

The Castle Guard would be pouring down the ramp into the city. He wondered how many companies would stay loyal to the Sea Lords, how many men his fisherpeople and the *eloish* would have to face. He wondered if Torold would keep his word and join their ranks.

He heard the clash of weapons and the shouting intensified.

He closed his eyes, turning his face up to the pale morning sun, seeking its warmth. He was beginning to shiver again. He pulled his cloak closer, and became aware of the woman's gaze.

She was watching him sardonically. 'Cold?' she said. 'There's plenty of action to warm you up by the Castle.'

'After you've let me in.'

'There's no one there, you know. They've all left. No priestesses pray to Astret now.'

'It doesn't matter.'

How much longer? He could, he supposed, simply pick her up and put her down elsewhere. It didn't have to be violent.

A movement high in the sky above them caught his eye. A hawk, wheeling in graceful spirals, carried on a warm thermal. The sweep of the wings, the powerful curve of it decided him.

He turned to the old woman, ready to move her with force if necessary.

She was gone. The chair was still tilted against the door, the knitting dropped casually at its side. He moved it out of the way and opened the doors.

It smelt unused, dusty and dank. In the light from the door he found candles and matches. He was shivering continuously now, and his fingers fumbled with the matches, dropping some on the bare wooden floor.

The picture over the altar was draped in white cloth. He pulled it aside and stared at the flawless face of Astret.

Silver shone in Her hair, glowed from Her eyes.

He had loved that face. Had spent much of his life serving the Mistress of the Tides, the graceful Lady of the Moon. The ebb and flow of Astrct's Rule had guided his every action.

Astret had been worth all their lives, imprisoned in the Stasis. It had been worth losing everything in that battle. But it was over. The Stasis had ended, the Boundary was broken. It was over.

And yet still, still lives were required. Relationships were forced, people lost identity in incomprehensible strategies.

Part of him wanted to kneel at the altar, and beg forgiveness for such thoughts.

'No.' He spoke quietly but it echoed through the empty warehouse. He had to force his jaw together to stop his teeth chattering. He felt cold and sick and old.

'No. Enough. I've had enough. Find someone else, Lady.'

The silver-black eyes watched him dispassionately, and he stared into them for a long time before finally replacing the white cloth.

He blew out the candle and went to the door.

The old woman was sitting there again, her chair tilted against the wall, still knitting. Her black stare followed him silently as he pulled his cloak closer against the cold wind from the sea, setting off back to the Castle.

He heard all around him, first in the click of her needles, then in the call of the gulls, and then in the treacherous rhythm of his own heart:

Too late. Too late, too late, too late.

Chapter Twenty-eight
Revolt

The streets were empty. It was as if everyone had been drawn towards the city centre, magnetically attracted by the noise and the violence. Lukas saw children staring wide-eyed from windows, half fearful, half excited, not venturing any further. No one else was around; the shutters of the shops were drawn, doors and windows firmly closed. The daily life of Shelt was suspended.

As Lukas approached the Castle, he began to meet people again, all going towards the harbour. Old men and women were helping the wounded back to their homes.

Instinctively, Lukas pulled down the hood of his cloak, not wishing for recognition. It was all he could do to stop himself acknowledging them for, as he neared the Castle and the streets became more crowded, he kept seeing faces he knew. The men and women he had trained in the deserted barns, people who had become friends.

Jarry Lindel, leaning heavily on her sister Rosa. There was a mess of blood clogging the side of her face where her right eye had been. Her head lolled to one side, and Rosa was crying, tears running over a white face. She was staggering under the weight, and for a moment Lukas almost forgot what he had to do.

He swerved away from them, through narrow streets and passageways. The tide had just turned, and the pavements were still covered with a stinking layer of slime and filth. The alleys were more crowded here, everyone carrying weapons or tending the wounded. Horses were stamping and snorting in distress as the sound of fighting became louder. He passed by the rush of bodies towards Castle

Square, down the wide street which led to the house where
he had left Felicia.

He would see she was safe, and explain that she did not
have to fall in with the plans of Mittelson and Torold and
everyone else. It *was* possible to refuse. There was no God-
given role she had to fulfil, nothing she had to do. He would
show her that she was free, and then go and fight with the
fisherpeople.

'Rosco! What in hell's name are you doing here?' A furious
voice at his side, a strong hand ripping the cloak back from
his head.

Philp Cammish, head of one of the oldest fishing families,
was staring at him, his sword hanging slack at his side, a
rough bandage around a gash in his upper arm. 'I saw you
at the Castle only minutes ago! How did you get here so
quickly?' He was a large man, shorter than Lukas, but heavily
built. 'Where are you going? They need you back there!'

He had no energy for explanation or prevarication. Without
hesitation, he drew back his fist and knocked his lieutenant
to the ground. Then he ran, down the long, tree-lined avenue
towards the great house at the end.

As he reached the door, up to his ankles in water again,
he looked back for a moment. Cammish was standing at the
end of the road staring at him, every inch of his body
expressing bewilderment.

The door swung open and Serethrun Maryn stood there.

'Where's Felicia? What have you done with her?'

At first Lukas could not take in the sense of it. Serethrun
was pale, his clothes filthy and torn, great circles beneath his
eyes.

'She's here, isn't she? I left her here . . .'

'Fuck you, Rosco, what did you do to her? Annis had never
seen her in such a state, not even after the Marqun!'

'She's not here now?' He was being stupid. 'Why couldn't
Annis bloody take care of her?'

'Why couldn't you?' Annis was standing just behind
Serethrun, her eyes grim and hard. 'I went to get blankets,
medicine. . . I was only gone for a few minutes, but she'd
disappeared when I returned. You've got a lot to answer for,
Rosco.'

He pushed past Serethrun into the house, through the vast hallway. He flung open doors, his eyes sweeping the deserted rooms. Then he ran up the curving staircase into the ballroom. He skidded across the polished parquet floor to the double doors onto the balcony.

Outside, looking over the city, he could see the whole of the square seething with fighting figures. Scarlet cloaks mingled with black jerseys, scarlet blood splashed uniforms and breeches. Huge, unsaddled horses reared high above the crowds, crashing down with sharp hooves. Their black-haired riders were whooping, an eerie, alien sound, clear and high-wrought through the clash of weapons, the shouts and the screams. The *eloish* were pushing their mounts towards the Castle, and all around the scarlet-cloaked men fell away, wounded and dying.

There, near the Castle gates, he thought for a moment he saw Mittelson, tall and bleak, together with another man wrapped in a black cloak, fair hair glinting in the midday sun.

He had no time to wonder who Mittelson's companion was. He stood on the balcony and called, low and long, the summoning for Astrella.

He wanted to find Felicia, to smooth that shocked look from her face, but he didn't know where to begin. She could be anywhere in the city, and nowhere was safe. High in the cold air, he and Astrella circled the city centre, deciding what to do.

There was chaos below.

The confusion around the Castle was complete. He could easily tell the fisherpeople with their dark knitted jerseys and fair hair. Women fought alongside men, for this was just as much their fight. These were the people he knew, the friends who trusted him. There was a steady flood of them from the run-down shanty towns along the river and harbour areas, fighting with the weapons they had made, improvised, or stolen. Many of them were swinging heavy boat-hooks or spades – anything. The struggle was focused on the Castle gates, where the Castle Guard was under severe pressure.

There was continual shouting. The fisherpeople were fighting for more than their livelihoods. Their families, their homes, their religion all depended on the outcome of this battle. They fought with inspired ferocity.

The *eloish* were also easy to identify from above, a swathe of dark, leather-protected riders sweeping in from the west gate. Their horses leapt and plunged through the crowd, their hooves battering down on people and weapons alike. Their riders carried and wielded short, broad swords with skill. Their wild cries grated on every nerve.

They were savage with a wild resentment that Lukas Marling recognised. The fury of the dispossessed, the explosive violence of a race crushed and then discounted. But there was also something of joy in their action, an exhilaration and blood-lust that was terrible to watch. They were enjoying it. There was a wild satisfaction in the spilling of blood.

But the real confusion lay within the ranks of the Castle Guard. They too were easily identifiable, with their vivid scarlet cloaks and gold braid. But scarlet fought with scarlet, and some stood in ranks alongside the fisherpeople.

Some of them had torn off their cloaks to join their families in the ranks of the fisherpeople. Others had put the scarlet cloaks on, wilfully insinuating themselves among the Guard and then turning on them.

Commanders shouted, drums beat, trumpets blared against the din, trying to make some sense of the attack, trying to work out who was fighting for whom.

Lukas Marling had no choice, He would never find Felicia in all this. And the fisherpeople needed him. He saw friend after friend fall beneath the superior weapons and professional skill of the Guard. He would have to play his part. There was never any real choice; it had all been decided months ago. The fisherpeople had to win, and then the trap would close.

No one noticed the huge hawk swooping down from the racing clouds, settling on the roof of some stables near the ramp to the Castle. No one saw Lukas Marling draw his sword for the first time, the hood of his cloak thrown back, running into the centre of the mêlée.

Nothing was as he anticipated.

As Lukas Marling fought, swinging his sword, jabbing with the knife, pulling and twisting and gouging and punching, he deliberately put aside all sense of caution. He ignored the carefully learnt tricks that he had passed on to the fisherpeople, all the devious feints and parries that helped ensure a swordsman's survival.

He didn't want to survive this. He wanted his friends to win, and he wanted out. He would cause maximum destruction at whatever personal cost. And then Felicia would be free of him, and Mittelson would have to find someone else, and Serethrun would no longer look at him with hatred and loathing.

His companions stared at him, amazed, shocked by this recklessness. And then, as they realised what was happening, fought with renewed vigour, with confidence and a strange fearlessness.

They saw that nothing touched him. He was invulnerable. No sword penetrated the careless defence, no knife thrust through to unprotected flesh. Blows seemed to glance aside, slashes to swerve and waver.

Lukas noticed it almost immediately, when a scarlet soldier cursed, losing his grip on a sword which had caught, clumsily, in his own cloak. A hurling axe, on a sure swing at his head, inexplicably lost volition and fell impotent at his feet. A knife ripping through the cloak wound round his wrist caught harmlessly on the neck clasp.

He was bruised, of course, scratched too. But no weapon injured him seriously, no attack from any number of men prevailed. He was untouchable, carelessly triumphant through no skill of his own.

He knew what was happening. He could almost feel the Silver Goddess, the dream he had denied, standing over him deflecting every blow. There was no free will left to him. His life was not his own.

A pawn, a toy, a victim. He was used, preserved to rule this city, bound to Felicia.

He looked about him with wild fury. He could see Torold in the distance, magnificently armoured, fighting with glorious, showy panache. He was going to get himself killed, thought Lukas. And then it really will all be irrevocable, because Shelt will need a leader, and I will be the only possible choice: bound to Felicia, riding a hawk, trusted by the fisherpeople, nominated by the Moon . . .

And still foolhardy members of the Castle Guard threw themselves at him, and he stepped aside over their bodies.

He swung his sword once and two men fell. He moved a little
to one side and a lance splintered into a door beside him.

He began to work his way through the fighting towards
Torold. Like Mittelson, he had one thought. Torold Westray
had to survive.

Chapter Twenty-nine
Dragon

As the tide turned, Dederic, the First Sea Lord, and his fellow Mages were standing high on the battlements of the Castle. Their backs were turned towards the fighting in the square. They had seen the third company, obeying Torold, strip off their cloaks and join the rebels. Their own loyal soldiers were disconcerted and it looked increasingly probable that they would not prevail at all. It was a bloody, chaotic mess, but the wasted lives, the violence and injury, were irrelevant to the Sea Lords.

The Sea Lords were unworried. There was no reason for them to depend on brute force: they could call on help from another source.

'Oh Ladon, Prince of the eternal ocean, come now!'

'Ladon, giver of life and health, reclaim your beloved, come now!'

'She awaits you in the city, held in the grip of the rebels. Defeat them, and take your heart's desire!'

They raised their spiral staffs towards the rising tide. They had one aim, one goal. To appease the dragon, and thus to ensure their own immortality. At one stroke they intended to put down the rebellion and achieve the ambition they had learned from Gawne.

Only one of them thought that there might be more to it than that. Only one of them, at this late stage, remembered who Felicia was and what her family was.

Brice Lammon, who had sworn to drive Javon's family from the City of Shelt, decided to take things into his own hands. As the incantations were spoken over the heaving grey seas, he slipped out of the long gallery and ran swiftly through the Castle to the garden gates.

He was going to find Torold. Ever the opportunist, he saw that this was his chance to rid Shelt of the usurpers. He hid his grey silk robes beneath a long cloak, and concealed his staff in the folds of the sleeves. Then he joined the press of people milling around the square, and began to look for Torold.

Ladon heard the wild summons, but it moved him not at all. The Sea Lords meant nothing to him; he could no longer be swayed by bargains or promises. This summons happened to suit him. He wanted his Moon child, his pale lover. With delight he approached the city, venturing into the shallow shelves of rock near the coast, inching along the jutting levels of the brigg, reaching out over sand and rock, running over brick and stone, ranging through mud and gravel in the heavy wash of the encroaching flood-tide.

He could feel the presence of the Moon in the square. He could sense a silver invulnerability hanging protectively over one figure.

Curious, he came closer, peering through the churning water, his multitudinous heads winding this way and that.

The Moon child belonged with the sea. Belonged with the tide, the tide which ran in her blood, turned with her will, moved with her breath.

Ladon had always recognised this. And nothing was going to stop him now, with the tide at its height for the last time.

Nearing Torold, through the crush, Lukas saw something else approaching from the Castle.

It was a dazzling blur, a sudden flash of light catching on sword and helmet, brightly turning vision away. The light was at first insignificant, a small glow, and anyone unused to Mage-power might have taken it for a mirror angled to the sun.

There was no sun in Shelt now. Lukas knew Mage-power when he saw it. Whoever it was was making for Torold with evil intent. A Mage was setting out to kill Torold, with or without the knowledge of the other Sea Lords. But Lukas needed Torold Westray to live, to rule his own kingdom. To let him off the hook.

He pushed through the crowds, his head lowered, his sword sheathed, making no attempt to defend himself. It was still unnecessary. The shield of invulnerability remained in place, deflecting every blow, every attack.

At last, he stood at Torold's side. The big man glanced at him.

'Rosco! What are you doing here?'

He was getting tired of this. He had never even met this man before. 'Where else should I be? *That*, Lord Torold' – he pointed – 'is not just a flash of sunlight. We have a fighting Mage on our hands.'

Torold had dismissed the captain of his own Guard who had been occupying his attention. He swung round, his sword and shield braced shouting, 'Where? Let me at him!' His eyes were shining with enthusiasm and determination. This was a man who loathed Mages, loathed their devious machinations.

Lukas felt a sudden liking for him. But the gleam of Mage-powered silver was now nearer, and the men around them were falling back. He stepped forward to stand in front of Torold, and laughed at it.

Bolting, electric charges sparked dangerously at him. He dodged and twisted, quick as running water, and hooked his sword tip into the spiral staff.

Separate a Mage from his staff, he remembered Mittelson saying, holding out his empty hands, and you have something else to reckon with.

He felt a wave of sickness running through his sword and up his arm. His whole instinct was to drop it, to throw it from him like the diseased and cancerous thing it now was. Nausea was almost bending him double. So he trusted in his strange, unwanted invulnerability, and fell forwards into the throbbing glow, pushing his sword at an angle up and to the side.

All at once the light died and the sickness faded and he found himself staring into the bitter, spiteful eyes of Lammon, the new Mage. The man who loathed Torold with more than a personal resentment.

The staff dangled uselessly from the tip of Lukas's sword. He raised the sword so that it slid down to his hand. As he reached out to take it, it fizzed and sparked and fell into a small pile of ash which ran through his fingers to scatter at his feet.

Lammon was watching him, a sour smile on his thin face. 'You can't have everything, Jolin Rosco. Kill me, if you wish. And know that I, dead, would not choose to change place with you, alive and victorious as you now are . . .'

He could not stand it, his own fears now voiced by others. The reality of it was becoming solid all around him.

'What are you waiting for?' Torold, at his side, was puzzled by the delay.

Lukas's sword point was resting on the small Mage's throat. He spoke without looking round.

'Torold. Rule your city. Take responsibility for it. You don't need me.'

'Who else can run Shelt now?' Torold's eyes were ranging over the turmoil in the city around them. The fighting in the square was grinding on, brutally fed by exhaustion and desperation. A fire had broken out by the Temple, and everyone was getting pushed closer together by smoke on one hand and the rising tide on the other. Some were standing actually in the water, but further away from the square, towards the harbour, there were screams and shouts.

Torold's voice went on. 'Only you, Rosco, have the support of the crowd. Only you can do it. It's too late to opt out now.'

Too late. Again. The hesitation was enough. Lammon moved suddenly, ducking deep to one side under the cover of his own cloak, and for an instant steel gleamed in his hand. Ignoring Lukas he lunged forward and threw the knife with unexpected skill straight at Torold's breast.

Surprise widened in Torold's eyes. He began to topple forwards, hands widespread against welling scarlet. He tried to speak.

Two movements: one to dispatch Lammon, a sword thrust to the side of his neck; then, falling to his knees, Lukas reached out to staunch Torold's wound.

He shouted commands to those around him, blood welling through his hands. A stretcher materialised, a broken door. A cordon of men, the remnants of Torold's own third company, kept cover as the stretcher was lifted, shielded it as it was moved through the struggle of fighting men towards the vortex of violence at the Castle gate.

Mittelson was there. Mittelson could heal, could mend broken bone, patch torn muscle. Lukas kept his hands fast to the wound, trying not to touch the knife. To pull it out would kill Torold. He closed his mind to the man's agony, to the big hands fluttering feebly at his side. He concentrated only on getting him to Mittelson.

His own hands were white-knuckled through the spreading red. Men pushed and shoved on every side, and their progress was painfully, desperately slow. But when he looked up from the ramp to the Castle gates, he saw Mittelson standing there, very close. Behind him the gates to the Castle were splintering, shattering inwards under the weight of a battering ram. As he watched, several planks gave way. A group of heavily armed fisherpeople poured into the Castle, led by Ferant and Alex Aldrich. Mittelson had taught them more than medicine, after all.

Next to Mittelson, blond hair blowing in the wind, directing the attack, vivid in action and authority, Lukas saw himself.

For a moment, his hands relaxed. Blood spurted. In shock he stared at his mirror-image beside Mittelson. He recognised it for what it was.

He shouted, white-faced, to the tall thin man by the splintered gates, 'Olwyn! What are you doing! It's a *Parid*!'

A man by his side took his place, trying to staunch the blood. Torold was now unconscious, his breath coming in faint gasps. Lukas started up the ramp, still yelling.

'Get away from it! This is madness, you can't deal with a damned illusion!'

There was a long moment of stillness as Mittelson looked at him. In the end, he spoke. 'What choice did I have?'

Lukas was by the gates now. He could hear the sound of fighting from within the Castle itself, but it faded into a distant background. He was watching the flickering form shifting through the air with familiar, sick horror.

No longer was the Parid simply a mirror-image. The force of Lukas's disbelief had shattered its frame of reference, and other creatures began to emerge. A spider, or was it a mantis?, praying claws high by its chin, a golden woman, hair wreathing like fog –

'Sharrak, get out of here!' His voice sounded raw and unfamiliar.

For a moment the shifting gold shape of a woman held steady, glowing in uneven contours in the clouded air.

Mist was rising up from the sea. The water in the streets was giving off vapours that stained the air. No one could see what the mist concealed, what the turning tide brought with it.

Sharrak's golden glow was beginning to run like paint in water, dissolving into the mist. It could spread its net wide like that, Lukas remembered.

'Mittelson! Stop it! Hold it steady or get rid of it – ' He was shouting words at the Mage.

Mittelson raised his hands once more in that curious, empty gesture. His triangular smile widened helplessly and, as if in response, Sharrak started laughing.

The curious, light, bubbling sound slid over the square. Storm clouds were no longer racing, but hanging heavy above the city. Each man and woman could hear the movement of the tide, slowly edging its way up street and avenue. And what with the sick sound of laughter and the black swell of the tide, the fighting stopped. The people of Shelt dropped their swords and looked, one to the other, in mutual dread.

This was a different enemy, a spreading golden stain, an undeniable nightmare for everyone there. They stood together under the threat, their divisions momentarily forgotten.

Torold lay unmoving on the litter. Lukas turned to Mittelson, reaching for the thin shoulders, shaking him.

'Come on, Olwyn, stop it! Any half-way competent Mage I've known can control this kind of thing!'

The gold stain was swarming towards him and it was all he could do to hold his ground.

'I have tasted your flesh, Lukas Marling, have waited long for this.' He could see its lips spread wide, the pearly teeth reaching, avid. It held a macabre fascination for him.

Mittelson was watching him with doubt; then his gaze slid beyond, to whatever was moving in the tide. Lukas did not turn around. He stared at Sharrak. He could not let it go; he had to find out. It seemed of urgent, undeniable importance. His words to it were whispered, private, from the centre of the confusion.

'Why did you let me go? What held you back in the Castle?'
Robard bleeding on a pallet, and Sharrak regarding him with
that strange expression. Its eyes had traced his every
movement. He now knew why. It had been rehearsing for
this surreal metamorphosis.

'What do you want, Sharrak? Why *did* you let me go then?
What are you doing now?'

'I want you – powerful, Lukas Marling. Earl of Shelt,
strong and invincible, grateful to me. Like your Mage friend
here wants you to rule in his debt forever.'

Like Astret, Silver Lady of Light, wants me married to
Felicia, loyal to the Moon eternally.

Why me? he thought. So absurd. So – arbitrary.

A sense of the futility of it all overwhelmed him. What
identity, what honour – strange concept – could he possibly
possess, given everything by the God? What was the use of
any of it?

There was a path left open to him. His knife was sharp.
Mittelson's eyes, watching him, held complicated secrets,
ambition, hope, fear. Sharrak, drifting in clouds of gold,
languorous mouth, smooth skin, watching him, wanting
him . . . Everyone in the square, the fisherpeople, the
soldiers, the *eloish*, all watching him . . .

And the cloud of invulnerability that preserved him from
injury and attack. Would it stop the knife from the vein,
too?

It did not stop that, no. But something else did. High-keyed
to the point of reckless and complete despair, he had raised
the knife, raised it to his throat in a silent, timeless movement
of grace. A last glance over the crowded square, where his
friends stood, appalled.

And then he saw her. A frail figure, guided by an old,
familiar, black-swathed fisherwoman. Knowing silver-black
eyes looked straight across the crowds to him, eyes that owned
and manipulated and used him. The fisherwoman thrust the
girl forward.

Felicia ran through the crowd. She was white and grey,
long pale hair streaming. She pushed through the men and
women with their drawn swords, their jutting knives, their
bloody clothes.

She was stumbling and uncertain but they cleared a path

for her. Up the ramp outside the Castle, shouting thinly
against the steady roar of the tide, 'Rosco! Rosco!'

Only his name, his false, lying, treacherous mockery of a
name.

She must have seen Torold, but there was no break in her
pace. She was almost at his side. And Mittelson, at last,
spurred into activity. His hands were weaving patterns of
light, looking from Felicia's white face to the cloud of gold
at his side. Some power sprang between the hands, the face,
the Parid . . .

Moulding and making. Shaping and designing. Kingmaker
and queenmaker, Mittelson spun the deepest spell of his life
to hold the Parid steady in some other guise . . .

Felicia had almost reached Lukas. She would have flung
herself at him, knocking the knife away, but the sea was
roaring now and the sound was overwhelming.

The sound shook the foundations of the city. Torn screams
ripped the air as the turmoil of the rising tide became
complete. The intruder arose.

Like a many-tentacled anemone, Ladon reared over Shelt.
Taking life from the tide, his heads and claws ran through
the narrow streets, the wide avenues, the sheltered parks.
He spread himself wide, threading through watery channels,
probing every secret place. He sought his prey.

And found her, white as moonlight, clinging to the man
he knew well.

So struck was he by this, so furious in his jealousy, that
he did not see the golden cloud coalesce into the flickering
shape of a woman just next to them. It moved closer to them,
as if it were trying to prise the two figures apart.

Ladon reared up and back, a cresting wave about to break,
a serpent poised to strike, a thousand voices suddenly
concentrated into will.

And the man, the Mage who used magic without staff or
spiral, knew what the dragon wanted. Knew its passion for
the Moon woman, the hope for all futures, for all peace. He
took the golden shimmering form of the Parid and whipped
it into shape.

And a pale woman, white-fleshed, pale-haired, languished
in the cold sea-water beneath Ladon's clutch. The Dragon
roared through a thousand voices, roared with triumph and

lust, and took the silver woman so enticingly offered.

Sharrak screamed too, a sound beyond the frame of ordinary reference, as Ladon seized its shifting flesh, the glimmering silver form. It ran multitudinous, foaming lips over the female body, and with the force of its desire held it steady, frozen forever in the likeness of the Moon's own princess.

Ladon and Sharrak, locked fast in greedy, myriad embrace, sank back through the waves, back over the rocky shelves, down to the deepest valleys of the ocean. The lost land of the dead, the realm of the flat nightmare, the high-pressured, rigid, inflexible prison of dark and cold.

No tide moved them there. No ray of Moon or Sun broke through those waters, where a dragon lay entwined with an illusion, locked together in a timeless, inescapable embrace.

Lukas turned to Felicia, trembling at his side. To stem the shaking, only that, he took her into his arms, holding her close to him. The knife dropped away.

Over her head he saw Torold's eyes flicker. He was watching them both with clouded eyes, his brow creased, his fingers clenched hard against the pain.

Mittelson was leaning back against the ruin of the gates, his hands slack and empty. He was grey with exhaustion, his eyes for once unselfconsciously revealed. This was the end, the limit of his power.

A sound behind him. The cross-bar on the other side of the gates was being lifted. Wearily, Mittelson stood aside, watching incuriously as the shattered, heavy wooden planks were pushed out of the way.

Figures stumbled forward, their hands tied behind them. They were dressed in grey silk, but no longer carried staffs. The Sea Lords stood there, all of them, with Dederic at their head. Members of their own Guard held the knives at their side. Ferant and Alex Aldrich stood behind them, frowning.

A pause and a silence. The square was quiet. The whole city waited, the sea-water now lapping gently at people's feet. The silence went on for far too long. Felicia was still shaking, so Lukas kept his arms around her, longing, suddenly and fiercely, to give her some peace, some comfort.

Feltham, commander of Torold's personal Guard, moved

forward past the line of Mages. He went to Torold's side and
knelt for a moment there. Words passed between them, but
Lukas didn't hear what they were. He saw Torold's clenched
hands suddenly relax, and heard that small, final sound.

They were all looking at him. One by one, in turn, he
looked down the line of Sea Lords, and each one of them
in turn met his eyes for a moment and then bent his head.

Torold Westray was dead. Feltham stood in silence for a
moment. Then he turned to face the square. He spoke only
three words, but Lukas, Felicia, Mittelson and everyone else
heard them.

'Earl of Shelt . . .'

And then the cheering began. The sound rose, augmented
by stamping feet, clapping hands, thumping on doors and
carts and barrels, a vast groundswell of noise that rang
through the city of Shelt.

Lukas looked only at Mittelson. His eyes were very cold.

'No,' said Mittelson softly in confirmation. 'No way out
now.'

Chapter Thirty
The Decision

Blythe moved swiftly and silently down the stairs. He wanted to test each step on the way so that he would not tumble into one of those terrifying drops, but that would have been too slow.

A door creaked open below him. The small light of a match, rosy glimpses of face and hand, rustles and whispers. Two, possibly three men, Weard's guards. Then the match caught, a torch flared, and light shot up from the bottom of the stair, pinning him like a trapped moth against the stone wall, his shadow leaping behind him.

Three men, twenty feet below. He was mentally prepared, but physically? There was only one way to find out. He ran, jumping stairs three at a time, and then launched himself out from the wall into their midst.

They were surprised, but in better shape. Armed with swords and knives. One of them, ragged and wiry in the flickering light, shouted, 'Get him! Now – ' but Blythe's fist caught him as he moved, and he stumbled off balance into the midst of his companions.

Blythe made no attempt to fight them. He just wanted a way through to the door he had seen on the other side of the small platform where they stood.

They were surrounded by barrels they had brought up from a lower level. As Blythe dashed past them, he saw that the bung from one of the barrels had come out. Dark liquid was spilling over the wooden staircase.

The three men had seen it too.

'The torch!' yelled one, urgently.

It was too late. A spark had flared along the creeping

dribble of liquid, reaching the barrel in an instant.

Blythe was at the door, pushing up the cross-bar, twisting the handle. As it gave, he felt the explosion behind him. Fire tore at the shirt on his back, and the force of the rapid succession of explosions as the other barrels went up threw him headlong into the world on the other side of the door.

Grey light, flat-packed earth underfoot, a faint breeze disturbing the dry, dusty air. The walls of unknown houses rose around him.

His shirt had charred on his back, his skin was sore and burnt. He was standing at the junction of three corridors. Drab houses stretched away into the dark on every side. A glass-encrusted pillar stood in the centre of the junction. Far down each passage he saw another such pillar, reflecting the faint echoes of light.

Which way? There were posters on the wall to his left, posters advertising ancient entertainments, dated performances. They were defaced and torn, their messages all dispersed. And then, further along the vaulted passage he saw the pillars of the theatre where he had lost Eleanor.

He began to run, his footsteps echoing, but the theatre was empty, the alleys all around it deserted. He peered through blank windows at empty rooms, dusty furniture, the discarded private lives of people long gone.

As he moved, he felt the wind blowing strongly down the corridors. The fire was underway, he realised. Dragging the air from the City of Stairs. The rags of torn posters wreathed around him like the Children of the Night. His hand was clenched, his knuckles white. God, what was Matthias up to?

He moved steadily through the swirling paper, steadily through the ruins of the city's frail pleasures. There was a constant feeling that he was not alone, that there were eyes behind the blank windows, following and tracking his every movement.

He felt that he was following ordained paths, guided somehow towards a crucial place, a crucial act. It was not quite a relief to find, at last, Thurstan Merauld. This meeting had been set up, he felt. This was planned . . .

Thurstan was staring at one of the posters, trying to make

out the text. The wind ruffled his fair hair, threw scraps of paper at him.

'Phin! Where have you been?' His blue eyes were clear, innocent and unaware. 'What is this place?'

'It's the city beneath Smintha, the City of Stairs. Where they went to get out of the Sun. Come on, Merauld, we've got to find Eleanor. She's here somewhere . . .' Blythe did not want to waste time. He wanted them to move on, to escape this closing trap. Thurstan seemed to be all right.

'And Lily – ' He was preoccupied.

'Who?' Blythe swung round to stare at him, taking in for the first time the disarray of his clothes, the unbuttoned shirt, bare feet. 'Where's your sword?'

'What? Oh, I left it somewhere . . .'

'Thurstan!' Blythe laid a hand on his arm. 'What have you seen here? Who is Lily?'

He smiled gently, disengaging himself. 'Someone – special . . . I ought to find her, Phin, but this place is so confusing. There are all sorts of other levels – '

'That doesn't matter. We've got to find Eleanor, and quickly. Your Lily, whoever she is, will have to wait. This is urgent – '

'So is this. She'll be here somewhere, Lily . . .' He smiled secretly. 'Phin, I think I'll just wait here until she turns up.' He was wandering off already, peering through the windows, looking for his lover.

Blythe caught his arm again.

'Don't be a fool, man, this is a place of hallucinations, of delusions. This is a set up. Lily could be just another deception!'

Thurstan paused, the same gentle smile curving the narrow lips.

'I know,' he said softly, 'but when I'm with her it doesn't seem like that . . .'

'What about now, Thurstan? She's gone, she's not here, there are other priorities – '

'Perhaps . . . But what do they matter?'

'It matters. It all matters. Eleanor is here somewhere, and Matthias. And unless we do something to stop it the Stasis will be with us once more. Don't you understand? This is not only about what happens to you. There's more to this than some woman.'

'No, no, Phin, that's all there is. That's all that matters, that's the only reality, what happens between men and women.'

Lycias and Astret. Phin and Karis. Eleanor and Lukas. Sun Emperor and Moon Empress . . .

Thurstan and Lily?

'You cannot be serious.'

'Oh, but I am. All I want, all I care about is – Lily.' His eyes were very cold. 'You hardly even exist. And nothing else matters a damn.'

Everything was very still around them. It even seemed as if the wind had ceased; as if, for a moment, the world was in shock, assaulted by a dread alteration, a deep rift in reality. The decision had been taken.

With abrupt, dagger-sharp insight, Blythe understood what had happened. The Rite would go ahead, the one chance Matthias was relying on had failed, and Thurstan had given it all away.

He had no option now. Looking past Thurstan to the end of the alley, he saw an ornate wrought-iron gate. The spiral stairs again. The wind blowing around them was being drawn to that doubtful portal, where a fire was burning. The city was surrounded by fire. The Rite progressed . . .

It was a context for experiences, for decisions, for emotions. A microcosm of life, where everything mattered and nothing was casual.

'Come on,' he said roughly, hustling Thurstan before him. 'Matthias. And the others. It's got to be stopped.'

Thurstan's face was blank with the residue of shock. Blythe was not at all sure that he understood what had happened. He pushed Thurstan ahead of him, and together they began to run towards the stairs, to the chasm which plunged from the Temple of Lycias to the realm of the Unseen One.

Quietly I wait. I lie in silence at the end of each dreaming life. My wings spread wide over dark trees. I welcome the homecoming of souls . . . I give rest to all. I wait. My Children are kind, and offer release from suffering. There are no lies here, no injustice. In purity, in peace, the quiet fields endure forever.

And long ages pass. The vanishing patterns of time, the intricate fingerprints of its passing, lightly brush the pale wands of asphodel.

There are sometimes disturbances in the patterns, troughs and promontories. Once the quiet flow unfolded, briefly held in a spiralling vortex.

Not for long. My wings, brooding, lift free once more.

I sing.

> They do not give up.
> They call again.
> The fire is lit.
> The Rite endures.

A thousand voices rang down the corridors. A wordless, ceaseless chant, washing like the tide through the channels of the City of Stairs.

The city wavered, indistinct, unstable, as the flood of chanting scurries flowed along every tunnel, down every staircase and well. Where light had run along the grid on which the city was strung, now the fluctuating murmur of the Rite swamped every space.

It filled their ears, broke into their thoughts.

The flood broke around their ankles. Suddenly there were scurries everywhere, swarming along the empty corridor. Thurstan and Blythe had to push through an unheeding flow of indeterminate matter. The scurries clogged round their knees, slid beneath their feet. It was like wading through a sea of mud, a sea of sound, and the walls and doors and windows wavered under the moving torrent of formless, changing flesh, the weight of wordless chanting.

They kept moving, but it was hard going. They were making for the central well, the double staircase. They were moving with the tide of scurries.

A wind blew all the time, and rags of paper caught in their hair and clothes. The air was becoming thick with drifting smoke. They were nearly there.

A door, emblazoned with iron. The scurries avoided it, dividing at the gate to follow the curve of the wall. Blythe pushed the gate open and went through.

They were on a spiral staircase.

Chapter Thirty-one
The Rite

Below them, the drop was lost in clouds of smoke. Far over the other side of the well they could see more stairs, winding upwards. There was no way of telling which staircase they were on, whether it would lead to the dubious safety of the iron-enclosed vestibule, or whether it would vanish into the world of illusion.

Perhaps it didn't matter. They only needed to go upwards, where the Mages stood. Their cloth-of-gold robes glinted with the flame of torches. Weard and Matthias on one side, Imbert and Edine on the other. And although they were not far away, they were untouchable in their concentration.

The flow of sound, the litany that inspired the scurries, was clogging the air. It was blotting out reasoned thought and clear-cut action. It came from the words they spoke. A low chant, an incantation, a summoning of irresistible potency.

For a moment Thurstan and Blythe stood there, trying to assimilate the structure of their surroundings. The smoke masked much, but it was broken, intermittently, by the wind being sucked into the circular stairwell. There were fires everywhere, all around the city, for the Rite was taking place everywhere in the City of Stairs, but there was a focus to all the energy. There was a centre to the Rite.

It lived in the double vortex of the central stairwell, and smoke wreathed from its heart.

Again Blythe looked down into the swirling mists. He was leaning over the wrought-iron banisters, gasping in the choking, laden air. He saw something else moving there, between the flames.

A bud of greenery, breaking into flower. It was joined by others, breaking and blooming and flowering through the smoke like water-lilies in a lake. Green leaves grew up through the flowers, swaying in the wind. He took Thurstan's arm, pointing silently downwards. Thurstan stared blankly for a moment and then said, 'What is it? Where does it come from?'

A shoot was winding up towards them, searching for something. As it swept across the width of the chasm, it caught on one of the iron struts supporting the staircase below them.

It fastened there, wrapping itself around the wrought iron, pulling itself upwards. Leaves and creepers trailed behind that original shoot. Within minutes the whole staircase was alive with greenery, blooming with small white flowers, seething and searching and climbing . . .

Twining tendrils had already reached the stairs where they stood. They were forced back through the gate, not trusting the inexorable movement. The creepers snatched at their legs before returning to the staircase. The Rose wound upwards to the Temple of Lycias.

Through the iron gate they watched the well fill with flowers. A green forest strung itself across the entire width, and all the time runners reached upwards, up to the Temple above, while smoke wreathed through the leaves and flowers.

And then a glimmer of white, of raven hair and smiling eyes. Through the smoke, a woman looked at them, and before Blythe could react, Thurstan had opened the gate and was out on the staircase once more.

'Lily!' She was above them, on the other side of the well. Beautiful, dusky and calm amidst all the chaos, she waited on the other staircase, her hand resting lightly on the iron banister. Her cream linen skirt was unsullied by the smoke. It moved and swayed as a flood of scurries broke around her feet. Her expression was quite blank, quite undisturbed. She did not look at Thurstan.

He began to clamber up the stairs, hauling himself up on seething branches. They writhed beneath his grip. Thorns tore his clothes. The staircase itself was twisting and buckling under the weight of the avid foliage. Blythe caught his arm, pulling him back.

'For God's sake, Merauld!' His hand was shaken off.
Thurstan did not even look at him, his eyes fixed on the
woman.

Which stairs were they on? Where they even on the same
staircase as Lily? Did it lead direct to the Field of Flowers,
or to the iron-enclosed vestibule? There was no telling, no
way of understanding the significance of where they stood.
That there was such a significance, Blythe did not doubt.

And then he realised that the curve was too acute, that Lily
and the flood of scurries had to be on the other staircase. He
saw how futile it was. 'Thurstan! She's on the other stairs,
you won't make it!'

He was shouting, but the noise from the chanting drowned
his voice.

The smoke from below wreathed with shadows, reaching
out to embrace her. Thurstan was no longer struggling against
the twining greenery. He hung there, his hands clenched on
the green stems, watching. He cried her name once more,
but there was nothing he could do.

Through the smoky shadows they saw her face change. The
features began to run, to melt, to mix with the pale dress
which dissolved in streams of flowing colour. Shapes were
suggested, things meaningful and meaningless, but all the
time the substance blurred, weakened, fragmented. Hands
and claws, eye and hoof blended together like the colours of
a paintbox.

Thurstan was white and bloodless, his mouth hanging
slack, his eyes staring.

Quickly, to stem the shock, Blythe pulled him back down
to the gate. 'It's not real, Merauld! No woman, that. No true
lover, not even human! Parid, that's what they're called,
you've heard of them. It was created by Imbert Cupere in
order to deceive you. It's not real!'

And you were willing to put everything aside for the love
of an illusion. You made the choice and took the whole
responsibility for it.

Dreams and memories ate through the substance of the
Parid. Wisps of drifting hallucination revealed a lock of dark
curling hair. Teased apart in darkness it was, diluted and
dispersed into creeping smoke.

*   *   *

I have taken back one who was stolen from me. I release the essence once more into the gentle mists. But the thief Mage risks more than dissolution.

He sends me fragments, a tide of formless matter to placate my anger. The tide carries the words he chants, the words which he hopes will please me.

I gather them to me, the pale formless ones, and quieten their silly noise. But he risks much, and knows it.

Unseen and unheard I move through different realms, along every life, tracking the minutes and hours. Years flow from the movement of my wings, catching up the dead, releasing the living.

I am not alone. My Children give peace in the shape of memory, flitting down the terrible paths of regret and guilt and madness. Few know that they are the Kindly Ones, the fruits of my spirit.

And the others, my dearest, my beloved ones, restore the balance. They fly between the Sun and Moon, beyond the violent glare of the day, beyond the deadly glow of night. The Arrarat are the children of my heart.

I release them to this world as necessary.

Sometimes, more is needed. The Rite progresses.

I am tempted to fly once more . . .

The Rose had reached up beyond the four Mages, up to the iron-fretted ceiling of the stairwell. A multitude of small white blooms turned away from Blythe and Thurstan, intent on the movement upwards.

The Mages did not watch. They were surrounded by leaves and flowers now, standing on the frail stairs. From folds within the cloth-of-gold cloaks they drew a number of glass shapes. Their lips framed words, their eyes were steady with concentration.

The central fire was raging now, flames flickering through the stems. Some of them were charring, shrivelling in the vast, gathering heat. And yet still the Rose surged upwards, pulling itself out of the depths of the well, striving to escape the furnace.

Wherein lay the essence of the Rose? Its centre, its mind, its wide and gaping mouth?

It stretched itself and tore down part of the staircase below

Blythe and Thurstan. It wrenched ironwork into strange fingers, imploring, eager hands raised to the darkness. Still it arose.

At its centre, shrouded in green, it held its precious burden, protected and hidden.

Masonry fell in its eager grasping. The first shoots had reached the ceiling now, hauling a vast weight up onto the iron struts. There was a sound of rumbling, a rapacious growling as the Desert Rose tore at the structure above them.

The blocks of stone that began to fall bounced against each other. Some crashed into the sides of the well. But the stones and bricks that fell on the limbs of the Rose were insignificant. The clouds of dust that disguised breath and sight mattered not at all. It was roaming through the Temple itself now, swarming over benches and pillars and altar alike.

Thurstan and Blythe, back in the corridor, saw through the iron gate chunks of brickwork and stone tumble into the well. Their ears were filled with the rumble of falling masonry. The Rose was shuddering as its limbs were crushed and severed by the weight. But still its centre was safely guarded, untouched by the collapsing, burning world around it.

Again it reached out its green tendrils, fastening on stone buttresses and arching supports, and then, at last, there was the massive crash of collapsing walls.

The roof caved in, pulled down by the clutch of the Desert Rose. The statue of Lycias fell through bright air, plunging down into the abyss of the great stairwell. The chasm was filled with vivid light.

The Sun beat down on them.

Flames leapt up through the twining branches to meet it. And there revealed in the sunlight was the Rose itself, the vast white flower with its open, naked face, moving ever upward, holding its offering in trembling, eager embrace.

As sunlight fell into the shaft, leaves began to uncurl. They peeled back like an unfolding bud, giving birth to new life, the hope that the Desert Rose might live once more in the glory of the Sun God.

The leaves fell away and the sunlight fell on her hair, gold on gold.

She stood there unmoving, and looked only at Matthias. Across the wide chasm, on a frail platform of leaves, she was cradled by the Rose, surrounded by smoke and flames and thorns and flowers.

Flame was eating its way into the Rose, and the lower flower eyes squeezed shut in agony. And yet still it thrust upwards, still bearing its precious offering, yearning towards the greater heat of the Sun.

Eleanor looked only at the blind Mage preparing to throw glass, and although the fire still burned around her, there was silence.

The scurries had vanished, back to their unknown home. Their chant was over. The Parid had been dissolved, unravelled. The Temple had fallen; there was no longer the rumble of collapsing wall and ceiling.

Phinian Blythe and Thurstan Merauld, watching helplessly at the side, heard her words.

'Matthias. How can you do this?'

And his reply, one word only. 'Wait.'

The glass shapes were thrown, glinting through the air. They seemed to throng around her head, to flash and sparkle. She did not move, did not even glance at Blythe and Thurstan. There was a movement of wings.

I am just, eternally wise. Knowing every secret, understanding every hidden thought. I am kind and offer, in the end, peace.

They are mischievous and foolish. They think the decision has been taken. They call, but they do not know what they risk. There are more ways to halt time than they comprehend.

Death halts time. Over my quiet plains there is no Sun and no Moon. For the dead, time ceases.

This is what they risk.

The Rite, all around her. The glass spinning, the fire burning, and the inexorable movement of the Rose still bearing her up towards the Sun.

She heard wings. She looked away from Matthias's empty face and narrowed her eyes. She heard wings: the familiar, steady, rhythmic pulse. A bright flame, high above her, wheeling in a descending spiral.

The Benu, blind arbiter of time, coming to take her to some other realm, some other dimension? Coming to take her home, coming to fall into a trap, a dizzying, whirling prison?

She almost cried out a warning, but something held her back. The plummeting hawk was coming for her, a fierce, burning, bright hawk of power, and she knew who it was.

Amery. The knowledge was like a song. Amery, Matthias's new-found hawk, released for just this one act, this one hope that visions could be interpreted in some other way.

Amery alighted next to Eleanor and looked at her. Their minds met, with nothing held back, no disguises or doubts.

Amery. Waiting to take her out of this, to take her away from the desert, to take her north, to Lukas.

The Rose began to curl up around them, seeking to hold on to its offering. They did not wait. Glass clashed somewhere around them, a frail scattering of no significance.

Together they flew, and left the Mages to the smoking ruins of their Rite.

'Traitor!' A wild scream of fury. Imbert was racing down the staircase towards Matthias and Weard, scrambling over the writhing stalks of the Rose. Edine surged after him, her face distorted with rage and disappointment.

'Traitor!' The scream cut through the air like a scythe, but Thurstan had seen what was happening, and he too was running towards Matthias.

He had been transfixed with horrors, but now he was impelled to action. He saw the fury on Imbert's face, and knew Matthias would have little chance.

'Come on!' he shouted to Blythe over his shoulder.

But Phinian Blythe had seen something else arising from the chasm. A shape of wings.

Matthias leant back against the wall of the stairwell, blank with exhaustion. He heard Imbert's scream and Weard's curses. It didn't matter. The Rite had failed and Eleanor was safe.

Only one thing mattered now. The presence of the shadows, swooping, waiting to alight, only a hair's-breadth from him. He could see nothing, but they betrayed themselves to every sense, not only to the eyes. They were fluttering with eagerness, ready now, drawn by guilt.

He knew that Weard had turned towards him, the spiral staff raised high. Matthias had no defence, no desire even to turn aside what would happen. He waited patiently . . .

A sudden flurry as Thurstan pushed past him, past Weard, rushing up the stairs to meet Imbert. Phin would be somewhere here too. The shadows knew him well . . .

Matthias waited, with empty hands and empty face, for the Children to take their toll. The air around him was foul with their presence.

They passed him by.

The shadows washed over Weard, staining him as they went. And Weard suddenly pushed past Matthias, running down the corridor, running as far, as fast as he could, in case they returned . . .

The Children had other prey. Matthias heard the bubbling moan, the muffled scream from the staircase.

Imbert. He had watched the shadows settle on Phinian Blythe once, long ago. He knew what would be happening. Imbert would thresh around, trying to ward them off, but it would make no difference. His arms would flail helplessly as the Children showed him the face of his guilt.

Matthias felt his knees weaken. They had passed him by – again. It was not his turn yet.

Like an old man, he followed Weard through the gate, out into the corridor, and then his legs gave way altogether and he sagged against the wall.

He heard the sound of screaming, high and agonised. He heard other footsteps on the leaf-encrusted stairs.

'Phin?' he said. More footsteps, and then a warm hand on his shoulder.

'Are you all right, Matthias? I must go and help Thurstan –'

'No. Stay here.' Matthias kept hold of his wrist. 'There's nothing you can do – '

'Imbert – '

'Will die. And Thurstan.' His voice was expressionless. 'And it is not necessary for you to watch this.'

But Blythe had pulled away. He was now at the edge of the staircase, looking through the flames at the figures remaining there.

*   *   *

It happened so fast that he almost missed it, and when he
tried to describe it to Matthias later, the details blurred under
the memory of smoke and flowers.

He didn't want to look at Imbert flailing around under the
weight of the Children. They were writhing around him,
whispering in his ears, flickering over his eyes, clogging his
mouth and nose. Blythe's hands shivered, helpless with
compassion.

He looked beyond Imbert Cupere. He saw a meeting,
Thurstan and Edine on the far side of the staircase. Still the
Rose bloomed all around them.

Fiercely protective, she stood between the two men.
Thurstan was speaking gently to her, his hands held out, but
Blythe could see that soundless tears were pouring down her
face. She was trying to keep him away from her lover. But
Imbert blundered past her, blind, wild with distress, and the
Rose snatched at his legs. He pitched forward, knocking
Thurstan off balance.

A deadly scrambling on the edge of the chasm, Edine on
her knees, the shadows chattering. And then the weight of
the Rose shifted once more, still yearning upwards, and the
two men toppled, falling, failing, down into the pit.

A shape of wings welcomed them. Blythe saw a darkness
so intense that the sunlight seemed irrelevant. The black
wings took on the colour of flame and lifted over the falling
bodies of two men. And then the wings sank, once more,
down to the Field of Flowers.

Edine looked at him. Across the burning Rose, through
the tapestry of its limbs, she stared at him for a long time.
Tears continued to fall, soundlessly, but her face was
expressionless. It seemed carved from pale stone, a statue to
grief. Then she stood up, turning away, and slowly walked
down the few steps to one of the exits from the stairwell.

She looked back at him, and he saw that the tears still fell.
He knew they would always fall. Then she opened the
wrought-iron gate and disappeared into the ruins of the City
of Stairs.

Phinian Blythe turned away from the stairwell, still covered
with burning greenery, back to Matthias. He helped him up
and then, stumbling, they made their way through the empty

avenues to other staircases. The heat everywhere was intense. He guided Matthias through the warren of passages beyond the ruins of the Temple of Lycias.

Slowly they made their way through corridors and stairways, up towards what remained of the city of Smintha. There was no sign of Weard anywhere. Blythe wondered briefly where he had gone, but it was no longer urgent.

At last they reached another door. It opened into the hallway of a large house. They crossed tiled floors to another, more elaborate door. This opened onto one of the radial streets running away from the Temple of Lycias. They had left the City of Stairs behind them.

This was the city of Smintha. Although it was no cooler above ground, unprotected from the burning sun, it was a relief to get out of the dead stillness of the underworld. The colours seemed hard and bright, the texture of sand was grainy and gritty.

It felt as if they were alive once more.

Blythe found a well not far from the Temple. There was still fresh water to drink, to wash away the marks of smoke and grime.

No sign of Weard or Edine.

At last Blythe spoke. 'Why didn't the Rite work? Thurstan made the decision, you know . . .'

'Yes. I know.' And then slowly, painfully, Matthias went on. 'He made the wrong decision on the wrong premise. His love was built on an illusion, a deception, a lie. It could be of no significance, it had no weight. Not a real woman, but a Parid. Not love, but infatuation. It wouldn't work on that foundation. The Rite could not hold against that.

'They were foolish, Imbert and Edine.' Matthias seemed to be thinking aloud. 'They could have done it between them. Theirs was a true love, something real. But no. Ever manipulative, they had to use someone else. *They* would not take responsibility. And so it failed.'

'And Eleanor – just whisked away by an Arrarat hawk. She'll be all right?' This was centrally important to him.

'Amery will take her north, to Lukas.' The exhausted voice was flat and expressionless.

Under the Sun once more, Matthias saw the future. Smoke clogged the air around them. They sat on the steps of one of the silent fountains and Matthias told him about the ring of bonfires all around the Desert Rose.

His voice was faint with exhaustion. But his words gave some relief, some shape to the events they had just witnessed.

'So strange, so bizarre that the Desert Rose is all that remains of the High Priest Lefevre. A unique metamorphosis. And a final one, I trust.'

'Don't you know?'

'No. That one is still hidden.' He paused. 'You swore an oath once, if I remember.'

An oath to kill the High Priest, whatever the cost, whatever the consequences. He had promised it in another life, another time.

Blythe stood up. 'I'll go and see,' he said. At the very least, he supposed, he should make sure that the Rose was finally destroyed. He had to make sure. He had to see for himself the end of Lefevre.

He left Matthias in the shade of a doorway and went back towards the Temple of Lycias.

Smoke blotted out the sun. The arena that had bloomed under water-lilies was now a pit of fire. Shoots and tendrils trembled on the edge of the chasm. Whatever remained of the Rose was still trying to drag itself out of the fire, up towards its God.

It was uncomfortably hot close to the edge, but Blythe stood there for some time, looking down.

The great white central flower gazed up at him, as a column of fire ate at its centre.

Words ran through his mind, the memory of another fire.

'Lefevre, Desert Rose, High Priest to Our Lord God, greet your Lord now. Unite in fire and glory, the ultimate gift of ecstasy.

'I remember, you see. You watched me burn in a cauldron once, and consigned my soul to the care of the Lord Lycias. I commend you now to your Master. Know your God, know the Master of All Fire, Flame and Passion. For you are the same now, the Fire of the Rose, the Fire of the Sun . . .'

The words stopped. He was not alone. As the Desert Rose still groaned, pulling and clutching and failing in its agony to escape one fire and find another, Blythe looked across the abyss and saw a slight figure standing there.

He was made of flame, His hair ablaze with fire. Green eyes glinted in the heart of it, flashing through the smoke to Blythe.

Lycias looked across the abyss to Phinian Blythe, and smiled over the fiery pit that contained their shared past.

'Greetings, Phinian Blythe.' The words were cold as ice from the heart of fire. 'What have you now for Me? Another wager? Or, having paid every possible price, having lost everything and endured the Children of Night, will you greet Me in peace?

'A hand in friendship now. Will you accept?'

The God of the Sun. The edge of His vengeance had wrecked so many lives, so many hopes.

And He did not necessarily deal in truth. How could one trust such a being?

But someone had to start it. Someone had to start climbing down, accept that the past was over.

Karis, Marial, Idas. Thurstan, Imbert, and a thousand others. Matthias, Eleanor, enduring so much. Could such a legacy be surmounted?

Blythe met the green eyes dancing in fire and paused. 'Yes,' he said. 'I accept. A new start, for us all.'

The green eyes were emerald bright. The figure faded into flame, and Blythe was left with the memory of brightness and passion.

A chance, it was always a chance. But the Benu was free, and anything was possible.

He turned away from the furnace and from the memory of brightness.

He did not see the final death of the Rose.

Chapter Thirty-two
Journeys

The child who had so recently existed in a baby's body now flew on the back of a golden Arrarat hawk. He had taken the guise of a youth, dark-haired, bronze-skinned. It stretched his new powers severely to maintain that shape for any length of time, but a baby's physique could not keep him steady on the soft, uneven feathers of the hawk. Together they skimmed through warm air, swooped and soared, catching the currents.

He had travelled a long way in the wake of the storm, following the great troughs in the desert where the sand had been whipped by its force. Boulders had tumbled from mountainsides leaving great gashes in the structure of rock, wounds and scars laid bare under the burning sun. Grieving, Coron saw cities crushed under the weight of the wind, set alight by the stabbing lightning, shaken by the ruinous thunder.

No one lived in these desert cities, with their sour wells and dried-up rivers. Forests of blackened stumps stood between the cities and the encroaching desert. The Stormbearer brought no rain, no relief to these exhausted regions. He brought only wind and hurricane, fire and violence, and the sound of howling accompanied him everywhere.

As Coron and Adila, Comyn's Arrarat hawk, began to catch up with the storm, the sky darkened around them.

He was not afraid, young Coron, although he knew the strength of shadows first-hand, had watched the horrors they brought. He wondered at the grief he had seen in others' eyes. He was saddened by the bewilderment and terror of so many.

But he was confident, coolly and quietly confident, that he could make everything right. He had lifted three ravens from the shoulders of Phinian Blythe, after all. He had created a playground for fishes in the middle of a burnt desert. He knew his Father was not intrinsically vicious, not wantonly cruel. Every act carried its own pattern of consequences, that was all. He knew that the Storm-bearer must have offended, and that that was why he was paying . . .

Further yet, the desert beneath him was broken by dying forests, farms still struggling, towns still scraping some kind of existence against the overwhelming sun. Coron and Adila were travelling northwards, north through the Empire of Peraldon towards the Malith Channel.

Everywhere they passed there was evidence of fire and wind. Whole areas were devastated by the power of the storm. Coron saw buildings collapsed over the bodies of young and old alike. He saw towns and villages wrenched asunder, road from road, house from house, tumbled, chaotic and ruined. He heard people crying, searching through the rubble for family or friends, or food, or water.

And still the Sun burned, complicating and worsening every effect of the Storm-bearer's passage. Coron smelt disease and plague souring the air of the stricken countryside.

Sometimes he halted. Swooping down to the parched land, he watched a man pull the body of his daughter from the rubble. His presence alone smoothed the path of the spade through the earth as the grave was dug. Water sprang fresh and cool in the wells and rivers where he paused. Fruit hung heavy from orchards as the trees suddenly blossomed and flourished. It began to rain. In such ways did Coron ameliorate the agony visited on Peraldon by the curse of his Father on the Storm-bearer.

He did not delay for long. Every hour he spent in attendance upon the sick and bereaved, the storm raged further through the land. It was an indulgence, grieving with these people.

Complicated emotions ran through him as he once more mounted his great hawk and followed the path of the storm. Pity, regret, fear, puzzlement. Why should it be so? Why should such suffering beset both innocent and guilty? He began to fear, not his Father, but the whole structure of this world, his home world.

Elsewhere there was delight. In other realms, other

dimensions, there was laughter. People and creatures and
rainbows spun fine images together. Balancing within a perfect
equilibrium, life was exciting and extraordinary, unexpected
and astonishing, and Sun and Moon lived in harmony.

People loved each other.

There was the truth of the violin bow on the string, the
brush on the canvas, the hand on the cheek, the delight in
clear eyes.

But here, here on his own world, all was sunburnt and
storm-torn. As the skies darkened around him, he knew the
storm was not far away.

Storm clouds were heavy over Shelt.

Serethrun watched it happen. From the back of the large
chestnut mare he had chosen after the raid on the stables,
he saw Felicia taken in Rosco's arms. His mind registered
that the fighting had stopped, that the sea dragon had gone,
entranced by that strange, shifting illusion. He realised that
the Sea Lords had been defeated and it mattered to him not
at all.

He had lost her. He knew it with unalterable certainty. He
had seen Felicia's eyes when Rosco spoke to her, listened to
her voice when she answered. She loved him, and now, in
front of the whole of Shelt, Rosco had acknowledged the
bond.

In despair, he dug his heels into the horse's side and yanked
on the reins. Blindly he pushed through the crowds, back
to the west gate. Although the cheering had stopped, there
was a constant murmur of approbation. It was broken, of
course, by other sounds – the groans of the wounded, the
grief of the bereaved – but most people were sighing with
relief. Their faces had relaxed, the bitter tension and
resentment briefly forgotten.

They were fools, he thought. Hoping that things would
be better, hoping that Rosco would make things right. Who
was he, anyway? What was he to do with Shelt, and Felicia?

Serethrun was almost at the gate now, but the open plains
were cluttered with tents and temporary, ramshackle
dwellings. Even the plains were sullied, spoiled by the
overspill from the city.

Better she had drowned. Better that the sea had taken her,

had kept her pure and free. Rosco didn't love her, of that he was sure. She would suffer and suffer again in an unequal, loveless marriage. It was a moment of clarity, of undeniable knowledge. She would be better off out of it . . .

He wondered at himself then, sickened by his own thoughts. He knew what the remedy was; he should leave Shelt and return to the *eloish*. To Irian, his sister.

She had not fought in Shelt; she had taken no part in the battle against the Sea Lords. It would not be fitting for the clan's shaman. She had counselled that the *eloish* fight with the fisherpeople, but there had been a warning with it. A warning for Serethrun alone.

It will do you no good, Irian had said, making Rosco Earl of Shelt. There is no happiness for you there . . . He spurred his horse on, galloping through the tents and shacks, out onto the plains. The wind in the grass followed him as the sun set. He left the city far behind.

He found her. Or was it a dream? Alone in the empty wilderness, attended by two women. She walked through the tall grasses towards him, her cloak flowing behind her, her body marked with the sacred paint.

Her eyes still held stars. Deep in the trance she gave him no acknowledgment, no greeting.

'There is one chance,' she said. 'You might just stop it. He loves someone else, someone from another place . . .'

Her voice became very faint, and he was aware that the two women waiting back at the camp would not be able to hear the words.

'Go south,' she whispered, 'to the Carald mountains. There are flames around her, but she walks barefoot over heather. If you can get her to Shelt in time, there will be no marriage . . .' As he watched her, he saw the stars fade from her eyes. She sighed, as if waking from a deep sleep. Her women moved forward, wrapping the cloak round her black-painted, naked body. She relaxed heavily against them, and Serethrun knew that she was now unconscious.

He dismounted, and helped the women carry her back to the small tent set at the edge of the camp. They stared at him, waiting for him to leave, but he waved them away.

'I'll watch with her – don't worry, I've done it before . . .'

'Don't wait . . .' Irian's voice was still quiet, unexpected at his side. Her eyes were open once more, bright with intelligence. 'Leave now, Serethrun. There's not much time . . .'

He took supplies, and a spare cloak. And then he set off, to cross half a continent, to find the stranger from another world, the stranger who walked barefoot over heather, surrounded by flames.

Chapter Thirty-three
The Wedding

The bells rang in Shelt that day.

The sound was almost lost in the howling of the wind. The banners flying from the great houses were whipped into rigid shapes. Frail lines of bunting were torn from their fastenings.

Olwyn Mittelson looked down from the Castle over the city of Shelt and watched the streets fill. Notwithstanding the storm, everyone would be out to cheer the brief procession from Castle to Temple and back again.

The fisherpeople would be there, of course, and the ordinary citizens of Shelt and its surrounds. The *eloish* were a notable absence, encamped again some distance from the city.

Serethrun Maryn's disaffection worried him. Mittelson had hoped to keep him close, to mediate with the *eloish*. But somewhere along the line he had misjudged it, and Serethrun had escaped the net.

He had disappeared after the shambles in the main square. He had been seen making for the south gate. Some weeks had since passed. No sign of Serethrun, no signs of any approach from the *eloish*.

But as Mittelson thoughtfully watched the cloaked and hooded masses beginning to gather around the barriers, he saw the unmistakable head and shoulders of Serethrun's chestnut mare appear high over the crowds. Slowly and carefully, she was edging towards the Castle. There were two riders on her back. He was expecting to see Serethrun, but he did not recognise the other, a woman with red hair.

He had no need of spiral staffs now. Delicately but rapidly

he sent his mind out towards the two people on horseback trying to assess their mood, their intent.

It was blocked, partly by the excitement of the crowd, but mainly because of something in the storm, the storm gathering over the city.

He shivered, pulling his cloak closer. He was distracted by the power of this storm. He turned away from the balcony intending to confer with Ferant Aldrich. For a while, he put aside Serethrun's reappearance and the strange woman.

There would be time to deal with them after the wedding.

Eleanor was high-strung with tension. Sitting on Serethrun's mare, she was impatient with the crowds, pushing and jostling all around them. She wanted to clear a swathe through them force a passage. And although she was tired, desperately weary, longing for rest and peace, she could not rest, would not, until she found him.

Lukas was here somewhere. He was here. Matthias had seen it, Amery had brought her most of the way, Serethrun had found her and helped her – everything had conspired to get her here swiftly.

She would find him today.

Serethrun left her with his horse at the Castle gates. She had wanted to accompany him, but no strangers were admitted to the Castle that day. Security arrangements were in force attendant on the Earl's marriage. Serethrun had had to use Mittelson's name to be admitted.

Eleanor had no chance. She had to wait in the chilling wind with the rest of the crowd.

She did not know why the crowds were gathering.

Serethrun had not recognised Lukas by the name she gave although he soon put it together when she described the Ararat hawk he rode. He told her about the vast bird winging over the top of the cliff, and Rosco, laughing, dropping Felicia into his arms . . .

Of course, Serethrun had his own reasons for wanting to stop the planned marriage between Rosco and Felicia although he did not tell Eleanor what they were. He did not even tell her that marriage was in the air. She was too vulnerable for such news. Anyway, they would get there in time, he was sure.

Serethrun had found her on a barren hillside to the east of the Carald mountains in the far south of Stromsall. He had ridden south, as instructed by Irian.

He found her at sunset. A blaze of fire framed a small figure, doggedly tramping over the scrubby grass and boulders, thin shoulders set hard against the biting wind.

He had watched her for a while from higher up, fascinated by the determination of her progress northwards.

She had stumbled on the rock and then he realised that she was barefoot. Shocked, for it was still cold, and the going was very rough underfoot, he had cantered down the slope and was offering a ride before he knew what was happening.

Together on horseback they galloped northwards over the wide plains, through Eldin and Hoel; Serethrun found them shelter and food on the way. She was insistent that they should never stop long in any one place, that they should push the chestnut mare Oriel to her utmost. Eleanor could not wait to find the man she loved. There was no need to tell her of the planned marriage. She'd find out soon enough.

Stabs of lightning accompanied their journey, and their rest at night was disturbed by distant thunder. Both of them were lonely, preoccupied and anxious, and did not recognise the thunder for what it was.

Storm-bearer.

Eleanor looked at the gates. Any minute now, she thought, he would come through. He would see her, she would see him, and they would be together. She could almost feel the warmth of his arms.

She was trembling. She turned away from the gates for a moment, unable to bear it. She felt sick with stress, a tight ball of tension knotting in her stomach. She could not bear the minutes stretching away.

Someone tapped her shoulder.

So taut was she that she shivered at the touch. She looked round. An old fisherwoman stood there, dressed all in black, petticoats fluttering in the vicious wind.

'I know a way, if you want to get into the Castle,' she said. Her eyes were piercing, shining black. 'This way.'

'I'm staying here.' Serethrun would bring him this way of course, because this was where she would be . . .

'They'll never let him out now, he'll be preparing for the ceremony . . .'

She never even questioned how the fisherwoman knew for whom she was waiting.

'What ceremony?'

'The wedding of Felicia Westray, heiress to the Earldom of Shelt and Eldin, to a man whose real name is Luka Marling. If you want to stop it, you'd better follow me. There's not much time.'

'He'll come here. He'll come to find me here. I can't go –'

'No messages will get through to him at this stage. He won't even know you're here; the marriage will go ahead because that's what's been planned. Your message will never reach him.'

Eleanor stared at the old woman, frantic with indecision.

'This way?' She held out an old, gnarled hand and, as if hypnotised, Eleanor took it.

'Where's Rosco?' Serethrun demanded roughly. Mittelson had been warm in welcome, but Serethrun had shaken him off. 'There's someone waiting for him outside. It's urgent –'

'Who? What is her name?' The red-haired woman, though, Mittelson.

'Eleanor. Eleanor Knight, she used to know him long ago –'

'The man's about to get married. The appearance of an old flame at this stage would be a major embarrassment. She can come to the party afterwards.' His words were light, but Mittelson remembered the name from Rosco's delirium, so long ago on that cold sea-shore.

He was still preoccupied by the storm raging just south of the city. It was driven by some force he did not understand relating to the storms that had wrecked Stromsall during the Stasis. He could not afford to be diverted by Serethrun's awkward reappearance, by this sudden manifestation from Rosco's mysterious past. Casually, he poured wine into a glass for Serethrun. 'Very well,' he said. 'If you insist, I'll go and tell him.'

Serethrun drained the glass and set it down on the table.

He started to follow the tall Mage to the door, but half-way there the floor shifted under his feet, rearing up towards him.

He fell, unconscious, to the ground.

It had changed.

She looked around her. Between the instant of taking the old woman's hand and this, there was nothing. Just one heartbeat after another within the space of a single breath.

It had all changed.

The cheering was loud around her, louder even than the storm rumbling overhead. It was almost dark, so heavy were the clouds with rain. The old woman had gone.

The banners and bunting hung in wildly fluttering rags overhead. She was shoved and buffeted by the crowds. People were throwing flowers. She could hardly stay upright in all the jostling.

Somehow she managed to get to the front of those pushing up against the barricade. Soldiers in scarlet stood shoulder to shoulder along it, holding back the weight of people from the wooden fences lining the road through the square.

Pinioned by the crush she could only raise her eyes to the procession passing in ponderous state.

Men on horseback first, in gaudy scarlet cloaks. Then the aristocracy of Shelt, in furs and velvets, riding in open carriages, one after the other.

The priestesses next, in black robes, billowing in the wind, austere and silent.

And at last two people on horseback, wreathed about with flowers.

She was fading as she stood there. Her grip on the barrier at her waist was slipping, slipping . . .

Lukas was talking to the thin girl at his side. He took a flower from the cascades that were showering all around them and handed it to her. His strange pale hair blew in the wind. The girl smiled.

He did not see Eleanor at the side of the road, only a few yards away. His eyes were blue and unconcerned, idly considering the crowd on either side, and already they had passed by on their way back to the Castle.

Eleanor fell, drowning, amidst the crowd.

She lay disregarded at the feet of the scarlet-clad soldiers.

No one noticed, no one knew. No one saw the pattern of revenge traced on wide-flung hands and unknowing face.

Except for one person. Following closely behind the procession, Olwyn Mittelson noticed the red-haired woman unconscious on the ground. Ever manipulative, ever curious, he signed to one of the soldiers, who bent down and lifted her up, taking her into the Castle.

The new Earl of Shelt would find her there.

JENNY JONES

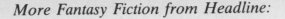

FLY BY NIGHT

Volume One of FLIGHT OVER FIRE

**'An extraordinary book. A vivid original. There is
something very special about Jenny Jones'
Michael Moorcock**

Eleanor Knight is a child of her age: spoiled, bored,
a stranger to commitment. From another world a
desperate rite of summoning calls and she
is carried on a whirling nightmare of hawkflight,
out of her self-indulgent unhappiness . . . to the
wind-lashed coast of the Cavers, worshippers of
the Moon Goddess Astret.

The Sun God Lycias and His High Priest Lefevre
maintain the Stasis which holds Peraldonia, an
ocean away from the Cavers, in a summery land of
light and eternal life. But the Stasis has a converse
side and it is in ceaseless night that the Cavers eke
out a barren existence − the rite of summoning is
their final despairing attempt to break Lycias' hold
on Time . . .

Disoriented and dismayed Eleanor wants no part of
the Cavers' problems, but the Moon Goddess will
not be denied. In the outsider's hands rests the
fate of a people: the final heart-rending agony of
choice will fall to her alone.

'Definitely something out of the ordinary, and
something good' Michael Scott Rohan

FICTION/FANTASY   0 7472 3398 5

More Science Fiction from Headline:

MEMORIES

MIKE McQUAY

The millennia-spanning masterpiece
of time travel

'A major achievement . . . unique' Norman Spinrad,
author of BUG JACK BARRON

MEMORIES

On a night when psychiatrist David Wolf's life is
falling apart, a woman comes to him, seeking help.
Her name is Silv, and she too is a psychiatrist – but
from Earth's distant future, a time when the planet's
surface is no longer inhabitable. And in her world an
experiment has gone drastically wrong: she has
unlocked the gates of Time – and through them has
slipped a psychopathic soldier, escaping to the
Napoleonic era, where he has the power to
manipulate the future. David and Silv must embark
on an awesome quest across Time before a tidal
wave of chaos sweeps through history.

MEMORIES

A sweeping, multi-layered odyssey filled with stunning
imagery, breathtaking intensity and high drama.

'Fascinating . . . this kept me reading all the way
through at one sitting' James P Hogan,
author of THE PROTEUS OPERATION

'Ambitious, complex and fascinating . . . takes the
reader on an ingenious roller-coaster ride'
Carole Nelson Douglas, author of PROBE

'Cause for great celebration . . . stands with a small
handful of science fiction novels which successfully
convey the pain and wonder of being alive.
It transcends the genre' LOCUS

SCIENCE FICTION   0 7472 3386 1

More Fantasy Fiction from Headline:

Sheila Gilluly

GREENBRIAR QUEEN

A GLORIOUS FANTASY EPIC

**The runes surged at once into flame so that the whole
length of the wand was limned with a brilliant glow.
In the dim room they watched as a second, spell-image
staff materialised out of the air, seemingly, and
hovered there above the real wooden stave in Llodin's
hands. Two ghostly hands appeared, a mirror of the
wizard's own, and seized the light wand. With an
abruptness that startled them all, the magic hands
moved quickly in the manner of someone breaking a
twig, and the spell staff snapped in two. In the gap
between the two pieces a piercingly bright gem
shone like a star, caught and held there, distant
and unattainable.**

The Dark Lord's reign is about to begin, for the age of doom
prophesied long ago is now upon the people of Ilyria. The
Greenbriar King is dead, his children have vanished, and his
treacherous bastard half-brother, Dendron, now holds the
throne. But more dangerous by far than Dendron is his
wizard adviser, the Fallen, who can free the dread Dark
Lord from exile and bring ruin to all the world.

The Fallen needs the blood of Princess Ariadne, the true
Greenbriar heir, to weave his spell. But a group of loyal
Watchmen would brave sorcerous evil and warriors' swords
to protect their future queen. For only she can wield the
magic Crystal, Ilyria's final weapon against the
Darkness to come . . .

FICTION/FANTASY   0 7472 3454 X

More Fantasy Fiction from Headline:

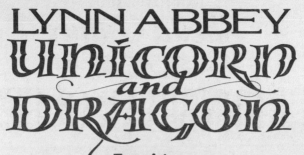

LYNN ABBEY
UNICORN
and
DRAGON

**Two sisters,
caught in a fantastic web
of intrigue and magic...**

Winter lies deep upon the land and evil forces are
at work: wolves howl malevolently in the forests, a
dying monarch cannot enforce the laws, and his
heirs circle like vultures, waiting to claim the
throne. The small castle of Hafwynder Manor is
thrown into chaos by the arrival of a mysterious
stranger, wounded by beasts both animal and
human, a man too ill to reveal his mission.

The forces of eleventh-century history invade the
Manor. Its safety, and that of all England, must
depend upon the deeds of the two Hafwynder
half-sisters: blonde, impulsive Alison, with her
talent to see into men's hearts, and the
dark-haired, cunning Wildecent, whose own rich
powers lie deeply buried and which now must stir
to life. With the forces of the outside world raging
at the castle walls, the two young women must
learn to shape their own destiny...

"Historic fantasy comes to life" Robert Asprin

**"Lynn Abbey is one of the most creative and
inventive writers of fantasy today"** C J Cherryh

FICTION/FANTASY 0 7472 3139 7

A selection of bestsellers from Headline

FICTION

RINGS	Ruth Walker	£4.99 □
THERE IS A SEASON	Elizabeth Murphy	£4.99 □
THE COVENANT OF THE FLAME	David Morrell	£4.99 □
THE SUMMER OF THE DANES	Ellis Peters	£6.99 □
DIAMOND HARD	Andrew MacAllan	£4.99 □
FLOWERS IN THE BLOOD	Gay Courter	£4.99 □
A PRIDE OF SISTERS	Evelyn Hood	£4.99 □
A PROFESSIONAL WOMAN	Tessa Barclay	£4.99 □
ONE RAINY NIGHT	Richard Laymon	£4.99 □
SUMMER OF NIGHT	Dan Simmons	£4.99 □

NON-FICTION

MEMORIES OF GASCONY	Pierre Koffmann	£6.99 □
THE JOY OF SPORT		£4.99 □
THE UFO ENCYCLOPEDIA	John Spencer	£6.99 □

SCIENCE FICTION AND FANTASY

THE OTHER SINBAD	Craig Shaw Gardner	£4.50 □
OTHERSYDE	J Michael Straczynski	£4.99 □
THE BOY FROM THE BURREN	Sheila Gilluly	£4.99 □
FELIMID'S HOMECOMING: Bard V	Keith Taylor	£3.99 □

All Headline books are available at your local bookshop or newsagent, or can be ordered direct from the publisher. Just tick the titles you want and fill in the form below. Prices and availability subject to change without notice.

Headline Book Publishing PLC, Cash Sales Department, PO Box 11, Falmouth, Cornwall, TR10 9EN, England.

Please enclose a cheque or postal order to the value of the cover price and allow the following for postage and packing:
UK & BFPO: £1.00 for the first book, 50p for the second book and 30p for each additional book ordered up to a maximum charge of £3.00
OVERSEAS & EIRE: £2.00 for the first book, £1.00 for the second book and 50p for each additional book.

Name ....

Address ....

....

....